# THE LAST TRAIN HOME

## Book Four

PETER A. MOSCOVITA

The Last Train Home
Copyright 2025 @ Peter A. Moscovita

Library of Congress Control Number: 2025916741
ISBN:   978-1-968069-75-9 (Paperback)
        978-1-969422-02-7 (Hardback)
        978-1-968069-76-6 (Ebook)



The views expressed in this book are solely those of the author and do not necessarily reflect the views of the publisher, and the publisher hereby disclaims any responsibility of them.

Olympus Story House

# CONTENTS

# Introduction

May 26, 1945, World War II was finally at an end in Europe, and a new phase was about to commence. Thousands of Allied troops from distant shores could finally return home, but repatriation was no easy task. Wave after wave of overloaded aircraft would wing their way to so many destinations. For many of those worn-out aircraft, it would be their last long distant flight, joining the countless thousands of American aircraft accumulating in the hot, dry Arizona desert and so many other places, their fate to be broken up for scrap. Throughout Europe and other sites involved in the field of war, vehicles would rust until they could be broken up, sometimes years later. Merchant shipping was also heavily utilized to transport thousands of troops back to their home countries. The English superliners Queen Mary and Queen Elizabeth carried as many as fifteen thousand troops on each transatlantic crossing. Many other transport ships would also undertake this mammoth task. For the Allied Intelligence Services, their objectives were far from over. Throughout Europe, thousands of German war criminals were running and hiding, knowing if they were caught, they would face charges of war crimes for the countless atrocities they had committed while wearing the German military uniform.

This daunting task would commence almost immediately after Germany surrendered, the BIS dispatching every available agent to Europe, undertaking long missions to capture these offenders. Timing was now a high priority as they moved quickly throughout the former German occupied countries, hunting down these offenders before they disappeared with new identities and travel documents.

Uncovering their hiding places was slow and frustrating work, as thousands of higher-ranking officers had already fled the shores of Europe.

They reappeared in many South American countries as well as countries in the Far East, their entry fee paid for with stolen gold and other precious commodities; finding them would be no easy task.

In their new roles, all Allied Intelligence organizations would reorganize from operatives in a hostile war to become hunters, combing the length and breadth of the European continent. This mission would become frustrating and time consuming. For those that had committed these atrocities against humanity, violating the conduct of the Geneva Convention would have consequences. The biggest hurdle facing these BIS agents was identifying the Gestapo and SS members before they simply disappeared, reappearing where German influence was very strong. These safe havens were mainly Argentina, Paraguay, Colombia, Brazil, Uruguay, Mexico, Chile, Peru, Guatemala, San Salvador, Ecuador, and Bolivia. Less frequent escape routes were into Spain, Switzerland, Canada, and even the United States. The escape routes were organized by the so called "Ratline," a vast, well-funded, and administered escape system. This organization was supported by the clergy of the Roman Catholic Church, managed by an Austrian Catholic Archbishop, Alois Hadal, the rector of the Pontificia Instituto Teutonico Santa Maria dell' Anima in Rome, a seminary for Austrian and German priests. He was also the Spiritual Director of the German people resident in Italy. In that organization, there were two primary escape routes; the first went from Germany to Spain, then on to Argentina. The second route was from Germany to Rome, then on to Genoa. The last leg would be to South America; eventually, these two routes would merge.

In 1944, Heinrich Himmler, Reichsfuhrer of the SS, realized that Germany would not be victorious in its conquest of Europe and Russia. In utmost secrecy, he established an independent organization, not connected in any way to the Ratline. This organization would become known as "ODESSA;" it was probably more like DNSS, which stands for DIE NEUE SS. The DNSS amassed enormous financial resources from assets looted by the Nazis from occupied territories to protect thousands of SS officers, who went underground until arrangements could be made for their escape. Those who were not so lucky and got caught faced interrogation by branches of the Allied Military Intelligence before facing a military court.

Major Karl Vita and fellow members of the British Intelligence Service would once again leave the shores of England for months on end, making emotional farewells to their families and loved ones.

They would scour the European countryside, following up leads on German personnel hiding in the most unlikely places. This new phase meant long months of tedious and frustrating detective work, sometimes becoming very dangerous. Like cornered rats, the hunted offenders vigorously fought back.

# CHAPTER 1

# The Hunters

The camp for the British Intelligence Service in Slough, Berkshire, was teeming with officers and servicemen, all gathering in the gymnasium for the first operational meeting on how to round up war crime offenders.

Before that meeting, many senior officers gathered in the lounge for a pint and a cigarette, relaxing with friends before the briefing commenced. This would be a long afternoon and, more than likely, a late night. The war was at an end; the Germans had unconditionally surrendered, and no one had given much thought to the task that now lay ahead of them. Major Karl Vita had returned to the camp the previous afternoon, his frame of mind solemn after another tearful goodbye at the Hitchin Train Station to his wife, Claire, and their fourteen-month-old son, Nicholas. These farewells were always difficult, not knowing how long the separation would be for them each time.

Karl was sitting with his longtime friends at their usual table; their former rowdy selves had changed to disgruntled, tired soldiers who'd had enough of war and those long periods of separation from their families.

Bill (Major William Lowes) approached the group; pulling up a chair, he looked around the table, sensing their frame of mind. He spoke, trying to bring some closure to their mood. "Chaps, I know how you are all feeling about now. The war is officially over, yet here we are, preparing to return to the continent for God knows how long. I'm with you, so ready to return to being a small-town lawyer. By the looks on your faces, I would venture to say you are all planning to resign your commissions after this next mission, am I correct?"

Gunther (Major Gunther Fisher) looked up, saying, "Bill, let me be the first to answer that question. My family and I will be moving to the United States. I have accepted a position in the diplomatic service commencing right after I leave the BIS. Thanks to Hazel's (Captain Hazel Collins) fiancée, Steven (Captain Steven Kowalski), for recommending me for this position. Steven has also volunteered to be our sponsor for American citizenship. My commission is scheduled to terminate in six months or so; we will depart shortly after that. My wife and children are really excited about this new start. So, my friends, that's our future. Herbert (Captain Herbert Werner), are your intentions still unchanged?"

Herbert had also been a German Army commissioned officer before WW2. Officers like himself deplored the direction of the Nazi party, electing to escape to England and offering their services to the British military, in his case, the Intelligence Service. Herbert nodded, followed by, "Like you, Gunther, I'm proud to be a German. I will stay with the BIS for as long as it takes to bring these Nazi thugs to justice. After that, my family and I will try to return to our village in Bavaria. I intend to play a part in rebuilding a new German military, one we can be proud of. Clive (Lieutenant Colonel Clive Knight) and General Jacks have been instrumental in recommending me for this new commission. Wearing a German officer's uniform will close the loop to my return. Wish me well, old friends."

Bill turned his attention to a very solemn Karl, sipping his pint of mild and bitter beer while listening to this conversation. "Karl, how about you? Are you still intent on returning to maritime duty after you finally leave the BIS?"

Karl slowly placed his beer on the table, then, clasping his hands together, waited momentarily before answering. "Well, if my wife Claire is still in agreement, I would like to finish what I started before this blasted war ruined my career in the maritime service. I still have regrets about terminating my position back in 1936. I so enjoyed being a first officer. So, my fellow heroes, it would mean so much to me if I could regain a similar position.

"The Langstaff Shipping Company is struggling to rebuild its merchant fleet as most of their ships have either been sunk or badly damaged. Those ships still seaworthy, I'm sure have been claimed as war prizes, more than likely in the service of the Russians, English, and Norwegians' fleets. So, what's our mission? For the ones still active in the BIS, our new roles will take on new objectives becoming hunters. And that objective will continue long after we have retired from the military; this next mission is becoming a global task.

"By the way, Bill, and for the benefit of these blokes at this table, let me congratulate you on becoming the newest partner in the law firm of McGivern, Tilbey & Morrison. It looks like we will become neighbors in Hitchin, and that move will make my wife and me so very happy. She gave me this news before I left yesterday, and I had to laugh, thinking those secret old ways of the BIS are still in play!

"As for Clive, well, he will update you on his decision to remain in uniform as a career officer. Right now, he is over in the gymnasium preparing for today's briefing. Poor chaps, they will be looking out at a sea of blank faces more interested in returning to their civilian lives than chasing those bad boys all over Europe," concluded Karl, taking the last swig of his beer.

One by one, they all stood, shaking hands, congratulating each other on still being alive and having firm objectives for life after the BIS.

Bill beckoned Karl to one side. He needed to explain his recent telephone calls with Claire over the last several weeks. "All right, Bill, you have my attention. I imagine this has to do with you joining Claire's law firm, correct?" Karl tried not to smile; he wanted the opportunity to see Bill squirm before he broke out laughing. On the inside, he was thrilled knowing Bill and his fiancée, Dorothy, would eventually become neighbors to the Vitas in Hitchin.

"Karl, I can see you are somewhat surprised at hearing about me joining Claire in her law firm, and by your expression, you're thinking, damn BIS secrets at it again. Well, let me put your mind to rest. This all started one afternoon about two weeks ago when I telephoned your house looking for you. Claire picked up and told me you would be back in about an hour. Striking up a conversation, Claire asked me if I had given any more thought to pursuing a carrier as a solicitor or, like Clive, would I elect to stay in the BIS as a career officer.

"I told her I was really looking forward to returning to civilian life, and yes, I would pursue a career in law once again. I also mentioned that finding a firm to retain me could become a challenge with so many chaps looking for the same positions after leaving the military. Karl, just like that, Claire asked if I would consider joining her law firm. Her two junior partners had expressed their intent to move up north to start their own law firm. They, of course, would stay on until she found a suitable replacement. I was utterly dumbfounded. I had considered approaching her but refrained from doing so. I didn't want it to appear that I was taking advantage of our friendship. Karl, it happened that quickly. We decided to keep it strictly confidential until I had a chance to talk to Dorothy about moving to Northern Hertfordshire.

"Claire was so excited, knowing we would be living close to that quaint town of Hitchin. Dorothy is very close to Claire; they write and telephone virtually every week, which made my answer very easy. I gave Claire my answer yesterday just before you were leaving to come here, and she told you. Karl, I hope you will accept this explanation. I'm so pleased knowing that I will be working with Claire. She is such an inspiration, and remember, I have been out of the law business for many years." Bill went silent, waiting for Karl's response, which always took a few moments.

"Bill, you have no idea how hard it was to keep a straight face. My dear friend, I could not be happier to hear that you will join the firm. I had thought about mentioning it to both of you a few months back, but I refrained from doing so. It is after all Claire's firm, and I didn't want her to think I was trying to persuade her in any way. Bill, I don't give a damn about who sees us, but come here and give your pal a big hug. Here's an idea for us to consider once you're settled into your new home; maybe we should consider joining the Letchworth Hall Hotel Golf Club. It should be a no brainer for you two solicitors to apply through the firm."

Karl was laughing, enjoying this wonderful news while walking away to join the group in the lounge, but first, he needed to call his wife. Headed to his office, he knew she would still be in hers. Sitting down, he picked up a picture of Claire and Nicholas, kissing it softly. How had his life changed since those years as a carefree merchant marine officer before the outbreak of war? A girl in every port was the life he loved until that life changing decision to leave his ship in Marseille, France, without prior approval from his captain. He escaped with his mother, sister, and nephew to England and into a new life as an intelligence officer for the BIS. Still holding the picture, he allowed his mind to return to the love of beautiful Kitty Johnson, killed on a mission back in 1937. It would be a long time before he opened his heart to another love, even though many tried, including Captain Hazel Collings. But no one could break the barrier around his heart until he met Claire. Within two days, he had asked her to marry him, he had found his lasting love. Happily married, Claire gave birth in March of 1944 to a beautiful baby boy, Nicholas, capturing Karl's heart. After one last look at the picture of Claire and Nicholas, he carefully returned the picture to the corner of his desk. Lifting the receiver, he dialed Claire's office.

"Morning, Barb; is the boss available?" Barb always recognized Karl's strong Austrian accent; it was that pronounced.

"Major, good to hear your wonderful accent. One moment while I find her for you. "Mrs. Vita, your husband is holding on two." Barb made sure Claire heard the word husband over the PA. "She will be with you in just a few moments, Sir. Hope to see you very soon; bye for now." Karl sat waiting for his wife to answer.

"Karl, darling, are you calling me with congratulations, or is there another reason?"

Karl, hearing this, smiled before answering. "Darling, I just wanted to tell you Bill and I spoke, and I could not be more pleased; joining your firm is a wonderful opportunity for both of you, so, you nervous solicitor, stop squirming." Karl was visualizing his wife at her desk.

"Karl, you always do that to me. You would think, by now, I'd be used to your games, yet here I am, still getting nervous over your next move. Bill has given you the rest of the details about him joining the firm, has he not? I asked him yesterday about the shingle on the building, did he have an opinion about keeping it the same out of respect for the founding partners? Guess what? He calmly replied that he would not have it any other way.

Darling, everything is working out for us, and I'm over the moon with happiness.

"Did he also mention he and Dorothy will drive you home on Friday? They'll be staying with us; isn't that wonderful? This way, you can return with them early Monday morning. Darling, I've already booked the private dining room at the George and Dragon for Saturday evening, and I've already spoken to Mama, Freida, and Ronny about joining us to celebrate."

Claire stopped talking, thinking, here I go again, getting over excited. I need to let my major get his two words in. "Claire, if you ever change, I will have to find another sexy lady with a spirit like yours. As for Bill and Dorothy driving me home on Friday, he has not told me that yet. I love the idea of gathering in Baldock this coming Saturday. You know how I feel about the George and Dragon, don't you? Did you say Ronny would be joining us? I didn't realize he was home on leave; he and I have not seen each other in over nine months. I must go, darling; the lads are waiting for me to join them for this long boring meeting. I love you, Claire; kiss our little terror for me and tell him his daddy is coming home at the end of the week; bye, darling."

Karl hung up the receiver and kissed the picture one more time before leaving his office to walk back to the lounge. "All right, lads, let's get this over with. It's going to be a long evening; you can be assured of that," yelled Karl as he rejoined the group. Their fire and spirit not as bright as in prior years, the tired band of brothers slowly headed toward the gymnasium and the briefing that would detail their upcoming mission. That dark cloud hanging over their heads in the lounge had started to diminish somewhat. Their plan for a peacetime future was the medicine they all needed to hear, realizing there would be a normal life waiting for them on their return from the continent, but that was still over eighteen long months away.

Clive, along with General Jacks, his staff, and members of the Allied Intelligence Services, stood behind the long table on the podium, waiting in silence until everyone had filled the rows of chairs. Over one hundred officers faced the stage, waiting for the order to be seated. From the back of the gym, a loud call for attention could be heard as Admiral John Gooding and three of his senior officers walked down the center aisle. Climbing the stairs to one side of the podium, they saluted the senior officers standing at attention.

"Gentlemen, please be seated," commanded the admiral. "Today, we start the final chapter in ending this war. From this day forward, we become military policemen; from here on, we will show our true stripes, not as spies but as hunters."

A loud cheer erupted as most of the audience stood clapping and yelling after hearing Admiral Gooding's opening statement. The admiral, while laughing, beckoned everyone again to be seated, enjoying the outburst.

"Chaps, this next phase will not be easy. In fact, it will be extremely frustrating. Finding those Nazi buggers who committed atrocities throughout the continent could well be the hardest mission for all of us. This afternoon, you will hear about our preliminary plans. Starting next week, we will dispatch groups to specific locations where those offenders have been reported to be hiding. Once again, let me remind you that this will be no easy task, so pay close attention to this briefing."

As expected, the briefing continued until almost 1850 hours; many faces had glazed over with tired eyes and overloaded brains. "Gentlemen, I can see from your faces that it's time to adjourn for today. We will reconvene here at 0830 hours' tomorrow morning. Thank you for your attention, and please, no stampeding out of here to the bar. We have plenty of beer and spirits available." With that, a very jovial Admiral Gooding bid them a good evening. After a quick supper, they regained their usual table in the lounge, tired but surprisingly upbeat.

"That chap Gooding is quite the character; wouldn't you all agree?" Bill said as he lit his pipe, puffing out a chimney of smoke. "I enjoyed his wit. He has a way of getting the gravity of this mission across, and I guess you could say they are preparing us for months of frustrating work. I must admit, I look forward to cornering those lying bastards and giving them a little payback. However, I would much rather shoot the buggers instead. How do you feel about that? The three of us have received injuries courtesy of the German Wehrmacht." Bill looked at Clive and Karl as he spoke.

"Bill, you know very well we will have to show a great deal of restraint if and when we corner one of those egotistical bastards. Just remember that when the urge to strike one of them overpowers your temper," replied Clive, concerned that many agents would lose their temper when confronted by the likes of highbrow Gestapo or SS blokes mouthing off about their superior calling. At 1930 hours, they all retired to their quarters for a good night's sleep.

The week dragged on to the point that most simply sat there, listening to a repeat of what was discussed the day before. The conference finally adjourned Friday at noon. "Gentlemen, thank you for your undivided attention. I can see you are now ready for the weekend. Just remember that next week, many of you will be heading out to your assigned duty zone, so enjoy these few days off, and remember, don't divulge what you will be doing." With that, Admiral Gooding left the podium and headed toward the exit.

Bill stood up and, turning to Clive, said in a boisterous voice, "All right, Clive, we're out of here. See you Monday morning. I understand Karl and I will be flying out with you blokes that afternoon, heading to Karl's hometown of Vienna for a month or so; our region also includes Salzburg for a few more weeks. We will have to play that by ear, I guess. Big hugs to Julie and the girls for us," concluded Bill.

Karl continued that sentiment by adding, "Yes, please tell Julie about Bill's future as a solicitor working with Claire. I'm sure she'll be pleased to hear that I know."

Their attention now turned to Gunther and Herbert, pleased that these two loyal Germans had finally reunited with their families after years of worrying about where they could be hiding. Clive informed Karl and Bill that Julie had invited

Gunther and Herbert to join them with their families Saturday afternoon at their house. "It will be so enjoyable, seeing those kids using sign language to communicate. Anyway, it will be relaxing for all of us. See you blokes on Monday morning." Clive was content that all his friends would have an enjoyable weekend before heading out for at least six months or possibly even longer.

Karl and Bill walked out the main door to see Dorothy waiting in the car. "There she is, always punctual. Got all our stuff in the boot, dear?" asked Bill as he swung his bad leg behind the steering wheel.

"Karl, sit up front; there's more legroom up there. I'll be fine in the back seat. Anyway, you chaps will be talking the whole way, I'm sure," commented Dorothy with a huge smile on her face.

Bill was about to give Karl some wonderful news. Once they were through Watford, he broke the silence by announcing, "Karl, before we get to your house, there is something we would like to share with you."

Karl stopped Bill from continuing. Turning in his seat with a big smile, he took Dorothy's hand as he completed Bill's announcement. "You two are getting engaged to be married, correct?"

Dorothy squeezed Karl's hand, replying, "Claire always says you second guess everyone, and here you go again, you hunk of Austrian spy; you are absolutely correct." Dorothy leaned forward in her seat, kissing Karl's cheek, tears of joy rolling down her cheeks.

After all these years, Bill had popped the question, but why now? Taking his eyes off the road momentarily, Bill turned to look at Karl's expression. "You old sod, you already figured that out when I told you that Dorothy and I will be moving to Hitchin once I leave the BIS, am I correct?"

Karl glanced at them, laughing loudly before replying, "You two know me so well. Of course, I knew. I'm willing to bet you five quid that Claire already knows. Bill, you were waiting until you had your future secured. That, my old friend, is simple intelligence thinking. I am so pleased that it's working out for you both, and it's wonderful to know we will still be together. Congratulations many times over!"

No sooner had they pulled into the driveway than the front door opened, and out came Claire with Nicholas in her arms. "Nick, look who's here; it's your daddy, Aunt Dorothy, and Uncle Bill." Picking up his tiny hand, Claire waved to them as they got out of the car. Karl rushed forward, throwing his strong arm around Claire's back, hugging them both, and kissing Claire passionately before kissing his little man.

"God, Claire, I hate these separations; they get worse each time I leave home."

Claire could never stop the tears each time her husband returned, and today was no exception. "Dorothy, we are so excited you two will have a couple of days to tour your new surroundings."

Claire was eyeballing Dorothy. Had Bill finally told Karl that they were getting engaged? Dorothy had confided to Claire and Julie two weeks before that the wedding would have to wait, adding, "It's still a long way off, but that's all right. We're already living together; living in sin can be fun," she concluded, laughing at this last statement.

Dorothy nodded in response to Claire. Just as she was about to speak, Karl interjected, "You two must think I'm dense. Of course, Claire knows, and so does Julie. You three tell each other everything, and that is a wonderful friendship. So now that we all know, what are we going to do about it?" Karl was really enjoying this, and he could tell the other three were as well.

"Dorothy, why don't you take those two bottles of Champagne out of the boot while I take the luggage up to the room? I'm assuming, first bedroom on the right, correct? Then, we have some celebrating to do," concluded Bill.

Hostilities had ceased, no more air raid warnings or fear of bombing raids, nor the new weapons the Germans were terrorizing the English people with. The new V-1 and V-2 rockets had no pilots. Instead, they relied on a gyro to guide them until they ran out of fuel; given time, these new weapons could have turned the outcome of the war. They were referred to by those in their path of destruction as the doodlebugs. The four close friends would have much to celebrate this weekend. Claire and Bill would spend Saturday morning in her office, outlining their new partnership in her firm of McGivern, Tilbey & Morrison. Karl and Dorothy took this time to visit the family in Baldock, which was always a wonderful time for Karl; he just did not see them that often. His mother, sister, and nephew Franchot met them at the front door. The last time Dorothy had seen them was at Karl and Claire's wedding; they hugged each other, and the mood was light and upbeat. Ronny had arrived back in Baldock the night before after being away for over nine months.

Karl embraced his brother-in-law, asking, "Remember me?" Dorothy stepped forward to embrace Ronny and gave him a big kiss on his cheek that left a perfect lipstick shape on his left cheek.

Ronny, laughing, yelled out to Freida, "See, darling, your old man can still attract the good looking ladies!" Freida was enjoying this reunion. Dorothy announced that she and her fiancé, Bill, had gotten engaged. The wedding, however, would have to wait until they had settled into a new home and Dorothy was successful in finding a new job. Mama hugged Dorothy, whispering something personal in her ear. Dorothy enjoyed whatever was said. Freida took Nicholas from Karl's arms. Franchot had already wheeled the pushchair outside, anxious to go walking with Dorothy and Freida, giving Mama and Ronny time alone with Karl.

"Ronny are you moving back to Baldock anytime soon?" asked Karl.

"Yes, thank God; I only have about three more months up north before we dismantle the base; our aircraft will be transferred to a larger base in Northern Scotland. As for my time in the RAF, I should be out sometime in December. The Americans are already planning to build new bases and recreational areas in Germany and Austria. I have accepted a full-time position administering and organizing new sites, some having golf courses. You know as well as I do that the big brass in the American military love their golf. The salary and benefits they have offered me are fantastic. The only snag at this point is I will be commuting till we are ready to return to Wien (Vienna) maybe when things get better; I can't see that happening till early in 1948." Karl looked at Mama, then back to Ronny, "Well, Mama, it looks like you will be going home. As for Mino, knowing my big brother, he is probably scheming to find a way of traveling back to the farm with Fritz, waiting there to make his move back into Wien to reclaim our property, assuming there's property still to be had. It's kind of ironic because I will be flying there with an investigation team next week, so I will be there much sooner than all of you. Hopefully, I'll be able to give you an accurate report on how bad things really are. If I can get some time off, I'll try to get a Jeep and, if necessary, an armed escort to drive out to the farm. Maybe I'll find Mino and Fritz there." Karl would not elaborate on the mission to hunt down war crime offenders hiding in Vienna and the towns and villages across Austria.

Karl drove them all to Baldock and the George and Dragon for an evening with the family on Saturday. Nicholas was already sleeping in his mother's arms. Karl let them off at the entrance to the lobby, then drove down Church Street to find a place to park the car. Walking back to the George, his mind took a detour back to 1937, when, arm in arm, he and Kitty (Lieutenant Kitty Johnson) had committed to marry. Tragically, that would never happen as Kitty lost her life in Germany on an undercover mission. Karl finding out about her demise when he and Gunther were on a fact-finding mission inside Germany. Poor Gunther, it was so difficult for him to tell me she was dead, thought Karl.

Entering the lobby, his mind still in the past, he looked up toward the wide central staircase, remembering clearly that last Boxing Day in 1937. Karl and Kitty stayed here before returning to their training base in Scotland. He stopped momentarily; his legs would not move as he continued to stare at that staircase.

A soft-spoken voice behind him said, "Darling, it's all right; I know what's going through your mind. I can see it in your face. Stay here until it passes; we'll be in the private dining room waiting for you once you have recovered your composure.

Remember, you're the lucky one; you're still alive and in one piece. Karl, you have a wife and son who love you so very much." Claire knew Karl still had bad memories and frightening nightmares about those early days in the BIS. They would become less frequent with time, but today, one had just happened. Leading him to a couch in the lobby, she made him sit down; stepping back, she maintained her distance while her husband battled his demons. Sensing the worst was over, Claire kissed him lightly on his cheek, squeezing his arm as she did so.

"Claire don't go; stay here with me, darling, just for a few minutes. I'm so sorry for this behavior. I have no right to spoil this day for all of you." Standing, he turned to Claire, placing his hands gently on her cheeks and then hugging her tightly, choking back the tears and fear raging within him. Claire stood perfectly still until she felt the tension slowly diminish from his arms. "I'm all right now, darling; what on earth did I do right to deserve a woman like you? I will never know."

Claire knew all too well that his recovery would be a slow process, so why keep returning to the George, where so many memories would capture his attention? The answer was simple: Karl loved this quaint hotel so very much. Strangely, it was therapy to him. Karl's expression had now changed back to his devilish look; he was back.

"Claire, you good looking mother, remember when we walked up those stairs for a wild passionate evening? Feel like letting them wait while we get a quickie?" Karl had regained his composure and mischievous ways as he kissed Claire passionately.

"Major Karl Vita, I'm your wife, not a quickie. No, I will not be a means to relieve your tension in some broom closet at the top of those stairs." Claire laughed heartily, thinking that if they did not have guests, she would have followed him willingly, but not today.

Inside the cozy private dining room, they all sat making small talk and enjoying a nice glass of French Chardonnay. Claire tapped the side of her glass to gain their attention before standing to speak.

"This is such a wonderful weekend! All of us are here together to celebrate the end of hostilities and the announcement of Bill and Dorothy's engagement. Join me in toasting Bill and Dorothy: may everything you wish for come true, congratulations again.

Now, we have one more announcement that dovetails right into this engagement announcement. Early today, Bill and I signed a letter of intent whereby he will join my law firm as a partner after resigning his commission in the BIS. Words cannot express my joy at having such a learned professional sharing the workload, although it will be a while before that happens. Let me welcome you aboard anyway. I believe you would like to add to this announcement; is that correct, Bill?" Claire sat down, reaching over for Karl's hand.

"Thank you, Claire, for making Dorothy and me feel very much at home. Joining Claire's law firm will be so exciting for me; it's been many years since I practiced law. Claire, I will be your shadow for a long time; I hope you know that. This new career makes it possible for Dorothy and me to plan for a new home right here in the Hitchin area. Dorothy asked me, if we are going to set up house in this area, why don't we plan our wedding right here as well? After all, it's going to be our home. So, Claire, when that time comes, can we impose on you to help Dorothy arrange the wedding plans at your church of St. Mary's? To conclude, thank you for this wonderful evening; we hope there will be more to come." Bill sat down, kissing Dorothy, a very, very happy man.

Sunday, after breakfast in the solarium, Karl excused himself to go upstairs to finish packing for the extended mission to Austria. The thought of being away from his family was making him angry. He'd had enough of being an intelligence officer.

Although, he was anxious to see how the Austrians were coping in this new peacetime environment. Vienna had suffered damage to many of its historic buildings, but compared to other cities in Austria and Germany, the damage could and would be repaired in the years to come. Carrying his kit bag and another suitcase downstairs, he placed them at the front door, ready to depart, then returned to the kitchen. Dawn had not yet risen, but the mood in the kitchen was solemn as he sat at the table.

"Karl, would you like some coffee before you depart?" asked Claire, her hands clasped together, a sign to Karl that she was getting anxious as their time together was almost over.

"No, darling, I would like to talk privately. I hope you don't mind, Dorothy," said Karl as he lifted Nicholas off his blanket.

"Of course, Karl, take whatever time you need. We will wait for you in the car. Claire, thank you both for a wonderful weekend; I can't wait to be neighbors," said Dorothy.

Bill also agreed, kissing Claire on her wet cheeks, "Things from here on will be far less dangerous, but separation is still hard to handle; stay strong, partner," said Bill as he carried their bags out to the car.

"Karl, Bill has put your luggage on the back seat. Now, go make a fuss over your wife and son," said Dorothy, walking out the front door.

Alone, Claire could no longer contain the emotions bottled up inside her. Since she was sobbing, the words did not come easily,

"Darling, no matter how many times we go through these goodbyes, I still have trouble. And this time will be another long mission; it will be almost Christmas by the time you return. Six months is such a long, lonely time when you love someone as much as I love you, darling." With her arms around Karl's neck, Claire realized this was not a good way to send off her man. Recovering quickly, she took Nicholas from his arms, trying to brave a smile.

"Claire, this may be an extended mission, but at least this time, there are no gunfights to return to. Please, don't worry about your old man. I will be careful; I promise you that." Karl loosened Claire's grip on his arm, then walked toward the front door.

"Ha, Sailor, how about one last going away kiss for your wife and son?" she asked, following him out to the waiting car.

Karl, his heart aching at this separation, turned around in front of the passenger's door, replying, "Any special place you would like that kiss, you oversexed woman?" Karl, with his arm around her waist, kissed her passionately. Then, taking Nicholas from Claire's arms, he kissed his son on the cheek, then his forehead, saying, "Take care of your mother, my little man; you two are my world, and I can't wait to spend more time with you both."

Bill started the car, and with the three of them waving out the windows, Bill turned right out of the driveway. Claire waited until the sound of the car's engine had faded, then with sadness, she looked at Nicholas, saying to her son, "At least I'm no longer home alone, Nicky. I will always have you, my precious baby boy. Let's go for a walk, shall we?"

# CHAPTER 2

# WIEN, DU WIRST ZURUCKKEHREN (VIENNA, YOU WILL RETURN)

The flight to Vienna was long and noisy, making several stops to offload personnel and cargo. Their Douglas DC-3 had seen better days. Nevertheless, it was still a more convenient way to travel than a noisy train that would take two days before reaching the Hauptbahnhof, Vienna's main train station, which was operating but still severely damaged. Karl and Bill made the first leg of the flight accompanied by Clive, Gunther, and Herbert, who got off in Hamburg, Germany. From there, they would travel by road to their duty station, about thirty-five kilometers east of Hamburg.

"Well, chaps, this is where we say so long. See you back in Slough sometime before Christmas, God willing," remarked Clive as he made his way to the back of the aircraft with Gunther and Herbert following.

"I hope you chaps are successful in your mission. These next few months will not be easy," Clive yelled before exiting the rear cabin door.

Gunther stopped momentarily at the door; turning, he yelled back, "Karl, keep your temper when you find one of those arrogant bastards. We don't need to see you in the hands of the military police for disfiguring a German officer." Hearing this, those traveling on to Vienna started laughing, brightening their day just a little.

"Up yours, you freeloader. Bill and I have the hard duty, so don't give me that. See you soon, God willing." Karl and Bill continued laughing as the RAF airman closed the cabin door, and once again, the big radial engines smoked back into life. The next stop would be the Schonbrunn Airstrip near the Schonbrunn Palace, east of Vienna. The RAF and the Americans operated this temporary air base between the Schonbrunn Palace and the Vienna River; it was the closest to the city. The Russians had control of upper Austria, which included Vienna, but by agreement, the city was divided into four zones, these being the Soviet Union, Great Britain, the United States, and France.

On this last leg, Karl decided he would study the latest occupation agreements, which, until now, had infuriated him, knowing his Austria and hometown of Wien were being carved up by the occupation forces. The document addressed the country's political status before the war and the latest agreement, which defined the Allied occupation, starting April 27th, 1945.

The Anschluss (Union), which commenced in 1938, defined the political union of Austria with Germany. The Allies, recognizing the events that had caused the capitulation of Austria to the Germans, unanimously agreed in 1943 to the document referred to as, The Declaration of Moscow. It stated that Austria would be regarded as the first victim of Nazi aggression. Once hostilities ceased, Austria would be treated as a liberated and independent country. Karl, reading this document, couldn't help thinking, if this is the case, why are all the Allies claiming zones? Reading on, he found his answer.

Until all the Nazi sympathizers and war criminals could be flushed out and political stability reestablished with a new government, the Allies agreed occupation forces would remain in Austria until the republic could be established on a date yet to be confirmed. Although divided into four zones, Vienna was policed differently from the rest of the occupied countries. The Allied Control Council collectively administered the central district. Germany, however, would not be given the same level of trust, being divided into four military zones with the Russians controlling Eastern Germany; this also included the encircled capital city of Berlin. In a show of force, the Russians cut off all road access into the city, virtually starving over two million Berliners. The situation was becoming a flash point for continued coexistence. The Allies tried negotiating with the Russians to no avail.

As Karl read that file, he had no way of knowing the muscle flexing would escalate to the point that the supply lines into Berlin were being choked off by the Russians. By June of 1948, Operation Vittles was launched by the Americans and British to supply the city. At the height of the airlift, transport aircraft were landing at Tempelhof Airport every 45 seconds around the clock, the most extensive aerial resupply mission ever recorded in post war history, and forevermore would become known as the Berlin Air Lift.

The Russians were infuriated by this bypass of their blockade, driving an even bigger wedge into the fragile treaty with America, England, and France. This would become known as the Cold War in the post war years. Karl came to the end of the file, and, closing it, he asked, "Bill, have you read this brief completely? I must admit, I hadn't, but now I'm glad I have done so. It all makes real sense to what's happening and why we are heading to Wien." Karl's rage had diminished as he realized what was happening in his beloved Austria.

"Karl, I briefly took a look at it the other day. I have not read it in its entirety, though. I think I'll do that right now while we are still in the air." Karl closed his eyes, allowing his mind to traverse the many events he had lived through. All these memories would be sidelined by the vision of his wife Claire and son Nicholas. Was he being selfish, wishing to return to the merchant marine service? That dream would always be at the back of his mind, waiting to become a reality, believing he had left before completing that phase of his life.

Claire understood that salt water was still running through his veins. He would never feel completely satisfied until he could retire from that deep blue mother ocean on his own terms. "Karl, wake up; we are descending into the airbase. You dozed off, and I let you sleep; you looked like you needed it." Karl just smiled; Bill thought I was sleeping, that's a joke.

"Karl, I agree with you. These documents I just reviewed really make sense. It's given me a clearer understanding of our mission in the coming months," said Bill as he returned the folder to his briefcase.

The DC-3 banked to the north, circling the grass runway, then banked even steeper. Descending over the tree line gliding down, it bumped twice as the undercarriage made contact with the grass runway. Karl strained his neck to look out the window at the wooden buildings and makeshift hangar left intact by the retreating Luftwaffe. Toward the left side of the runway, he could see a line of damaged, abandoned Fokker Wolfe-190 fighters, and further down, a few Heinkel-111 bombers stood unable to fly, one laying where it had landed on its belly, the props bent backward. Other aircraft wrecks used for parts littered the field leading up to the hangar. The Germans must have abandoned this base in record time as trucks, half-track armored vehicles, a few Kubelwagen, and a few Mercedes sedans lined the apron. Further down, an assortment of BMW motorbikes lined up, some laying on their sides; others had sidecars left behind, their service no longer needed.

As the plane taxied, it rocked in protest as it rumbled over the uneven grass; squealing brakes brought it to a complete stop, followed by the two Pratt and Whitney radial engines spooling down into an uncanny silence. The cabin door opened, followed by an RAF sergeant speaking loudly. "Gooday, Gents! Would Majors Lowes and Vita please identify yourselves?" yelled the sergeant in a strong Scottish accent.

"Here," replied Bill as they made their way to the rear of the aircraft. "Good afternoon, sirs; my name is Sergeant Thomas McKenna. I have been assigned as your driver for your time here in Vienna. I have a car waiting; could you please sign in at that administration building over there before we depart? I'll wait by the car while you take care of that; look for the car with the big white C on the driver's door. Sorry for the mess the Jerries left us; believe me, it looks much better than two weeks ago. Shall I take your luggage to the car while you sign in?" asked McKenna.

"Thank you, Sergeant," replied Bill as he identified his and Karl's bags. The car assigned to them was a dark grey Mercedes Benz 170V, recently repaired by the base mechanics. The German markings had been hastily painted over and replaced with hand painted British identification numbers. Outwardly it looked really rough, but the inside was surprisingly clean.

"The blokes in the motor pool found the best one from those staff cars parked over there. With some creative magic, they managed to get this one running again. The wheels came off that one on blocks, and from what I was told, the base commander used this particular car. It had a blown head gasket, so when those krauts hightailed it out of here, it was left behind with the rest of the vehicles," explained the cheerful Scotsman.

Once his passengers were onboard, McKenna started the engine. Turning toward the main gate, he took a sheet of paper from his canvas bag, studying the directions to the hotel where they would be staying. "Sorry, Sirs, still finding my way around Vienna. I think I need to go past the palace, then out on the Schonbrunner Strasse," announced the confused sergeant.

"McKenna, I'll direct you if you give me the hotel's name and street address. I was born and brought up in Wien, so no worries about getting us around for the foreseeable future," remarked Karl.

Bill broke out laughing as he listened to Karl giving their driver directions and correcting him on his German pronunciation. "McKenna, people from Vienna refer to the city as Wien; the letter V is a problem for German speaking people, including myself."

Looking into his rearview mirror, McKenna was taken aback that this major wearing an English field uniform was, in fact, an Austrian from Wien. Karl gave McKenna directions that took them past the Schonbrunn Palace. Gazing out the car window, Karl recalled a time nine years earlier when he drove past this historic palace with his mother, sister, and nephew. Fearing the worst, they escaped Austria before the Germans swept across the border with no resistance.

"It looks like the British have requisitioned the Schubert Hotel near the Prata," said Karl, looking at McKenna's directions.

"Excuse me, Sir; what does the Prata stand for?" asked McKenna as they continued driving toward the city.

"It means fairground or amusement park. The Prata is famous for having the largest Ferris Wheel in the world; it was built for the 50th jubilee of Emperor Franz Joseph in 1897. Not sure what it looks like now, but originally, it was designed to have 30 cars holding eight to ten people each. Oh, by the way, it's a whopping 65 meters high; that's 213 feet for you two."

Totally fascinated by Karl's knowledge of local history, McKenna replied, "Blimey, Sir, that's bloody high; those Austrian engineers must have been brilliant to design that big thing?" McKenna was really enjoying having such a learned guide in the car.

"On the contrary, old man, the design engineers were English: Walter Bassett and Harry Hitchens."

Entering the city's suburbs, Karl braced himself, remembering how the city looked during that final battle between the German garrison and the advancing Russian military. In the closing weeks of the war, Karl and Gunther had been sent there to assess the strength of both sides and report back on the outcome of this last-ditch attempt by the German and Austrian military to hold off the Russians. Now, many of the main streets and boulevards were closed off or simply impassable due to collapsed buildings blocking traffic access. Looking down the streets, they could see rows of trucks and an army of workmen feverishly clearing rubble; many of those vehicles had been loaned by the occupation forces. On the other hand, some side streets were virtually untouched by the bombing and street fighting, allowing traffic to pass freely.

Karl navigated from memory and his trusty pocket compass, finding streets that would take them in the general direction of the hotel. Turning onto a wide boulevard, they continued toward Stephan Platz (St. Stevens Place), eventually arriving at the once magnificent opera house, now encased in scaffolding as workmen worked to rebuild the ornate building to its former splendor. It would not reopen completely until April 1952, although limited performances did commence in December of 1948.

"There it is: St. Stephen's standing majestically in the center of the plaza." It, too, had been heavily damaged but, like so many other historic buildings in the city, was being faithfully restored. "When you get to the square, turn left; the hotel will be about half a mile if my memory serves me correctly," directed Karl, his insides churning at having to see the cathedral in such a state. In time, he would again be in awe of its beauty. At the hotel entrance, two armed military police stood checking every person entering.

"Looks more like a military headquarters than a hotel," remarked Bill as he stepped out of the car.

"McKenna, you will be staying here with us, won't you?" asked Karl as he walked toward the police guards.

"Yes, Sir, I will, so I'll be your driver any place you need to go while you're here. I believe only officers occupy the upper floors; the noncommission types and drivers will be billeted in the staff quarters downstairs. When will you need me next?" inquired McKenna.

"Not sure, but we'll find you probably tomorrow after lunch. If you go out, leave a note at the desk about how to get ahold of you. I don't think we'll be going anywhere for the rest of the day. Thank you for getting us here," concluded Bill.

"I think we should thank Major Vita for his directions," replied McKenna as he unloaded the luggage. Inside, rows of desks lined either side of the lobby. Army noncombatants were manning the noisy typewriters; rows of files lined the outer walls to accommodate the various teams of investigators operating from this location. "May I please see your orders, Majors?" asked a very young lieutenant sitting at the very first desk. Karl and Bill presented their orders, then waited while the lieutenant reviewed them. He removed two large, sealed envelopes from a filing cabinet, both with a sign-off sheet attached to the front. "Sirs, these envelopes contain all the documentation, passes, and vouchers you will need for the next two months, after which additional ones will be issued. You have been assigned adjoining rooms, 3012/3013. Not sure if the elevator is working again; we had problems with it yesterday, so just check it before climbing the stairs," concluded the young officer.

"Bill, how's that leg of yours? Will you be all right to climb those stairs if that elevator is still out?" asked Karl.

"One moment, Sir, does Major Lowes have a medical issue? If so, I could move you both to ground floor rooms. They are not adjoining and perhaps a little smaller, but most of the teams have not arrived as of yet, so it's not a problem right now," concluded the lieutenant.

"Well, if it's not a problem, that would be easier for me," replied Bill, returning his and Karl's keys. Walking down the hall, they were surprised to see local chamber maids busily making up rooms. "Well, at least they are being paid. We must help the local civilians, mustn't we?" said Bill as he arrived at his room. The young maid looked flustered, having not finished this room yet.

Karl, smiling, spoke to her in his best Viennese accent. "Young lady, please do not alarm yourself; we are only dropping off our bags into the rooms, so you can continue your work. It's time for a steinkrug (glass of beer) anyway.

"Excuse me, Sir, your Austrian accent is perfect! Did you live or study here in Austria?" asked the young maid.

With a big smile, Karl laughed and answered her, "Young lady, thank you for asking me that. I've had mixed feelings since arriving earlier today, but you've made my day. I was born and raised only a few kilometers from here, near the Prata. I'm home in my beloved Wien. It may be battered right now, but soon, it will rise again." Karl's spirits had taken a giant leap, his mood changing as he lifted the young maid off her feet, swirling her around and seeing the next generation of Wiener already paving the way forward. What is your name, dear?" asked Karl loudly.

Bill was standing there laughing, watching his friend's confidence bounding back.

"My name is Gretel; pleased to meet you, Sir. I am somewhat shocked to find out you're really a Wiener; welcome home, Sir," answered Gretel.

"The name is Karl Vita; sorry to scare you like that. Seeing everyone working like this is making me feel so much better. See you later. By the way, you are a charming young lady, but then again, look where you're from!" With that, they left, allowing Gretel to finish preparing their rooms.

# CHAPTER 3

# THEIR FIRST CAPTURE

Karl rose early at 0500 hours, deciding to use the bathroom first at the end of the hall. Returning to his room, he dressed in his field uniform. Reaching for his canvas shoulder bag, he walked down the hall and out into the lobby. Clerical personnel were already at their desks, waiting for additional military personnel to arrive. "Excuse me, young man; is breakfast being served in the same room as supper last night?"

"Yes, Sir, they are still setting up, but I'm sure you can get a hot drink while you're waiting," said the cheerful corporal. Karl entered the dining hall; civilian contractors were busily getting ready for the 0600 hour opening.

In German, Karl asked if he could get a big mug of coffee while waiting. Sitting at a table, he started to think that this hotel probably was used by the Germans, and these same people had waited on them. This angered him somewhat until he rethought it. Making a living, regardless of who the masters were, that's what hardworking people really cared about. Had Gretel worked here during the occupation, and how did she view those Germans? Interesting, he thought.

Taking his steaming cup of coffee, he walked outside, saluting the military policeman as he passed. The weather would be nice today; dawn was shedding light over the buildings. Karl was considering that, if time permitted, in a few weeks, he would like to visit the Vita homestead first. He did not expect anything had been done since he saw it last but seeing the family home was pulling at his heartstrings. Walking slowly along the pavement, he looked at the boarded up shops, thinking how beautiful these streets had once been. Now, look at them; what did this war accomplish other than destroying cities, towns, and families maybe never to be the same? Turning left at the corner, he stood in shock; the street was in its original state other than empty shop windows and the noticeable absence of vehicles. It could have been 1938 again.

Looking at his watch, he returned to the hotel and joined the others who would make up the investigation team. "Morning, all; I trust you all slept well. What time are we scheduled in the meeting hall?" asked Karl as he pulled up a chair.

"0730 hours according to this schedule," replied Captain Arthur Harrison, better known as Archie.

"What's on the menu? Anything worth eating?" asked Karl. "Well, old man, you probably will enjoy the sausage and black bread. Unfortunately, the eggs are still powdered; we can't have everything, I guess," concluded Archie as he stood to get another mug of tea.

Twenty-five British and Canadian officers assembled in the noisy meeting room, waiting for the director of British Operations to arrive. "Gentlemen, please find a seat, so we can begin," barked Colonel Martin Albeon. "Our task in the coming months is to scour this city and surrounding towns and villages in the designated search area assigned to this specific group. This operation is a joint effort by all the Allies. We have five investigation teams in this room; each team will be given a list of war crime offenders we suspect are still hiding in the city or may have already moved to a remote location somewhere in Austria. The Ratline has already dispatched over two hundred or so into Italy. Our search groups are chasing them down as we speak.

"Personally, I feel we are too late. They are probably on their way to South America by now. Your job will be to hunt down those still waiting to escape and bring them in. Let me make this perfectly clear: at any time, if you suspect these individuals are showing signs of armed aggression, then, in that case, you are authorized to eliminate them. These types are like cornered rats; they will try to harm you before you can react. Each team operating in the field will have an armed squad. Do not get in their way if a gunfight erupts. Do not,

I repeat, do not put yourself or your team members in harm's way. The war is over; we don't need any more dead heroes. Let's take these villains alive if we can then go home. Are we clear on our objectives? This world will be better off if these thugs leave it sooner than later. Now, I'll take questions if you have any," concluded Colonel Albeon.

"I have one, Sir," said Bill, standing to address the colonel. "The information you are providing each team, how current is it? I'm asking because chasing down cold leads will waste valuable time."

Colonel Albeon nodded his head in agreement, saying, "Excellent question. Unfortunately, it's a hard one to answer. We are going by information gathered from many sources, so I can't really give you a definitive answer; sorry about that."

Over the next seventy-plus minutes, questions were asked, many having the same results. The flood of questions exhausted Colonel Albeon, and he adjourned the meeting. Each team retired to their assigned operations room; their work was about to start.

"All right, chaps, we have our list of bad boys. Let's start at the top, shall we? Hauptmann (Captain) Hans Gruber, a Gestapo officer, has roots right here in Vienna, and from this report, he still has a family living in Linz. The Americans interviewed his wife recently, but they did not get anywhere with her. According to this report, he supposedly has been spotted within the last several weeks in this district. It looks like it's up to us to find this rat.

Major Vita, you're the local chap in this group. Why don't you take the lead on where we should start?" asked Archie with a sarcastic smile.

"Archie let's put that big map on the wall. That way, when we have finished canvasing one block, we can mark it as complete or some other term that identifies it as done. Also, let's take the most current information and start from there. Does that sound like a plan to you all? Now, I'm assuming you all can speak basic German; am I correct? If you can't, that will hinder the investigation," said Karl as they spread the large map across the wall, Archie stapling it into the plaster.

"Karl, every one of the team members has a good command of schoolbook German. May I suggest, as we start our investigation and uncover a potential strong lead, you can take over? How does that sound?" asked Bill as he spread the paperwork in front of them.

"Good move, Bill; now, can we start this mission because, at this rate, our friend Gruber will be long gone. In addition, as we canvas the areas and streets in our zone, let's mark places where the other four could be hiding if they are stupid enough to remain in Wien, that is. We should be able to cover more ground doing it this way. Okay, let's get this show on the road. Are our transport and armed guards outside?" asked Karl, reaching for his canvas shoulder bag.

"I believe so," replied Archie, strapping on his sidearm belt and checking his .45 pistol.

Outside, the weather cooperated with dry, sunny skies; it was a good day to go hunting. "If no one has an objection, I'll sit up front, seeing as I know my way around this city," suggested Karl. Crossing the city was a challenge, with the same diversions as yesterday. Arriving at their first location, Karl told McKenna to park the lorry at the north end of the wide boulevard. "Chaps, from here, let's divide into two search groups. Archie, you take the left side with Lieutenant Gray and five guards. Bill and I will start at the other end on the right just in case we see someone trying to make a run for it." McKenna dropped the first team off, then drove to the next intersection and parked the covered army truck. "McKenna do not leave this vehicle for any reason, and make sure the safety on your sidearm is off," commanded Karl.

Bill stood smiling, watching Karl leap into action and thinking, you can always rely on Karl to be the leader. He's a natural at operations like this. "Ready, Bill? Take the safety off your sidearm, and you five blokes should have your rifles at the ready," commanded Karl as they started walking to the first block of four-story apartments. In a low voice, Karl told Bill to take three guards and secure the courtyard. Then, with the two other guards, he walked up to apartment number A-102. Knocking loudly on the door, he yelled, "Apartment inspection, please open this door!"

Anxiously waiting, it felt like five minutes instead of the twenty seconds it was for the front door locks to be opened and the door opened in slow motion, only enough for the old woman inside to look through the gap. Speaking his perfect German with that distinctive Viennese twang, Karl asked the old lady, "Fraulein, sorry to disturb you like this. Would you open the door, so we can enter?" His right hand was resting on the stock of his sidearm.

"Yes, I'm always cautious about strange people at the door," replied the old lady as she opened the door wide. Karl and his guard rushed in, Karl yelling, "Frank, check those back rooms down that hall. I will check these front rooms."

Satisfied there were no others inside the apartment, Karl asked the frightened old lady to take a seat, then asked her, "How long have you lived in this apartment? And more importantly, can you help us? Have you seen a German officer reportedly residing in this apartment block? His name is Hans Gruber." Karl watched her facial expressions, and her hands clasped together tightly.

"I don't need trouble. I've been through too much already. Leave me alone; I beg you." Karl hated himself for pushing her like this. She was old and frail, worn out by years of fear and hunger; she just wanted peace at this point. Satisfied he would not get any useful information, he ordered the guard out into the courtyard and on to the next apartment. Over the next three hours, they went from apartment to apartment, then on to the next street, until the sun was setting. Meeting up at the lorry, a look of disappointment was on everyone's face.

"Tomorrow is another day, chaps; let's head back to the hotel," said Bill as they all climbed up the tailgate.

"Karl, when Gray and I were questioning an elderly gentleman on the fourth floor, he told us he overheard a conversation yesterday between two angry men. The taller one pointed his finger toward the hills, referring to them as the Wienerwald. Does that mean anything to you?"

Karl stopped dead in his tracks. "It means a whole lot to me; that word is German for Vienna Woods. If what you're telling me is accurate, our man has slipped away up into those woods. I'm willing to bet he knows his way around those woods, but guess what? So, do I. When we get back to the hotel, we need to meet with Colonel Albeon immediately to authorize at least fifty to sixty men to comb the entire Wienerwald. Well done, chaps; we may be onto something. It's getting dark right now. I'm willing to bet if our man is up there, he is waiting to meet up with agents of the escape organization known as the Ratline. He could also be connecting with people from Odessa, another organization set up by Reichsfuhrer Heinrich Himmler's secret service back in 1944, with escape routes through Madrid, Spain. That organization provides escape routes for higher ranking Gestapo and SS officers," explained Karl.

"At the crack of dawn tomorrow, we must be in position around the Wienerwald. I believe we have earned a grosser beer stein; let's get going. Bill banged on the lorry's rear window for McKenna to get going. Karl's mind was racing with planning tomorrow's operation. "Chaps, once we get back to the hotel, I must call the central police department immediately for their assistance in the morning. I'm sure they would love to be part of this arrest, assuming there is one."

Karl walked down the hall in the early morning hours to meet up with Bill and the others in their squad. "All right, lads, are we ready? Let me get a strong hot mug of coffee. I'll meet you outside," said Karl as he entered the dining hall. The breakfast line was long, but Karl spotted Bill pouring two large mugs of coffee at the urn. "Hope one of those is for me, Bill," yelled Karl over the noisy morning chatter.

"Here you go, boss, nice and hot, two sugars with a splash of milk, correct?" replied Bill.

"So, when did I get a promotion?" asked Karl, trying to be sarcastic enough to get a laugh out of Bill.

"Well, old man, this is really your operation this morning. The rest of us will be following your lead. You're the only one who knows where he is going, right? By the way, we have over forty-five regulars waiting by their lorries outside." Bill was enjoying this early morning banter with his friend.

Walking outside, Karl rallied all the soldiers around him, saying, "We will divide into five-man teams. The maps I had made up last night each have a team number on them. That will be your search area, so take the time driving up to the Vienna Woods to familiarize yourselves with the area. Now, to assist our search, I have arranged for a detachment of Viennese Police Officers to meet up with us at the base of the Wienerwald. They have excellent knowledge of those hills. They are only assisting as guides. They will not be involved in any other capacity; is that absolutely clear? Now, do we have enough two-way radios for each group? We must stay in touch at all times," said Karl, receiving a positive answer from one of the lieutenants. "Right, let's get this show on the road, shall we?" concluded Karl, his adrenaline pumping at the prospect of making an arrest. Karl joined Bill in their Mercedes, and in a spirited voice, Karl gave McKenna directions, the convoy following through the streets toward the Wienerwald.

It was now daylight, with the promise of a very warm day. The drive took only forty or so minutes to reach the rendezvous point. The police, in their gray and bottle green vehicles, with Polizei on the sides, were already waiting. Karl hopped out of the car and approached the officer in charge. "Good morning, Captain. I'm Major Vita of the British Intelligence Service; I am so pleased to make your acquaintance. Thank you so much for making these last-minute plans happen." Karl was enjoying being amongst fellow countrymen.

Once the search parties were organized with their police officers, the search commenced, with the police officers using sign language to direct the teams. Karl's team was approaching the main lodge from the west. They stopped to inspect several small chalets and continued climbing up through the trees. "Team five to command, we are at a chalet about halfway up. The fireplace is still warm with signs of food being heated; please advise?"

Karl took out his master map to locate where team five was operating. "Team five, from command, fan out and continue your search up the hill. If you get to the main lodge, do not enter. Instead, surround the building until all the teams converge there; command clear." Karl was getting concerned that they were too late. Two hours had passed since that radio message, and now all the teams were arriving at the lodge. Karl's mind was racing. His gut was telling him their Nazi had made his escape, but in what direction? "Captain Muller, is that small regional train station still operating near Grinzing?" Karl's mind was in overdrive, thinking about what routes they could be using, assuming they left on foot from the Wienerwald at first light.

"Yes, it's still in use mainly for local trains; why do you ask?"

Karl looked at his map again before asking. "What time do you think the next train would be passing through there and is there a way of finding out where its final destination will be?" asked Karl.

"Major, sending your troops to that station could scare off Gruber if he is heading there. If I take two officers and wait at the station, it will not raise suspicion. Why would it? We are Austrian policemen. We will take one of your radios, and if we see any sign of suspicious characters, we will radio you to surround the station," advised Muller.

"Excellent thinking, Captain. What are your thoughts on this, Bill?" asked Karl, now feeling they had not wasted the morning.

Captain Muller's driver parked the police car in plain view of the station, making it look like it was a routine inspection. Walking calmly toward the station office, he stopped to pick up a schedule, casually looking at the arrivals for the next train arriving at 1130 hours; its last stop would be in Graz. Waving to the stationmaster, he returned to the car, saying, "Radio this information to Major Vita immediately, then join me on the platform. Fritz, you walk down to the other end of the platform and make it look like you're in no rush. Alright, let's get going; remember to look around the platform as you go."

Back at the base of the Wienerwald, Karl got the message about the time of the next train. Turning to Bill, he said, "This could be it. We need to surround the station, but every effort must be made to stay concealed." While Karl was standing there, he got an idea. Speaking in German, he said sharply, "Officer, I need your uniform right now. I'll explain later. For the time being, you can play being an English Major; now, move it." The confused policeman removed his uniform, exchanging it with Karl's.

"Bill, I am going to take one of their vehicles and meet Muller at the station. You disperse our boys around the station; no one is to move once we see that train pulling into the station. Is that clear enough?" Karl was in control mode, and all his focus was now on that train. Jumping into the police car, he told the driver to waste no time getting to the station. Parking the police car to one side of the station allowed Karl to walk down the platform toward Muller, standing with his hands behind his back.

Speaking loudly, he said to Muller in German, of course, "Sorry to be late, Sir; I got a late start."

With a strange look on his face, Captain Muller played along with Karl's front by answering, "That's alright, Corporal; our guests have not arrived yet, so no harm done." Muller asked in a hushed voice, "Is everyone in position?"

Without turning his head, Karl answered, "They will be in about five minutes or so. Have your officer go right to the engine's driver with orders not to depart until released by you." Muller slowly nodded, then walked off toward the other officer farther down the platform.

The train's whistle sounded as it closed the distance to the platform. For a moment, Karl allowed his mind to return to the Hitchin Station and the sight of Claire holding baby Nicholas in her arms. How his heart ached at being apart like this; then, just like that, his mind returned to this operation. People in the waiting room started to wander out onto the platform. Muller and Karl were eyeballing the travelers. Karl began to think this was a wild goose chase when Muller walked back toward him, his eyes making a sign that further down the platform there were three men carrying suitcases who did not appear to be civilians. Karl casually turned. Walking down the platform, he could see the men were getting nervous as he approached. Karl was ready to leap into action if they got worried enough to make a dash for an exit.

The British troops were now in place, surrounding the station and the open areas across from the station. Others had already stealthily hidden in the waiting room. Muller looked at Karl, nodding that he thought they should make their move. Karl and Muller walked down the platform just as the suspects climbed into a carriage. "One moment, please," yelled Muller. "I need to ask you a few questions." With fear on their faces, they pushed themselves into the compartment, then lunged to the opposite side, throwing the door open and jumping down onto the track.

Karl blew his whistle loudly, signaling everyone to move in quickly. Karl and Muller followed the three suspects, jumping out the door to the tracks below, their revolvers at the ready. Muller fired his gun into the air to stop the three Germans as they ran across to the opposite side, climbing the steep grassy bank. At the top, they froze, throwing their arms into the air. They had run right into the rifles of twenty-five or so British soldiers, their guns at the ready. Karl reached them first, yelling, "Hauptmann Hans Gruber, you are under arrest on the charge of war crimes. If you make one wrong move, it will give me great pleasure to send you right to Hell."

Muller handcuffed Gruber while soldiers from the squad handcuffed the other two Germans. Gruber was now screaming that he was only a corporal in the infantry stationed in Wien and did not know an officer by the name of Gruber. Karl was tense with anger, almost ready to pistol whip this coward standing in front of him. "Get him out of my sight and back to headquarters."

Bill arrived on the scene, cheerfully saying, "Nice job and a well-executed plan. Captain Muller, you and your men have played such a big part in this capture. I will make sure you receive the appropriate credit for your assistance."

The drama was over. While they were standing around talking, a British officer approached the group, saying in German, "Major Vita, we should exchange uniforms, don't you think? I could get used to being a major." His Austrian humor was coming through. With the operation a complete success, Karl had overlooked the fact that he was still wearing an Austrian police uniform.

Roaring with laughter, he slapped the policeman on his back. Still laughing, he finally said, "There's a shed over there. Let's make the exchange in there, shall we?" Back in their proper uniforms, they walked back to the group. Karl approached Captain Muller. He spoke loudly for all to hear, "Today, Captain, you and your officers have reinstated my trust and love for Austria, my homeland. As a former Wiener, I have wrestled with what happened here during the war. Collectively, we have all learned a lesson. Never again will Austrians and other Europeans allow bullies like Herr Hitler and that swine Gruber, along with so many others, to use their uniforms and rank to commit untold atrocities against the innocent people of Europe. I was torn with my loyalty to Austria, thinking how could its citizens allow these things to happen? Over the last several weeks, all of you have reinstated that love I had and now have again. With time, those evil times will become bad memories never to be repeated. Thank you all again for assisting us today." Karl saluted the police officers standing in front of him, then shook hands with each before leaving with Bill to go back to the car and on to the next offender on their list.

The weeks clicked by, and the job became harder with every passing day. The four remaining Germans on their list managed to elude them. Each time, they got close to making an arrest but never close enough. They eventually managed to detain several more Nazis; one was badly injured trying to shoot his way out in an alley gunfight. The trail was becoming colder as the weeks dragged by, chasing down leads to the whereabouts of the others. Maybe one day, they will reappear in some distant city in South America. The weather was getting miserable. Karl always found time to write to Claire, trying to remain upbeat about his remaining time away from home. Christmas season was almost upon them, and right now, he had a few days off. He decided to request the use of the Mercedes to visit the family farm, the family factory, and finally, he would visit the family home in Wien.

Although the house was not that far away, he still had visions of seeing the horrendous conditions it was in during those last few days after Soviet forces had overrun the city. Although it was close to his hotel, he had not been able to bring himself to visit it, making excuses he was too busy chasing Nazi war offenders.

Making his way back behind the hotel, he found the military drivers and their mismatched assortment of former German vehicles. Calling out to his driver, he politely asked, "McKenna, good morning. I have a few days off and thought I would drive to my family's farm. I don't believe I'll need an armed military escort, though. I'll visit our family's property here in Vienna on my return. I'll take the Mercedes, which will give you some time to explore. Just be careful, as not all the districts are totally safe yet. Who do I see about using the car, and where can I get some petrol coupons if that's what I'll need to fill the tank?" asked Karl.

McKenna had come to admire this commanding officer. He was a man who made things happen, remembering how he had orchestrated the capture of Gruber. "Sir, I'm your driver. I understand how you might like to visit your family's properties on your own. It's very personal for you, and I'm sure it will also be quite upsetting. Would I be out of line if I asked to tag along, as I have not been out of the city since arriving? I will understand if you prefer to go alone. I just thought I would ask." McKenna waited in silence for Karl's response.

"Tom, I thought you would be delighted to have a few days off. Of course, I would enjoy your company under one condition. Once we are away from here, you drop calling me Sir, alright?" Karl had considered asking McKenna to drive him around for a couple of days but felt he needed some time off as well. "Well then, grab your kit bag, make sure the old jalopy is running alright, and don't forget to fill the petrol tank. See if you can scrounge a couple of jerry cans while you're at it." That triggered an old memory from back in 1936 when he was in Marseille for that last time. He purchased a little German Opel Cadet car during his shore leave. Included in that purchase, he had asked for four jerry cans of benzene fuel. Reliving that, he shook his head. Could it really have been more than nine years ago?

"Everything alright, Sir?" asked Tom, unable to fathom the blank look on Karl's face.

"Yes, Tom, sorry, I drifted off. Mentioning those jerry cans reminded me of a time back in 1936 when I wore the uniform of a German merchant officer, leaving my ship without permission. That action still haunts me to this very day."

Tom stood there dumbfounded. "Blimey, Sir, I had no idea you were in the German merchant service before the war. Maybe you can tell me about those times while we are driving if you feel like sharing those old memories."

"Tom, I think I would enjoy airing those skeletons with you." Karl decided he should start being more open about his past life. Back in the hotel, he walked into their operations room to find Bill. "There you are. How is your research going on the whereabouts of that bastard, Wendell Schneider? Any closer to narrowing down his whereabouts?" asked Karl, feeling a little guilty about leaving Bill to hold down the fort.

"Karl, please stop worrying. We'll be fine. You deserve a few days away from here; now, be off with ya!" said Bill as he waved his arm for Karl to leave.

Karl walked out to the front of the hotel to find McKenna talking to some of the other drivers. "Ready, Tom. I will enjoy driving to the farm this morning if you don't mind. I promise not to scare you too much; is that alright with you?" Tom had already opened the passenger door, believing Karl would tip his cap in a casual salute before sliding into the passenger seat.

Feeling a little strange at hearing Karl's request, he chuckled before answering his commanding officer. "Blimey, this will be a first for me, Sir. It's not every day a major in the BIS plays chauffeur to his sergeant, is it?" Karl, in high spirits, laughed out loud as he started the Mercedes.

Driving their way through the streets of Vienna and negotiating their way around the wrecked buildings and vehicles, they finally reached the open roads of the countryside. In parts, the landscape looked almost untouched by the battle that had raged in Vienna. The twisting, narrow streets looked serenely quiet, with virtually no traffic other than an occasional truck and maybe a horse drawn cart here and there. The only blemishes were the occasional burned-out vehicles that still lay off to the side of the narrow road. The sun was high in the sky, and the road was becoming steeper with wonderful winding turns through the countryside. This was the medicine Karl needed; it was so very enjoyable. It brought back additional memories, painting a clear picture of another time driving through similar winding hills when he made that life changing decision to leave his ship, driving from Marseille to Vienna. That time was a very strenuous period, with the ever-growing fear of being overrun by Germans looming over the people of Austria.

Along the way, he stopped in Innsbruck to see his old girlfriend, Annie Lourie. Openly smiling, Karl remembered that passionate evening with her at her parents' house so very well. Karl had asked her to return to Vienna with him instead of taking the train. That drive was a happy time. Unfortunately, it would come to an end when they arrived at her parents' house in Vienna, both saddened that the chances of seeing one another again could and would be many years in the future.

"Are you alright, Sir? You look like a bad memory has crossed your vision," Tom asked as he watched Karl's expression change from a broad smile to a solemn one.

"Tom, I'm sorry; I guess I drifted off into those old memories again. Now, let me finish telling you the story of how I ended up in the BIS, and I promise not to drift off again." Rekindling those bygone memories helped Karl in so many ways, thinking about how much he had to be thankful for. His wife Claire and their son Nicholas may never have happened if not for all those events that shaped his future. "Tom, I am really enjoying this drive. How about you? Are you getting bored yet?" asked Karl as he slapped Tom on the shoulder.

"Bored, Sir? Not on your nelly. Seeing all this countryside is breathtaking; thank God it's nice and sunny, even though it's a little chilly right now." Tom was from the western suburbs of London, raised and brought up in a congested row house with virtually no grass or trees to break up the drab brick buildings that seemed to surround the families that called those streets home. "Sir, until I joined the air force, I only got to see trees and grass when my parents took us kids on a coach to the seaside in the summer. Once I joined up, I got to see so much it saddened me that, as a youngster, it was only a couple of times a year. You have no idea how you're making this drive for me so delightful. Thanks, Sir, for bringing me along with you today."

Karl, listening to Tom, was thinking that men like him are the heart and soul of all nations, honest as the day is long and, sadly, the ones that get hurt the most in times of armed conflict. "Tom, talking like this, we nearly missed our turn. Hold on; I need to turn right into this lane. We are less than two kilometers from the farm. Sorry, it will be a little bumpy; this lane is not paved." Karl enjoyed the familiar surroundings as he drove slowly up the lane toward an opening in the tree line. There, in front of them, the familiar farmhouse and its outbuildings stood out against the backdrop of the mountains now covered in snow. Stopping for a moment, they both took in the distinctive smell of an operating farm.

"God, I miss being at this farm, Tom; it made my childhood so magical." Stopping like this gave them the time to take in the beauty and solitude of the surrounding countryside. Pulling up to the front door, Karl got out, telling Tom to wait in the car for a few minutes. The old door knocker was still there with the letter V at its center. Before he could use it, the door opened, and out came Otto Manfred.

"Master Karl, I can't believe it's you!" he exclaimed, throwing his arms around the youngest son of Herr and Frau Vita. "I did not expect to see you until things had returned to normal if there is to be normal. Anyway, we prayed daily for your safety. What is this uniform you are wearing? Is it the free Austrian Brigade?" asked Otto inquisitively.

"No, Otto, it's the uniform of the British Intelligence Service, which I joined back in 1936. Is Frau Manfred home this morning?" asked Karl.

"Of course, she is. Where would she be milking the cows?" laughed Otto. Karl beckoned Tom to join them as they entered the house. Tom walked up to Otto with his hand outstretched, receiving a firm handshake in return. Karl explained that Tom did not speak any German and he would translate for him.

"Please, come into the kitchen; I'll make coffee once I have found my wife. By the way, you may be surprised at who is staying here with us." Otto left them, heading to the barn.

Taking in the surroundings, Tom asked, "Sir, this is beautiful; is that man the manager of this farm? He appears to be a real nice chap," continued Tom as he sat down in one of the big rocking chairs near the fireplace.

"Otto and his wife have been with my family for as long as I can remember. When I was a youngster, my sister and I would stay here for a month at a time. The summers were wonderful, but I really enjoyed the wintertime. We get a great deal of snow up here, and going for sleigh rides is a memory I will always cherish."

The front door opened, and the voice of a young boy began yelling, "Uncle Karl, Uncle Karl, where are you?" As the kitchen door flew open, standing there full of excitement was his nephew, Fritz. "It's really you!" yelled the excited young boy, leaping through the kitchen and jumping into the waiting arms of his uncle.

"Fritz, you have grown so big since I last saw you in Wien. Slow your talking down; we have much to catch up on!" Karl laughed, tears of joy cascading down his cheeks. "Fritz, please speak in English and say hello to my fellow soldier; his name is Tom McKenna."

Fritz, freeing himself from Karl, walked over to Tom and, with his hand outstretched, said confidently, "Very pleased to meet you, Herr McKenna; please, excuse my poor English. I really don't have many opportunities to speak it, until today, of course."

"Fritz, how did you get here, and where is your father?" asked Karl, also explaining the relationship to Tom.

"Papa will be here shortly. He went to buy some more things to take with him to Wien. He is planning on leaving in about ten days," answered Fritz, still very excited at meeting up with his uncle again.

The front door opened again, and in walked Frau Manfred. Speaking loudly, she said, "Where is that little terror, Karl?"

He stood and walked over to the elderly lady, his outstretched arms ready to encircle her. "Millie, you are such a sight for sore eyes. Come here and give me a big hug." With his arms around the old lady, Karl kissed her repeatedly, those tears of joy shared by two. "May I ask where your son and daughter are or is that something too sensitive?" asked Karl, expecting a sad response.

Millie lowered her arms, then led Karl to the long kitchen bench and sat down before answering. "Karl, I'm sorry to tell you this, but Otto Junior was killed in the last battle for Wien; he was only seventeen. We tried to find out what happened to his body but never could. As for Greta, she is in the village teaching school. She normally comes home on weekends. She will be saddened to find out she missed you next time, yes?"

Karl made himself a mental promise to use his position in the Intelligence Service to find, if at all possible, where Otto Junior was buried. "Karl are you going to introduce me to your friend, and does he speak German?" asked Millie as she stood, her hand outstretched toward Tom.

"I am pleased to meet you. Karl, would you translate that for me?" Karl explained to Tom what Millie had said.

"Coffee, Herr Tom?" asked Otto as he passed around the big mugs full of strong, hot coffee. Tom decided to practice his limited German by saying thank you. The time was going quickly, and the aroma of Braunschweig sausage frying on the stove, along with some sauerkraut, was making them all hungry. As they sat eating they heard the sound of a truck approaching the farmhouse.

"That must be my brother," said an excited Karl, finally being able to see his oldest brother after all these years. Outside, Karl could see his brother inspecting the Mercedes, wondering who it could belong to. "That, Herr Vita, is British Military property; please, do not touch it." Karl tried not to laugh as his brother spun around toward the person speaking.

"Karl, my snotnosed baby brother, I can't believe it's you. My God, the last time we saw each other was in the courtyard of Mama's home in Wien back in 1936. The two brothers embraced, relieved that they had survived the war. Mino, you have been a constant worry to me. Mama and Freida will be overwhelmed to hear you are back in Austria. When I return to my headquarters, I will get word to them that you and Fritz are here at the farm, unharmed. Now, where is your wife, Mina?" asked Karl as they turned toward the farmhouse.

"That I'm not sure of; the last time I heard from her, she had made it to her mother's house outside of Prague, and from there, they were going to the mountain home of her sister. Karl, that was in November of 1938. I see you are in the Intelligence Service, and the badge on your uniform signifies the rank of a major. Is that correct?" Mino asked, looking at his brother's field uniform.

"Mino, I have been in the British Military Intelligence Service since arriving in England back in 1936. I'm married to a wonderful English girl by the name of Claire, and we have a son named Nicholas. Mama, Freida, and Franchot love Claire and Nick immensely, as does our brother-in-law, Ronny. By the way, he is a captain in the RAF until early next year. After that, he will retire from the service. He has accepted a position working for the Americans in Munich, Germany. It's a hell of a position; he will be in charge of all the recreational golf facilities around the country. As for our two brothers, they are both well, living in England and serving with the Free Austrian Brigade. I arranged for them to work in the supply depot. As for Mama, she can't wait to return to Wien. Any idea what the house looks like right now?" asked Karl as they stopped to talk further before joining the others.

"Karl, I'll have it looking presentable by about February or March of next year. Have you seen it yet? All that stuff in my truck is for the house. I intend to return to Wien in about ten days," concluded Mino.

"When you return to Wien, big brother, come see me right away. I'll give you my hotel address and phone number. You can stay with me; it won't be a problem, seeing as you're my big pain in the ass brother." Both brothers started laughing. Other than not knowing the whereabouts of Mina and the sad loss of their father, they were all safe. "Now, once you join me at my hotel in Wien, I will be able to patch a telephone link to Baldock, so you can talk to everyone, including your new sister-in-law, Claire. She speaks fluent German, just like a Wiener."

Back in the house, they all had a wonderful meal with merry-making, laughter, and stories flowing freely. "Tom, old man, it's time for us to think about returning to our base," said Karl as he stood, ready to say his goodbyes. Mino, remember to head over to the Hotel Schubert after you have dropped off your repair supplies at Mama's house. I'll leave word at the front desk to give you a room key if I'm unavailable. Otto and Millie, thank you so much for all you have done over these terrible years of hostility, and you, Fritz, I'll try to get back to see you, conditions permitting, in a few weeks, alright?"

Mino followed Karl outside. Pulling Karl's arm, he guided him away from Tom, saying in his broken English, "Tom, excuse us, I need my brother for just a few minutes, all right?" Karl followed Mino to a safe distance away from the Mercedes. "Karl, next time you visit here, I think you, Otto, and myself should look inside that cave, don't you agree? Remember, Papa moved a lot of things in there for security back in 1936? Everything was wrapped and securely covered, but who knows what the damp has done to them. So, bring some old clothes along, or you can use some of mine, all right?"

Karl thought for a moment about what his brother had suggested, then answered, "Mino, I can see you're anxious to get into that cave, but quite honestly, if you were to remove any of those things, what would you do with them, or where would you take them for safety? Surely not Wien; it will be a while before you can call that city safe. I advise that we leave everything hidden until this country is back on solid ground; then and only then can all of us come together with Mama to open it. Mino, that hiding place has been sealed since 1936. If any damage had occurred, it would have already happened. No, big brother, it's far safer remaining sealed until we can all make a family event of it." Karl put his arm around his brother, waiting for a response.

"Of course, you are right. I suppose I'm getting a little anxious about that cave, my little brother, the major in the Intelligence Service. Who would have thought you would turn out to be the brother in military uniform, our own spy?" Mino chuckled at his last remark.

Karl hugged his older brother again, then walked over to the car, saying, "All right, Tom, let's get going, shall we?" The drive back felt so different. Tom was talking about how he had enjoyed his day. On the other hand, Karl was miles away, processing what needed to be accomplished in the following weeks before his brother arrived.

The following morning, Karl rose early again, meeting Bill in the breakfast area. "Karl, I thought you were staying overnight at your family's farm?" asked Bill.

"Change of plans. Today, I'm going over to my mother's house. I had an unexpected meeting up at the farm with my oldest brother. Can you believe that bugger traveled from Trieste, Italy, to Salzburg here in Austria? He is such a wheeler dealer; he managed to buy a used German truck there, then drove with my nephew to our farm. What a wonderful surprise that turned out to be. I told Mino he could stay with me when he returns to Vienna in about ten days. I think that will be all right, don't you?"

Bill nodded his head in agreement. Karl slugged back his coffee, gobbled a roll, and then left to visit his mother's house. Karl had provided Tom with a city directory, telling him to have a nice day but remain vigilant of his surroundings. The drive to the house was relatively quick. Pulling into the courtyard, the sight in front of him flooded his mind. Workmen were everywhere, repairing the building and refurbishing the apartments. Locking the Mercedes, he asked a man he believed to be the foreman if his car was in the way.

"For an Englishman, you speak like a Wiener?" said the cheerful foreman.

"That's because I am a Wiener, just like you," he said, pointing to the Austrian shoulder patch. Walking into Mama's apartment, Karl was tensing up, remembering the deplorable state he saw it in last. There in the hallway, two men were applying fresh paint over the repaired walls. The ceiling had already been painted white. Speaking in German, Karl asked the older man, "What a big surprise to see how far the repairs have gotten. I'm assuming my brother Mino is behind all of this, am I correct?"

The older man looked at Karl, then with a broad smile, said, "Master Karl, have you forgotten us already? Have we changed that much?"

Karl focused on the man's paint splattered face, then smacking his hands to his face, he said loudly, "Herr Muller, I am so sorry for not recognizing you right away. It has been over nine years since I saw you at the factory. Please, forgive me, will you?" Karl felt embarrassed at not recognizing the former office manager of his father's company. Some intelligence officer I turned out to be, thought Karl. Then he asked, "Did my brother have anything to do with you working on this apartment?"

Herr Muller smiled, looking up at his son still on a ladder, paintbrush in hand, and simply responded by saying, "Your brother has created jobs for us and others from the company. It gives us a chance to start over again. We were barely making it through each day after the war was finally over. We lived without running water or heat during this last winter and finding food was our biggest daily challenge. My wife came down with pneumonia and died last March because of those conditions. Your brother came along when my son and I were about to give up. We had decided the best thing for us to do was to walk out of Wien into the countryside, where the chances of surviving could only be better. We are so thankful for his generosity."

Karl was sickened to hear yet again about what the poor people of Wien suffered because of the actions of the Nazi regime. Karl made his goodbyes, telling the Muller's he would return once his brother returned to Wien. His next stop was the family factory, which was about an eight-minute drive. Turning into that familiar boulevard, he stopped. Parking the Mercedes, he continued on foot toward the three-story building. About fifty or so yards further down, at the barricades in front of the entrance, Karl ducked beneath it, then continued up the five steps to the main entrance doors, thinking I would have thought these glass doors would have been broken. The building looked untouched from the outside, with no signs of bombs or street mortar fighting.

As he reached for the door, a loud English voice yelled out, "Sir, you can't enter this building; it's been requisitioned by Allied Command as a control center." The British Military Policeman crossed Karl's path.

"Corporal, I am with the British Intelligence Service; as such, we have access to all buildings in our sector of Wien. For you English types, Wien is the Austrian word for Vienna. By the way, for your information, this particular building belongs to my family. As for me, I'm also an Austrian, regardless of this uniform." Karl restrained his irritation to the questioning, realizing the young corporal was only doing his duty.

"My apologies, Sir. I did not notice your insignia. Please, be careful when you enter the building; it's a real shamble right now. The workforce inside is mainly ex-German and Austrian military, cleaning up and removing old furniture and plenty of damaged machinery. I was told the new command will arrive in a couple of weeks." Karl touched the tip of his cap in a casual salute as he reached for the door handle. Inside should have felt familiar, but right now, it felt like a cold, drab foyer. Whatever it was previously was no more.

Walking down the hall, he reached his brother's office, which had been repainted, and was waiting for furniture to make it a viable work area again. Farther down the hall, he reached his father's office with its large windows. The smell of new putty around the glass created a vision of what it looked like only a few weeks earlier. A new sign had been hung on the office door that read Command Headquarters. Karl spent the best part of an hour touring the entire building, talking with many of the workers who were more than polite at seeing this English major roaming the floors. Before saying goodbye, he wished them all good luck for the future.

Returning to the car, he thought, I'm not sure I will ever enter that building again, even after it reverts back to our family. He pondered for a moment. It's still early, so I think I'll drive to Annie Lourie's parents' home; maybe it's been spared. Navigating his way, he continued to be amazed at how people were working to restore their beloved city. He remembered when he was here last; how many of these women were raped and their homes plundered? *I guess I'll never know the answer to that question, will I?*

Pulling up to the closed wrought iron gates, he saw a big chain and lock preventing him from driving further. Walking over to the side gate, he was surprised to find it unlocked. Karl entered, walking down the drive toward the once beautiful home of the Lourie family, now looking more like a shabby reminder of what the German occupation had left behind as they hastily vacated the house and the city.

Someone yelled, "Stop right there; this is the police." Karl slowly removed his military identification card, waving it in the air for the police officer to see. Taking the card, the officer asked, "What is your purpose here?"

Karl politely told the officer he was a close friend of the Lourie family, as well as being a former citizen of Wien himself. Hearing Karl's story, the officer returned Karl's ID card, asking him if he intended to visit with Herr Lourie, inside directing his workmen.

Karl could not believe what he was hearing. "Herr Lourie is here. When did he arrive? Does he have any family members with him, or is he alone?"

The policeman smiled, saying, "He only arrived this morning. I'm not sure who is with him; I'll walk you up to the house. Herr Lourie has hired off-duty officers to patrol the house and grounds day and night now that it is being renovated."

Karl could feel the excitement building as he entered the house. "Excuse me, Herr Lourie; this officer is here to see you," said the police officer.

Turning quickly, Herr Lourie could not believe his eyes at the officer standing before him. "Karl, is that really you? I can't believe it. My wife and maybe Annie will arrive tomorrow; they will not believe me when I tell them I saw you after all these years. Come, let's go and find someplace to have a cup of coffee, shall we?"

Over coffee, Karl told the elderly gentleman about his experiences, leaving out the times he nearly became a fatality of war. Finally, he summarized how he met his wife and about their son Nicholas. "Herr Lourie, you must know I'm anxious to hear all about Annie. Did she marry, and does she have children?" Karl was hoping to hear her life had been filled with only happy times.

Herr Lourie slowly shook his head and took a moment to compose himself, then answered in a slow, saddened voice. "Karl, I wish I could have a better story to tell you, but unfortunately, I don't. Three years ago, last October, Annie and her husband Helmut were going to a birthday party given by their friends for their daughter. Julie was seated on Annie's lap, and the road was wet with patches of ice. A delivery van approaching the intersection slid right through it, slamming into their car and sending it into a spin. Helmut tried to correct the spin, but his actions made it that much worse. They rolled down the embankment, the car landing on its left side. Annie was the only survivor. Karl, she has never really got over the loss of Julie. Such a sweet girl. We all loved her so much. Anyway, now you know and will be prepared when you see her in a couple of days. She is going to be ecstatic at seeing you again. As for poor Helmut, well, that marriage was doomed from the start. They both worked hard to make it work, but let's not mince words. She will always be in love with her first love, and that, Karl, will always be you."

Karl sat up; his pain was written across his face. The old man reached over, taking Karl's arm he said softly, "Karl, it's a fact, but you should not feel guilty. We can blame this damn war for many lost opportunities, and you and Annie were among those fatalities. When you escaped to England, it made it impossible for that relationship to survive. She was already pregnant when she arrived in Switzerland. My wife and I comforted her as much as we could, but you know how headstrong she can be. She insisted it was her problem and no one else should carry that burden.

Helmut was a nice chap, and he knew she was expecting someone else's child, but he wanted to marry her anyway. At first, it was wonderful to see them together. Unfortunately, that did not last long once Annie gave birth to Julie." The elderly gentleman stopped talking, waiting for Karl to process what he had been told.

"How far along was her pregnancy when she arrived in Bern?" asked Karl.

"Five months, I believe. Are you thinking Julie could have been your daughter, Karl? I personally don't believe it could be. After you left, she started seeing an officer in the Austrian Army, but that didn't last very long either. All serving officers were called up, but who really knows what happened back then? Annie would never talk about it, and now Julie is lost to us forever. Whenever we bring up Julie or Helmut, she becomes defensive and even more evasive." Herr Lourie changed the subject, confirming how pleased he was to see Karl again. "I can only imagine what you have experienced. Those ribbons on your uniform tell me you have seen more than your share of atrocities. No need to answer that, Karl; the expression on your face tells me all I need to know. I'll get a message to you when Annie and her mother arrive. Where are you staying?" Taking a small pad and pen from his jacket pocket, he took down Karl's information.

Looking at his watch, Karl said, "You must excuse me, Sir. I must return to my hotel; I did not realize the time. It was truly wonderful seeing you safe and in good health, and I look forward to hearing from you soon." Karl shook hands, then left without looking back.

Back in the hotel, Karl headed for the bar. Loud voices and smoke made it a happening place. "Karl, over here, we were wondering if you would be joining us," said Bill, pushing a chair out for his friend. "Well, did you get to see everything?" asked Bill.

"Just about got a few surprises, though," replied Karl, slugging down his first beer. "It appears that Annie Lourie will be arriving tomorrow. Earlier this afternoon, I spent some time with her father. He's a wonderful old bloke always liked him." Karl refrained from saying anything further; there were too many around them. "I'll tell you more over dinner. Drink up. I'm famished; it's been a long day."

The dining room was surprisingly quiet as they walked in. "It's still early; it won't be like this in about another hour, so if there is sensitive stuff you want to share, do it now," said Bill as he sat down at a table in a quiet alcove. After telling Bill about Annie and her tragic loss, he sat with his hands clasped together, his face wrestling with a nagging question. Could Julie have been his daughter? "Bill, Herr Lourie is convinced she was the daughter of an Austrian Army officer. I'm wrestling with a big decision right now. Should I see her, and if I do, could it stir up old feelings, making her emotional stability that much worse?"

Karl continued eating, waiting for Bill's opinion. "Karl, that's a difficult question to answer. If it were me, I would make an effort to mend bridges. I think your friendship right now would go a long way to helping Annie heal those hurtful memories. Talking about all those good times when you were together will go a long way to changing her current frame of mind. Does that answer your question? I'll cover for you tomorrow if you decide to make that visit," concluded Bill.

As usual, Karl rose early, then proceeded to the lobby to post his letter to Claire, looking for familiar faces in the breakfast area. Seeing no one, he asked for a mug of coffee and a buttered roll before proceeding to the courtyard to get the Mercedes.

"Morning, Sir, will you require me to drive you today?" asked McKenna.

"No, Tom, not today, but definitely tomorrow morning," answered Karl as he started the car. He took the time to explore other places he wanted to visit, killing time before heading to see Annie. Looking at his Lecoultre watch, he was satisfied it was the right time to make that visit to see Annie at the house. The wrought iron gates were now open with a police guard on duty. Pulling up to the officer on duty, he presented his identification card, receiving an immediate salute.

"Drive on, Sir; the Lourie family is expecting you." The policeman waved his arm for Karl to proceed. Karl's mind was racing, remembering those many times he had driven down that long driveway. Parking to the side of the front door, he got out, straightening his uniform. Then, placing his cap on his head, he approached the steps to the big front doors. Ringing the doorbell, he stepped back, feeling the tension build. The door opened, and there stood Annie, immaculately dressed, but her face said something else. The tortured expression had aged her.

"Karl, you darling man, you have already brightened my day. It is so wonderful you came to visit us. It's going to take a little while to get used to seeing you in an English Army uniform instead of that handsome dark blue maritime one. Come here and give me a big hug."

Karl stepped forward, his strong arms enfolding her slender form. For a moment, they stood there in the doorway. He held her tightly, sensing that she was fighting back the tears and tension, which started to make her shake. "Damn it, Karl, look what you have made me do. I promised myself I wouldn't do this; now, look at me." Looking up, she looked right into his eyes, those silent words telling him what he was not prepared to acknowledge.

"Annie, it's so wonderful to see you again after nine horrible years of war! I can remember so clearly saying farewell right here on these steps, having no idea what was in store for either of us in the years to come." As they entered the makeshift dining room, Annie's mother was excited to see Karl once again.

Hugging him and kissing his cheek, she spoke, "Papa, why don't we leave these two alone; they have so much to talk about. Karl, shall I bring you your usual very strong coffee?"

"Madame Lourie, you know me so very well. Please, that would be nice." Karl felt Annie taking his hand and guiding him into the living room. The workmen had been dismissed until after Karl had left.

"Come, sit next to me, and tell me all about your family. Father told me you had told him about them yesterday; do you have pictures?" asked Annie, a little more relaxed now.

"Yes, I do, Annie, but I really have a question to ask you before we do that."

Annie took his hand once more. Tears flowed down her cheek as she spoke. "Father has told you about Julie and Helmut, and you're concerned my daughter could have been your child. That's what's scaring you, am I right? You can relax, Karl; she was the daughter of a man I fell in love with right here in Austria. I left Wien with his child growing inside me. We communicated briefly, and he knew I was carrying his child. We were both excited at the thought of getting married and raising our daughter. After Hitler's forces took over Austria, I lost contact with him altogether. Believe me, I was almost tempted to return to Wien. Thank God, my father stopped me. I found out later that his unit had been reassigned to a regiment of the German army. I fear he met his fate someplace. I will never find out, will I?" Annie felt better that Karl had heard the answer to the agonizing question he had been concerned about since the day before. Karl was hurting as he continued to listen to her story. With a stone face, he moved his head slowly from side to side in disbelief. Annie was looking at him, thinking he is feeling guilty about how he left me. "Karl, now that you have heard about my life, show me those pictures."

Karl snapped out of his current frame of mind. From his inside pocket, he removed three photographs from his wallet, handing them to Annie. "Karl, your wife is beautiful, and your son is truly a Vita. In years to come, the ladies will have to watch him just like I had to watch you, correct? This picture of Claire looking back over her shoulder in her sports car is really striking. What's the story behind that picture and car?" Annie was throwing question after question at Karl.

Karl, smiling quietly, said to her, "Slow down; I can't keep up with you."

Annie apologized for her excitement that covered up her broken heart and continued by asking, "Now, tell me all about how you left Wien and all the details in between, leaving nothing out."

Over the next ninety minutes, Karl gave her all the details, including the time he was within minutes of taking his own life as a prisoner of the Gestapo and the other times he was mortally injured. Still holding his hand, Annie was visibly moved, hearing he almost did not see the end of hostilities.

With tears in her eyes, she spoke, "Oh, Karl, we may not be together anymore, but I don't believe I could face going on if you had been killed. Claire would be the same. She and I have a lot in common, and that, darling, is you."

Karl stood, and looking at his watch, he looked down at Annie, kissing the back of her hand as she said, "Karl before you leave, promise me you will bring Claire and Nicholas to see us one day when things return to normal, will you do that for me?"

Karl, seeing her like this, was feeling even more guilty for all the things he had done wrong over so many years. Annie took his arm and walked him to the dining room to say goodbye to her parents. Karl said, "I am so pleased we could connect. Let me say this; I may live in another country with my own family, but there will always be a private place in my heart for this family and my city of Wien. We'll meet again and thank you for allowing me to visit here today."

Annie walked him outside to his car, not really saying much. "Karl, I haven't said this to you in so long, but indulge me one more time. I am and will always be in love with you. Kiss me goodbye once more; I need to have that to comfort me and what could have been." Annie turned in front of him and, putting her arm around his neck, reached up, kissing him on the lips. Karl did not move as she did this, thinking if this will help her, why not?

"Annie, that was wonderful, but you obviously realize it can never be repeated, don't you?"

Annie, still holding him, replied, "Yes, Karl, I do. Goodbye, my lost sailor."

# CHAPTER 4

# HOME TO ENGLAND

Karl, along with his brother Mino and nephew Fritz, arrived at Vienna's Westbanhof Train Station with plenty of time to spare. Karl had arranged for them to visit the family in Baldock for Christmas. Mama and the family had not seen them since leaving Wien in 1936, and this would be a glorious reunion for them all. Standing by the compartment door, Karl made sure everything was correct.

"Remember, when you get off the boat train in London, we will be waiting for you by the exit gate in Victoria Station. Have an enjoyable journey; it looks like it's time for you to be boarding. Fritz, give your uncle a big hug." Karl turned to Mino, hugging his big brother, then, with a wave, he walked back down the platform. Outside the station, he waved to McKenna, who was waiting with the Mercedes further down the curb.

"Well, Tom, this will work out nicely. By the time they arrive in London two days from now, I will already be home. Those DC-3 transport planes may be uncomfortable and noisy, but it cuts the travel time down with only one stop to six hours or so. It's a real shame I couldn't take them with me because it's a military flight. Now, let's get cracking; I have a plane to catch."

Bill had arrived at the airdrome earlier, taking Karl's luggage with him. Looking at his watch, Bill was thinking, come on, Karl; you're cutting it close. From the gate, Bill could see the Mercedes approaching the aircraft, which had already started boarding.

They were finally heading home for Christmas after a deployment of nearly six months. Jumping out of the car, Karl thanked McKenna for taking such good care of them and promised to stay in touch. Climbing the ladder, he yelled back to McKenna, "Tom, hope that old girl keeps running until you leave next year; thanks again."

On the tedious flight home, he had a lot to think about, including the ones that gave meaning to his life. His last thought looking out the window was a sad one as he bid farewell to his beloved Wien and his first love, Annie.

Claire and Dorothy made sure they arrived early at RAF Bevington, almost an hour before the scheduled arrival time. They were waiting there, eyes focused on the end of the runway for the first sight of the lumbering DC-3 descending toward the runway. Dorothy had followed Claire in Bill's car. Between the four adults, the baby, and all that luggage, there would not be enough room in one car, so they decided to take two. In the operation room, the big potbellied stove kept the room nice and cozy.

"Mrs. Vita, the tower just informed me your husband's plane will be touching down in about fifteen minutes; they're almost home." Claire thanked the sergeant. She could feel the excitement building to see her husband climb down that ladder, realizing that this was his and Bill's last deployment for the BIS, or was it?

"There's the plane, Dorothy just about at the trees. I can't believe they're almost home. Bill will be so relieved being demobbed this coming January. As for poor old Karl, he won't get out until June of 1947, and that could be extended into July. Next year will be a year of change for all of us. The best part is that you two will live close by to us in Hitchin and that will be wonderful." The Dakota taxied over to the hangar; applying the left wheel brake, it spun around, so the cabin door faced the operations room. The two big propellers had wind milled down to a stop before the cabin door opened, followed by a crew member attaching the boarding ladder. One by one, the passengers disembarked, walking quickly to their loved ones. Claire, getting impatient, turned to Dorothy, saying, "Don't tell me they're not on this bloody plane. I'll kill him if he pulls that one again." Dorothy just smiled; she knew her friend so very well.

Two figures appeared by the open door: Karl and Bill, both with big smiles on their faces. "Come on, Bill; let me help you down.

Give me your walking cane first, then be very careful; this ladder is slippery and steep." With Bill's feet firmly on the tarmac, Karl turned toward the terminal when he was hit by two arms wrapping around his neck, not a good thing to do to an officer who still suffered from shell shock.

"Karl, my darling husband, you're finally home! I can't believe it after all this time! Bill, did you watch over my crazy Austrian?" Claire was her usual self, the excitement clearly showing all over her face.

Dorothy had also thrown her arms around the normally composed Bill, kissing him profusely and yelling, "Come on, Bill; loosen up. Just wait until I get you home later." Bill looked at Karl, both laughing at their excited ladies.

"Claire, where is my little man? You did bring him to meet us, didn't you?" Claire turned and pointed to the WRAF girl standing inside by the window. Karl kissed Claire on the cheek, then walked in to get his son. Bill was looking on, thinking, what a change from that cocky maritime officer Clive and I met in Dover so many years back. The BIS will have a hard time finding anyone else with his capabilities and commitment. I'm not sure how I will tell him that Clive wants him to be a key witness in June for the trial of the Gestapo officer responsible for torturing him and Jean Yves. He won't like that either, but it should only be for a couple of weeks, though.

Karl entered the operation area, his arms outstretched and ready to take his son. "Nicky, come to your Papa! Thank you, Miss, for holding him. I'll take him from here. Nick, how you have grown over the last six months!"

Claire and the others entered the building, enjoying how Karl was twirling his son around. Claire spoke, "What say we all head home? It's been a long day so far."

"What time do we have to be at Victoria Station tomorrow, darling?" Karl asked.

"We should be alright if we get there about 1400 hours," replied Claire.

"You didn't say anything to Mama or Freida, did you?" asked Karl. "Darling, have you forgotten already that you are married to a solicitor? Secrets are my business," Claire replied with a smirk.

"Bill, I guess I'll see you next at your new house. I bet Dorothy did a great job preparing it for her returning hero." Bill looked at Karl before they both broke out laughing.

"Returning hero, my ass," replied Bill as he walked away arm in arm with Dorothy.

Like so many others, Karl had missed Christmas and New Year's so many times. This year would be different; the family would be reunited, including Claire's sister with her family. They all had much to celebrate; the war in Europe and the Pacific was finally over. Claire drove home, so Karl could bond once again with his son. Claire smiled as she frequently glanced at her husband, thinking, poor bloke, what demons he shelters from me.

Finally, she spoke, "Darling, after Christmas, what say we think about trading the good old Wolsey in on a new car? She is starting to show her age." Karl nodded and laughed, in a sign of agreement. "What is so funny about buying a new car?" she asked.

Karl, still laughing, finally responded, "The last time I purchased a car, I ended up marrying its owner." Claire tried hard to restrain the temptation to come back with a wisecrack remark but decided not to.

"Karl, you can be such an idiot. Now, be serious; what's that car you saw in Baldock before you went off to Wien?" Karl smiled when he realized Claire was talking to him in German.

"Claire, I know you are almost fluent in German, but my English still needs some work, so English, please." Karl was still amazed at how quickly she had mastered this second language.

Later that evening, after Claire had made a wonderful roast beef dinner with all the trimmings, thanks to their friends at the farm who supplied them with the ingredients, their bellies were full. Karl put Nick to bed before returning to the sitting room, finding Claire on the floor in front of the crackling fire with only a few candles to set the mood. Claire and Karl loved listening to classical symphony music, and in that firelight, the magical music of Rachmaninoff and Puccini had a soothing effect on them both. Sitting on the floor, leaning against the settee, sipping a glass of Brandy, they were in a new place. The topic of war was now replaced by what would be their new challenges as they looked toward the new year.

Claire cuddled against Karl's arm. Speaking first, she asked if he had thought any more about returning to the maritime service.

"Yes, Claire, I have been thinking about that quite a lot recently, but when I do, I feel guilty about pursuing that dream. Darling, you have been patiently waiting for me to be home on a full-time basis. Returning to sea duty will leave you alone once more. That, Claire, is selfish on my part, so I really am wrestling with what to do once I say goodbye to the BIS. If you remember, I have already been approached by the English and American diplomatic services about joining them. These career opportunities won't stay available very long, so I really don't know how to proceed. Claire, speak your mind on what I should do at this point."

Claire stood up, returning with the Brandy bottle and topping off both their glasses before responding. "Karl, you have always been your own man; that is something I love about you. Darling, let me say this, you have done so much for this country, your family, Nicholas, and me. Maybe this new phase of your life should be pursuing your old passion, returning to the deep blue ocean. If you are serious about this, do it soon before our children grow up, but hear me loud and clearly, I will agree to this for no more than three years. Is that agreed?" Claire saying that, sent him a message that Karl heard loud and clear.

"Claire, you just said something that has me wondering what you're trying to tell me. You said children, not child. Was that a slip or wishful thinking?"

With a suggestive look on her face, Claire smiled as she put her arm around Karl's shoulder. "No, Karl, that was not a slip. When I had my scheduled appointment with Doctor Burgess, we discussed having another child and that you could be returning to merchant service once you retire from the BIS. His suggestion was, if we want another child, we should be thinking of becoming pregnant sooner than later, regardless of whether you are away at sea." Claire took another sip of her Brandy and stroked her hand on Karl's cheek as he processed what she was saying. With the likelihood of lasting peace, Claire and her husband Karl were finally allowing themselves to plan for a new life where danger had no place.

"Claire, God, you are strong, saying that like you did. In one sentence, you are sending me off to sea, with the likelihood of leaving you with a bun in the oven. I guess you better get ready for some long nights to make that happen; that's the best Christmas present you could give me. But Claire, are you sure about this? You know I always talk of having a girl before Nick gets too much older, but that's a lot on your shoulders, darling? Do you feel like getting a head start tonight? I'm a little out of practice, so you might have to help me in that department." The old Karl that Claire loved was starting to arouse her again after six long months. With a smile, she reached down and unbuttoned his trousers.

The following morning, they bundled up Nicholas, driving him to spend the morning with Mama in Baldock, giving her the excuse that they were meeting some BIS friends but would return for a late lunch. The drive to Victoria Station took a little over an hour. Parking the car, they walked into the busy station, hand in hand and over the moon that their family could expand in the coming year. Outside the iron gates at the head of platform number five, they waited patiently for the first sight of the boat train arriving from Dover. Karl kept looking at Claire, wearing a stylish tweed coat over a straight skirt, which, when open, showed off her figure very well. Against the cold, she had a wool jumper set to finish the look. He loved how she carried herself, stylish and always the classy lady. Standing beside her, he smiled, watching her become excited to meet her brother-in-law and nephew for the first time. The thought of potentially becoming a mother once again was beaming across her face. Seeing her like this, Karl pulled her close, kissing her affectionately.

"Wow, Karl, I did not see that coming. Darling, let's not make a spectacle in front of all these people, shall we?"

Karl, laughing, answered her by saying, "Never stopped you before, you good looking woman. Look, here comes the train. Are you ready to meet the head of the Vita family?"

Claire answered in German, "I hope they approve of your English wife."

With his arm around her waist, Karl whispered in her ear, "Darling, you have won the hearts of all the other family members. What makes you believe my big brother will be any different?"

Claire kissed his cheek, then turned to watch the engine slowly approach the buffers at the head of the platform. With smoke and steam hissing from its sides and funnel, the train came to a complete stop. The carriage doors started to open as the passengers began exiting. Karl and Claire moved to the side of the gates, looking for familiar faces. "There they are, Claire, waving at us." Karl took his wife's hand and moved to the center of the gate, waving at his brother and nephew. Karl moved forward to hug his brother, then his nephew. "Mino, Fritz, welcome to England. Let me introduce you to your sister-in-law, and Fritz, say hello to your Aunt Claire. Don't be shy; give her a big hug."

Claire stooped down, reaching for the young lad's arms, then hugged him tightly, saying in a calming tone, "Fritz, you and I will become really good friends; you wait and see." Standing up again, she turned her attention to Karl's big brother; with a glowing smile, she said, "Mino, Karl talks about you constantly. May I kiss you on the cheek and maybe a real big hug as we Vitas like to do?"

Mino's face gave him away; he was so impressed with his new sister-in-law. Answering in German, he said, "Claire, it is such a thrill finally to meet you in person. Your German is almost perfect; I hope my family did not teach you any bad words, or did they? Thank you so much for meeting us today and making us feel so welcome."

With a smile, Karl finally spoke again, "Mino, let me help you with those suitcases. We need to get going, or Mama will give us a mouthful for being late for lunch. Imagine her shock when she lays eyes on you two!"

Arm in arm, they walked back to where the car was parked. Holding his aunt's hand, Fritz thoroughly enjoyed the many sites around the station. To this young boy, the excitement of seeing all this activity versus the depressing sights of broken countries they passed through on the train was helping him feel alive.

Arriving at the bungalow, Karl laid on the car's horn, announcing their arrival. Mama was in the kitchen, preparing the food. Hearing the car horn, she said with an aggravated tone, "Who on earth is making that annoying racket out there?" Wiping her hands, Mama marched out of the kitchen, followed by Freida, with Franchot in tow. She opened the front door, about to give whoever was responsible for that disturbance a mouthful when her eyes fell on her oldest son and grandson. Speechless, she stood frozen in the doorway.

"Mino, I can't believe my eyes! Can it really be you? How did you get here?" Mino stepped forward, wrapping his arms around his mother's neck. Fritz did the same except around her waist.

Mino turned his head toward Karl, then said quietly, "Thanks to my baby brother, this Christmas will have a new meaning. Other than my wife, Mina, not being here, we are all together."

Freida and Franchot welcomed Mino and Fritz in the same manner, Freida showing her emotions of relief that her brothers were all together once again. With her arm still around Fritz, Mama turned to Karl, finally saying, "Claire is right. Our own spy can make things happen, and, son, thanks to you, we will all have a wonderful Christmas together a family at last."

1945 would be the first time in over nine years that the Vita family would celebrate the Christmas holidays together. Sadly, Papa would never be with them again.

# CHAPTER 5

# 1946 THE YEAR OF CHANGE

Christmas would be hectic and crowded for the Vita family now that Claire's sister's family would stay at the house. Sleeping arrangements would be challenging, but that closeness made it much more enjoyable.

On Christmas Eve, Claire, without Karl's approval, announced that she and Karl had decided to have another child with God's help and Karl's stamina, but this could be months or years away. Both families were ecstatic at hearing this. With a smile on his face, Karl was thinking; I hope I'm around for this next one. Claire crossed the room, happy as she could be, wrapping her arms around Karl and whispering in his ear, "Darling, this was the perfect place and time to share our intentions. Don't you agree, even if it's a little premature?" Karl just smiled back at her. Things were changing fast, and he had to prepare himself for a new life outside the BIS. Going into the new year with the prospect of an expanding family could have a profound impact on their future.

Mino would leave in early January, leaving Fritz behind with his grandmother until conditions were more favorable for them to return to Vienna. Once again, like so many times before, Karl's time in Hitchin had also come to an end. Packing his small suitcase, he went downstairs to find Claire dressed, ready to take him to the station. Karl picked up young Nicholas and kissed him, finally saying, "Son, soon, your daddy will be a civilian, and your mummy will have to get used to having him around until he decides on a new career."

Claire listened and, shaking her head, finally spoke, "Karl Vita, stop feeling sorry for yourself. Leaving the BIS is all you can talk about lately. Having a new challenge is what you need. Am I right? And while we are on the subject of a career change, don't forget to call or write to that nice man James McGinley if he can help you get an interview with his shipping company. I can't imagine you out of uniform. You always get me going each time I see you wearing one." Claire continued by reminding him that if he returned to sea duty, it would be for only three years. Contacting Captain James McGinley was the right man to help him make that happen.

Arriving back in Slough, the transition from wartime to peacetime operations had already started. While Karl was still on leave, Major William Lowes had started transferring his command to the new incoming base commander, Major Nigel Mason. His retirement would finally take effect on the last day of January 1946. Bill's staff was throwing him a hell raising party two days before his departure. Karl, Clive, Gunther, Herbert, and General Jacks would also attend. Many others who had stood shoulder to shoulder through the dark, dangerous days of WWII would make this such a memorable evening for Bill. On his return, Colonel Clive Knight had directed Karl to assist the new commander by organizing the files for the remaining field agents. The dramatic reduction into a peacetime force had thrown operations into chaos, so Karl reviewed each agent by their abilities before making his recommendations to Nigel and Clive.

In many ways, this was a sad task for Karl. Over the years, he had closed the files on so many agents who would never return home, and now he would say goodbye to those leaving the BIS for new careers in civilian life. On that last day, Bill was clearing out his desk. Clive asked Karl to join them for a last glass of Bill's finest Whiskey. Sitting around the desk, Bill nodded to Clive that this would be a perfect time to broach the subject of Karl traveling to Nuremberg, Germany as an expert witness regarding German torture methods used on Allied Intelligence prisoners.

"Karl, what I am about to ask you may anger you at first, but after hearing me out, I believe you will see it as a way of closing the loop by being able to testify at the war crimes tribunal against those that did you harm. Karl, this is not really a request. It's an order, straight from the top; is that clear enough for you?"

At first, Karl displayed signs of irritation and anger, but processing Clive's orders quickly made him agree. The thought of coming face to face with those Nazi thugs would finally bring closure for him. "Clive, you are so right. Why is it that when you two meet up with me, you have already decided on what I should be doing?"

Clive, raising his glass, answered, "Major Vita, this may be the last order you receive from me. I wish we could be going with you!" Clive was saddened by the realization that both his friends would be out of military service, starting with Bill at the end of January 1946.

The Nuremberg Trials were a series of military tribunals following World War II, commencing November 20th, 1945, and continuing until October 1st, 1946. The first and primary trial the tribunal was given was to try 24 of the most important political and military leaders in the Third Reich, which the International Military Tribunal conducted. Further trials of lesser war criminals were conducted under Control Council Law No. 10 at the U.S. Nuremberg Military Tribunal, referred to as the NMT. In preparation, Clive asked Karl to take the time to document the harsh treatment and torture administered by the Gestapo, including the extent of his wounds. Later that day, Clive and Bill had time to reflect on how documenting that fateful time would finally help Karl to close that chapter of his military career.

The new peacetime operations would give Karl the luxury of a flexible schedule, allowing more time at home. Some weekends stretched to being three to four days long. Like all those times before, Claire, with baby Nicholas, would pick him up at the station. Bill and Dorothy had moved to a new home, allowing them to spend evenings frequently with Karl and Claire. Bill had started a law relicensing course, followed by intense training with Claire and members of the law firm of McGivern, Tilbey, and Morrison. Things were falling into place quickly. Claire was radiant, thinking about having another baby; when that time came, Bill would handle her caseload.

One morning, Nigel entered Karl's office carrying a brown paper envelope. "Here you go, old man, your orders to appear as an expert witness in the trial of Gestapo Officer Major Rudolph Becker on June 12th. By the sounds of it, you will be over there for about ten days after that. When you return to camp, you can start transferring your command to your replacement, Major Roger Arnold. Karl, I have not had the privilege of serving with you very long, but I wish I could have. You're quite the hero in this camp. Colonel Knight talks so very highly of you each time your name comes up. Would you consider having dinner with my wife and me this coming Thursday evening? I really would like her to meet you."

Karl looked up from his stack of folders with an approving smile that said yes. "Nigel, that would be delightful; where shall we meet?"

Nigel replied, "Do you know the Charter Arms?"

Karl could not contain himself, breaking out laughing and answering, "Do I know the Charter Arms? What would you like to know about it?"

Nigel, looking confused, asked, "Is that a yes, then? How about 1800 hours? We will meet you at the bar if that's all right with you. By the way, now that we have a date, are you alright with me inviting Colonel and Mrs. Knight along? My wife is still finding her way around Slough, and spending an evening with you all would help tremendously." Nigel smiled with satisfaction as he left Karl's office, closing the door behind him. Karl, putting his arms behind his head and his boots on the edge of the desk, started to think back to the time he and Claire stayed there before they were married, and she met his friends for the first time. Now, it seemed like only yesterday. Karl picked up the envelope and, removing its contents, studied the agenda and travel documents before focusing on the location and time to appear before the Nuremberg Military Tribunal (NMT). His eyes stopped scanning when he came to the name Major Rudolph Becker, Gestapo. Sitting there thinking, he tried to relive the events that almost cost him his life back in 1940. He and Captain Jean Yves Jerva of the Free French Army were masquerading as a Kriegsmarine and Vichy French officers. Both were tortured at the hands of the Gestapo. Feeling the anger and painful memories building up within him, he allowed that near death experience to unfold in his mind. The thought of seeing that pompous Gestapo swine was causing him to feel hate once again something he was trying to put behind him now that the war was over.

Leaving home on June 9th, he was driven by faithful Charlie back to the camp after a wonderful four days at home. Two days before, Dorothy had invited Karl and Claire to their new house in Letchworth about a twenty-minute drive from Hitchin. Letchworth was a wonderful Garden City, the first such town in England to be given classification. It was perfect for raising a family, and their new home was perfect for just that. Driving home, he smiled while thinking of Bill in civilian attire waving goodbye to them, his arm around Dorothy's waist. Over a light lunch, Dorothy had told Karl about the wedding arrangements she and Claire had started, Bill adding his input when time permitted.

The wedding would probably take place in early August of 1948. Bill was up to his neck with coming up to speed with the practice, thankful he had Claire's help and guidance. Claire's excitement showed through as she continued helping Dorothy decorate the new house and, when time permitted, make additional plans for the wedding. "Dorothy, shall I call Julie, or is this something you would like to do? She is marvelous at planning wedding activities," said Claire.

Bill interjected by saying, "Claire, I believe Dorothy should be making that call, don't you agree?"

Taking Dorothy's hand, Claire simply answered, "Of course, my excitement, as usual, is taking over; sorry for that." Dorothy, Bill, and Karl broke into laughter; they all loved Claire's excitable ways. Karl was thinking, who would have thought all those years ago when I first met Bill that he would become my wife's partner, living only a few miles up the road?

Two days before Karl was scheduled to fly to Nuremberg, he met with Clive and General Jacks at the General Staff Headquarters. "Karl, it's nice to see you again; it's been quite a while, hasn't it?" asked the general.

Karl answered, "Almost two months, Sir."

"We asked you here today to go over the trial. By the way, your friend Jean Yves will be your co-witness at the trial. Make sure you both have all the details clearly mapped out. We need that despicable individual to spend many years behind bars. Now, I need your input on Captain Nigel Mason. How strong is he? Moreover, is he the right man for the job of base commander? I have to make a two-month status report on his performance." General Jacks was using this trial meeting to get an opinion from Karl on Nigel's ability to run the Slough Operation.

"That is a loaded question, and quite honestly, that answer should be coming from Colonel Knight, not me," replied Karl.

"Well, I have Colonel Knight's report right in front of me. I just wanted your input before proceeding; thank you, Karl." Watching the eye contact, Karl sensed that poor Nigel might be on thin ice, but running an intelligence operation would never be easy, even if Bill Lowes made it look that way. I better wish him luck as I leave tomorrow; he may not be there when I return.

Early the next morning, Charlie drove Karl to RAF Bigging Hill for his flight to Nuremberg. Waiting to board the aircraft, Karl started thinking how different traveling these days was no more anxiety or fear of coming home in a box. These next ten days will give me closure. There is a side of me that is starting to feel sorry for that blighter. His days of freedom will not happen for many years. I don't think they will hang him, but then again, I have no knowledge of what other atrocities he is accused of.

The flight was noneventful. In fact, Karl was bored. Arriving at the hotel, he asked if Major Jerva had checked in yet. To his surprise, he was told the major had arrived that morning and left Karl a message: Karl, I will meet you at the bar at 1730 hours. We have much to catch up on. By the way, Monica sends her love.

Karl smiled as he waited for the small elevator to take him to the third floor. Opening the door to room #311, he was surprised at how nice it was with the faint smell of fresh paint. Washing up, he brushed off his uniform, then went back downstairs to have some quiet time with a glass of beer before Jean arrived. Sitting at the bar, Karl noticed how people were so much friendlier than when he was in

Germany last. It must be because they don't have to worry anymore about bombs falling and Gestapo and SS soldiers threatening them. It makes me feel good to see this change of attitude. A tap on his shoulder made him jump momentarily.

"Karl, my old friend, it is so wonderful to see you again. Buy me a beer, you bloody Austrian; then we can catch up."

Karl gripped this tall Frenchman's arm, hugging inappropriate in a bar. They moved to a corner table. "Well, old man, how is my girlfriend, Claire? Sorry, I meant your wife." Karl was beaming, enjoying that French way of being funny.

"Jean, she sends her love and told me to tell you not to be a stranger now that travel restrictions are being lifted. Jean, in your note, you mentioned Monica. Is there something I don't know?" asked Karl, searching the expression on Jean's face.

"Well, Karl, I wanted to see if that intelligence mind of yours still knows how to connect the dots. I guess you are still that devious agent, aren't you? Monica and I are becoming very serious about the future. She has risen through the nursing ranks and now is a department head at the Charles de Gaulle Hospital in Paris. Karl, I want her to become my wife, and there is no one else I would prefer to be my best man when I make Monica Mrs. Jerva."

Jean stopped talking, waiting for Karl's response. "Jean, you know how I feel about Monica. She contributed so much to saving my eye. Remember our time at the farmhouse after that mission? She and I have a history from way back in 1936, but she has already told you that. Jean, I'm surprised, but then again, I'm not. Monica is a wonderful, sweet lady; you better take good care of her, or you will be answering to me." Karl put his arm around Jean's shoulder and, in his best French, said loudly, "Congratulations! Have you told any of our limey friends yet, or was I the first?" Jean laughed at Karl's behavior.

The following morning, dressed in their best uniforms, they reported to the British judge advocate office, temporarily housed in the enormous Palace of Justice, miraculously undamaged other than numerous bullet holes on the outside walls. That same complex also housed the large prison, now overcrowded with accused Nazi war criminals waiting to hear their fate. The Allies were very much opposed to a common protocol for the trials. In late 1943, during the Tripartite Dinner Meeting at the Tehran Conference, the Soviet leader, Joseph Stalin, made an outlandish proposal. He felt that 50,000 upwards to 100,000 German staff officers should be executed. U.S. President Franklin D. Roosevelt countered that, making a joke out of this ridiculous statement by saying, "Perhaps 49,000 would do the trick."

Prime Minister Winston Churchill did not share in this behavior, believing them to be serious. He denounced the idea of the cold-blooded execution of soldiers who fought for their country and said he would rather be taken out into the courtyard and shot for such a thought. However, he also stated that war criminals must pay for their crimes.

Sitting in the waiting area, they waited for the assigned prosecutor. "Majors Vita and Jerva, I'm pleased to make your acquaintance. My name is Captain Alex Parker, and I am one of the prosecutors on the team for the Allies. The one you are here for is docket #4500079, the case against Gestapo Officer Major Rudolph Becker. Have you brought the support documents I requested? We have a few days to perfect our case against Becker, so that will work out just fine. Once you have given your testimonies, you will be required to stay here until the case is dismissed. Don't look so worried; it won't take long. We have hundreds to prosecute and many more that will be testifying against Becker. We can't linger on a low-level case like this one. Right now, the first session is being presided over by Soviet Judge Nikitchenko; the prosecution indicated there are 24 major war criminals and seven organizations that represent the leadership of the Nazi Party. That session is already in process. Hermann Goring is not taking this too seriously. I wonder what he will be laughing at if the outcome is a death sentence."

Karl and Jean were called upon to give testimony on the appointed day. Following an American military policeman, Karl and Jean entered the courtroom, which was substantially smaller than the main one at the other end of the building. "Major Jerva, you will testify first, just like we rehearsed. When I ask you to describe the torture methods, please emphasize the electric torture and other barbaric methods you suffered. It's important that this court hears the extent the Gestapo was prepared to use to break a prisoner's will."

Captain Parker intended to paint a very bleak picture for the court. Jean was close to breaking down; the two-hour session had made him relive that fateful day. Sitting with his hands clenched, Karl stared at Becker, who looked more than scared at what was being told about his conduct.

A uniformed court official next called Major Vita to the stand. "Please enter the witness box, Major, and refrain from speaking until asked to respond," requested the official, saluting before stepping back to assume his station to one side of the witness box.

Jean, who had regained his composure, was directed to take a seat in one of the bench seats to one side of the elevated witness box. Looking up, he winked at Karl, a smile on his face that told Karl he felt good at having had the opportunity finally to face Becker. He finished his testimony by saying, "If it weren't for the intervention by the French Resistance, I would not be here today."

Captain Parker stood up from the long row of military prosecutors below, asking, "Major Vita, please state your full name and serial number for the court stenographer. Now, you are fully aware of why you have been summoned to attend this tribunal today, are you not?"

Following the instructions given to Jean Yves and himself a day before by Captain Parker, Karl replied, "Yes, I am." As he said that, Karl moved his gaze to Becker, sitting in the defendant's enclosure.

"Major, I apologize for making you relive these horrendous events, but the court needs to hear first-hand the methods used to make you talk. So, please, take us through the events you and Major Jerva endured on that intelligence mission back in 1940, and please direct your answers to the court."

Over the next two and a half hours, Karl described in detail their capture and the torture methods used by Becker's men to extract the mission objectives. Karl skillfully described the torture methods that nearly blinded his left eye permanently.

Captain Parker's final question was, "Major Becker claims you wounded the two guards that tortured you. Is that correct, and, if so, please describe that incident."

Karl tensed himself, believing that incident would not be brought up, answering, "That is true. I was in a state of blinding rage at what they had done to me. I reacted totally out of control." Karl stood, waiting for the next question, which did not happen, so Karl continued.

"War is hell, and I pray the world will learn from this waste of lives. I will always resent Major Becker as someone drunk with power using brutality to acquire information. Did he administer that torture directly? No, he did not; however, he had full knowledge of the methods used on me hour after hour. One of his last remarks to those two thugs under his command was, 'Call me when you have broken him.' Major Jerva and I were spying on German maritime sites in France, wearing Axis uniforms. We are fortunate that our lives were saved. We both accepted the high risks we were undertaking. Becker believed he was doing his duty for his country. It's not my place to judge him and all the other Gestapo officers on trial, but they need to be taught a lesson they will never forget; thank you."

"Major Vita are there any other closing remarks you wish the court to hear before I dismiss you?" asked Captain Parker. His face was sending Karl a message that he had stepped outside what they had rehearsed. Poor chap had no idea of how Karl always spoke his mind. "Thank you, Major Vita; you are dismissed."

Karl turned to step down from the witness box, briefly stopping to eyeball Becker, standing in his uniform, not looking very spiffy without all those insignia. Karl tapped his left eye with a smirk across his face. Karl would never forget Becker, but that hate had now turned to pity. Karl and Jean would spend the next six days attending the trials of the former Gestapo officers that would continue for many months to come, but right now, they both wanted to leave Nuremberg behind them. They had given their testimonies to the best of their ability. The following morning, Jean and Karl made their farewells, promising to spend time together but that would be many years from now.

# CHAPTER 6

# Farewell to British Military Service

For the next four months, Karl worked on the mountain of documentation and files he would transfer to the officer replacing him. Changes at the camp were happening almost weekly, with new faces replacing those leaving for new careers as civilians. His replacement had been redirected from a posting in Singapore. Until he arrived, Karl would remain in command.

Earlier, Clive had approached Karl about extending for a few more months. This request fell on deaf ears; Karl would not stay one more day than he had to.

A knock on the office door got his attention. "Come in!" responded Karl. The office door opened, and there was Clive with a younger officer at his side.

"Major Vita, I hope we are not disturbing you from that rather large stack of folders in front of you. Let me introduce you to Major Eric Lang; he just arrived this morning. With the time you have left, you two will be extremely busy transferring the many duties you are responsible for." Looking at Karl's face, Clive knew that look that told him Karl would be very professional but not overly friendly. This command had been his life for so many years and handing it over to someone else would be extremely difficult for him.

Karl stood up, extending his hand to Eric. "Pleased to make your acquaintance, Major. I'm glad you arrived earlier than scheduled. This transfer will take some time and many long hours."

Clive turned toward the office door, saying as he went, "See you two later in the lounge for a pint, same time, same table. By the way, Gunther said to remind you that he will be leaving for orientation at the American Embassy in London. After today, we won't be seeing him at our little gatherings."

Karl stood and walked around to the chair next to Eric. Sitting down, he smiled before saying, "I hope Colonel Knight didn't fill your head with swashbuckling stories of slaying that dragon, Herr Hitler, did he? Now that we are operating in peacetime conditions, I can assure you that things are changing very quickly for the better." Karl had a very devious smile on his face.

The office door opened once again. Clive stuck his head back inside, saying, "Major, one last point, please don't scare Major Lang off; it took my department a tremendous amount of time and effort to find your replacement." Clive laughed, knowing how Karl enjoyed ruffling newcomers.

Karl took his tunic from the coat rack and slapped the young major on the shoulder. "Come on, old boy, let's get that mug of beer, shall we? Tomorrow, we can start your orientation in earnest." They arrived at the congested lounge, thick with cigarette, pipe, and cigar smoke. In an upbeat voice, Karl yelled to Clive, "It's your turn to buy that first round, and Eric, it's almost after hours, so drop the formality of calling us by rank. Soon, I will be getting used to being called Mr. Vita."

At the table, Clive stood, speaking loudly and announcing, "Chaps, give me your attention for a moment. Today, we have a new member. Will you all welcome Major Eric Lang to our staff?" All those around the table stood one by one, extending their hands in friendship to Karl's replacement.

Gunther turned toward Karl, asking him if he could talk privately outside. "Of course, you can; chaps, we will be back shortly," replied Karl.

Outside, Karl and Gunther sat on the wooden bench by the front door. "Karl, you and I haven't seen much of each other lately, so I'm pleased we can talk like this before I leave for London tomorrow morning. You and I have been together through many good and bad times, through the hell of espionage missions, facing death on more than one occasion. Old friend, we made it, didn't we? This next phase is much harder than everything else for me to face, having to say goodbye to my closest friend. After my orientation at the American Embassy, I will fly to Washington for more training before I find out where my duty station will be someplace warm, I hope. As for my family, they will remain here in Slough until that happens, then join me, wherever that is." Gunther was becoming emotional, sitting on that bench, facing Karl, and waiting for his response. For this former German military officer, pouring his heart out like this was not easy for him to do.

"Gunther, I did not know your departure had been moved up to tomorrow. Why do I have a sneaking suspicion there may be more to this than what you are telling me?" Karl, the devious intelligence officer, was at it again, trying to second guess what Gunther had just told him.

"Karl, please don't ever change. You know very well that everything I do from here on will still have some form of intelligence attached to it. Is that why you turned down the Americans some time back?" concluded Gunther.

"Old friend, every story has another side to it, and that way of thinking will be tough to change once I am out of the BIS. Gunther, like you, I feel a part of me will be missing starting tomorrow. Please, promise me we will stay in touch. With your German discipline, it will be easier for you than me to keep up, so feel free to yell at me when you don't hear from me, okay?" Karl was also thinking that regular communications will be hard to maintain when I'm out at sea.

"We better get back to the others before they think we deserted them," replied Gunther. After they all wished Gunther Godspeed in his new life, the group called it a night. "Herbert, see you tomorrow, same time, same table; have a nice evening." Karl shook everyone's hand before making his final farewell to Gunther. Speaking in German, they wished each other a peaceful life and promised that the families would try to meet up, maybe the following year.

The following morning, Karl met up with Eric in the main office to start the tedious job of transferring his command; Karl asked for everyone's attention. "Would you all please join me in welcoming your new commanding officer, Major Eric Lang? Although I will remain here for a while, I will not be directing the day-to-day operation of this department. This is also the perfect opportunity to thank you all for the unwavering support you have always given me during those difficult war years. I will never forget your loyalty and help on those occasions I returned a little banged up. Again, thank you will never be enough. Major Lang, would you like to address this scruffy bunch?" Karl always enjoyed teasing the staff, and not doing it today would be a big disappointment to them.

"Well, Major, I don't know about scruffy; they all look very well dressed. I hope that's not for my benefit. Major Vita is leaving a very big pair of boots for me to fill. His reputation will be very hard to follow, so please feel free to help and guide me when I get off track. Later, I will give you my history in the military and how I was asked to join one of the highest performing intelligence arms in the service. As I said, Major Vita and all those others who were here during the war years make me feel rather inept about now. Thank you again for your attention."

Karl turned to return to his office, followed by Eric when a big cheer erupted from the entire office staff. Sally yelling, "Karl, it's been a pleasure having you as our boss! Have a great second career back on some ship out there on the ocean." One by one, they all gathered around Karl, now visibly taken aback by this show of affection. Sally threw her arms around Karl's neck, kissing him and saying, "I've waited years to do that a second time." Everyone was laughing, enjoying this spontaneous outpouring of affection for their departing boss, Karl Vita.

Later that evening, Karl sat quietly at the small desk in his room. The first letter he would write would be to his wife, Claire, then a second to Hazel in America, and finally, he took a blank sheet of paper and fed it into his typewriter. He sat composing a letter in his head to James McGinley of the Clyde Shipping Company before starting to type.

*Dear James,*

*I hope this letter finds you well. My time in the Intelligence Service is rapidly coming to an end. As such, I'm starting to explore my options moving forward, and returning to sea duty is very much at the forefront of that search.*

*Last time we were together, you had mentioned that if I intended to return to maritime service, I should contact you first. Well, Jim, that is why I am writing this letter, hoping your offer still stands.*

*It's so very hard to believe it's been over ten years since I left my ship, the Tristian, in Marseille. As I write this note to you, I find myself wondering what steps will be required to get my ticket reissued. If you can give me some guidance in that department, it will be very much appreciated. As of June 19th, 1947, I will be a free agent looking for a ship. Do you have one looking for an officer?*

*Considering future communications, the best way to proceed is by telephone. Please contact me here in Slough until I depart the BIS. I'm looking forward to seeing you again very soon.*

*That scent of sea air is already filling my conscious mind; do I sound like a schoolboy?*

*I Remain Sincerely Yours,*
*Karl Vita*

*P.S. What is the status these days of the Clyde Princess? My home address and telephone number are attached.*

Karl reread his note, wondering if it was too short and to the point. Should he have elaborated more, or was this note enough to express his desire for the future? Addressing the envelope, he inserted his calling card with his letter. Walking to the main lobby, he got a stamp from reception, then held it momentarily, thinking, will this be the start of a new phase for me? I'm praying it is. Each day,

Karl would search the mail for a letter from Claire and another from Captain McGinley.

The following week, Karl walked over to his office, enjoying the early morning fresh air. Sitting at his desk, he placed a call to Claire at home before Eric arrived. "Claire, my thoroughbred woman, how are you, darling, and how is my little man doing? Have you talked further with Doctor Burgess about becoming pregnant?" asked Karl, waiting for the usual stream of things happening at home.

"Darling Karl, you sound sad, are you? Is it the realization that your time in the BIS is coming to an end? Bill asked me to tell you he has applied to the Letchworth Hall Hotel Golf Club for a membership, for the firm, of course. He is not wasting any time, and lover boy, he is really doing a fantastic job at the office. It must be that military training of his. When you return this weekend, Dorothy wants us to go to their house for dinner. Karl, you think I was excited about arranging our wedding. Well, Dorothy has me beat in that department. Caroline, my adorable little sister, has been on my case for us to visit them in Oxford one of these weekends, so think about that one, will you? Don't mean to bug you, dear, but did you write to Jim McGinley yet?" Claire went silent, thinking, I do this every time we talk on the phone. I get too excited, I suppose.

"Claire, good on the golf application; yes, on dinner at the Lowes; yes, on going to Oxford; yes, on writing to Jim. Now, for other news, Eric Lang is working out nicely. He's a little green still, but that will pass with time. As for me, well, I'm a little melancholy at this point. I guess that's to be expected after so many years in this line of work. Darling, do me a big favor; could you call Bert at the garage and have him pick up the MG? I would like it serviced before I arrive home Friday. You and I, Frau Vita, are taking that little MG on an outing; perhaps Freida could watch Nick for us? I was thinking of punting on the river again in Cambridge; reliving our first date will be medicine for both of us."

Listening to her husband, Claire was thinking his frame of mind was giving him away. He's grasping onto happier events that will take him away from the cloud over his head. It saddens me to hear him talk like this; he's driving himself crazy, thinking about all the changes coming in his life.

"Darling, if that's what you want to do, then that's what we'll do. Reliving those first few days will be wonderful, but you over sexed Austrian, no mucking about under the table at the fish and chip shop. That's one day I will never forget. See you Friday, darling; please bounce back into that cocky bloke I love so very much. Goodbye for now, darling."

Karl returned the receiver to its cradle, thinking, Claire knows me so very well, and she is right. I need to get out of this mindset I seem to be in. Chuckling, he vividly remembered that night at the fish and chip shop. Since you know me that well, my sweet Claire, that episode will definitely be repeated!

Another Friday rolled around, and Karl took his small travel case with him to the office. He was more than ready to head to the train station. Even though Charlie had been instructed to drive him home, Karl wanted that alone time before reaching Hitchin Station. The train leaving Welwyn Garden City was the signal for Karl to reach overhead for his case, knowing it would only be fifteen minutes to the Hitchin Station. Listening to the bumpers banging in protest as the train slowed into the station, Karl wished a fellow passenger a nice weekend.

Looking through the open window, he could see Claire and Nick standing on the platform. Before the train came to a complete stop, he allowed his mind to recall events from the past. He remembered the ever constant cloud of uncertainty each time he returned home that always hung over him with that nagging question would he become another fatality to add to the thousands who had died in action? But today, it was just another weekend at home with his family.

In time and good fortune, he would return home wearing a different uniform, the uniform of an officer in the maritime service. That thought put a big smile on his face as the brakes squealed and the train came to a complete stop. There on the platform was Claire, leaning over Nicholas, waving his little hand at his Papa. Looking at Claire, his last thought was how calm she appeared to be now that there was no more war or secret missions to worry about.

Jumping down, Karl walked quickly toward his wife and son. "Darlings, give me a big kiss; I have missed you so much. As for you, my little man, what do you say to your Papa?" Karl reached down, swinging Nick into his arms and kissing him on the cheek. Nick put his small arms around his father's neck, squealing with delight. Claire drove home, giving her two men a little travel time together. Stopping the car in the driveway, Claire could not stop laughing, watching her husband and son playing next to her. Walking around to the passenger side, she reached down to take Nick from Karl's arms.

"Claire, was that getting out of the car for my benefit? You knew I would look, didn't you? God, you always corner my attention when you do that. Those legs of yours are what I think about sitting at my office desk." Since their very first date, Karl would remember the wonderful sight of her thighs, clad in sheer nylons, as he helped her down into the boat to go punting on the river in Cambridge.

"Karl Vita, I can see from the look on your face that there is no way I can escape you tonight, but then again, who said I would resist?" replied Claire, her spirits high at having her family together for another weekend. Standing in the driveway, they held each other with poor Nick squashed between them. This new feeling of safety allowed them to look toward the future without the fear of Karl being killed in action. Inside the kitchen, Claire, with a big grin on her face, took a letter addressed to Major Karl Vita off the table, saying, "Darling, you may wish to open this letter right away?" Claire had looked at the sender's address on the upper left corner, which read Captain James McGinley with the address of the Clyde Shipping Company under his name.

While Claire prepared fresh coffee and sandwiches, Karl sat holding the letter, his heart racing about what the contents of that letter could be. He slowly opened it, ensuring he did not rip through the return address. Unfolding it, he started to read with Claire watching from the counter. She brought over two steaming mugs of coffee, then sat down next to her husband. She softly put her arm around his shoulder as she watched his facial expression change from concern to a very broad smile.

"Claire, Jim has asked me to travel up to Glasgow for an interview with the directors of the Clyde Shipping Company. Claire, I could be returning to sea duty."

# CHAPTER 7

# CLYDE SHIPPING COMPANY

After almost ten years in active service with the British Intelligence Service, Major Karl Vita was within two weeks of retiring from the military. His new life would be back in the merchant service, reclaiming his former position as a maritime officer in the service of the Clyde Shipping Company. Two weeks earlier, he had taken the night train to Edinburgh, Scotland, leaving from London's King's Cross Station, then a local train the following morning for the last fifty miles to Glasgow. Jim McGinley had made a reservation at the Taffy Arms in Edinburgh for Karl to rest up in before picking him up at 1100 hours the following day in Glasgow. Karl had slept on and off most of the way up to Edinburgh. The rest of the time, he studied the material Jim had sent him on the Clyde Shipping Company.

Rising early, Karl went downstairs for a quick breakfast before heading to the station to catch the train to Glasgow. Looking out the carriage window, his mind drifted back to that fateful mission in 1945. He and Gunther, along with a detachment of S.A.S. troops, had undertaken the suicide mission to commandeer a German merchant vessel carrying equipment to be used in the manufacture of a new German weapon, the atomic bomb, delivering that ship to Aberdeen, Scotland.

Over the years, he had played a vital part in so many missions. Today, he was back in Scotland to apply for a peacetime maritime position, returning to the life of a sailor. How quickly things have changed, he thought. Hearing that familiar bumping of the carriages meant they were pulling into the station in Glasgow. Stepping down onto the platform, Karl searched for a British sea captain. What he saw was a well-dressed Scotsman in a tweed suit.

"Karl, welcome to Glasgow. Did you have a pleasant trip? I hope you enjoyed staying at the Taffy Arms. My wife and I stay there when we visit our daughter in Edinburgh. We can leave if you have your luggage; my car is parked around the corner." Jim reminded Karl of what a Scottish gentleman should be like, honest as the day is long and fiercely proud of his Scottish heritage.

The Clyde Shipping Company headquarters was in a walled brick compound; the main building, some four stories high, had numerous smaller buildings around it. In the lobby and central main hall, the walls were decorated with pictures and paintings of ships that had been part of the company's fleet since 1862, starting with beautiful sailing clipper ships. Jim smiled, watching Karl as he studied each picture. "Here we are, Karl. Did you have time to review the package of documents I sent? I hope so because how this interview goes, so does your potential position with the company." Jim smiled as he asked Karl that question.

"Yes, I did, Jim. I read through them again on the train last night, just to be on the safe side," replied Karl. The inside of the headquarters was drab, with not too much in the way of color, but that did not matter to Karl as he was not looking for a land position.

"Karl, make yourself comfortable. Sheila, my assistant, will bring refreshments shortly. She also notified the management that you have arrived." Sitting in the long conference room, Karl started thinking, what's my plan B if this doesn't go well? I guess I could always accept that position in the diplomatic service the Americans offered me. Unfortunately, either position will require me to be away from home for extended periods. Jim returned, followed by Malcolm Finley, the company's managing director.

"Major Vita, I'm so very pleased to meet you at last. Captain McGinley speaks very highly of your maritime accomplishments and the accolades bestowed on you by the British Intelligence Service. Please, have a seat; did you bring the documents Jim asked you to bring with you?" Karl could feel his tension melting away as he sat back down. "Mr. Finley, it's a pleasure to meet you. I hope Jim didn't build me up too much; I was just doing my job. Now that my time in the BIS is coming to an end, my aspirations are to return to my second love after my wife and son. That's my expectation for today's meeting: returning to sea duty." Karl stopped talking; he thought his last statement should make his intentions perfectly clear.

"Well, Karl, is it alright if I call you by your Christian name?" asked the jovial Malcolm Finley.

"Of course, you can if I may also call you Malcolm?" Karl was now feeling comfortable, and Jim could see these two would get along very nicely. Over the next four hours, Malcolm and Jim mapped out what the Clyde Shipping Company was prepared to offer should Karl agree to the terms of employment.

"Karl, we will take care of all the paperwork for you, including updating your maritime ticket. However, you will have to sit for a written exam at the British Maritime Board; there's no way around that. It should be a piece of cake for you, though. We will also require copies of your nationalization document and your military discharge documents. Once you have them, include this application document, and mail them back to Jim's attention.

Jim took over the interview by adding, "The Clyde Princess is in dry dock for a long overdue major overhaul. That's why I was available for this meeting. If you decide to join us, you will undergo extensive orientation before joining me on the Princess as its third officer. In that position, you will basically be in training until assuming the position as my second officer. Does this fit into your expectations?"

"Karl now is the time to voice your concerns or any questions for either of us," asked Malcolm.

Karl waited momentarily before answering them. "Gentlemen, what can I say except to thank you for this opportunity? Just a couple of questions: can we discuss further the compensation package and the average time at sea during a contract? With a wife and small son, I need to factor that into any position I accept. Other than that, I believe at this juncture, you have covered everything that I need to know," concluded Karl.

Malcolm answered each question, followed by, "Karl, does our proposal meet your expectations, and can we consider this to be a deal?"

Karl stood, reaching over the table to shake both of their hands. "Gentleman, may I take the liberty of using a telephone? I need to call my wife. She is a solicitor, and you know what they're like; they need to know everything," said Karl, smiling at the outcome of this meeting.

"Of course, Karl. Why don't you use my office? Let me show you the way," replied Malcolm, also feeling good about the outcome.

"One thing, Karl, keep an eye on your watch; I need to get you back to the station to catch that train back to Edinburgh if you're going to make the night express back to London," cautioned Jim.

"Jim, this will be a quick call. I'll be right back." Jim nodded his head in response. "Claire, I'm heading home. I think everything went really well. I should get a confirming letter and contract in the mail within a week or so. I love you both. Now, I must go if I'm to catch that express back to London; see you tomorrow." Karl made his goodbyes, then followed Jim out to the car.

"Karl, old man, I must admit to you right now that when I first met you in Ostend, I wrote in my logbook: Had an interesting passenger today, an Austrian chap in the German merchant service. When questioned about being on my ship, he told me he had left his ship to save his mother, sister, and nephew, who were still living in Vienna. Commander Vita told me his entire story, leaving nothing out. I thought this is a fine officer willing to sacrifice his maritime career to save family members. I sincerely hope our paths cross again. So, you see, Karl, I was hoping we could serve together at some point, and here we are about to start the next chapter on the old lady, the Clyde Princess. Here we are at the station; your tickets are in this envelope. Don't waste any time; the train is already in the station. Out you go; we'll talk tomorrow."

Karl jumped out of the car, thanking Jim for making the next stage of his career happen, then sprinted to the ticket counter. He waved back at Jim, standing in front of the car, watching to make sure Karl had made it in time. Jim was thinking, there goes the next generation of European sailors, loyal, dedicated, and committed. The Clyde Shipping Company is lucky to get an officer like this chap.

Seeing Karl climb into a compartment, Jim got back into his car, started the engine, and drove off.

Arriving in Edinburgh, Karl opened the envelope, removing the first class ticket for the express back to London. The Flying Scotsman was a legend for luxury train travel in the United Kingdom. Karl presented his ticket to the ticket collector at the gate, who told him his compartment was toward the front. Karl felt like a young boy as he walked the length of the train to the first class carriages at the front of the train. A uniformed train conductor asked for his ticket, then, with a real Scottish accent, said, "Your compartment is in this carriage, Sir; dinner starts at 7:15 p.m. Have a pleasant journey to London."

Karl thanked him, then asked one last question as he climbed up into the entrance, "What time does the bar open?"

The conductor smiled, then answered, "Our bar opens about thirty minutes after the train departs the station. It sounds like you'll be wanting a wee dram of Scotch Whiskey, is that right, Sir?"

Karl laughed, replying, "Am I that obvious?" The interior was very luxurious; the compartment had comfortable upholstered individual seats. Karl stowed his small case overhead, then walked into the next carriage to claim a seat at the bar, even though the liquor shelves were still closed. Looking around, he watched numerous high ranking military officers talking merrily at a window table. I feel strange out of uniform; it's like I'm invisible to those chaps. Two well-dressed ladies climbed onto the bar stools next to Karl, laughing about God knows what, Karl still feeling invisible. A shrill whistle from the engine, followed by the familiar jerking of the carriages, announced the train was leaving the station. The women next to Karl turned, smiling at Karl and asking, "Are you heading to London on business?"

Karl perked up at having these ladies to talk to. "No, I'm returning home. My family and I live in Hitchin in Hertfordshire. I came up to Glasgow yesterday for a job interview. How about you two? By the way, my name is Karl Vita, and I'm pleased to make your acquaintance." Karl's mood changed immediately.

"Nice to meet you, too, Karl. My name is Roberta Murphy, and my friend here is Susan Mann. What is that accent I'm hearing?" Karl knew that was coming; it always did each time he met someone new.

"I'm Austrian from Vienna. I joined the British Military back in 1936. Soon, I will retire and return to my previous position in the maritime service." Karl did not offer more; the intelligence agent in him would not volunteer more until he felt comfortable with these two fellow travelers.

"I'm sorry; I didn't mean to pry," replied Roberta.

Karl lifted his hand, a sign of no harm done. "How about you two ladies? That's not a Scottish accent I'm hearing?"

Roberta and Susan looked at each other and laughed before replying, "We are both from New Zealand. Our time in England is ending, so we decided to visit Scotland while we're still stationed in England. This first-class return ride on the Flying Scotsman has used up most of our savings, but chances are, we will never be able to repeat this. We report back to our unit in Uxbridge, Oxfordshire, tomorrow morning, then back to wearing a uniform. Next month, we will board a ship that will take us home. It's a long bloody way but going home will be wonderful. We'll see our families for the first time in three years.

"Ladies and gents, the bar is now open; what can I get you?" asked the cheerful server in his crisp white jacket.

"Ladies, may I buy you a drink?" asked Karl.

"Oh, that's so generous of you, Karl. Could we have a pink gin, if that's alright?" answered Susan as she moved to the opposite side of Karl, saying, "There, that's better; now, I can see you better. You're a lucky chap tonight you've got a lady on either side. Am I being too inquisitive by asking you what you did in the Intelligence Service?"

Karl reacted, thinking, the damn war is over; I need to stop being so secretive. "Susan, I am still a serving Major in the BIS. Now, you can tell me what you ladies do in the military."

Roberta spoke before Susan could, "We're in the army. Up until the end of the war, we deciphered German communications, so in a way, our responsibilities were like yours, but probably a lot less dangerous, I'm sure. Care to join us for supper, Major?"

Karl smiled back at his travel companions, answering, "That's an offer I can't refuse." The food was all right, but that didn't matter;

the company made the difference. Karl looked at his watch. They had been talking for over two hours. Standing, he said, "As much as I have enjoyed your company, it's time for me to get some shuteye. Thank you for a delightful evening. Now, if you would excuse me, I think I'll head to my sleeper compartment."

As Karl walked away through the dining compartment, Susan turned to Roberta, saying, "What a nice bloke he is."

Roberta smiled back and with a devilish smile answered, "I would have loved to join him in his sleeper. I can assure you he would be very tired when we arrive in London. Oh, well, I can dream, I guess." Susan smiled and nodded her head in agreement.

Karl could not sleep well; he kept thinking about joining the Clyde Shipping Company and the nice time he had with his two lady friends. If I was still single, that Roberta would have said good night to her friend Susan, telling her she'd see her in the morning. Thinking that made Karl smile, remembering his former life. With that thought still fresh in his mind, he instantly relived his first few dates with his wife, Claire. Any other thoughts vaporized as he drifted to sleep once more with a vision of Claire and Nicholas.

The following morning, Karl shaved and washed up before getting dressed. He left his suitcase on the seat and headed to the dining car for breakfast. To his surprise, the compartment was quite busy. Looking around, he found an empty seat. "Tea or coffee, Sir?" asked the friendly waiter.

"Coffee, please, and could I have some bacon and eggs if they are available?" Karl took a small pocket pad from his inside pocket and started to write himself a to-do list.

"Care for the paper, Sir?" asked another waiter.

An announcement came over the PA, letting all the passengers know that the Flying Scotsman would arrive at King's Cross Station in less than one hour. Upon hearing this, Karl returned to his compartment to retrieve his case, then waited for that familiar sensation of the train slowing down into the station. From here, he would walk to the other side of the station to catch the train back to Hitchin.

Walking down the platform, two voices behind him made him jump, "Karl, we thought we had missed you. It was really nice spending time with you last night. I suppose we will never see each other again, so, you handsome chap, have a wonderful life with that family of yours. Your wife is a lucky lady, and from the sound of it, so are you," said Roberta. Reaching for his hand, she pulled him in, kissing him on the cheek. Karl returned that kiss to both, and then, smiling, he headed off toward his train.

# CHAPTER 8

# WEDNESDAY, JUNE 19TH, 1947

Karl was starting to feel like an outsider with no responsibilities or authority. With only two days left as a serving officer in the BIS, he spent these days writing updates on field personnel and menial tasks requested by Eric Lang. His office now had a new, stenciled sign: Major Eric Lang. Karl had moved into the transient officer's area for the few days he had left. Tuesday evening, after depositing his briefcase in his room, he walked to the lounge to meet up with his friends. Opening the door, he was hit by an unsuspected surprise. Over the bar, a long banner read, We Will Never Say Goodbye. Karl stood speechless as everyone started clapping and yelling saucy comments.

Clive stepped forward, talking loud enough to be heard over the ruckus coming from all in the lounge. "Karl, surely, you didn't think we would let you go without a hosing from all of us remaining. In about an hour, I want you to go back to your quarters and change into your dress uniform. Tonight, my friend, your close friends will spoil you at your favorite inn in Slough, and that is the Charter Arms. Now, go and enjoy yourself with this mob, but don't drink too much; we have a party to attend this evening." Clive slapped Karl on his back, then gently pushed him into the waiting arms of some female officers. He was happy for his longtime friend but sad the group would lose yet another wartime member.

His spirits were again high from the attention he had received in the officers' lounge. Karl changed into his dress uniform, thinking, tomorrow, I will wear this one last time as an officer in the Intelligence Service. So often, I thought I would never see the end of hostilities, never mind leave the BIS. Considering this, Karl sat on the end of the bed, the sadness overcoming him as he lowered his head, trying to control the tears rolling down his face. I should be ecstatic about now, so why am I feeling like this? A vision opened in his mind: poor Kitty would never know what we suffered or the overwhelming feeling of relief on the days Germany then Japan surrendered. Karl felt guilty thinking about Kitty, but then again, because of Kitty, he found the love of his life, Claire. Thinking more about that, he smiled and thought, can you imagine if they had met before the war? I know they would have become close friends. I wonder where that would leave me. The thought made Karl chuckle.

Clive had asked Karl to meet him in the main lobby; from there, they would drive together to the Charter Arms. Entering the lobby, Karl got yet another surprise. There, waiting for him to arrive, Gunther and Herbert stood in their smart dress uniforms, smiling at the shock on Karl's face. "Gunther, I thought you would be halfway to America about now, you bugger!

Herbert, you knew all along he would be here, didn't you? You're both sneaky spies."

"Well, Karl, this is partly true. I am leaving early next week, but there is no way I would miss this party. Herbert nearly slipped a couple of times; that tells me our days of being spies are really over!"

Clive, outside leaning against his big Humber staff car, was laughing out loud, saying, "Bet you didn't expect to see Gunther and Herbert waiting in the lobby, did you? Come on; let's get this show on the road." In the car, their spirits were high. What Gunther had said about not missing this party was resonating in the back of Karl's head. Parking the car, they walked into the foyer of the inn. Clive told the maître d' they were here for the Vita party.

Karl tensed himself as he eyed the half empty dining room. "Gentlemen, please follow me," instructed the very proper maître d', leading the way. Clive stopped in front of the private dining room and put his arm around Karl's shoulder.

Seeing the expression on Karl's face, he said, "Ready, old man? This has been in the works for many months now." Something was telling him there was more to this party than they were letting on to.

Karl's unique ability to read situations told him he needed to prepare for more surprises. The door opened, and there, in a semicircle, were more of Karl's friends. In the center of the group stood his wife, Claire, Karl's mother, his sister Freida, and brother-in-law, Ronny. On the opposite side stood Claire's sister Caroline, Clive's wife Julie, Dorothy, and Bill. Another shock was seeing General Jacks with his wife, Mary. After the clapping had died down, Claire stepped forward with that same look of love she had for Karl all those years ago here at the Charter Arms.

"Darling, are you shocked to see all your friends and family gathered here to give you a memorable sendoff?" Claire, the ever constant diplomat, took Karl's hand and turned toward the group, announcing, "I'm sure, by now, you have heard Karl will be returning to his love of the ocean as an officer for the Clyde Shipping Company. Let's give him a big round of applause and best wishes in this career he is returning to!"

Claire's emotions overflowed with love and pride as she circled her arms around her husband's neck. Karl had difficulty holding back the tears before addressing this gathering. Speaking would be a challenge in this state of emotion.

Finding that composure and holding Claire's hand tightly, he finally spoke. "My wonderful wife has a way of putting me on the spot. This evening is especially difficult because I will leave you and the BIS tomorrow afternoon. Thank you all for making this such a special event for Claire and me in such a fitting setting.

Being amongst such special friends and having our family here as well is such a shock. I can only say I must have done something right to be at the receiving end of this going away party. Please forgive me; I'm too overwhelmed right now. Thank you again for such a memorable evening."

Clive stepped forward, asking everyone to join him in a Champagne toast to a returning seaman. Karl and Claire made a point of talking to and thanking everyone for attending. Mama was sitting next to Dorothy, thinking Karl is his father in every way. Tears welled up in her eyes. Dorothy, seeing this, asked, "Mama, are you alright? Are those tears of relief now that Karl is out of danger, or are they purely for this wonderful couple we all love?"

Smiling, Mama took both her hands before answering. "You are correct, Dorothy. Seeing them together like this reminds me so much of my husband Amilcari Vita and myself before the children came along. Those early years were so magical, evenings out at favorite restaurants and waltzing into the early morning hours. I can only relive those wonderful times now in my mind. Watching these two allows those memories to happen once again. Karl's father would be so proud of him tonight; that's why I have these tears of happiness," explained Mama, kissing Dorothy's cheeks.

Karl started to wonder, if they were all here in Slough, where would everyone be staying tonight, and where are the children? "Claire, are we staying here tonight? Knowing how you operate, I would say we are? Did you bring Nick, Franchot, and Fritz along as well?"

Claire smiled back at him, saying, "The children are at Julie and Clive's house; their house sitter is taking care of them. Don't worry; they will be at your passing out tomorrow afternoon. As for Mama, Freida, and Ronny, they are staying here with us. Dorothy and Bill are staying with Julie as well."

"Claire, why is it I have a feeling you have booked that honeymoon suite again? Have you?"

Grinning, Claire reached over and kissed his cheek, saying, "What do you think, Sailor? It's a special occasion, and tonight, you will make it even more special, won't you?"

The party was winding down, and people were saying their farewells. For some, it would be a long time until they met again. Tomorrow would see Karl's military separation become a reality, fondly referred to by those returning to civilian life as being demobbed. Arm in arm, they went upstairs to relive that first evening at the Charter Arms. Entering the darkened room, Claire turned on the lights, flooding Karl's memory with that evening so long ago. "Karl, Clive insisted I bring your newer formal uniform with me. The one you wear around here is really showing its age. Then again, who knows when you will wear it again? Darling, I know how you are about surprises, so please don't be mad at me." Claire was playing Karl, and he knew it.

Karl started laughing, finally saying, "Claire, you are such a manipulator! How on earth could I ever get mad at such a conniver? Tonight, you can show me how sorry you are."

Beaming, Claire threw her arms around Karl, saying loudly, "Sailor, what is it I should be doing?" Karl walked over to the bed stand, turned the light on, then switched off the main room light overhead. In the dim light, he stood silently watching as Claire started removing her dress, glancing at him as she removed her slip, panties, and bra but not her suspenders or stockings. Karl was more than aroused by the way she was teasing him. Karl had fallen madly in love with this complicated beauty from that very first day. As he watched her, he knew those feelings grew even stronger with each passing day. "Karl, am I the only one getting ready for bed? Or are you going to stand there all night?" Taking the upper hand, Claire knew shortly she would become putty in his hands.

"My darling, I cannot pass up a chance to see the best strip show I have ever seen. Now, I'll undress. Think I'll need pajamas tonight?" Claire, going along with this foreplay, smiled. Rolling her head to release her hair, she sat upright, waiting for her man to make passionate love to her. Somewhere in the back of her mind, a thought cropped up. Soon, Karl will be heading to Scotland to start his new position, and once again, I will wait patiently for that smoking beast to return him home to me in about five or six months. At least this time, I won't worry about him on some spy mission.

After hanging up his uniform, Karl slid under the covers. Facing Claire in that dim light, she was everything he could hope for, the perfect wife, lover, and fantastic mother to Nicholas, and one day, another child would complete their family. Karl softly pulled her to him; he could feel she was becoming anxious for that first kiss or touch. With deliberate movements, he put his arm around her neck and kissed her. She responded by thrusting her tongue into Karl's open mouth. Karl would let her have her way, thinking everything comes to those who wait. Kissing her neck, he moved down her heaving breasts, placing his mouth over the left very erect nipple and cupping the other with his hand. Claire was breathing heavily. It had been some time since they had been alone like this, making love, and she was more than ready to have him inside her.

Laboring to speak, she started to beg Karl, "Darling, it's been so long; don't make me wait any longer." Pushing Karl onto his back, she parted her legs to straddle him, and in the softest voice, she lowered her face to speak into his ear. "My darling man, you have had your fun turning me into a babbling nymphomaniac.

Now, it's your turn to need it badly." Claire returned to an upright position and placed her right hand around his erection. With deliberate movement, she guided her hand up and then slowly down. Karl's chest was heaving, but Claire was watching his face for a sign he was about to explode. Each time he started to tense, Claire would stop, waiting for that heavy breathing to subside. Karl was about to speak when Claire lifted herself, then lowered herself down over his penis. Claire moved slowly up and down, building that sensation they would share together only moments away.

"God, Claire, you are a sneaky vixen." Karl put his hands on her hips to hold her down, then thrust into her. That's all it took for them both to explode into an orgasm that left them both completely spent. Claire rolled off Karl and snuggled up to his side, kissing his chest.

Chuckling, she made a comical remark, "Darling, this orgasm could have definitely started something, but not tonight, wrong time of the month. For a minute, I thought that sperm was going to come out elsewhere."

Karl sat up laughing loudly, saying, "Claire, only you could deliver that line. Come here, you vixen, and kiss me. Then it's lights out; tomorrow will be a big day for us." In that darkness, two people lay in each other's arms, confident they had a future to look forward to.

Karl and Claire had risen early; not wanting to rush, they got themselves ready. Karl dressed in his newer formal uniform for the last time, and Claire wore a floral dress with a dark blue fitted jacket. Together, they made a handsome couple. "Claire, take my camera and take plenty of pictures. Don't worry; everyone else will be doing the same. Thank God the fifteen of us leaving today will not be required to go to the demobilization center. If that had happened, the closest would be the one in Guilford. General Jacks and Clive have made these arrangements. They're still concerned about security for serving agents and officers in the BIS."

Downstairs, they met up with Mama and the family. Earlier, Bill and Dorothy had brought the children over. They all sat around a long table, drinking tea and coffee while they waited for Karl and Claire to come down to join them. Seeing them entering the dining room, Franchot and Fritz ran over excitedly to hug them. Dorothy, carrying Nicholas in her arms, was right behind them. Mama smiled as Karl greeted the boys, then took Nick from Dorothy. This will be a good day, she thought.

After breakfast, Karl went back upstairs with Ronny to collect the luggage. Then, after packing the cars, they all headed up to the camp for the last time. At the gate, the military policeman approached the car, saluting Bill even though he now wore a civilian suit; he knew him so very well. "We will miss you, Major Vita. Today is the day, correct? And Major Lowes, always good to see you again. Pass on through; I'll clear your family in the car behind." Saluting again, he waved them through.

Karl turned to Bill, asking him, "Bill, why don't you take them all to the main hall? Clive said all relatives and friends are requested to gather there. You might as well drop me off first at the administration building. See you all in about an hour, maybe less."

With a spring in his step, Karl climbed the stairs two at a time to the lobby entrance. "Morning, Gladys. I'm just going down to communications to say goodbye, so if anyone asks for me, you know where I'm at." Karl opened the door to his former department to find everyone waiting for him, Major Lang out in front.

"Major, we are so pleased you took the time to say goodbye." Eric was speaking for the group.

"Thank you, Major. I could not leave without saying goodbye one last time. One by one, they trooped by to shake hands with their old boss, most hugging Karl, and Eric not objecting. When Sally approached, she was already crying at having to say farewell. "Sally, please don't cry. I'm sure we will meet again. For now, though, come here and hug me," said Karl. Sally had been the closest to him throughout those difficult years, and now, deep in his heart, he knew there would not be a next time, so he kissed her cheek, saying quietly, "Sally, there will always be a place in my heart for you. Remember that always, and Sally, have a wonderful life." Karl stepped back. Saluting Eric, he extended his right hand to shake the hand of his replacement, then turned and left the department without looking back. He did not want anyone to see the tears in his eyes.

At the end of the hall, he walked into the smaller office attached to the main conference room. "Good morning, Major; please take a seat." Some fourteen other officers were already seated, waiting to be called to the long table in front. Major Nigel Mason was sitting at the end to thank them for their service to King George VI. Alphabetically, the assembled officers were called up; once they were processed, they were free to join the reception in the conference room. "Major Karl Vita, you're next," called the friendly Lieutenant. Karl had been sitting there for the best part of an hour, and he was more than ready to get this over with. "Please, be seated; this will go quickly as you have seen from those before you. May I have your documents, including your identification card and sidearm?" Karl slid the folder and brown paper bag in front, then placed his identification card and trusted sidearm on the table.

"I will sure miss that pea shooter," said Karl, making light of this demobbing process.

The lieutenant ticked off each item, then slid two signed receipts in front of Karl, "One for you, and one for our files. One last question, do you still have any additional rounds for your sidearm in your possession, or are the ones in that paper bag all of them? According to the sign-off, there should be thirty?" Karl opened the bag, counting exactly thirty. "That's it, Sir; let me sign the triplicate release documents. The top one is yours. Goodbye, Major; enjoy civvy street." With that, the lieutenant stood, saluting his superior officer.

Karl returned the salute. Moving to the end of the table, he saluted Major Mason, followed by saying, "Goodbye, Sir. I really didn't have much time to spend with you, but I wish you all the best in your new command."

Major Nigel Mason smiled back, adding, "Thank you, Major Vita. I'll try my best to live up to the exceptional standards set by all of you that are mustering out today. That discipline will be hard to follow. Again, I thank you for your outstanding service to the BIS and his Royal Highness, King George VI. I understand you are returning to your previous profession as an officer in the merchant service; is that correct?"

With a confident smile, Karl answered, "That is correct, Sir." Karl stepped back, making his last salute, then headed for the open door, his emotions running extremely high.

As he entered the conference room, everyone started clapping as another officer crossed over into civilian life. Looking around, he spotted his family members sitting on the opposite side of the room. Getting over there would be challenging with all the outstretched hands and well-wishers. Politely, Karl kept moving in the general direction of Claire, holding their son. Her excitement would be hard to miss. Karl stopped short, seeing General Jacks to one side. Turning on his heel, he saluted, then extended his hand, saying, "General, you were there at the start, and you're here at the end to see me leave. The words I'm looking for elude me right now, so I'll simply say thank you, Sir, for guiding me, but most of all for the unwavering trust you gave me, a foreigner to England throughout those war years."

From that very first day, General Jacks always believed in Karl, not only as an exceptional officer but also as a true friend. "Karl, from now on, please call me by my Christian name of Arthur, or if you prefer, Art. I want to think our friendship extends beyond the military commitment you made. Good luck, and please drop me a line once you have your ship; don't forget!"

Karl turned with a smile, moving closer to his family standing at the back of the hall, enjoying the attention their soldier was receiving. "Claire, getting close to you and the family was like a combat mission, well, maybe not combat," yelled Karl over all the merrymaking going on around them.

Mama moved forward, dwarfed by so many taller men in uniform. "Karl, you make me so proud. If only your father could be here to see this; maybe, he is. Come here and put those strong arms around your mother." Looking at her husband with his mother, Claire could not help thinking that Mama was the foundation and bedrock of this family. The reception was winding down, and Julie, worried about the traffic driving through Watford, suggested they should consider leaving. Ronny, Freida, Franchot, Fritz, and Mama had just left.

Freida's parting comment was, "We will see you all tomorrow in Baldock. Dorothy, don't bring anything; we have prepared a feast for all of us." Less than fifty people were remaining, and Karl was having a wonderful time introducing his wife and son.

Bill did not want to break up the merrymaking, but it was time to leave, so he made light of his announcement, "Mr. and Mrs. Vita, your ride back to Hitchin is waiting to leave. Say your goodbyes if you please." Karl looked at Claire, then broke out laughing at seeing Bill and Dorothy pointing toward the exit.

Karl's sense of humor kicked in replying loudly, "All you retired military types are alike still giving orders!"

Bill and all the others in the room started repeatedly yelling, "Vita, go home!" until Clive, still laughing, hugged his two friends with a final comment. "You said it best, Karl; we were there at the start, and we are all here together alive at the end. Now, will you please go home?" Hearing this, Karl held tightly to these fellow officers, remembering their first meeting in Dover in 1936 aboard the Clyde Princess, a ship he would soon be serving on as one of its officers.

CHAPTER 9

# TIME AT HOME

Summers in England can be wonderful, with the scent of colorful flowers and vibrant shades of green. After so many years of living for those few days at home before returning by train to his base in Slough, Karl had decided that he would take the rest of the year off. He gave himself this gift after all those years in military service, clearing his decision first with his new employer. Having this time at home, doing anything he pleased, allowed him and his family the time to enjoy each other before traveling North to Glasgow to join his ship in January 1948.

Taking advantage of this extended time at home, Claire had planned a first ever summer holiday for them. In preparation for that event, she spent more time in the office with Bill and her staff transferring cases, mainly to Bill, with the help of her assistant Beverly. Claire was beyond ecstatic at the thought of finally having time away with her husband and son. In anticipation of this, she had booked a suite at Talland Bay Hotel in Cornwall, the very same hotel where they had spent their honeymoon. On the other hand, Karl thoroughly enjoyed treating each day as just another ordinary day.

One afternoon, sitting out in the garden with Claire, Nicholas playing in front of them on a blanket, he thought more about the upcoming drive to Cornwall. Finally, he said, "Claire, if we are heading to Cornwall on holiday, maybe we should consider that new car we talked about. What do you think?" Claire loved how Karl was enjoying this new freedom.

Smiling back, she hugged his arm, responding, "Karl, I told you that a while back, so yes. Let's go looking—nothing crazy, though. I still need a business looking car. Remember that when you start getting carried away."

With a big grin, Karl reached for her hand, replying, "Claire, you realize we will have to try out the back seat? Otherwise, there's no point, is there? And for the record, the old Wolsey never was used as a passion wagon, was it?"

Claire's reaction was, "Not that you would know about anyway." Karl was enjoying watching his wife's face as they teased each other. "There you go again, Vita. We are looking to exchange our Wolsey for a newer family car. On the other hand, you are already thinking about steaming up the windows on some country lane." Claire was enjoying herself, thinking, that crazy bugger of mine will definitely make that a priority if we get a new car, but then again, it will probably be me who makes it happen!"

They drove to Baldock to drop Nicholas off at Mama's house on Saturday morning. Then they left to look at cars. By the afternoon, they had looked at five different makes, finally returning to the MG dealer in Cambridge. The car they really liked was a new MG four door saloon, model YA-1, in British racing green with a dark brown leather interior. The price on the windshield was a whopping 735.00 pounds. "She really is a beauty, wouldn't you agree, Miss?" asked the salesman.

Claire replied, "It's not me you have to convince it's my husband that chap looking under the bonnet." The salesman excused himself, approaching Karl. Claire wandered around and looked at a new model from MG, the TD two seater sports car, thinking how this model had changed from theirs. Karl was still drilling the salesman, so she decided to try the back seat of the car he was looking at. Smiling, she thought, this bugger has our name written all over it.

"Excuse me, Madam, may I answer any questions for you?" the young salesman thought, I've got him convinced; now, I need to convince his wife.

Karl closed the bonnet, then replied, "Well, we'll need to drive this car. Then, let's talk seriously about what it's going to take to trade our Wolsey. Why don't you look at our car and see how far apart we are to make a deal; how does that sound?" An hour or so later, they had a deal.

"Mr. Vita, now we have a deal. I can have it ready for you on Monday, late morning, if that fits your schedule."

"My wife will be working, but I can be here after 1000 hours. Sorry, I meant 10:00 a.m.; old habits die hard," replied Karl, pleased as punch over their new acquisition. Driving back to Baldock, Karl kept talking about how the new car drove and how nice the interior was.

With a wicked smile, Claire said, "Darling, while you were negotiating, I tried the back seat. It's very comfortable, or had you forgotten that specification?" Laughing, Claire reached over, put her arm around her husband's neck, and said, "If you are happy, darling, then so am I. Now, we will be a two MG family, won't we? I'm ready to pick our boy up, and so are you."

On Monday morning, before driving Claire to the office, Karl made sure all their personal items had been removed from the Wolsey and the logbook was in the glove box. In the courtyard, before getting out of the car, with a tear in her eye, Claire quietly said, "Goodbye, old friend; I hope you go to a good home." Karl stood watching her, knowing she was saying goodbye to that special link to her departed parents.

Arriving at the dealership a little after 10.00 a.m., there on the forecourt was the spiffy new MG. Excited to drive it home, Karl could barely contain his enthusiasm. The transaction complete, Karl and the salesman sat in the car, reviewing its instrumentation and the strict engine running in notice for the first five hundred miles. The drive home was enjoyable but a little frustrating for Karl as he really wanted to open it up. Parking in the courtyard of the law firm, all eyes were looking at the Vitas' new car. Bill and Claire walked out to see Karl with a schoolboy smile on his face, saying, "Well, Bill, what do you think? I think once it's run in, it will go like the clappers. It handles more like a sports car than a family saloon."

Watching, Claire shook her head, smiling and thinking, this is why I fell in love with him. He can be tough sometimes scary to those who cross him and yet so sweet and loving with that spark of excitement like right now. "Karl, darling, you know I will be using this MG on Monday, and you can use your little MG sports car?"

Karl laughed out loud, agreeing that his MG needed to be run anyway. "Claire, here, you take the keys for this one, and I'll get my car out of the garage and drive it home right now. Bill, old boy, make sure she doesn't scratch it turning around in the courtyard, will you? See you Wednesday evening for that card game?"

Karl drove home in his little MG, the canvas roof down and the wind blowing through his hair. He was enjoying life with no clouds in the sky or in his life.

Two weeks went by very quickly, and now it was time for the Vita family to head out on holiday. Loading the car, Karl filled the left side of the back seat with baby stuff and some luggage pieces. The boot was not as big as the old Wolsey's, but that was fine. He returned to the house for the last piece of luggage and yelled up the stairs, "Honey, let's get moving; we don't have all day."

Claire knew her husband so well when he was on a mission; everything was always by the schedule and clock. Claire had dressed in a light pink blouse, a matching floral flared skirt, and a wide dark pink belt finished the look. "Ready, darling; I'll be right down just finishing dressing our little monster." Grabbing a white jacket from the chair, she took Nicholas by his hand then hurried downstairs, locking the back door as she went outside. Karl was already behind the wheel, studying a road map.

Looking up, he smiled at his wife and Nick waving his little arms at seeing his papa. The new MG still had that new car smell, which they both loved. This would be an enjoyable day of driving.

"All right, you two, let's get going, shall we? Claire, I've marked the route for you to follow. By the way, did I tell you how sexy you look this morning?"

Claire, smiling at his attention, he never missed a trick. "Behave yourself, Vita. See this little guy on my lap? He's like his dad—doesn't miss anything and always playing with my buttons."

The drive was long but very pleasant, with the sun shining brightly. It bothered Karl's left eye somewhat, even while wearing sunglasses. Crossing into Cornwall, their spirits were high, knowing they would be at the Talland Bay Hotel in less than an hour. "Karl, look; there's the sign for the hotel. We made really good time even with the traffic. Darling, I love our new car, even though you drive a little on the fast side."

Karl just smiled, allowing a memory to enter his mind. The last time they were here was on their honeymoon; unfortunately, when they returned home, he would leave his new bride for almost nine months on a training mission in Canada. With a smile, he thought, when we leave this time, it will be to return home until January anyway, then off to Glasgow to join my ship and another five months away from my family. This thought saddened him, but then again, he was going to sea, not back into war torn Europe. This will be a wonderful two weeks, he concluded.

Claire sat quietly, knowing her husband had momentarily drifted into thought. Reaching over, she softly grasped his arm, knowing he would look at her. "My dear complicated man, are you someplace in your past?"

Karl smiled as he answered, "I was thinking about the last time we stayed here. This time, we have our little man with us, and a new car loaded with so much stuff. Just think, Claire, we have two whole weeks of family time. No, Claire, those bad memories are behind me, or should I say us? Now, let's go register, shall we?"

Walking slowly into the lobby, Karl holding Nicholas's little hand, they couldn't help but notice there were definitely more holiday makers than the first time they were here. But, then again, that last time, a world war was raging. Claire had her folder ready, saying in a very proud manner, "Mr. and Mrs. Vita checking in it's so nice to be returning. The last time it was on our honeymoon. I'm assuming my request for a suite will be no problem; is that correct?" Claire was polite, but that edge of sarcasm made her wishes for this stay perfectly clear.

"Yes, Mrs. Vita, your instructions were clear. You will be in our very best suite, overlooking the beach. As for the crib, it has already been placed in your room sorry, I meant suite. Please, sign the register for me. Call downstairs when you have settled in; we have Champagne and refreshments waiting for you a gift, I believe, from your office," said the young man behind the desk, somewhat intimidated by this elegant, well-spoken woman. "May I have the keys to your automobile and please point it out for me?"

Claire smiled at the young man, saying, "It's the dark green MG over there; you can't miss it. Karl, darling, can I please have the car keys?"

Karl always loved the way Claire acted in front of strangers. She is such a sexy vixen; I bet that young chap will be watching her as she leaves the lobby.

"Your suite is ready for you. John will be up shortly with the luggage. We're glad to have you back with us again."

Claire took the room keys and smiled, thanking the young man. Walking down the hall, Karl started laughing out loud as he swung little Nick up in the air, screams of happiness erupting from his son. "Steady on, Sailor; you'll pull his bloody arms out of their sockets doing that," cautioned Claire, the protective vixen of her cub.

Karl, still laughing, answered, "Nonsense, you overprotective woman, he's a strapping young lad, and yes, he's a momma's boy, but then again, so am I. Did you look back at the chap behind the desk? He couldn't take his eyes off your exquisite backside, but then again, neither can I."

Claire could sense that the way Karl was talking was the sign she was waiting for. He was emerging from those controlled BIS ways to a carefree husband and the father she had waited so long for. "Karl Vita, as I have always told you, you are a dirty old man, and I love it. I hope Nick is really tired," concluded Claire with a smirk as she unlocked the door to their suite.

The next two weeks were everything they hoped and dreamed about, with their days spent building sandcastles and walking along the beach. They had lunches at the hotel or sometimes in some quaint harbor side restaurant. Each day, Claire made sure that Karl had time to relax. Sleeping in the sun was rebuilding him; even though externally he looked like the handsome chap he was, over ten years of being an intelligence officer had aged him so much. With luck, this holiday would return the man he must have been before the horrors of war gave him those scars and black bags under his eyes. Karl needs this holiday more than he realized. She prayed that after these two weeks, her husband would return to the man he had been full of life once again.

Their love making had taken on a new phase; no more rushing or acting with spontaneity. Now, it was making love slow and long, which Claire thoroughly enjoyed; how she loved being married to this crazy Austrian. Occasionally, in those peaceful moments when her two men were sleeping, she allowed her mind to travel back to when she was married to Patrick.

What would her life have been like if he hadn't been killed during the Battle of Britain? And poor Kitty would never experience a life like this on holiday with Karl and a child much like Nick in her lap. These thoughts she would keep to herself, thanking God for the blessing he had given her and the second chance for a happy life with a man she could only have dreamed of. In her mind, she continued to thank both Kitty and Patrick for the gift they had given their lives for.

# CHAPTER 10

# TEARFUL GOODBYES

Karl's extended stay at home had come to an end. Their holiday had done so much to revitalize their spirits; however, all good things must have an ending. The time was rapidly approaching for Karl to start preparing for that long separation. Using one of the guest bedrooms, he organized the clothes and other items he would take with him on his first voyage. Downstairs, he heard the back door open, and Claire announced loudly, "Where are my two men?"

Karl smiled as he walked out onto the upstairs landing. "Up here, darling. I think you have woken Nick. I'll be right down."

Claire did not want to wait; she had a gift for Karl to wear when he left for Scotland. "Darling, hurry up, will you? I have a present for you down here." Karl, hearing this, thought, what did she do this time? Claire had gone into the sitting room, hanging a long brown paper bag on the open door with "Vita" scribbled across the front. "In the sitting room, darling," she cheerfully yelled out.

Karl, the intelligence chap, braced himself for this surprise from his wife. "So, what is it you have you done this time, Mrs. Vita?"

Although saddened by her husband's departure, Claire was enjoying herself, having just picked up the long awaited package. "Darling, sit down here in your chair, and please indulge me by letting me finish before you fly off the handle. Hopefully, you won't do that, as it would spoil my surprise." Karl had already spotted the long bag hanging on the door and guessed its contents. With her hands clasped together, Claire continued, "About six weeks ago, while you were out, you received a telephone call from that nice man, Jim McGinley.

"He had called to tell you that on your arrival in Glasgow, he would take you to the company tailor to get fitted for your uniforms. Hearing this, I asked him if it would be acceptable to allow me to have our tailor make those uniforms for you while you were still here at home. He agreed it would be an excellent idea, so long as the color and style matched the company's uniform code. I asked him to forward the insignias, brass buttons, company ties, and a size nine and a half cap to my office address, along with a list of whatever else I should consider. I concluded by asking if there were any charges to include an invoice in the package. Before ending the call, I said to him, 'Let's keep this our little secret, shall we?' He is such a nice man; I hope we can meet one day.

"Do you know how he responded to my questions? He said, 'Mrs. Vita, or may I call you Claire? There are absolutely no charges. I will have those items sent to you post haste, and please call me any time until Commander Vita and I set sail.'"

Karl's hands supported his head as he smiled, looking up at his wife with her hands giving her away as she fidgeted, waiting for an answer. "You did say commander, did you not? That bag hanging on the door contains my new uniforms. I suspected that when I walked in. Claire, please never lose that excitement. I had started to regret leaving you and Nick alone again. Seeing you like this makes me realize that as much as I love being home with you both, this next phase of my working career is not forever I just have that burning feeling inside to finish what I started so many years ago. I love you, Claire, for all that you continue to do for me; now, let's make sure they fit, shall we?"

Karl stood up, reaching for Claire, he wrapped his arms around her, holding her tightly, then kissed her as if it was the first time until a little voice behind yelled, "Mama, Papa." Nicholas was standing at their side, his little arm reaching up Claire's skirt to hold her leg.

"Karl Vita, what have you been teaching your son?" Hearing this, Karl scooped Nick up in his arms, kissing his cheeks and laughing at what Claire had just said. Karl walked over to the bag hanging on the door. Taking one of the two uniforms out of the bag, he examined the insignia and bars on the sleeves before putting on the trousers and jacket.

"Perfect!" remarked Claire. "Now, go upstairs and put your shirt and tie on, and here, take your new cap with you while I get out my camera. Nicky, we are going to take pictures of your daddy." Claire set up the camera on a tripod, so she could take pictures of Karl, then others with him holding Nicholas, and finally, a series of family pictures. After sitting and playing with Nick, Claire stood, turning toward the door, and in walked Karl, looking so much different in a maritime uniform than the military one he had previously worn in the BIS. "God, Karl, you look really smashing. It makes me want to devour you. Stand over there so the light from the window doesn't throw a shadow."

Claire took numerous pictures from different angles, then the family shots with the timer. The following morning, they headed to Baldock. It had been almost ten days since seeing the family.

Ronny was in the driveway, cleaning his car, "Hi, you two! I haven't seen you in some time. Your visit is very timely; we have lots to discuss."

While Freida and Claire went to prepare some coffee and pastry, Mama, holding Nicholas on her lap, had tears forming, which caught Karl's attention immediately. "Mama, what is upsetting you like this?" he asked.

Ronny, standing behind Mama, answered for her. "Karl, when you leave to join your ship, we will prepare to leave about a month after your departure. It's time for us to head back to Wien! Mino sent a letter telling us that the house is totally repaired and looking better than it did before the war. Your brothers have been helping Mino with the house and the other property since arriving back in Wien a few weeks back. As for my new position, my American boss needs me to move permanently instead of commuting like I have been doing since joining them. That commuting, according to him, causes me to lose a week in every six. I got a letter from him telling me they won't continue like this any longer, so if I still want this job, I need to plan on moving post haste."

Karl sat down next to Mama, asking, "Mama, is this something you are ready for? Have you decided to return to Wien, or would you prefer to stay here with Claire and me?"

Mama kissed her grandson on the forehead, then grasped Karl's hand and replied, "Karl, it's time we went home; as much as I hate to leave Claire and Nicholas once more on their own after you leave. Going home will not be easy, rebuilding our lives back in Wien. Living here in England was always temporary; we all knew that didn't we?" Mama looked up to see Freida and Claire hugging each other; their tears were of joy and the pain of separation. The excitement Karl and Claire had experienced the day before was shattered by this latest news. Even though they knew this departure was rapidly approaching, they didn't believe it would happen till much later. The rest of the day was spent deciding how to close the bungalow. Claire's firm would handle renting it furnished for the next two years just in case problems in Austria could warrant their return. After which, it would be listed for sale.

With only a couple of days left, Karl and Claire spent this precious time in Baldock, helping with packing for that long road trip of 1,500 miles back to Wien. Claire took charge of filling out the forms needed to ship four large crates to arrive in Wien about two weeks after they arrived. This last visit brought tears and heartache. It was like the family was breaking up again. Taking a break for coffee, Claire decided it was not the best time but the only time to make an announcement saying, "Two days ago, I had a doctor's appointment; something wasn't right. To my surprise, Doctor Burgess informed me I was six weeks pregnant. Karl, you're going to be a father again, and Mama, another grandchild."

Silence and shock filled the sitting room until Karl yelled out, "All that hard work has paid off!" The gloom they were experiencing had changed to excitement; Claire had delivered the most wonderful news. Karl, over the moon with excitement, announced, "I need to make sure I'm back home for when that bundle of joy you are carrying decides to make an appearance." He held his wife tightly; Karl and Claire had gotten their wish, and the family had an event to look forward to, making their goodbyes a little more cheerful, but now, it was time to head home. This last tearful farewell for Karl left them emotionally drained as they drove back to Hitchin. Claire promised she would be over to help more once she had seen Karl off at the station. The following morning, Karl made one more check to make sure he had not forgotten anything. Closing the two suitcases, he put on his maritime blazer and cap, then walked downstairs to find Claire dressed and making breakfast for her sailor.

"Darling, are you hungry? I hope so; you must be famished after using up all that energy last night. I don't think I will be able to make love for at least the next four or five months, you sex maniac. Nick was having a good old time, banging his spoon against the table. Karl lifted him onto his lap, making every minute count. Bill and Dorothy arrived at the house early enough to spend some extra time with Karl before heading out. At the station, they stood watching Karl as he purchased a one-way ticket to Glasgow. Smiling, he thought, I guess no more buying a ticket to Slough.

This morning was already becoming taxing for Claire, having to adjust her life once again, living alone with her son in that big house. Covering up the sadness, she held on tightly to her husband's arm, neither making small talk that would only make parting so much harder to bear. "Karl, while you're away, Dorothy and I will make sure Claire and Nicholas are well cared for, so please try not to worry too much." Bill was trying hard to make conversation without too much luck.

Karl, sensing the tension, said, "Why don't you all leave? Staying will only upset you more waiting around like this; please, do this for me?"

Claire put her arms around his neck with a tearful smile, answering, "Karl Vita, during the war, I saw you off every time. I always stayed until that train had turned the bend. Today, you are leaving again, but not back into some war zone. No, Karl, we will stay until you have turned that bend. Is that perfectly clear? Now, kiss me while you still can." Karl held her tightly, feeling the tension she was hiding. Bill and Dorothy held Nicholas back, giving them a little more time together. The public address announced the arrival of the express train to King's Cross, arriving on platform three. It was time to make those last farewells.

"Claire, I never thought it would be this difficult. It's worse than when I was in the BIS. Right now, darling, I'm not sure I can do this for three years; I love you much too much." Karl broke away from her arms to say his goodbyes to Bill and Dorothy.

Making light of this farewell, he said, "Bill, just think; when I get back, those flowers you planted last autumn will be blooming around the new house. Thanks again for all you are both doing for Claire and Nick."

Dorothy had been holding Nick, his little arms outstretched for his papa. She passed him to his father. "Nicholas, my little man, I will miss you so very much. Kiss your papa?"

Standing next to Karl, Claire took Nicholas from his father, saying, "Darling, you need to board the train; it's getting ready to depart." With tears rolling down her face, she tried very hard to keep a cheerful smile on her face.

Picking up his two suitcases, Karl walked to the nearest open compartment. Climbing in, he placed both cases on the overhead rack, then like all those times before, he lowered the window in the door, and in a loud voice, yelled out, "Claire, how I love you and Nicholas. Don't forget to write often, so I'll have letters waiting for me when we dock in some foreign port." The train lurched as it slowly moved down the platform, its whistle blowing. Waving madly, she stood there until the train turned the bend, hiding the platform and those still standing there.

Claire turned to Dorothy. Seeing the pain in her face, Bill held her tightly, telling her to let it all out. "I'll be all right, Bill. I think right now I'd like to head to Baldock. I should be in the office by early this afternoon after I've dropped my little terror off. Ready to drive me home?" concluded Claire as she regained her composure.

Karl sat down, taking out a manual on the Clyde Shipping Company. He held the manual in his hands, but his eyes were not looking at the pages; he was someplace else. Changing trains, he settled in for the long ride to Scotland. Jim McGinley had booked a room at the same hotel for the overnight stay before boarding the train for Glasgow the following morning. Although the hour was late when he arrived in Edinburgh, he had to talk to his wife. In the lobby, Karl called Claire, reversing the charges. He heard that familiar voice answering, "Hitchin 4567," the operator asking permission for the charges. "This can only be my husband, Karl, right?"

Feeling better hearing her voice, Karl answered, "Yes, Claire, it's me. I'm sorry for calling you this late; I just needed to hear your voice before you turned in. Claire, what the hell am I doing? Life is so short, and here I am about to go off on a bloody ship. I'm so stupid, just thinking of myself like this. At King's Cross Station, it took all my willpower not to turn around and head back home. Claire, tell me everything will be all right, leaving you like this?"

Hearing her husband talking with a tone of defeat in his voice, Claire started thinking, this is not the tough bloke I married, nor the same man that looked danger in the face so many times. He has got to put his fears aside about leaving Nicholas and me alone. "Karl, my darling man, please stop talking like this. Remember, it was my suggestion you return to sea duty, if only for three years. Karl, please shake off your mood right now; stop worrying about us. We will be fine. It's not like those war years when there was always the possibility I would receive a telegram from the war department telling me that you were missing or died in action. Karl, are you listening to me? Throw me a big kiss before we hang up. I'll decide where that kiss will land. Now, say good night, and please try to get a good night's sleep. You have a big day tomorrow."

Claire waited until she heard the line go dead. Standing next to the door with the telephone receiver still in her hand, she thought he was feeling guilty about this separation. All those months of being at home had to be the reason for him acting like this. Back in the kitchen, she made herself a cup of hot cocoa, then headed upstairs to an empty bed.

After arriving early at the station, Karl decided to buy himself a cup of hot tea and a bacon sandwich, still feeling completely alone. Thinking about Claire's scolding last night brought a smile to his face; sitting and sipping his tea, he continued to think. She can be so sweet, but she can be as tough as nails when needed. I guess I showed her a weak side of myself; I won't do that again. I forgot that she always admired how I handled bad situations. I sure did not do that last night. With a smile, the old Karl started taking over once again.

Thanking the girl behind the counter as he paid the bill, he noticed three attractive ladies sitting at a window table. They were in their early twenties, and he could feel them staring at him. The old Karl was starting to return to his cocky self. On the way out, he stopped at their table; smiling, he touched the brim of his cap, saying politely, "Ladies, thank you for those admiring looks, but see this ring? It means I'm spoken for. I just wanted to thank you anyway; have a wonderful day. With shock on their faces, the women continued to stare as he walked out.

Arriving in Glasgow, he could feel the difference in temperature this far north. At the end of the platform, he spotted an older gentleman holding a sign with Commander Vita written on it in large letters. Seeing the sign, he thought, being referred to previously as major to now being referred to as commander will take some getting used to, I guess.

"Morning, I'm Commander Vita, and your name, Sir?" asked Karl as the driver reached to carry Karl's cases. "I'll carry this one; sharing the load will be easier on both of us."

"Nice to meet you, Commander; my name is Arnold Nickels. Our car is right behind that entrance, and we should have you at the company offices in no time."

Reaching the car, Karl asked, "Mind if I sit up front with you, Nickels? I like to see the road ahead." Arriving at the company's lobby entrance, Karl could not help seeing the big superstructure towering over the offices. I wonder if that's the Princess, he thought. Thanking Nickels for the ride, Karl followed the young receptionist down the same hall and into the conference room.

"Karl, it's wonderful to see you, and may I say, your uniform is going to overshadow the one I'm wearing. That's quite the lady you're married to; she's so friendly. Come and sit next to me so we can go through all the documents together. We have five or six days here at the dock before we shove off, and don't worry; Arnold will deliver your luggage to your cabin. Don't expect it to look like the one you had on the Tristian. Let's start by reviewing this first trip and the port calls enroute, shall we? This trip won't be long because we are scheduled for a new refrigeration system on our return. However, it's a good way to familiarize yourself with that old girl behind us. When we cast off, the first stop will be in Marseille. Hopefully, we won't lose you this time." Jim was remembering the first time they met back in 1936 in Ostend, Belgium. "Our schedule has us dockside for five days."

Karl looked at Jim first with a solemn smirk, followed by a boisterous laugh, which was precisely what he needed.

"From there, our schedule takes us to Alexandria with a full load. I expect we will be there for approximately a week. We will also take on fuel for the longest leg to Boston, Massachusetts. It is not the best time to cross the North Atlantic, but it is what it is. During the first two legs, you will be our acting third officer, reporting to Arnold Simms, the current first officer. He will show you the ropes; however, he will leave us in Alexandria to take command of the Northern Lights, returning to Glasgow for a major overhaul. By then, you will be ready to assume the position of second in command. How does that sound to you? By the way, I gave your lovely wife the details of this trip, so she always knows where you are. Welcome aboard, Karl; I'm really looking forward to sailing together. Ready to meet the staff officers in my office? Then, we can grab some lunch before boarding the Princess. It's ironic to think that after all these years, you will be serving on the same ship that first took you to England all those years ago."

Karl, with a smile on his face, replied, "Lead on, my Captain." Jim introduced the staff, repeating the same story in each department as he introduced Karl. The time now was approaching 1400 hours.

Obviously pleased with the addition of this new officer, Jim looked at his watch and said, "Karl, you must be starving. Let's make our next stop the cafeteria. I think Malcolm and some of his people would like to join us, so be prepared to be bombarded with questions. You are somewhat of a novelty around here right now, being the first foreign officer to serve with the company since prior to World War One."

Lunch was as expected, a string of questions that tired Karl, having to answer them politely. "Gentlemen, you must excuse us; Commander Vita and I have much to do aboard the Princess."

Walking out onto the dock, Karl sighed with relief, saying to Jim, "That was more like an interrogation than a lunch meeting."

Jim, clasping his hand on Karl's forearm, replied, "Sorry about that, old man. I didn't expect them to bombard you with so many questions." Walking along the dock, the side of the Princess looked enormous; her fresh paint gave her a new ship appearance. At the boarding ramp, Karl stopped. Looking up, he was enjoying the memories this ship had given him. "Let's get on board, shall we? I'll show you to your cabin, so you can unpack and settle in, after which you can meet up with me in my day cabin. You do remember where that is, don't you?" asked Jim.

Karl smiled and nodded, saying, "Shall we convene in about an hour?"

Jim replied, "Sounds good to me. Call me if you need additional time; my extension is #109. See you later."

Karl removed his jacket and tie in his cabin, then sat down at the small desk. Looking around, he saw that the space had been refurbished, including the furniture. Putting the two cases on his bunk, he started removing their contents. He thought the hanging space was a little tight, but the storage drawers were more than ample. He placed the picture of Claire holding Nicholas in her arms on the shelf next to his bunk. Then he put the first picture Claire had given him next to it. Looking at that picture, he could feel her presence. With his index finger, he touched her lips, then placed them on his own. This separation would be tough, but the times at home in Hitchin would mean so much more. The last thought that crossed his mind was that the next three years would go by very quickly, and when I leave this time, it will be with the consent of the Clyde Shipping Company. Karl had found the composure he had lost temporarily the day before.

# CHAPTER 11

# RETURNING TO SEA DUTY

The next few days would be taxing for Karl, spending almost the entire first day with the engineering officer, climbing in, out, and over the machinery and the many systems that made up the ship. Day two would have him with the second officer Arnold Simms, familiarizing himself with the bridge equipment and the other duties a second officer is responsible for, including maneuvering responsibilities. That afternoon, he spent most of his time with the navigation officer, a kind chap who had made many dangerous Atlantic crossings during the war. Raymond Murry was a wealth of information and obviously happy to have Karl join the ship's company.

Before Karl knew it, they were on the last day before setting sail. Captain McGinley called a meeting for all officers to attend, as this would be the first voyage for the Clyde Princess since her major refit. Karl was getting that old feeling of excitement as they all discussed the many aspects of operating this large vessel. Later that afternoon, Karl walked over to the company offices to call Claire. This would be the last call he could make until they docked in Marseille, France. Karl looked at his watch, deciding Claire would more than likely still be in the office. With the assistance of the switchboard operator, he dialed the office number, hearing the familiar operator answer. "Maggy, it's Karl Vita; is my boss still in her office?" he asked jovially.

"Yes, Commander Vita, she is; please hold while I locate her for you." Karl, with building anticipation, waited until he heard Claire's voice.

"Darling, I was wondering when you would call today. How's it going? Getting to know your new ship must feel strange?" Claire stopped talking, allowing Karl to answer.

"So far, it's going well; sometimes, it's a little overwhelming. There's so much to learn in just a few days. Jim and his crew are wonderful; they have welcomed me with no remarks or reservations about me being a foreigner with an accent. How is my little man doing? Does he look around the house to see where his papa is hiding? Give him a big hug, will you? Darling, when I spoke to you yesterday, I never had time to apologize for how I sounded off. That's not like me, but thanks to that kick in the backside from you, I'm in a far better place right now. So, darling, no need to labor over that any further. Would love to kiss your belly so that baby knows its papa. Throw me a big kiss before I hang up, will you?"

Feeling relieved that Karl had regained his confidence once again, Claire continued by saying, "Karl, my darling man, I am missing you very much. Going to bed alone is hard, but I'm getting used to that until you're back here next to me. It's not like I haven't done this before, is it? It's so different this time. You're away on an extended voyage, but I don't have that horrible empty fear I always had each time you left before. There was always the strong possibility you may never return, and that concern is no longer with me. You're out of sight, doing a job you love, so I'm all right with that. Just remember, I have a calendar that I'm crossing off month by month for the next three years. Then, Commander Vita, you're all mine once again. Do you hear me? When you return, I'll be showing that bump; someone in there needs to feel their father kissing my belly." Claire was laughing, enjoying this bantering they had a way of doing on the phone.

"Claire, it's so comforting to hear you talk like this. It makes me feel so much better that you will be all right until I return. Good night, darling; I'm not sure I will be able to call you tomorrow, but I'll do that once we are dockside in Marseille. I love you, Mrs. Vita; Nick and our new baby make my life so wonderful; bye, darling." Karl hung up the receiver, returning to the ship with a confident smile. Claire sat at her desk smiling. Holding Karl's picture, she continued thinking, I accept that I married a sailor.

At 0930 hours, the Clyde Princess was coming alive, ready to set sail for Marseille, France. Captain McGinley gave the order on the bridge, "Number One, make ready to cast off your lines. Commander Vita, please assist."

"Aye, aye, Sir," came the reply. On the wing deck, holding a bullhorn, First Officer Arnold Simms barked his first order to the maneuvering gangs and dockside workers, "Single up on the bow and stern spring lines." When that was done, it was followed by, "Let go aft sprint and dock line." A tug positioned itself at the stern of the ship, ready to push the big freighter away from the dock. The last command Simms gave was to let go the bowlines. The second tug moved in, ready to push the ship into the harbor channel. "Helmsmen, come twenty degrees to port. Make shaft revolutions for three knots."

Clearing the breakwater, the Princess increased speed, signaling the two tugs to stand off, thanking them for their assistance. The old ship gathered momentum to a cruising speed of thirteen knots.

The captain, satisfied with the departure from Glasgow Harbor, turned to Simms and Vita and, in a jovial tone, said, "Well, don't you two think we deserve a nice cup of tea about now? What do you say to that?" This first voyage to Marseille would take approximately three to four days, depending on weather conditions.

Karl was regaining his confidence. Out on the wing, he placed both hands on the railing; momentarily closing his eyes, he allowed that familiar clean ocean air to fill his lungs, energizing every fiber of his being. Karl was home out at sea once again.

Back in the wheelhouse, Jim and Arnold sat sipping their hot tea, watching Karl through the window. "Arnold, he has so much to adjust to; this time aboard the Princess will recharge his batteries, that's for sure. Did you know he was the recipient of two war medals while he was in the British Intelligence Service? Those military chaps tried very hard to keep him for another tour of duty, but once a sailor, always a sailor, right?" said Jim, clinking his mug against Arnold's.

"You are so right, Captain. Once that saltwater is in your blood, it's very hard to turn away from it. So, let's help him get his sea legs back, shall we?" concluded Arnold. On the fourth day, Karl had the third watch. The dawn was slowly breaking, and the weather conditions could not be better to make their arrival in Marseille. As he stood in front of the helm, looking toward the bow, he knew it would be a glorious day.

A sailor interrupted his thoughts, saying, "Captain on the bridge." Karl turned to welcome his captain. "Morning, Sir; I trust you had a restful night?" Karl had enjoyed the quiet he experienced on this watch.

"Karl, the navigator informed me we should see land in about forty-five minutes. Your watch is almost over. How do you feel about taking on the responsibility of docking the old girl?" asked Jim, hoping to see that confident look on Karl's face.

"I was hoping you would let me take that on. Thank you, Sir." Whenever they were within earshot of the crew, they would always refer to each other by rank. This morning, Captain McGinley would stand ready to assist his new officer, even though he knew Karl was more than capable of doing this and so much more. In time, he would rely on Karl to run the ship completely. "Land sighted off the port bow, what are your orders, Sir?" Karl looked at Jim, confirming he would be in command of maneuvering operations this morning. Arnold Simms entered the bridge with a cheery greeting to everybody on the bridge. With a hot cup of tea in his hand, he sat near the navigation table, ready to assist if needed.

Karl barked out orders one after another. Jim looked at Arnold, nodding with his approval. "Pilot's aboard, Sir, and on his way up to the bridge," said one of the sailors assigned to bridge duty.

"Very well, Roberts, stand by; Mister Thompson, ring up three knots when I order. We will stay on this course toward the entrance, then standoff until the tugs are alongside." Karl, totally in control, greeted the pilot in French, making their communication easier for the pilot, turning maneuvering over to his control, and watching as the pilot gave precise instructions to the helmsman and the sailor on the ship's telegraph. Karl walked out onto the bridge wing, and with a bullhorn in his hand, instructed the deck crew to stand ready with the heaving lines fore and aft. Three tugs took up their positions, two at the bow and one at the stern. Slowly, the tugs pulled and pushed the Clyde Princess toward its assigned dock. Leaning over the wing railing, Karl yelled, "Let go forward spring line," followed by, "Let go bowlines." In quick succession, he repeated the instructions to the stern crew. Then he commanded them to secure all mooring lines until secured by dock lines. Karl's last command was, "Done with engine; helmsman, secure your helm." With a cocky smile, Karl turned to face the captain and the first officer, saying, "Well, how did I do? It's been ten years since I landed a ship in Marseille." He had a look of confidence written all over his face.

"Commander, that was perfect and by the book; make sure you make your entries in the log before leaving the bridge. After all this time, I would imagine you will be going ashore. Is that correct?" asked Captain McGinley.

"Yes, Sir, I hope to find the people who helped me back in 1936. With luck, they are still living here," replied Karl.

Captain McGinley replied, "Excellent, maybe later you will be up to having a drink with Arnold and myself. Shall we say at 1800 hours? Will that give you enough time?" asked Jim.

"That will be perfect, Jim sorry, I meant Captain. Meet you at the main gate."

Still in his uniform, Karl walked down the boarding ramp, his mind overloaded at remembering leaving the Tristian for the last time back in 1936. At the guard house, he presented his ID, then walked up the Boulevard Du Littoral to see if the Langstaff Shipping Company building was still standing. Turning the corner, in shock, he looked at the row of bombed out buildings the length of the boulevard. Karl turned onto the Rue Du Refuge, taxing his memory of where the garage was where he bought his trusted little Opel Cadet car. He hoped it would still be standing.

Finding the alley, he tensed up in anticipation of finding more bombed out buildings. To his surprise, the garage was in front of him, looking so much better than when he saw it last. Walking to the side door, he found it unlocked. Opening it, he saw the same disarray of vehicle parts and two old trucks left over from the occupation. In the dim light, he searched for Claude. Finding no sign of him, he yelled, "Hello, is there anyone here?" Hearing no reply, he called out again. Still, no answer waiting there he was about to leave when the door that led into the home opened, and out came Martine, her hand over her mouth in total surprise.

"Monsieur, I can't believe it; you are still alive! Claude will be so happy to see you again. We talk about you often, wondering if you made it to England." Martine was obviously overwhelmed at seeing Karl again. "Please sit down in the office; Claude will be back in about ten minutes. He just went to the scrapyard to find parts for one of those old German trucks out there. How about a nice cup of coffee while we wait?"

Karl stepped forward, hugging Martine and kissing her on either cheek before saying, "Thank God, both of you are alive and well! When I got off the ship, I expected to see some bomb damage, but nowhere near what I saw. What did you do to survive?"

Martine looked down, and grasping his arm, she spoke, fighting back the tears. "The Germans really didn't bother us too much; we were just small fish to them. I found work in a café. I only stayed about a year; it was terrible. The Germans, feeling superior, thought they had the right to manhandle me, and the other girls tolerated their behavior. After leaving there, I got a job in the fish factory, where I remained until the Germans left the city. Poor Claude barely managed to keep the garage open. The occasional repairs managed to keep him with work for a while, but that dried up very quickly, eventually he found work on a farm about eight kilometers from here. With no benzene to be had, he was forced to use his bicycle, regardless of the weather. I remember vividly waking up in the middle of the night to the sound of heavy equipment on the main road heading north out of Marseille, leaving it a ghost town. By midday, the church bells started ringing, signaling the Germans had left."

Karl sat quietly, listening to the sad story Martine was telling. Karl was about to ask a question when the side door opened, and in walked Claude. Not expecting to see Karl sitting with his wife, he was dumbfounded. "Monsieur, I can't believe my eyes! After all these years of war, you remembered us." Overwhelmed with excitement, he wrapped his arms around this seaman, his emotions stopping him from speaking. Karl felt like a massive weight had been taken off his shoulders, reconnecting like this. Karl looked at his watch, then asked them if he could buy them lunch at the local inn. That way, they could continue exchanging stories. A wonderful afternoon would soon come to an end. The time was getting late, and Karl had to return to the harbor to meet his fellow officers.

"My dear friends, I'm so sorry to leave, but I must meet my fellow officers. I will stop by before we depart the day after tomorrow." Standing, he hugged them both.

With tears in her eyes, Martine whispered in his ear, "Our prayers have been answered! We are so happy to hear you're married and have a son. Please, write to us when you can, God bless you, Sir." Karl paid the bill, then looking over his shoulder toward them, he touched the beak of his cap as he left the inn. He was relieved they had survived but saddened at the thought that their struggle would continue as the people of France struggled in bankruptcy to rebuild their country.

The following morning, Karl entered the small office that serviced the Clyde Shipping Company's needs in Marseille, asking the women behind the reception desk, "I need to make a call to England. Could you place it for me? Here is the contact and number."

"Please, take a seat, Commander, while I place the call for you." Karl smiled at hearing this. "You can use the phone in that small office if you like; it will be a little more private. Press two when you see it flashing, then your party will be on the line."

Karl promptly entered the office, closing the door behind him. He waited while the operator completed the connection. "Claire, can you hear me? It's your sailor still in Marseille. How are you and the little terror doing?"

Claire's heart skipped a beat at hearing her husband's voice. "Karl, tell me more about your first voyage. Was it what you expected? Did you manage to find that couple you always talk about who sold you the Opel Cadet? When I spoke to you yesterday morning, you appeared to be concerned about their welfare. We don't have long, so write a letter before you leave and drop it in the post. That way, you can tell me everything. I did not hear you say the most important thing."

With a soft tone to his voice, Karl laughed and then replied to Claire, "There is never a minute of the day that I don't thank the Lord for the gift he has given me, and that is you, not forgetting Nicholas and of course the new baby. I love you very much, Claire. Are you still having morning sickness? That must be miserable day after day."

Claire, hearing this, was having a hard time responding. "Karl, you always know the right things to say, especially when we are on the phone. My makeup is a mess right now. Karl, we love you. Now, before you sail, why don't you write more details in that letter?" Karl agreed he would find time later that day, posting it in the morning before they sailed.

Their time in Marseille had flown by; now, the crew of the Clyde Princess made ready for the next leg of the voyage to Alexandria, Egypt. As promised, Karl would go ashore in the morning to post his letter from the company office. Back on board, he met with the captain, first officer, and the navigator to review the manifest and their plotted course across the Mediterranean Sea to Alexandria.

"Karl, you will take charge of maneuvering, Arnold will be assisting just in case something goes haywire. We will cast off our lines at 1045 hours, so let's get ready, shall we?" directed the captain. At 1000 hours, the company agent came aboard to give the first officer a packet of documents. In his French accent he wished them bon voyage, then left to go back down the boarding ramp. Karl and Arnold went out onto the bridge wing, ensuring the maneuvering gangs were in place and ready. Once that was done, Karl barked out through his bullhorn the instructions to cast off, Arnold making sure the tugs were in position. "All stations in position, Commander, awaiting your orders," said Arnold, being very professional in his address to Karl.

"Very well, Number One; let's get underway," replied Karl as he gave his first maneuvering order. This next leg would take them 1810 miles at eleven knots, and with a following sea, it would take them approximately six days. The weather was turning nice with plenty of warm sunshine, and Karl was starting to enjoy himself. Arnold had removed himself from his duties as first officer, allowing Karl to take command. Captain McGinley had a habit of remaining on the bridge for long periods, observing how his new number one would perform his duties.

Feeling confident with the watch crews, he spoke out as he slid off his bridge chair, "Number One, I have things to do in my cabin, so I'll leave the ship in your good hands. Try to spend time with the junior watch officer before you go off duty, will you?"

Karl smiled and gave his captain a casual salute, thinking, Jim just called me his number one. I guess Arnold will be a passenger for the rest of this leg. Karl was still sleeping when he was woken by the steward saying, "Sorry to disturb you, Sir, but the third officer has instructed me to tell you we are about forty-five minutes from the rendezvous point. Here is your hot coffee and a buttered scone to keep you going until later."

"Thank you, Frank; tell the watch officer I will be up in about twenty minutes, will you?" replied Karl, still a little groggy.

Dawn was on the horizon, changing the dark Saturn sky into a burst of blue and crimson. This would be a marvelous day to arrive in Alexandria. Karl dressed in his white summer uniform and went up to the bridge. To his surprise, Jim and Arnold were already there, drinking their morning tea. "Morning, chaps; glad to see you played it safe by turning up early in case I didn't appear in time." Karl's warped sense of humor was back in full force, giving all on the bridge a good reason to have a laugh.

"Number One, join us. Harold still has the watch, so no need to rush. Frank is bringing you another cup of coffee and should be back in a jiffy," said Jim, pushing a chair out from the desk.

Alexandria was a magical place and was still under British rule. Their stay would not be long but long enough to get some sightseeing in and a couple of letters off to Claire.

"I say, chaps, now that the sun is up, I think today will be a hot one, too hot for these wool uniforms. I think I'll follow Karl's lead by changing," said Arnold, standing up to leave the bridge to go back to his cabin to make ready to leave the ship once dockside. "I'll catch up with you both once my packing is done. Then, old man, the Princess will be your responsibility under Jim's command. From what I've witnessed, the old girl is in good hands." Arnold walked to the door, saluting the seamen operating the helm and the telegraph.

Jim looked out the bridge window with a view over the bow. "I will miss Arnold, but now you will assist me with the Princess, so Number One, take her in if you please." Captain McGinley climbed back into his bridge highchair as Karl started giving maneuvering instructions. Dockside, the captain and Karl wished Arnold a safe voyage aboard the Northern Lights back to Glasgow and his long overdue four-month leave.

"We'll miss your laughter and that dry sense of humor. Please, stay in touch, Arnold. I have enjoyed sailing with you," said Jim.

Karl shook his hand, and his parting words were, "I would have liked to spend more time with you, old chap. I hope to see you back in Glasgow, and I wish you calm seas on the way home."

Arnold shook their hands one more time, then proceeded down the boarding ramp to the dock below. "Chaps, sound the whistle when you leave, so I can take pictures as the Princess passes by the Northern Lights, will you?" Jim and Karl gave him a thumbs up in response. Karl walked into the wardroom; most off duty crew were off the ship, so the compartment was empty. Making a cup of coffee, he opened his writing case and started writing to Claire.

*My Dearest Claire,*

*We are scheduled to depart Alexandria at 1600 hours tomorrow afternoon for our last stop in Boston, Massachusetts. Arnold Simms left us this morning to assume command of the Northern Lights. He was a wonderful officer to learn from. He will be sailing back to Glasgow, then off on leave for four months. As for us, well, we are getting ready to make the transatlantic crossing. The long-range weather forecast looks favorable, so it should be a trouble free trip. Have you spent much time with Mama and the family? Is it next week that they leave for Wien? When I return home, it will be strange not going to visit them in Baldock. I worry about you being on your own for a few months until I return. Our little terror will not understand that his grandma has left, poor little chap.*

*Claire, I miss you so very much. As much as I love my new job, I miss my night job of keeping you fired up if you know what I mean. Thinking of that makes me quite excited.*

*In Boston, we expect to be docked there for the best part of a week. I would have loved to meet up with Hazel as she is only a couple of hours away in Rhode Island. Have you heard from Gunther yet? He must be in training in Washington about now. In his last letter, he mentioned he had put in for a duty station in London or maybe Berlin. Has he told you any more about his posting yet? Must go, darling. I'm meeting up with Jim in about an hour. I will put this in the mail when I go ashore, so the next one will be from Boston.*

*All my love, kiss our little terror for me.*

*Love always,*
*your husband Karl (now First Officer Vita)*

Karl walked to the dock office to meet up with Jim. He had changed into a sports shirt and slacks, feeling good to be out of his uniform for a while. "Why, don't you look touristy?" said Jim, also in casual attire. "If you're in agreement, I thought we could visit some Egyptian ruins before getting a bite to eat; the food is very good here. I have a favorite restaurant down by the pier. I think you will like it. Ready to leave?" said Jim, walking toward the office entrance.

"Lead on, Skipper," replied Karl, following right behind him. This time off was wonderful, and his friendship with Jim was getting stronger, making his time apart from his family that much easier to bear. Touring the magnificent Egyptian ruins was exciting to these sailors. To Jim, it meant so much more. Exploring historic sites was more like a passion, admiring the accomplishments of the ancient Egyptians. Later, as they walked along the pier toward the restaurant, Jim continued to share his knowledge of this ancient port city, with Karl listening intently to all Jim had to say.

"Karl, the restaurant is down there, but before we proceed, do you recognize this dock we are approaching?" Jim studied Karl's face as he asked that question.

"Jim, I remember being here during the early part of 1936, but no, I must admit this particular dock does not have any significance to me." Karl could sense he should know what Jim's question signified. It had to have a meaning to him, he thought.

"Karl, when I first laid eyes on the Tristian, it was berthed right here at dock #203."

Karl looked at the surrounding buildings and the entrance to the harbor. "Oh, my God, Jim, you are so right. What an amazing memory you have; now, I recognize everything." Standing there, Karl's memories flooded his mind. He could see the Tristian lying at the dock and himself leaning over the bridge deck, directing the dock gangs as they made ready to leave. His mind raced forward to that last voyage to Marseille, France, and that fateful day he would leave that beautiful ship without the captain's permission back in 1936. Karl's mind was racing through those events, feeling the pain of desertion.

"Karl, I didn't mean to hit a nerve. I only thought you would enjoy seeing where I first saw your ship." Studying Karl's face, Jim realized this may not have been the right thing to do, even though his intentions were harmless.

"Jim, it's alright. I was not prepared to relive those bygone days of so long ago, but I'm so pleased you did because here we stand, fellow sailors sharing a memory that could never be changed." Over lunch, they discussed how the war had changed the maritime industry. "You know, Jim, I often wonder what happened to the Tristian. Did she make it through the war, and if so, where is she now? I can only imagine what shape she could be in. Maybe it's best I don't know." Looking at Karl's face, Jim decided he would not mention that she was moored outside of Montevideo, Uruguay, in desperate need of major repairs. Over a delicious lunch of lamb, the two talked about their war experiences and the destruction left behind.

"What say we head out back to the old girl; tomorrow is a workday for both of us. I hope you enjoyed this day of relaxation," said Jim, standing up to pay the bill, Karl asking to split it. "Let me get this one, Karl. I'll take you to a really nice restaurant in Boston, which you can pay for," laughed Jim.

The Princess, still loading cargo, was sitting much lower in the water, ready to leave the following morning. Karl rose early; the dawn had not yet broken, but his energy was fully charged at the thought of leaving later that day. The ship was still in darkness. Very quietly, he entered the wardroom and poured a big mug of fresh coffee. Then, he climbed the stairs to the bridge. The sunrise would be spectacular and the perfect way to start the day. There would be very little time for himself once the ship's company started preparation for their next leg across the North Atlantic to Boston, Massachusetts. A hand on his shoulder made Karl look around to see the navigator standing next to him. "Morning, Number One; it's going to be a marvelous day to head out. We should have smooth seas all the way. Have you ever been to Boston? I understand it's a grand city to visit, and I'm quite looking forward to time off there." Graham White was much younger than Karl. He had entered the maritime service at the tail end of hostilities. As an enthusiastic junior officer, he was very much at home in his capacity.

"Graham, I did not hear you coming out onto the wing. I'm glad to have the company though, and you're so right; today will be a wonderful day to get underway." All day long, the remainder of the cargo and fuel were brought aboard; by lunchtime, they were ready.

On the bridge in his highchair, Captain McGinley issued orders to Karl, "Number One, make ready to cast off if you please."

Karl and the other officers were standing ready for their orders. "Aye, aye, Sir," replied Karl as he walked out onto the wing to direct his orders to crew members below, waiting at their stations. The tugs kicked the waters of the harbor against the Princess's hull as they pushed her out into the harbor waters of Alexandria before taking up stations at the bow and stern. The big freighter's propeller thrust into the water, moving her slowly forward.

"Helmsman, when we pass the Northern Lights, give it a long blast on the ship's whistle if you please," commanded the captain. Karl and several other officers watched as they moved slowly by the

Northern Lights. Hearing the whistle, Arthur replied with the same long blast of his ship's whistle, waving goodbye to his previous ship.

With his bullhorn, Karl yelled, "Have an uneventful journey back to Clyde Side. Hope to meet up with you there on our return." The captain came out onto the wing to bid his farewell to his previous first officer.

"Number One, take her out to sea. We need to stretch her legs, then join me inside." There was a cheerful manner in the captain's voice as he said that.

"Make your revolutions for ten knots. The captain needs to feel those deck plates vibrate." As much as he missed his family, at this moment, Karl felt the joy of being in command of a big merchant ship, heading northwest into the clear blue seas of the Mediterranean then out through the Straits of Gibraltar into the North Atlantic. After so many years away from this life, Karl felt at home once again. As predicted, their passage was uneventful. Other than the occasional passing ship, the sea was empty; Karl was a happy sailor once again.

"Land Ho, Sir, three points off the starboard bow," yelled one of the bridge spotters.

Karl answered, "Very well, Navigator; give me your latest position, please. Signal the pilot boat that we are reducing speed. Let me know when he's aboard."

Jim looked on from his captain's chair in admiration as Karl gave precise orders to the bridge crew, thinking, I always knew Karl Vita would be the perfect officer. Sooner than later, the company will give him his own command. As much as that thought saddens me, he is more than ready to assume command of his own ship.

"Pilot is aboard, on his way up to the bridge, Sir," yelled the yeoman. The pilot entered the bridge, and in a jovial voice, he announced, "Welcome, guys, to Boston. My name is Marcus O'Brien. Did you have a nice crossing? Would anyone mind if I smoked?"

Jim replied, "Go right ahead, and welcome aboard, Mr. O'Brien." Marcus gave the bridge crew the course and speed to enter the channel. "Have any of you guys been here before?" asked Marcus, taking a sip of coffee.

Jim answered, "I have been here many times before and after the war on this very ship, making those dangerous convoy crossings of the Atlantic. Boston is really a wonderful historic city."

Marcus, a man very proud of his city, commented on the islands as they steamed toward the harbor entrance. Karl had his eyes firmly on their progress toward the entrance. Seeing the tugs approaching, he turned to Marcus, saying, "Thank you, Mr. O'Brien. I believe your job here is done. It looks like the pilot boat is coming alongside and thank you for the history lesson. We really enjoyed hearing about all that English tea that landed in the harbor. Thank God I drink coffee."

Marcus first had a straight face as he looked at Karl, then he broke out laughing, "Where are you from, Sir? You're definitely not English." Karl was enjoying this rough and tough Bostonian.

"Marcus, I'm originally from Austria, now living in England and married to an English girl." Karl could see by the expression on Marcus's face that he might be thinking this guy was probably in the German Navy.

While watching where this bantering was going, Jim interjected by saying, "Mr. O'Brien, my first officer here, prior to joining the Clyde Shipping Company, was a decorated major in the British Intelligence Service, in case you were thinking something different."

Karl, standing by the entrance, just smiled. He was used to going through this kind of questioning. He turned toward Jim with a nod of gratitude.

"Sir, I hope you did not take offense to what I just asked. It was not my place to inquire about your accent."

Karl, still smiling, said, "That's alright, Marcus, no harm done. While we are on the subject, what did you do in the war?" asked Karl.

"Sir, I was a navigator on a minesweeper based right here in Boston; nice to have met you both." Marcus casually saluted Karl and Jim before leaving the bridge.

Still with that sarcastic smile, Karl looked at Jim and finally said, "Thank you, Captain. I kind of enjoyed that, didn't you?"

Karl took up station on the port wing along with the second officer, ready to convey his maneuvering instructions to the deck below. Jim came out onto the wing as the lines were secured to the dock. "After you have secured the ship, let's you and I have a chat, shall we?" Captain James McGinley had decided the time was right to share his intention to retire from being a ship's captain with Karl. For some time, the company had encouraged him to move ashore to become the director of operations and fleet commodore over their growing fleet. In this new position, he would replace Malcolm Finley, moving up to a new position as vice president. Although this restructuring would not take effect until the following spring, the need to have a plan in place was high on the priority list of the company's board of directors.

"The ship is secure, Sir."

Karl loudly made his final command, "Done with engine, secure the helm," as he returned the bullhorn to its holder. Down on the dock, the workmen swung the boarding ladder into place, locking it into position for the customs and port authority officers waiting patiently to board, welcomed by the third officer.

Jim and Karl were waiting on the bridge for the authorities to enter, standing without saying a word. Karl was reliving that day in Dover when he waited to be questioned by customs and intelligence personnel with the expectation of being granted asylum. The bridge door opened, and in walked four officials, ready to inspect and clear the ship.

After the port authorities had left, Jim turned to Karl, saying, "Why don't we get some coffee, then have that chat in my day cabin, shall we?" suggested Jim as they left the bridge. Karl followed, but that look on Jim's face was giving him away. Why was Jim asking to have a private chat? In his cabin, Karl sat on the couch, holding his hot coffee and waiting for Jim to sit opposite him. "Karl, take that worried look off your face; today's chat will make you a very happy fellow. Believe me when I tell you the company and I could not be more pleased with how you have adapted. What I'm about to share with you is highly confidential. As a former intelligence officer, you are used to keeping confidential information secure.

"Karl, I have been a ship's captain for longer than I care to admit. When I received your letter about finding a maritime position, I was more than delighted, thinking you would be an excellent candidate to join our staff of qualified officers. Karl, next summer, I will hang up my captain's cap, moving ashore as the new director of operations and the fleet commodore. That will leave an opening for a replacement captain for the Princess. Karl, there is no one more suited to this position than yourself. Arnold Simms will assume my position as the principal captain; from what I have seen, you two will have no problems sharing that captain position on this ship." Jim stopped talking to take a sip of the hot liquid, allowing Karl to speak.

"Jim, I am truly honored to think that after such a short time serving on the Princess, you have the confidence in my abilities to take on the responsibilities of being this ship's relief captain. As much as I have dreamed of being a ship's captain, there is a preexisting condition that could make you reconsider that promotion. When contemplating a return to sea duty, I talked extensively with my wife about the sacrifice she would have to endure during the long periods when I was away at sea. She agreed with only one condition, and that condition was that it could not be for more than three years. So, as much as I'm humbled to hear I am being considered as a relief captain, in all consciousness, I cannot accept." Taking a sip of coffee, Karl searched Jim's face for that disappointed look, which did not happen.

Instead, Jim smiled at Karl. Nodding his head, he replied, "Karl, I know all about your understanding with your wife. Some time ago, when I was doing my due diligence, I called your wife to make sure she would be alright with you being away at sea for extended periods. Claire confided in me that, as much as she was thrilled to hear the company was considering promoting you, she needed to disclose that your time at sea would be short. Karl, we have carefully considered that stipulation and believe it could be a blessing in disguise. So, no need to labor that thought any further.

"Karl, your wife is amazing; her legal mind gave me such a clear picture of your need to return to the sea, and when the time came to leave, it would be on your own terms. She is really someone to be admired. Maybe one day, we will see women commanding big ships like the Princess. Unfortunately, that could be a few years in the future. One last thing, Karl, then we can move on. I asked Claire not to bring it to your attention; blame me if you must. I needed to see how you would fare on this first contract." Jim had delivered his intentions, feeling somewhat relieved it went so well.

"Now that's out of the way, let me explain how you and Arnold will command this ship together. The contract schedule for both you and Arnold will be for five months on and four months off. The ship will be out of commission each year for about two to three weeks. When that happens, the captain still on duty will oversee that overhaul. Captain Vita, for the second time, do we have a deal?" asked Jim, standing up to shake Karl's hand. Karl was already standing, the look on his face giving him away. He was ecstatic, knowing he would take command of this ship in the future.

"Jim, it appears you and Claire have planned my career for the next three years anyway. I'm glad you decided to make a move on that plan."

Over the next hour, Jim explained that he and Arnold would have trainees traveling with them on most voyages, effectively ensuring the fleet would always have new officers in training for the future. "Karl, we are six hours behind England here in Boston. If you want to telephone your wife, you should be doing it soon, as it's almost eight o'clock in England. Walk with me; I have business with our agent, and I know where the office is located."

Jim smiled and walked toward the door; he turned to Karl with a remark that shocked Karl momentarily. "Karl, I have never told you this before, but I think we are good enough friends now to tell you this. When we sailed from Ostend to Dover, I did, in fact, contact customs about you being on board. What you don't know is that I asked to be transferred to the port intelligence people. I told them I had an officer on board wearing a German maritime uniform, trying to get this mother and sister with her baby to England, and asked if they would come aboard once we docked. I told them I was impressed with your honesty but thought you could also be a very well-rehearsed spy for the Germans. So, you see, Karl, I asked them to interrogate you before allowing you off the ship." Jim was still smiling, waiting for a reaction.

"Jim, I would have done the same. Just think what I could have fed back to the German intelligence?" Laughing, they left the ship, knowing there was a bright future for Karl as a fleet captain.

The office occupied by the port agent for the Clyde Shipping Company was small, with desks jammed back-to-back; the office manager had an equally small office. This surprised Karl as they entered, removed their caps, and Jim said loudly, "Morning, I believe you will remember me from the last time. I'm Captain McGinley, and this is my First Officer Commander Vita; here are the manifest and fuel requirements for the return trip. Commander Vita here needs to place a trunk call to England. Is there someplace he can talk privately?"

The office manager stepped forward. He was a cheerful chap, wearing a bright, colorful sweater. "He can use my office. Dial one eight for an overseas line; you may have to wait a few minutes to be connected. This way, please."

Karl followed while Jim sat with the agent who would process the cargo documents and arrange for a fuel barge to be brought alongside. Karl dialed the number, waiting patiently until the operator asked him for the overseas number. Again, a few minutes passed before the operator answered, "Go ahead, Sir, your party is on the line; sorry for the delay." With that, she hung up.

"Claire are you there or am I talking to an empty line?" asked Karl. "Darling, I'm here! It's wonderful to hear that Austrian accent of yours! I love it so much. Wait a second; someone wants to say hello to his dad." Karl could hear Claire talking to Nicholas, encouraging him to say something.

"Papa come home; papa come home," came that little voice from three thousand miles away in Hitchin. Hearing him, Karl started choking up, but his son needed to know his papa had heard him.

"Nick, your papa will be coming home soon. Say it again, Nick." Karl heard the phone rattle as Claire took the receiver from her son's little hand.

In the background, Karl could hear Nick yelling, "Papa come home." Karl waited as Claire composed herself, saying, "Karl, he misses you so much! He looks for you everywhere. How long will the return trip take? And will you be able to leave right away? Darling,

I have some wonderful news to share with you. Yesterday, I had a checkup appointment with Dr. Burgess. Although it's still very early, we could be looking at this coming August, but it's too early yet for an actual delivery date. So, Mr. Vita, tell my good friend Jim to push the Princess as hard as he can." Claire sounded upbeat, knowing Karl would be at her side for the birth of their new baby.

"Claire, this is exciting news! I still hope it's going to be a girl. I miss you and Nick so very much, mainly at night. During the day, I have very little time to think. Once our fuel bunkers are replenished and the last of the cargo loaded, we will depart for home." Karl did not mention the discussion he had with Jim. This was not the time or place. "Darling, I must go. I have a ship needing my attention. Jim sends his regards."

Karl hung up the telephone, his face one big smile. Very soon, he would be a dad for the second time. Later that night, he wrote to his mother, full of excitement, to remind her she would soon be a grandmother once again. As he addressed the envelope, he broke out laughing, thinking, I'm willing to bet she already knows everything. That wife of mine always keeps the family informed, and the arrival of this new baby will be no different.

The time was 1230 hours; the Princess and her crew were standing ready as the pilot had just boarded. "Welcome back, Mr. O'Brien, we are ready for you to take us out," said Karl.

Marcus replied with a big smile, "Aye, Aye, Sir." He then conveyed instructions for a course to enter Boston Harbor. Next stop, Glasgow.

Karl was sitting in Jim's highchair as Marcus instructed, "Maintain three knots till I give you a new course." Marcus, sipping his coffee, turned to Karl, saying, "Well, guys, that was a quick turnaround. Next time, stay longer. Helmsman, make your course 080 degrees until we clear the breakwater, then come left to 030 degrees and maintain that heading until we are at the rendezvous point. Increase revolutions for five knots, if you please, Quartermaster." Karl studied Marcus as he gave the crew directions, thinking he's such a jovial chap. I hope next time I can spend more time in his company.

"Pilot launch coming alongside, Sir," yelled a seaman.

"Very well, ring up all stop until the pilot launch has cleared. Thank you, Marcus; be careful climbing down that ladder, will you? I hope to see you on our next visit," said Karl, extending his hand to the rough and ready harbor pilot. Standing on the portside wing, Karl watched as Marcus leaped aboard the pilot launch. Turning, he waved, and Karl waved back. Back inside, he gave orders to maintain course and ring up revolutions for eleven knots." Karl was thinking, next stop Scotland, and then home to my pregnant wife.

# CHAPTER 12

# CHANGING TIMES

Karl had turned in early. They had been at sea for six days, and the weather had been kind to them so far. With a following sea, they were planning for an early arrival the next day, and that thought made Karl a happy sailor.

Entering the wardroom at 0530 hours, he saw Jim already having breakfast. "Morning, Karl, did you sleep well? I went out like a light until 0415 hours. Come, sit down; I think Gaines is already getting your coffee. I think you should join me in this delicious bacon and eggs. I must admit, American bacon is so different from ours; I think I prefer it. Next time you're in Boston, put some aside in that new refrigeration compartment in the number one hold being installed once we return home. I don't think the customs blokes will take any notice, do you?

"Karl, I checked with the navigator. All going smoothly, he said we could be tied up at approximately 1530 hours. So, are you all packed and ready to go on leave? I'll call ahead to have a car standing by to take you to the station. With luck, you'll make the 1715 hours' train to Edinburgh. Don't worry about the customs inspection or the other things that need the captain's attention. Remember, until later today, I'm still the skipper of this vessel," challenged Jim, reinforcing that this was his last trip as the master of the Clyde Princess.

Like clockwork, the maneuvering went smoothly, and now an anxious Captain Vita was heading down to the gangway, saying goodbye to all he passed getting there. As soon as the customs officers had inspected his passport and company identification papers, he was cleared to disembark. He took one last look back to see Jim and others gathering on the bridge wing, waving him farewell and best wishes for a healthy new baby. Walking briskly, he climbed into the waiting company car.

"Is that all your luggage, Sir, or do you have more we need to wait for?" asked the driver before he closed the rear passenger door.

"No, whatever I missed will have to wait until I return," replied Karl, excited finally to be heading home to Hitchin. The drive to the train station was relatively quick, giving Karl ample time to buy a suspense novel for the long trip to London. The train from Glasgow arrived in Edinburgh ahead of schedule, so he had no need to rush. He took the time to browse through a couple of shops, looking for a toy for Nicholas and a really big teddy bear for the new baby. Finding a compartment toward the front of the Golden Arrow, Karl placed his suitcase and teddy bear overhead and his topcoat on a window seat before walking forward to the dining car. Karl was amazed at how few people were traveling this evening; it was so nice and relaxing.

"The bar is not open yet, Sir, but you're welcome to sit at the bar until we are," said the bar steward. "Going home, Sir? Have you been away very long? By the look on your face, I would say you're more than ready to be at your destination, am I right?" continued the steward.

"Yes, you're absolutely correct. I've been gone over five months, so this extended leave will be wonderful. My wife is expecting our second child sometime in August," replied Karl. A loud shrill from the train's whistles told them they were about to depart.

"Here we go, Sir, right on time. There's no one around, so here, bang this one back." Moving toward the end of the small bar, the steward was turning a blind eye to Karl downing the glass of Scotch Whiskey. Karl was quietly laughing and thinking, someone up there is taking good care of me. Whoever you are, thank you for the life I'm living. Two naval officers were getting a kick out of Karl as he chugged down his glass of whiskey.

"I say, old man, are you traveling alone tonight? If you are, care to join us for a drink before supper?" asked one of the naval officers as he moved down to sit next to Karl, extending his hand toward him. "My name is Reginald Hemmings, and this chap is John Wright.

I think we are doing the same thing as you going home on leave. Merchant service, I see?"

Smiling, Karl answered by saying, "Yes, I am. What about you two? I see you're in the Fleet Air Arm, am I correct?" asked Karl, not really expecting too much of an answer from these naval officers other than a friendly nod.

They were still sitting at the bar two hours later, drinking up a storm. John finally said, "Chaps, if we don't sit down for dinner soon, it will be too late. So, drink up, or take your drinks with you. I need to eat something before that alcohol hits my brain."

The three sat down, Reggie ordering three glasses of Champagne to toast Karl's announcement of the new baby. The dining car was closing, so with cheerful goodbyes, the two naval officers headed down the corridor to their compartment, leaving Karl sitting at the table, finishing his coffee. The following morning, Karl rose early, got himself presentable, then headed to the empty dining car for coffee and, of course, bacon and eggs. Arriving at King's Cross Station, he looked for his new friends but didn't see them. He thought I guess we were passing ships in the night, never to meet again. But then again, he had said that so many times before.

Leisurely, Karl walked down the platform for the quick train ride to Hitchin. People, mainly ladies, commented on the giant teddy bear under his arm. Karl laughed and thought, never thought about doing this when I was still single too late now. Thinking more, he said quietly under his breath, "Thank you, God; I could never dream of a life without my Claire and our little terror. I'm still guessing whether we'll have another boy, or I'll get my wish for a daughter."

"Next stop, Hitchin," came the announcement over the speaker in the compartment, and the train started slowing. The familiar squealing of the brakes meant the Hitchin Station was only moments away. Karl stood up and retrieved his luggage and teddy bear from the overhead rack before putting his topcoat on, ready to exit the carriage once the train stopped. For a glancing moment, he allowed his mind to travel through all the times he had returned to this station, always wondering if the next time he left, he would never return. Those war years were no more, for now anyway. Walking to the taxi rank through the familiar, dimly lit tunnel, he headed to the first in line. Climbing into the back seat, Karl gave the driver the address, then, in a jovial voice, told him not to look so disappointed. He was going to give him a big tip for the short three plus mile trip. Karl could hardly contain his excitement at thinking about Claire's face when she opened the front door to see him standing there. I'm willing to bet she's going to give me hell for not calling her to pick me up. Seeing that look on her face will be worth it.

In the driveway, true to his word, Karl gave the driver a five-pound note, saying, "I told you this would be a good fare, didn't I? Thanks." Karl retrieved his front door key, and opening the door, he found the house deadly quiet. He thought Claire must be on her way to pick up Nick from the babysitter's. I can't wait to see their faces when they come through that door. While I'm waiting, let me check the garage. I'm willing to bet she has already brought over my MG sports car. Back outside, he opened the garage door. There in front of him, with a big yellow bow on its radiator, was his beloved MG the car that introduced Claire to him so many years ago.

Not lingering, he went back inside the house to make himself a cup of coffee and a cheese sandwich. He laughed again at seeing the pantry fully stocked, ready for the returning hungry sailor. That sandwich satisfied his craving for food. He took his luggage upstairs, thinking he would empty the cases before Claire and Nick arrived home. No sooner had he started doing that when he heard a car enter the driveway. Quickly, he went downstairs, picking up the teddy bear and the bouquet of fresh flowers he had bought at the station. In the kitchen, he stood waiting for the door to open.

Outside, he could hear Claire calling Nicholas to take one of the smaller shopping bags. Karl reached for the doorknob. Opening the door, he said softly, "Madam, allow me to help you with those bags."

Claire stopped dead in her tracks with her mouth wide open. She was speechless and very much in shock. Before she could speak, Karl wrapped his arms around her, one of the bags spilling over onto the step. "Karl, darling, I can't believe you're already home. I didn't expect you until later today. You bugger, this is just like you; kiss me before I slap you." The warmth of her lips sent an electrifying feeling across his face. A small hand was also pulling the leg of his trousers, yelling, "Papa, me too!"

"Nicholas, come here, my little man. You are speaking more words! Has mummy been teaching you those?" Karl lifted his son under his left arm, his right around Claire. "Let me look at you, darling; you are glowing must be that package you're carrying. Nicholas was kissing his face and pulling his hair, excited to have his father home again. Karl bent over to pick up the contents of the shopping bag before following Claire inside.

"Karl, there's a little green car in the garage, ready for you to go driving tomorrow. I had it serviced last week; she is ready for you, darling. I'm still in shock. It never entered my mind you would be here when I got home. Come here, you wonderful man. I need to feel your arms around me; it's been too long." Karl put Nick down, and with his arm around her, he kissed her again. "Karl Vita, where did you buy that big teddy bear? It's so cute, just like my big Vita bear."

From the corner of his eye, Karl could see Nick reaching for the box on the table. "Wait up there, you little thief. It's for you anyway; let me open it for you." Nicholas insisted he could open the box by himself, and he pulled at the paper around it. "Wait! You're so impatient. You didn't get that from me; it must be your mother's side." Karl opened the box, and Nick's face had excitement written all over it. He took the toy car out, unsure what to do with it. Karl laughed, enjoying being a dad once again. He showed his son how to wind up the car. Then, putting it on the floor, he turned the front wheels, which were operated by a long tube with a bulb on the end.

"Nick, take this in your hand. When you squeeze the bulb, the front wheel turns left to right. Karl showed Nick how to release the brake; then, with Nick walking behind it, he managed to hit all the furniture, making him yell with delight.

"Oh, Karl, you have opened Pandora's Box. He will drive us mental with that toy," laughed Claire, sitting at the kitchen table, smiling and watching her two men playing.

"Darling, you have no idea how often I have thought of being here, doing just this." Karl sat next to her, his arm around her neck. She looked radiant with that baby bump.

"Once we have had supper and put Nick to bed, we can relax in the sitting room uninterrupted. You can tell me about the exciting places you have been; how does that sound to you?" asked Claire, realizing it was useless to talk until Nick was asleep. Karl carried Nick upstairs, staying with him until his eyes could no longer fight the feeling of sleep. Claire had made a plate of sandwiches and biscuits for them to share, along with a pot of hot coffee.

"Alright, Claire, let's look at that list of Christian names we compiled before I left. My top three are Emily, Amanda, and Christina, in that order. If it's a boy, how about Karl Junior?"

Claire, reaching for his hand, continued, "Let's make this easy; if it's a girl, I love the name Emily. I agree with you; Karl Junior would also be my choice if it's a boy. There, that was easy. Karl, I was thinking next summer, when you're home on leave, let's plan on driving to Vienna with our kids. What do you think? I miss having the family close by, most of all Mama. Darling, she needs to see her grandchildren, and we need a holiday, not in Cornwall, but in the city where you grew up. Let's do this, shall we?"

Karl sat, gazing into her eyes, finally answering, "Claire, if that's what you want, then that's what we will do. Why don't you write to Mama and Freida, telling them our plan, and if we do this, we can also consider stopping in that town of St. Sebastiana in Germany to fulfill the promise I made to you at the George and Dragon, remember? We'll give Kitty a fitting headstone on her grave. I still have the document with the name she was buried under, Gretel Manton." Karl once again searched Claire's face for a sign of agreement. For a moment, they sat holding hands, not saying a word, Karl keeping his gaze on his wife's face.

"Darling, that's a given. Now that the war is over, she's still buried under that fictitious name in that graveyard. Why don't you contact her mother and tell her what we plan on doing? I'm sure she will be very happy to hear we are doing this for her oldest daughter. Make sure you tell her we will also take pictures for her."

Again, Karl smiled at the unselfish generosity of his wife, wanting to do this for someone she never knew. But, then again, there may be a spiritual connection.

With her arm around Karl's shoulder, Claire continued. "Now, let's talk about Dorothy and Bill's wedding; it won't be long now. Bill has been a real peach, helping Dorothy and me with all the preparations. She is trying to keep it to about fifty or so people; good luck with that idea," said Claire, laughing as she remembered what happened at their wedding. "Darling, please call Bill tonight or first thing tomorrow morning. He will be glad to have an extra pair of hands to help with the arrangements. He really misses you, Karl. He often brings up that first meeting between you, Clive, and himself. That meeting created a bond of friendship that will never be divided. Just think, we may have never met if you hadn't joined the BIS. Where would you be right now if that hadn't happened?" Karl, looking at her, was having the same thoughts.

Claire pushed herself up, saying, "Ready for bed, darling? It's been a long day for you, and I'm ready to have my husband back in bed beside me. Feeling the warmth of your body against mine will be wonderful. If you're not too tired, I would love to take care of you. It's been a long time, and you need the relaxation. What do you say to that, Sailor?" Claire was giving him that mischievous look that left little to his imagination.

"Claire, don't you think that's a little risky right now?" asked Karl as he followed her upstairs, tapping her backside on every step.

"Keep that up, and you'll find out what a pregnant woman is capable of doing," replied Claire as they entered the bedroom, closing the door quietly behind them. Karl took a long hot bath, feeling the hot water calming every muscle in his body. Claire had taken hers first, giving him time to finish emptying his cases. Karl thought this dry-cleaning bill would be a whopper for sure. Claire came out of the bathroom in her bathrobe and looked at the pile of uniforms and shirts on the floor, smirking "Good thing you came home. How long had you been wearing that uniform you arrived home in today?"

Looking at each other, they both laughed quietly, followed by Claire saying, "In you go, Sailor. I need a very clean husband next to me tonight." Fifteen minutes went by. Lying on the bed, Claire decided to check on Karl, hoping he hadn't fallen asleep in the tub. Wearing a very sheer light blue nightgown, she walked in.

Standing over Karl's head, she said softly, "Haven't seen that little chap in a long time. I hope he's not taking a nap. Maybe he's forgotten his other job, taking care of your wife! What do you think, handsome? Will he be up to the task tonight?" Claire sat on the side of the bathtub, her right hand extending into the hot water, encircling Karl's limp penis.

"Claire don't start something you can't finish. Remember, I've been on a ship with no women around for over five months and teasing me like this will only lead to you having to satisfy that pent up need for lovemaking," said Karl, standing up in the tub. Claire took a towel to wipe him dry.

"Darling, no need to put your pajamas on; you'll only have to take them off again in a few minutes," Claire said with a devilish smile, which Karl loved, as she returned to the bedroom. That wonderful feeling of having his wife's warm, soft body alongside his was arousing him. He wanted her so very much.

"Darling, how are we going to make love? On your side, or maybe from behind. This is a new one for me. What did we do when you were pregnant with Nicholas?" asked Karl as he held his wife close to him.

"Karl, I keep telling you I'm very pregnant, which makes me even hornier. Just think, tonight, you can get rid of all that dirty water. No need to take precautions; I'm already pregnant. Now, stop keeping me waiting." Karl kissed her softly, sensing that eager response, her mouth open, ready to feel the sensation of each other's tongues. "Karl, I want you so badly. Please, let me feel you inside me. I've waited too long for this moment." Karl rolled Claire onto her side, kissing her breast as he did so. Moaning softly, she held his erection tightly, skillfully helping him enter her. Karl responded with short, slow thrusts, then longer, more forceful ones, getting faster with each movement. On the verge of an orgasm, Claire whimpered quietly for Karl to do the same.

"I need to feel you inside me, please. Please, darling, do it now." Hearing her talk like this, Karl erupted with a deep thrust, giving in to what she had waited for all those long months. Sweating and breathing heavily, they lay in each other's arms, feeling content and satisfied that sleep would come easy this night.

Very early the following morning, Karl placed a call to Bill's home in Letchworth. "Bill, it's Karl. I wanted to catch you before you left for the office. I'm sorry it's a little early. I had too much going on yesterday, so apologies for not calling you sooner. How does lunch today sound to you? I'm dropping Claire off at the office; then, I think I will make a stop at the farm. Shall we say 1145 hours? I'll pick you up. Claire has a lunch meeting, so it will be just the two of us."

Hearing his old friend on the other end of the telephone, Bill was delighted to see his old comrade in arms again. "Looking forward to getting together as well this Saturday. I guess Claire hasn't told you we have a reservation at the Letchworth Hall Hotel at 1900 hours. It's a welcome home dinner for you, my friend, with two surprise friends joining us." Bill left out who those guests could be, chuckling to himself, knowing Karl would be racking his brain to figure out who they could be. "See you at lunchtime then, Captain Vita?"

Karl returned the receiver to its cradle and stood there, smiling. He already knew who would be joining them. His intelligence mind was still as sharp as ever. It must be Clive and Julie, he thought as he entered the kitchen to see his wife busy in front of the counter. "Claire, only you can make a maternity outfit look sexy. Come here and kiss me."

Claire walked over to her husband when their son Nicholas ran in from the dining room, yelling, "Papa, Mama, I need a hug as well." Karl scooped Nick into his arms, and Claire and Karl embraced their little terror.

"Darling, we must leave a little earlier to drop Nick off at the babysitter. Then, you can drop me off at the office. What did Bill have to say? I forgot in all that excitement yesterday to mention we are joining them for dinner this Saturday; did he tell you that?" Saying that, Claire bent down to put on Nick's coat and cap. "Ready, darling. Why don't you get my car? It's parked on the side of the garage."

Karl nodded his head in agreement. Putting his driving coat on, he walked out into the cool morning air, sliding his hand over the curves of their MG-Y saloon car. Karl started the engine and raced it to warm it up quicker, patiently waiting for Claire and Nicholas to exit the back door. Claire placed a duffle bag full of Nick's toys, clothes, and other things he would need on the back seat, then climbed into the passenger seat, placing Nick on her lap. "Claire, if we are going out to eat Saturday evening, who will watch the little chap? Is it Sheila?"

Claire nodded as she fussed over her son, "Yes, darling, she suggested we drop him off for the evening, giving us some quiet time alone. I told her we would pick him up Sunday morning, then go straight to church, if that's alright with you. His clothes are in that bag, so he will be ready at about 9:30 a.m. Sorry, you're still on military time 0930 hours." Smirking, she muffled a laugh as she said that. The drive to Sheila's house took only minutes. Pulling up in front of her house, Karl walked around the car. He opened the passenger door and picked up his son from Claire's lap. Sheila and her husband came out to greet them at the front door.

Nicholas called out, "Aunty," and reached out to Sheila's waiting arms.

"Captain Vita, it's so nice to see you again. How long has it been? Over six months, I believe?" asked Sheila.

"Time flies, Sheila at least I'll be here for the arrival of the new baby. We really appreciate you taking care of our little terror." After some small talk with Sheila's husband, Harry, they headed for the office.

"Claire, if you don't mind, I think I'll go in with you to say hello to everyone. Is that alright with you?"

Claire reached for his hand to help her out of the car, saying, "Darling, that's a great idea. They will all love seeing you. It's been quite a while since you were here last." Looping her arm through Karl's, they walked up the steps into the small lobby. "Everyone, look who I found outside! He's come to say hello." Claire was touched by her staff's reaction.

After greeting everyone, Karl asked if Bill was in the office yet. Barb answered, "He's at a deposition in Luton this morning, but he told me he'll be back in time to meet you for lunch."

Karl walked into Claire's office to say goodbye, noting the picture on her desk. "You still have that first picture I signed on your desk? You old sentimental softy."

Claire answered, "That picture pulled me through many difficult times when you were off on some mission. So, as long as I'm in this office, that picture will remain right there as a reminder that I'm one of the lucky ones that still had a husband after the war ended."

For a split second, Karl could see her sitting at that desk, tears in her eyes, counting the hours until she could meet him at the station, safe once more, even though it would be just a few days until he would leave again. "I'll be off then, darling; do you need anything?"

Smiling, Claire could see that picture had brought back memories from their first meeting. "Don't forget to pick me up around 1600 hours. We are on our own. What say we head to the Fox for cocktails and some supper? I know how you love that place," said Claire, placing her briefcase on the side of her desk. At the door, Karl looked back at that briefcase, remembering a cold, snowy day in St. John's, Canada, when he had that case made for her.

Karl had never closed or transferred his Lloyds Bank account in Baldock, even though he always intended to do so after the family had left to return to Wien. Nothing in Baldock had changed much since he had been there last. Parking the car in front of the Black and White Café, he crossed the road, taking in the aroma of hops from the local brewery.

As he walked, he started remembering all those times he had returned to Baldock after some mission, his nerves a complete mess and all those nightmares he would experience, the fear of sleeping a constant concern. He felt his breathing becoming short as he relived the time he almost took his own life to prevent the German Gestapo from brutally beating him to obtain his mission objective. Taking his glove off his left hand, he reached for his left eye, thinking how close he had come to losing the use of that eye completely. Stopping in front of the confectionery shop, he stared at the window display, not really noticing it. In his mind, he was back in 1941, reliving the horror he experienced while in France. After what seemed like an eternity, his anxiety slowly subsided, that black cloud dissipating. Taking a deep breath, he continued to walk toward the bank.

At the service window, he said, "I would like to open my safe deposit box, please. Here is my account number." Karl showed his ID and bank book to the lady behind the desk.

"This way, please; do you have your key ready?" she asked as they entered the safe deposit vault. After the clerk had inserted her key, Karl did the same, removing the long gray metal box, then placing it on the table behind him.

"Right, Captain, I'll leave you to your business. When you're finished, press the attendant button." With a smile, she left the vault. Karl looked at the box; he couldn't remember the last time he had opened it. Inside, he reviewed the contents, then removed the manila envelopes stuffed with British Pounds Sterling, his eye zeroing in on a folded note he did not recognize. As he unfolded it, he immediately recognized the handwriting.; it was Mama's. He started to read the letter, in German, of course.

*My dearest Karl,*

*It's sad you were not here to see us off, but I know you're happy once again somewhere out on the high seas.*

*I didn't need any of the money you left in these envelopes. In fact, your brother Mino, before he left to return to Wien, gave me all his English money, so you will be pleasantly surprised at the new total.*

*Son, please don't stay away from your family too long; we miss the three of you so very much. I already miss my grandson, Nicholas. I'm sure Claire will write once the new baby arrives. I pray every day it's a girl. Karl, I know my youngest son so very well; that look on your face told me you are hoping for a girl as well.*

*Karl do not fret about Wien. It will come back stronger than ever. Always remember, your roots are buried deep within this city's heart. I will wait patiently to hear from you once you have read my note.*

*Your loving Mother,*
*Alga Fischer Vita*

Karl, read the note several times, then kissed it before he returned it to the envelope and put it in his briefcase, along with the remaining contents of the box. Pressing the bell, he waited for the attendant to return. "Miss, I now live in Hitchin, so I will not need this box anymore. Could you please close it out? As for my current account and savings accounts, I'll retain them through the Hitchin branch. After signing the transfer of accounts, he thanked the service manager for her help, then left without looking back, closing another wartime chapter.

Karl parked the car, then walked into the office, asking the young receptionist, "Did Major Lowes make it back yet?"

With a warm smile, she answered, "Let me check for you, Captain Vita. I believe he only arrived back about ten minutes ago." She dialed Bill's extension, then said, "Major Lowes will be with you shortly. Can I get you a refreshment while you wait?"

"You must be relatively new. I can't remember seeing you here before. What is your name, young lady? I'm not so good with names, but I never forget a pretty face," teased Karl.

"My name is Gwen Adams, Sir; it's nice to finally meet the infamous Major Vita, or should I now I refer to you as Captain Vita?" Gwen blushed at the minor blunder she had just made.

"That's perfectly alright, Gwen. You can call me anything but never late to receive a smile from a beautiful young lady."

With a timid smile, Gwen answered, "Your wife told me you were a charismatic flirt. She is so right, but I can tell from your face and that picture on her desk that you two are very much in love with each other. I hope one day I can have that as well. All of us here in the office are getting excited, waiting for the new baby's arrival. Is it a boy or girl you are hoping for, Sir?"

Karl was just about to answer her when the lobby door opened, and out came Bill, his raincoat over his arm. "Gwen, watch this bloke; he's a charmer and one of the best friends anyone could hope for. Karl, you rascal, have you been charming Gwen?"

Karl smiled, then laughed, answering, "Bill, how can you say such a thing? We were discussing the new baby, and to answer your question, Gwen, we are hoping for a girl. One of each would be a dream come true. Thank you for keeping me company while I waited for this bloke. Welcome aboard, young lady; you're a delightful addition to the firm. You most certainly brighten up this lobby."

Bill chuckled as he listened to Karl. "Let's go; I think you have embarrassed Gwen enough for one day. Gwen, I should be back before two. If my 2:30 arrives early, put him in the small conference room with my apologies for not being here to greet him," concluded Bill as they headed to the front door.

"Bye, Gwen, thanks for being a good sport," remarked Karl, holding the door open for Bill. Gwen smiled at having finally met Claire's lovable husband. Over lunch, Karl and Bill discussed at length his new position and the first voyage on the Clyde Princess followed by small talk and chat about the new baby.

"Karl, I need to ask you this. I hope you don't take offense at me asking this again. Clive and I have been close friends since our time at the Army War College, and training together for the Intelligence Service. While you were away, I asked him to be my best man. This was difficult because you are also a very close friend, and God knows we have been through a lot together. I'm repeating this, I know, but telling you in a letter is not the same as face to face, so I'm sorry if I'm repeating myself. There, I'm done; no need to belabor that explanation further."

Karl sat quietly, respecting Bill's time before answering. "Bill, that letter I received from you while I was in Boston made me extremely happy, knowing you were finally putting a ring on that wonderful Dorothy's finger. Of course, Clive should be your choice for best man. For God's sake, you two have a long history, way before I came on the scene, so stop beating yourself up over this. I thought I conveyed that in my return letter. Now, what are we going to do to make your bachelor party one you will never forget?" asked Karl, laughing, remembering what they all did for his bachelor party.

"Oh, no, I don't need a repeat of that evening; you blokes were off your rockers. Dorothy told me to light up the town one last time because, after that, there will be no repeat performances." Bill reached over the table, gripping Karl's arm. With a look of sincerity, he said, "Karl, for as long as I live, I will always cherish the bond of friendship we three have. What saddens me is remembering those days in the BIS that dark picture of seeing the limp form of Kitty inside that van after it rolled over. Claire told me what you plan on doing next year, giving Kitty a proper headstone. What you didn't know was Clive had requested that her remains be returned to England after the war. Because of stupid bureaucracy, that request was denied with some lame excuse about disturbing the grave of a fallen officer." Bill had taken a big chance at bringing up Kitty's demise, knowing the hell Karl went through for so long after he was told she had been killed on that fateful mission before the war. Bill sat quietly while Karl gathered his composure.

"Bill, thanks for telling me that. I, too, had thought about bringing her home to England, but then again, we both know she is not there only the remains of a remarkable woman who will always own a special part of my heart. I am so fortunate that fate introduced me to Claire, so much like Kitty in a way. There is a connection that I can't explain, but in my darkest hours, they connected, and that is why I will keep my promise to give her a fitting headstone next year. Bill, why are we being so solemn, talking like this? Lighten up, will you?" Karl raised his hand to the waiter to bring two more glasses of mild and bitter beer. "Let's talk about your plans for the honeymoon even if it's still a long way off, then you can tell me about the future you and Claire are planning for the firm, shall we?"

"Well, you may have no plans for this afternoon, old man, but I must get back to the office. Claire will be all over me if I'm late for a meeting starting in forty-five minutes. Until Saturday, then."

Bill stood up, and as he turned toward the door, Karl wished him a successful meeting, concluding with a sarcastic remark. "Tell Clive we are looking forward to seeing him and Julie this Saturday."

With a smirk, Bill slowly shook his head, replying, "Bloody spy, always second guessing everything, you old sod." Karl was enjoying the interplay with this close friend. After he dropped Bill off, Karl looked at his watch, thinking, I've got three plus hours. I guess I'm going to take a ride through Ashwell; then, on the way back, I'll stop at the farm for some fresh eggs. I wonder if Claire needs anything else while I'm there. Karl sat in the car, then thought, I can do those things tomorrow with Claire. Let me call Sheila; I haven't spent time with her since before I left for the ship. I think she would enjoy the company. Getting out of the car, he returned to the lobby to place that call.

"Sheila, it's Karl Vita. I was wondering, if you're not too busy, maybe my little man and I could have afternoon tea with you? We have not seen each other in quite a while. I hope I'm not putting you in an uncomfortable spot. It's your call," said Karl.

"Captain Vita, that would be wonderful! You're in luck; I've just baked some scones. Nick is going to be thrilled to see his dad." Sheila was also thinking that Karl is the perfect person to talk to about Harry and those nightmares that scare him to death. I'm glad he called. Karl returned to the car and drove straight to Sheila's council house on the eastern side of Hitchin. After parking the car on the street, Karl knocked on the front door, stepping back off the front doorstep. The door opened, and there was Sheila, smiling but with a strange look on her face. "Captain Vita, please come in," she asked, with two small screaming boys at her side, excited to see Nick's father at the door. Nick was overexcited, pulling on Karl's leg.

"Ha, Nicholas Vita, where are your manners? Calm down," said Karl, laughing as he lifted his son into his arms. Sheila had made a pot of tea and had a side plate of homemade scones on the kitchen table.

"Please, Captain, have a seat, will you?" Karl sat, then asked Sheila to start calling him Karl. "My dear, no need to call me Captain. Karl will be just fine. I can't remember if I have visited your home before. I must say, with little children running around, you manage to keep your home very tidy. What time does your husband come home from work? I would really like to see him."

Sheila sat down next to Karl, pouring the hot tea. Then, looking at Karl with tears in her eyes, she finally answered. "He works the night shift, 3:00 p.m. to 11:00 p.m., and usually puts in two hours of overtime twice a week. That extra money in his pay packet goes a long way right now. The problem is, since he returned home, it has not been easy for us. He is not the same man I married. The war has changed him so much. He gets terrible nightmares; that's why he prefers to work nights. He is still scared he might harm me if he is home in the evenings."

Karl knew exactly what her husband was going through. Taking Sheila's hand, Karl carefully asked, "My dear, many of us have the same problem, me included. I am fortunate that mine have become less painful and few and far between. Would you mind if I talked to Harry? He may listen to me, and it may help that I was a senior officer suffering from similar nightmares." Still holding her hand, he could feel the pain in her trembling hand.

"Karl, I'm so sorry for bringing this up. As I said, living with this problem is making our life together intolerable. Claire had mentioned to me weeks ago, when Karl returns home, let him talk to Harry. He will more than likely suggest he makes an appointment at the military hospital in Hitchin. Karl, I would be so appreciative if you could find the time to meet with Harry." Sheila looked at her watch, saying, "Blimey, you better get going, or Claire will be waiting outside the office door for you."

Karl stood up, then softly put his arms around her, holding her tightly before saying, "Sheila, you also need to let it go. Now, hold me tightly, and let those tears of relief flow." At first, Sheila resisted this strange feeling of being held by another man. She had held back all that tension for so many months; she could not hold back any longer. She surrendered herself into Karl's arms, letting the tears and tension go. Holding Karl tightly, she felt that tightness finally melting away. Regaining her composure, she stepped back, somewhat embarrassed at what had just happened.

"Karl, I'm so sorry; please forgive me for holding on to you like that. You have made me face up to the problem I was trying to hide. Thank you again and for offering to talk to Harry. When do you think that could be arranged?"

Karl lifted her head, and, wiping the tears from her eyes, finally said, "Let's make it this coming Sunday. I've been through a similar situation and talking about it helped me immensely. You must be strong in making Harry confront that demon and admit to himself there is a problem; it will be very hard for him to admit he is in trouble." Karl picked up Nick, kissing his cheek before handing him back to Sheila. His parting words were, "Sunday afternoon, I'll pick you all up say about 12:30 p.m. including Nick instead of taking him to church with us. How does that sound? Sheila, I've been there; I know what he is not willing to admit to himself. Left unchecked, this trauma will only worsen; the longer you look the other way, the harder it will become to help him. Now, I really must be off, and thanks for those delicious homemade scones. Karl kissed her on the cheek before he lifted his son into his arms, saying to him, "Nicholas, say goodbye to your papa."

Karl walked down the path to the gate. As he opened it, Sheila called out, "I should call Claire to make sure this Sunday is alright with her, don't you think?"

Karl simply waved his arm, answering, "Nonsense, she would be the first person to invite you, especially knowing what you're going through. See you Sunday." As he drove off, he started thinking how many thousands of men and women from all branches of the military around the world were facing this same problem, trying to hide it from their families. God knows I did, and thanks to Claire, I'm almost in control of this demon well, not totally yet.

Pulling the car into Claire's reserved parking place, he chuckled at seeing his surname on the sign. Entering the lobby, he smiled at Gwen, saying, "Gwen, how is your day going so far? I bet there is a young man waiting patiently for his date to arrive later this evening, is that right?"

Gwen, blushing a little at the attention from this charismatic gentleman, replied, "I'll announce you, Sir. Why don't you head down to your wife's office? It will be a lot more comfortable waiting there than here in the lobby," answered Gwen, feeling a little uncomfortable.

Claire was just wrapping up a meeting in the conference room. Hearing the public address in the hall, she stood, shaking hands with her clients and saying, "I'll try to have this issue wrapped up in about two weeks. Thank you again for coming in today." Claire opened the door for the elderly couple, directing them toward the lobby, then walked in the opposite direction toward her office. When she opened the door, there was Karl, relaxing on the couch, "Darling, I did not expect you so early," she said with a smirk.

Karl answered, "I thought a little office romance was in order. But then I thought about your employees getting the wrong idea."

Claire always enjoyed his teasing comments and answered him back, "Kiss me like there's no tomorrow, you bloody Austrian lover boy."

With both arms around her, he kissed her, saying, "Really missed you today. Let's go home; I've got a lot to discuss with you."

Claire, pulling back, answered, "I thought this was a date night without our little terror. Or did you forget we planned to go to the Fox in William when we leave here?"

Karl, laughing and slapping his forehead, replied, "Sorry, my love, I completely forgot. Well, no harm done; you're here and in command as usual."

Claire could never stay aggravated with her husband; he had a way about him. "Karl Vita, sometimes you scare me—forgetting things. God knows how you find your way home when you're driving that ship all those thousands of miles. One day, I expect to get a telegram telling me you landed in Cuba!" She also remembered that James McKinley had told her that Karl was a natural navigator and, without doubt, amongst the very best captains in the fleet.

On their drive to the inn, Karl told her all about his time with Sheila and why he asked her to join them for lunch on Sunday while Clive was still in town. With the help of three senior officers, who had all suffered injuries at various times during the war and suffered similar nightmares, they just might connect with Harry, getting him to admit how scared he was of cracking up and possibly hurting his wife.

"Darling, with all your clowning around, there is a side of you I adore the compassion you have for others in trouble. Of course, you three should do your best to help Harry, and please insist he gets professional help, will you?" replied Claire.

Parking the car in their usual spot, they walked briskly toward the entrance of the Fox. Inside, the roaring fire gave off a soothing glow. The bar only had a few regulars sipping at their pints and conversing with Harry behind the bar.

"Well, will you look who is back home? Commander Vita.

Claire, your worries about him out there in the Atlantic Ocean amounted to nothing, at least he is home at your side for when the baby arrives. I told you there was not an ocean big enough to keep him away from being by your side," said Harry, pouring Claire an Orange Crush and a pint of mild and bitter for Karl.

Claire corrected Harry, so proud to announce that her husband had been promoted to captain. "Well, blow me down," replied Harry. "Drinks on the house. Now, are you going to have supper with us tonight?"

Claire looked at Karl before saying to Harry, "Surprise us, Harry. We are easy tonight, so whatever you suggest will be delicious, I'm sure." Sitting at the table by the fire was magical, together again and excitedly talking about the addition to their family.

Karl held Claire's hand and quietly continued, saying, "My darling, Claire, we have been coming to the Fox since that first day we met. But darling, each time, it's the same that picture of you taking my hand outside on that bench and confessing your intentions to make that meeting permanent always makes me thankful that my single life was behind me. What we have now can never be replaced. Thank you, darling, for making that first move."

Claire, smiling at him, replied the way she always did, "Karl, there was no way you were getting away from me. You were mine, and that will never change; let's head home, shall we?"

Claire unlocked the outside door to the kitchen while Karl parked the car in front of the garage. Entering the kitchen, Karl suggested, "Let's have some port in front of a blazing fire, shall we? You can have a sip of mine if you like. I'll get some firewood from the shed. Back in a minute?" Claire went upstairs to change into her housecoat. Returning to the sitting room, she sat on the couch as Karl started the fire, then lit the candles, turning off the table light. "There, that's a little more soothing," he said as he sat next to her, his arm around her shoulder.

Once more, they talked about how lucky they were, and the terrible burden Sheila and Harry had to face. Claire grasped Karl's hand, asking, "I know we talked about this at the Fox, but indulge me one more time. You did explain that you went through similar nightmares and what we did to get you to face it?" inquired Claire.

"Yes, I did. However, I think Harry has it much worse than I did. If you can keep the girls busy in the solarium, Bill, Clive, and I will try to get through to Harry. It just might make him confront those problems. I think he will pay attention to three former intelligence officers." With a grin, Karl said, "Obviously, I have figured out who the mystery guests will be for dinner Saturday evening. So, what do you think of my idea?" concluded Karl.

With a satisfied smile, Claire answered, "You bugger, is there nothing you can't second guess? Maybe you should work for our firm as an investigator instead of driving that bloody ship of yours?"

Karl started laughing as he poured another glass of port for himself and a soft drink for Claire. "I think I prefer the sailor's life, thank you very much," responded Karl.

Claire reached for his hand and, in a soft voice, replied, "What did I do to deserve you? With all your clowning around, you still take the time to help others. I'll call Sheila in the morning. I will have to be careful, though, what I say as she is on a party line. I'm never sure who could be listening."

Taking both her hands, Karl asked, "Tell me again what Doctor Burgess said about your due date?"

Taking a sip from her drink, Claire answered, "I guessed you were almost asleep when I told you the night you arrived home. All going well, it could be early August. If you remember, in my last letter, I asked my sister what she thought about staying with us a few days before my due date. I should have known better; she insists she stay here for a minimum of two weeks. I told her we would pick her up at the train station about two weeks before that due date. I think she plans on returning again toward the end of November or early December. David and their kids will drive here, arriving December 23rd. Karl, I know my baby sister so well; she is going to stay much longer, wait and see if I'm right. Now that you are alert, you can store that information in that mind of yours."

Karl smiled back at her before asking, "What train will she be taking? I should know that by heart, considering all the times you picked me up there. How could I ever forget that excited look on your face each time I saw you through the carriage window? That is a picture I will cherish forever. Claire, it's going to be hectic around here just before Christmas. Our hands will be full with the baby and your family staying with us; it will be challenging to say the least. Claire looked up with a big smile on her face, saying, "Ha, tough guy, you can handle it; now, let's go to bed."

Karl was up early on Saturday morning, as usual, letting Claire catch up on some overdue sleep. Looking at her relaxed face, he smiled, thinking, she needs this rest so desperately. She is on the go nonstop; no wonder she was looking forward to this alone time. Downstairs, he made coffee for himself. Footsteps on the stairs told Karl his wife was heading downstairs. Entering the kitchen, she walked behind her husband and wrapped her arms around him, placing her head between his broad shoulders. In a soft voice, she said, "Morning, Sailor; how long have you been up? I think I'm going to have a pot of tea instead of coffee; care to join me?" asked Claire.

"Claire, can I ask you a pointed question? And It's very much my business, so indulge me for a few minutes, will you? When we see Bill on Sunday, I'm going to ask him for his help. Claire, we need to ask him to consider taking over all your responsibilities for at least six months, effectively assuming the position of managing partner. Next week, I will drive you to the office to make that transition happen. Claire, take that look off your face. I know it's your firm, but you're my wife. I feel bad enough being away at sea for months on end; that is something I intend to address when I return to my ship." Karl was displaying his leadership side, and at this very moment, the decision maker had kicked in.

Claire was intelligent enough to know that when he got into that mode, it was best to remain quiet until he asked for her input. "Darling, I'm sorry for pulling rank like this. It's not a great way to start a Saturday morning, is it?" Karl turned to pour Claire a mug of tea, remaining silent until he returned to the kitchen table.

"Karl Vita, as head of this family, I know when you talk like this, it's best to remain quiet, my commanding officer. I like it when you display that authority; it makes me feel secure. You are absolutely correct. I have been putting this off for too long. I guess you saw how tired I've become. Bill is a darling, in as much as he has already broached that issue, suggesting we make plans very soon, which I have been reluctant to address. So, next week, I will make this happen. Darling, I have a question that is now bothering me. You just said, when you get back to the ship, you are going to do what?"

Karl's tone had returned to that quiet way he had of talking, "Claire, I'm not sure I can stay at sea for another two years in light of all that is going on here."

Hearing this once again, Claire took the high road by responding in a very aggravated voice, "Bugger it, Karl, we have been down this road a few times before. If you remember, it was my bloody idea in the first place! As much as I miss you terribly when you're away, these days, it's much easier to handle. After all, you're not going off to war, are you? I keep telling you, I'm all right with this arrangement for the next two years anyway, and let's face it, when you come home on leave, you're here for at least four months no more five or six days, then off again. Karl, I can also be a tough businesswoman when the need arises. Now, come here and give me a real kiss not that peck from earlier." Claire was glowing; this kick in the backside was what she needed.

Karl stood against the kitchen counter, grinning profusely. This is the woman he had fallen in love with not that many years ago. Someone or something above had given him this new life, erasing all those bad times he had struggled through, excluding the brief magical times he had with Kitty.

Saturday evening, dressed in their finest, they drove to the Letchworth Hall Hotel to meet up with their friends. Karl dropped Claire at the lobby entrance, then parked the car.

Walking into the bar area, there they were: the gang of four. Karl stopped momentarily to remember his wedding to Claire not many years ago. How beautiful she looked in her cream-colored wedding dress, surrounded by her bridesmaids and all the military attendants in dress uniform. Those memories would always be attached to this hotel. "What a motley bunch you lot are," said Karl as he embraced his former commanding officer. "Did you really think you could surprise me like this? It's wonderful to have you join us this evening. Doesn't Claire look wonderful? We are praying for a girl. I hope someone up there is listening."

Julie, holding Claire and Dorothy's hands, smiled with approval. Answering Karl, she spoke, "Karl, you're an incurable romantic. So long as the new baby is healthy, would it really make a difference?"

Clive moved behind Bill and Karl and put his arms around their shoulders before announcing in a boisterous voice, "Here we all are, friends in perpetuity. The war was devastating in so many ways, but it brought us all together, did it not?"

With those piercing eyes, Claire looked at her husband with a smile that told him how grateful she was for those painful events that brought them together. "May I add to that, Clive? There are two departed souls Karl and I need to be eternally thankful to. They gave their lives and, in doing so, opened the door for Karl and me to find each other two broken souls that now have a wonderful life and family. Kitty and Patrick, in my heart, I know you two have played a part in making this happen." Claire searched all their faces for a sign of approval.

Julie kissed Claire on the cheek and, in a voice that labored as she spoke, responded by saying, "Claire, that was truly a wonderful thing to add. Shall we toast everyone who gave their lives so others could live in peace and happiness?"

Listening to his wife Julie, Clive looked at Bill and Karl. That look told them that peace would be short lived as another war was about to erupt on the Korean peninsula. "I say, you bunch, this is getting a little too serious. Let's go eat, shall we? "Over dinner, Clive stood, announcing he had some wonderful news to share. Clive was a master at making speeches, and this one would affect them all. "I'm the only one here that didn't jump ship from the BIS; no pun intended chaps. Julie and I have lived in Slough almost as long as we have been married. Six months ago, I was asked to head up a new branch that will absorb the remaining units of the BIS into the joint intelligence service to become known as MI-5.

"Here's the best part: that new branch will be based in Cambridge, only forty-five minutes up the Royston Road. What are the chances of that happening? We are so thrilled that we will be close to you all once again." Bill already knew about the move but was sworn to secrecy until it became official.

"I'm willing to bet these two already knew all about this move," said Karl, looking at Bill and Dorothy. "From our very first meeting, there was always something going on between these two spy blokes. Today is different; we are so pleased to hear this wonderful news, aren't we, Claire?" said Karl as he looked at his wife with a big grin on her face.

"Karl, we all knew about the move but decided if Julie and Clive were to be the surprise guests, then so should this wonderful news be part of that secret. That intelligence nose of yours got fooled for once."

Karl, shaking his head, looked at them solemnly, followed by, "You're all bloody spies. Who cares because this is the best news!" After a marvelous dinner and stimulating conversation, it was time to leave. After saying their farewells, Karl went to get the car. As he drove up to the lobby, he looked at his pregnant wife waiting by the door, thinking from August on, things could be very interesting for Claire.

Sunday, after they had gone to church, Karl dropped Claire off at home, then drove to Sheila and Harry's house to pick them, their children, and Nick up for lunch. Nick, recognizing the car as it pulled up, ran down the path into his father's arms. "Nick, where are your manners? You should have escorted Sheila to the car," said Karl, his son not really understanding what his father had just said.

"Harry, so nice to see you out of uniform. Let's go have some lunch, shall we?" Arriving back at the house, Karl parked in front of Bill's car, commenting, "Looks like our other guests have already arrived. I hope you're hungry, and I bet your son is. Am I right, Graham?" Karl kept looking at Harry, who did not say much. He simply smiled at Karl's remarks. Inside, Karl introduced everyone, then led them out into the solarium. Before going to church, Karl had turned on the electric heaters, making it very comfortable out there.

"Karl and I thought it would be roomer out here because we are eight adults and three children. Please, have a seat, Dorothy. Julie and I will bring out some fruit to get us started." Lunch was more like a late breakfast, with everyone enjoying telling their stories, except Harry, who sat quietly enjoying the food.

After lunch was over, Claire excused herself, taking the ladies with her into the sitting room, saying, "Gentlemen, I will get you some coffee in about an hour." With that, she closed the French doors, leaving the four men to talk.

Clive, armed and ready, struck up a conversation almost immediately. "Harry, Karl told us you were in the army during the war; is that correct?"

Harry, feeling uneasy in the company of high-ranking intelligence officers, sheepishly answered, "Yes, Sir, our battalion was formed right here in Hertfordshire. We saw action in France; then we were part of the rear-guard action at Dunkirk. We lost forty brave men in that action. After three weeks' leave, we were shipped out to North Africa to join up with Field Marshal Montgomery's forces. I served there almost two and a half years and got one amazing suntan." Chuckling as he said that Harry felt much more at ease now.

"Harry, old man, no need to stand on ceremony with us. Please, use our Christian names; you'll feel much more relaxed doing that," said Clive, getting ready to launch his next ploy to get Harry to talk about his nightmares. "Karl, you had some bad times during and after the war, if my memory serves me, right?"

Karl, hearing this, knew that was his cue to tell how he, along with the help of his wife and trained medical support, learned to face those nightmares. Bill described to Harry his time as a prisoner of the Gestapo before the outbreak of the war. Clive kept his focus on Harry as Bill concluded his ordeal. "Harry, in what you told us so far, you must have seen some horrible things during the war years, am I right?" asked Clive, ready to open those horror stories.

"Sir, sorry I meant Clive; these are things I'm trying to put behind me; the war is over. However, my war is still with me day and night. I'm almost at my wits' end and don't know what to do about it." Harry was starting to let the trauma through.

Clive moved closer to Harry, putting his arm around this poor soul's shoulders. "Harry, you are lucky the three of us have been through those same horrors; you're not alone. Let us help you face those demons together right now. Tell us exactly what those nightmares are that scare you so badly. Then, tell us about the action you saw. Don't hold back; let it all out, and please don't feel embarrassed doing so. You are amongst fellow soldiers. All right now, slowly relives those visions for us."

Over the next hour, Harry described the most horrific tales of the carnage he had witnessed in the battle of El Alamein the one that was the main culprit was the hardest for him to tell. Breaking down in tears and shaking profusely, he stopped, allowing Clive to grip him tightly, saying, "You're doing good, Harry; take a deep breath, and when you're ready, tell us what happened in El Alamein."

Harry took a sip of whiskey Karl had put in front of him, then, with both hands clasped together, told them what scared him so much. "Dawn was breaking, and we knew the Jerries would do a full-frontal attack with Tiger tanks and what looked like a full battalion of ground troops. The shelling started about 0600 hours; we were ready for them, or so we thought, behind our wall of sandbags. Suddenly, two or more shells burst in front and in our foxhole. I was thrown to one side by the blast; I thought I was a goner. My friend from school was next to me at the start. When I gathered my wits, I saw Collin lying on his stomach with blood all around his head. I yelled out to him as I crawled over to help him." Harry was shaking badly as he relived this nightmare.

Karl placed his hand on his arm, saying, "Harry, take another slug of that whiskey before you're ready to continue."

Harry sat, sipping the whiskey, then said, "I'm all right now. When I went to lift his head up, it came off in my hands. 'Oh, God,' I yelled, 'someone, help me,' but as I looked around, they were all dead except me. This is the first time I've ever told anyone about that day when I thought I was in Hell. Clive, I need help. I can't forgive myself for feeling I should have died with my pals; the guilt is more than I can handle. I'm scared to tell Sheila in case I get out of control and do something dangerous to her."

Bill stood, pulling Harry to his feet with his arms around him. Bill, now in tears, his voice laboring with anger, finally spoke, "Harry, next week, I will arrange for you to meet with the people that can help you right here in Hitchin. In the meantime, lean on Karl and me. We will be there for you, day or night. Harry, are you listening to me?

You're no longer alone; let your friends and wife help you face these demons. With the right treatment and medication, you will conquer this. You survived, Harry; now, learn to enjoy your life and family."

Karl poured four large glasses of whiskey, then made a toast, "To all of us who survived, never forgetting those millions that didn't and died in the pursuit of peace." The four stood clinking glasses, watching Harry start the process of living life again.

"May I ask you three a question? Did you have this planned? Because I feel so much better. Here's to you, Collin, and all the other blokes I left behind in North Africa."

Sipping their drinks, Bill said, "Hear, hear to all those we hold dear; may they always enjoy the freedom we fought so hard to win."

Claire knocked on the door, asking if they were done, as Sheila would like to return home. Harry replied, "I'd like to go home as well. I need to be with my wife and kids this evening." The girls entered the solarium sheepishly to see if the coast was clear. Sheila looked at her husband's face for a sign he was feeling better. Moving over to face him, she reached for his hands.

With a smile, Harry said loudly, "These blokes have really helped me, Sheila. Bill here is going to arrange for me to get help at the hospital. Sheila, you're a remarkable wife and mother. You don't deserve the hell I've put you through. Let's go home and make a fire, shall we?" Harry put his arms around his wife and kissed her properly for the first time since returning home.

Sheila could not believe her husband's transformation and started laughing, commenting, "Harry, let's get the kids to bed, then enjoy that fire. Maybe there's a new spark in both of us." This was a perfect day for all of them.

Karl drove them home. As Harry got out of the car, he said quietly to Karl, "Thank you, Sir. I'm so fortunate to be in the company of England's best. Thanks again; see you real soon." Karl watched them walk up the path, holding hands, thinking that a life and marriage were saved this day.

Monday morning, Claire resisted the request of her husband to stay home. "Darling, I'm all right. I made a promise to the Ellies that I would finish their filing before I left this week. Now, get your coat while I bundle up Nick, ready to drop him off at Sheila's house. I bet Sheila has things to tell me." Claire giggled at what might have happened after the children were put to bed the night before.

Pulling up in front of Sheila's house, Claire suggested Karl remain in the car with the engine running while she gave Nicholas to Sheila. Using the door knocker, Claire waited in the damp morning air for the door to open. "Claire, sorry it took so long to answer the door. It's been a little hectic around here; please, come on in."

Claire looked at Sheila's flushed face, which gave her away. Smiling, she said, "By the look on your face, I would venture to say your frozen assets have melted completely. Am I right, or should I mind my own business?"

Sheila took Nick's bag of things from Claire, then blushed again, saying, "Last night, he had me feeling like a schoolgirl again. He woke me up very early this morning for more. I hope to hell I'm not pregnant after these episodes. All those years of storing those juices makes me wonder." In the hallway, these two friends were enjoying each other's company.

Back in the car, Claire was laughing profusely as she relayed Sheila's tale of her husband's rebound. "Karl, do you miss those days and nights of passion, or are we becoming a boring married couple?"

Karl reached over to her, always enjoying her honesty. He took her hand, then, with his wicked smile, said, "My wonderful, sensitive wife, passionate lovemaking may have to wait a few months before we can resume those hot and heavy nights. However, you still have those wonderful, moist lips that are going to waste. There is nothing stopping you from using them, is there?" Karl squeezed her hand, waiting, as usual, for a sarcastic response.

"Karl Vita, I'm not a slut. Well, let's say I enjoy pleasuring you with my lipstick." Looking ahead, she pointed to a very narrow lane, saying, "Turn left down that lane and park behind that hedgerow." Karl, as always, enjoyed winding her up, and by the look on her face, she intended to make him pay for what he had just said. Karl parked behind the hedgerow; shutting the engine off, he waited for his wife to make her move.

Turning in his seat, he said, "Alright, Claire Vita, you were saying?" Claire took off her coat; moving as close as she could to Karl, the hand brake and gear shift were still in the way, so she pushed the gear lever forward into second gear, then lowered the hand brake out of the way. Karl remained very still, not saying a word, fearful he would interrupt his wife's little game. Claire skillfully opened his coat and blazer, then unbuttoned the front of his trousers. With a fiery look in her eyes and that wicked smile, she removed Karl's very erect penis. First, she stroked it softly, then with her thumb, she circled its tip. Karl laid back with the seat reclined and closed his eyes as Claire worked her magic; her mouth encircled him all the way down. This was too much for Karl to control. Letting out a deep sigh, he erupted, making Claire even more excited, not allowing Karl to recover from that orgasm. Seeing Karl tensing, Claire stopped, her mouth still over his erection.

Sitting back again in her seat, she asked, "How was that lover boy? Feeling a little better now?" as she rearranged her coat.

"Claire, for a proper Englishwoman, I swear to God, you put the women I've known to shame. I really needed that."

Still fixing her hair, Claire quietly responded, "My darling Karl, I need to keep you in line, so those ladies out there with wandering eyes won't stand a chance around my man." Karl laughed as he buttoned up his trousers, then closed his blazer. Turning the car around, they headed back down the lane.

Still laughing, he looked at Claire, saying, "Darling, you forgot to fix your lipstick. You better do that before we arrive at the office. Right now, you don't have any on at all."

Claire looked in the sun visor vanity mirror, then, with a giggle, replied to Karl, "Well, I know where to find some, don't I?"

Karl looked at her and replied, "No, you don't. That lipstick is there for the rest of the day, and for the record, I'm completely empty, so no replays."

Claire, of course, always ready with a saucy comeback to his sarcasm, replied, "Well, darling, I will agree with you. Right now, lunch is out of the question. I've had way too much protein for one day; thank you very much."

Karl parked the car, both of them in stitches at her last remark. Hand in hand, they entered the lobby, Claire saying, "Morning, Gwen. Would you please call Mr. Lowes and ask him to join us in my office?"

"Glad to, Mrs. Vita. May I get you both some coffee?" Karl nodded, then replied, "That would be wonderful. Mrs. Vita, I suppose you'll have tea instead, is that correct?"

Bill entered the office, carrying a large mug of steaming tea and a notepad, saying, "Morning, you two. You're looking very chipper, I must say. That lunch and being able to help Harry the way we did has put me on top of the world." Sitting down in one of the big leather chairs, he continued, "Is this meeting anything to do with the plan Claire and I put together last week?"

Claire smiled at Karl, replying, "Bill, yes to your question. However, I need you to do me a big favor. Could you take over completely on the Ellis case? His royal highness here is demanding I start my maternity leave right now. With everything going on, I'm becoming increasingly fatigued, and Karl is getting worried about my health trying to do too much. As usual, he is correct. This document, which I've already signed, effectively turns management of this firm over to you for a minimum of six months. After that, we can revisit this arrangement." Claire handed the folder over to Bill to review and sign. Making a quick review of the document, he signed it, handing a copy back to Claire. He always trusted her judgment completely and was more than ready to assume the position of managing partner.

"Claire, you need to address the staff; now is as good a time as ever." Claire smiled, nodding her head in agreement. She called Beverly to make that announcement for her. When Claire opened the door, the staff, all standing in a circle, had a card signed by everyone, and a big colorful box tied up with ribbons. Two of the girls had a long sign stretched between them. It read: to Claire, Karl, and Nicholas, the very best for a beautiful new healthy baby.

Stunned at this gathering, Claire looked at Bill, then Karl with tears of total happiness. She struggled to thank them all, saying, "I don't know what to say except thank you all for the love and devotion you have always given me, and now the same for my partner, Mr. Bill

Lowes. From this day forward, and for at least the next six months or more, he will be assuming the position of managing partner. I know you will give Bill the same dedication and hard work you have always given me; again, I thank you all." The staff waited for her to finish, then crowded around to give her their farewells. Bill and Karl stood back, watching the love being bestowed on their boss.

Returning to the office, Claire tidied up her desk, then put some personal things into her case, including the first picture Karl had given her. She looked up, saying, "Well, Bill, it looks like you're the new boss. Remember, I'm only down the street if you need me. Most expectant mothers work right up until they're due. With all that is going on, I guess I've worn myself down." Karl had remained quiet through this entire time. He may be Claire's husband, but today, it was all about the firm and its employees.

"All going well, before the end of summer, you will be an uncle and Dorothy a new aunt," concluded Claire, feeling melancholy at departing on this extended leave.

The following morning, Karl quietly opened Nick's bedroom door. He lifted him out of bed while he was half asleep, making sure he could not wake his mother. Putting Nick in his chair, Karl gave him some juice in his special drip proof cup, then made his breakfast, which Claire had prepared before going to bed the night before. Karl sat at the kitchen table, holding his son's little hand, placing his finger over his mouth for Nick not to make any noise. They had breakfast in silence—not an easy task for a young boy.

With breakfast done, Karl poured another mug of coffee; then, with Nick under his arm, they went into the sitting room. On the couch, Nicholas sat snuggled up under his father's arm, fighting the strong desire to fall back asleep. Karl smiled as he watched his son finally give in to sleep. Laying him on the couch, Karl carefully placed a throw blanket over his little man.

Standing there, he looked intently at the next generation of Vita men, saying softly, "Son, I hope you never see or do the things I have had to do to safeguard our family. This new world must remember all the terrible things we suffered through and how close we all came to being annihilated by an atomic bomb. Sleep in peace, my son."

His emotions overcame him as tears welled up in his eyes at saying those last few words. Back in the kitchen, he decided to prepare some toast and more coffee before sitting down at the table, only to be startled by Claire standing in the doorway, tears in her eyes after listening to those last few words her husband had spoken to his son. Those words had so much love in them; there was a private side to her husband only a few would ever see. "Sorry, darling, I didn't mean to startle you like that. I should know better but seeing you two together like that was too personal for me to break that magic you showered on our little Nicholas. Next time, I would love to join you." Crossing the room, Claire pulled Karl away from the kitchen counter. With her arms around his neck, she kissed his cheek, hugging him with all her might, saying softly, "Karl, having you home is the magic I miss the most. I could never have imagined that intensity when I was married to poor Patrick. God forgive me for thinking that. I can't find the words to express this feeling I have right now it must be the pregnancy thing, I suppose." Still in Karl's arms, Claire was experiencing maternity emotions overcoming her normal strong mannered self.

Looking at her in his arms, Karl was trying to feel what his wife was going through. The thoughts of having their second child and the release of anxiety she had borne through those months of separation had caught up with her. "Look what you're doing; only a few days back from sea, you have turned me into a slobbering idiot. Let's get some coffee and feed this baby with some breakfast." Those few brief moments had left an indelible thought in Karl's mind: with the baby still a few months away, it would become harder and harder for Claire to cope. Making her take an early maternity leave was the right thing to do. Thank God Bill is taking over the firm. At least she doesn't have to worry about that. Smiling, he thought, that's like telling an elephant it can fly.

The months passed by quickly, Karl keeping busy with a new project expanding the one car garage into a two-car garage for the two MGs, a bigger undertaking than he realized. Claire, against Karl's wishes, had started working at home on cases Bill had asked her to stay abreast of; in one way, this kept her mind occupied and out of Karl the carpenter's hair. During the latter part of July, the weather had turned nice again after a gloomy, wet June, just in time for Bill and Dorothy's wedding. The ceremony, conducted in the same church Claire and Karl had made their vows in, brought memories back for those that attended their wedding. Dorothy, in a white fitted knee length wedding dress, looked spectacular. Julie, the maid of honor, along with the two bridesmaids, wore pale blue dresses, also knee length. Bill, against Clive's suggestion to wear his dress military uniform, elected to dress in a traditional morning suit, whereas his best man, Clive, a serving officer in MI-5, wore his military dress uniform.

The reception was held at the Letchworth Hall Hotel, Dorothy limiting the attendees to only sixty. The wedding not as boisterous as the Vita wedding but was enjoyed by all with good food and wine with plenty of dancing. Later than afternoon, Dorothy and Bill changed into their travel outfits, ready to head out in their car no later than 4:00 p.m. Karl and Clive had decorated Bill's car with streamers and the traditional tin cans attached to the rear bumper.

While the newlyweds were on their honeymoon in Cornwall, Claire had demanded she take over the daily operations of the law firm until Bill returned in ten days' time. Bill was reluctant to comply so close to her giving birth. Right after the wedding, Karl journeyed to Glasgow for ten days at the request of the commodore for captains not out at sea to meet at the corporate headquarters to discuss crew allocations and revised fleet maintenance programs for the growing fleet. Karl, although reluctant to leave Claire, complied, thinking as long as I'm home for the arrival of new baby.

# CHAPTER 13

# EMILY

"Claire, let's move it, or we'll be late picking up your sister." Claire was still fussing around upstairs, making sure the bedroom was ready for Caroline. Karl was playing a game in the sitting room to keep Nicholas occupied.

Hearing Claire coming downstairs, he picked up his son and walked into the kitchen. "Nick, look at your striking mother. Isn't she beautiful?" Karl helped Claire with her jacket, then helped Nick with his. "Darling, wait here while I back the car out." The weather in Hitchin in August can be inclement; however, today's weather was brisk almost clear blue skies with virtually no wind. Karl pulled up in front of the train station, saying to Claire, "Why don't you take Nick into the waiting room while I park the car? It's best you stay in the waiting room until the train arrives. Once I've collected Caroline, we'll come back for you. There's no need for the three of us to wait out on that platform, is there?"

Nothing much had changed at the Hitchin Train Station except the peacetime conditions of fewer men in uniforms and more business commuters in their pinstriped suits and traditional black bowler hats. Karl walked down to the platform where Claire had waited for him so many times during the war years. Finding an empty bench, he sat waiting for the announcement that the express from King's Cross would arrive on platform two in seven minutes. Looking at his watch, Karl thought, right on time. Standing up, he heard the familiar banging of the carriage bumpers watching as white steam and smoke mixed to form a cloud for those passengers looking out from their compartment windows. Karl, standing there, started thinking, how many times did I strain my eyesight looking through that cloud for the first sign of Claire? A gloved hand vigorously waving caught his eye; smiling, he knew it had to be Caroline.

Almost leaping from the compartment, Caroline, with her left arm outstretched and the right carrying her suitcase, embraced Karl, saying in an excited voice, "Karl, it's marvelous to see you again. How long has it been since we saw each other?" Caroline was so different from her older sister always bubbly and usually very saucy with her remarks. Today was no different. "Karl, what did you do to my big sister when you were last here on leave?"

Karl, waiting for a remark like that, answered, "Well, Caroline, your sister is a sexual piranha. As they say, absence makes the heart grow fonder. God, it's wonderful to have you here with us again. Come on, give me that suitcase. It's too noisy and stinks of smoke on this bloody platform. Claire and Nick are in the waiting room. You can update us once we are in the car." Caroline adored her brother-in-law and the way he took care of his family. Looping her arm through his, she pulled him close as they walked down the platform toward the waiting room.

Caroline remembered so very clearly the day Claire received the news that Patrick's Hurricane had gone down in the English Channel during the Battle of Britain, and he was presumed dead. How devastated Claire's world became months and months of loneliness and despair until the day she decided to start living again. Her first act was to sell Patrick's MG sports car to an intelligence officer from Austria. Like a flash of light, they fell in love, and here today, she was attending the birth of her sister's second baby. Looking at Karl's facial expression, she saw that same penetrating smile on his face. Claire had hit the jackpot, meeting her sailor. "Karl, how is that big boat doing with its new captain at the wheel? Sorry, I meant helm. I know how particular you are when it comes to correct terminology," she said. Pulling Karl to a stop, she reached up to kiss his cheek, saying, "Karl, I am so proud of you and so very lucky to have you in our family." Kissing him again, she couldn't resist saying, "Captain, if I had the bollocks and a little more daring, I think I would kiss you on the lips. But you know I won't do that, don't you?"

Karl enjoyed her daring ways always pushing the envelope. "Better not let Claire hear you talking like that. She's likely to make you sleep in the garage." Searching Karl's facial expressions, she thought she had crossed the line for a split second until Karl, squeezing her tightly, laughed loudly at her last comment.

"Karl, it is so wonderful to be back home in Hitchin with my big sister and favorite brother-in-law. Here we are, and there is my very pregnant sister by the window."

With Nicholas in tow, Claire almost ran out of the waiting room, calling out, "Caroline, my baby sister! Come here and give me a big hug and a kiss!"

As they stood there hugging, a little voice screamed out, "Can I get a hug too?" The two sisters looked down at Nicholas, laughing as Caroline lifted him into her arms.

"Nicholas, your Aunt Caroline is here to take care of you. Look how fast you're growing up; you're almost a young man, aren't you? Can you hold my hand walking through the tunnel?"

Before leaving for the station, Claire had prepared supper, knowing Caroline would be famished when she arrived. Sitting in the kitchen, devouring the hot stew, they had time to catch up on both sides of the family. Caroline loved this old house; the home she and Claire grew up in was now ready to share some exciting news that would give her more time with her sister.

David, her husband, knew so well that she was missing her hometown of Hitchin more with every passing day. Oxford was a wonderful city, but it wasn't home. Their kids were growing up fast, and both David and she had decided they wanted them to grow up in Hitchin. Being closer to Claire and her family influenced their next major decision. Just before she left for Hitchin, David received the transfer he had applied for over a year before.

"Ready for some wonderful news, sis? Last year, an opening became available at the Searle Research Laboratory in Baldock. Well, David knew I was missing living here, so he threw his name into the selection hat. A few days ago, he received a letter informing him he had been selected for this position."

"Oh, my God, Caroline, this is wonderful news. Have you given any thought to where you're going to live?"

Grinning profusely, Caroline replied, "Well, sis, I was going to ask Karl about the bungalow in Baldock. Is it still being rented? If so, when will that rental end?"

Karl looked at Claire, replying, "Caroline, Claire is the rental agent for the bungalow. Why don't you ask her?"

Claire looked at Caroline, asking, "When will the transfer happen?" Caroline was ready with her answer, replying, "Next year around the end of June. Is that a problem, Claire?" Caroline searched her sister's face as Claire excused herself to retrieve a folder labeled Blackett Baldock Property from the sitting room desk.

"Well, Caroline, how do you feel about living here for a couple of months? After that rental is over, we can move you into the bungalow. Ronny and Freida may even be interested in selling it, knowing it would be going to my sister and her family. This is turning out to be a wonderful day. Can you believe we will be back together after all these years?"

Karl was happy at what had just happened; however, there was sadness for a moment as he thought, *I'll never again live in my hometown of Vienna, Austria, will I?*

The following Thursday morning, Claire and Caroline took Nicholas shopping in Luton, giving Karl time to finish a house maintenance project, replacing the sink stopper in their bathroom. At about 1:30 p.m., the phone rang. Sliding out from under the sink, he ran for the telephone on Claire's side of the bed. "Hello, Hitchin 4567; who is calling?" he asked.

"Karl, thank God you're still at the house. It's Caroline. We are at the Lister Hospital; we were almost back in Hitchin when Claire's water broke. I got her into the passenger seat, then drove as fast as I could to the hospital. The nurse in the maternity ward called Dr. Burgess; he should be here in about thirty minutes. Don't worry, Karl; she is fine at this time, but the contractions are getting closer. How fast can you get here?"

Looking at his watch, Karl answered, "In less than twenty minutes. Who is looking after Nick?" Caroline had forgotten to mention that a friendly nurse was watching him until Karl got there. Not waiting for an answer from Caroline, Karl changed quickly, then ran downstairs, grabbing his driving coat and keys as he rushed out the back door. Driving his MG sports car very quickly, he arrived at the hospital in record time. Karl parked the car in a no parking area, yelling to the police officer at the front door, "Sorry, Constable; my wife is almost delivering. I hope you don't give me a parking ticket."

The friendly policeman, laughing loudly, yelled back to Karl, "Best to use the stairs, Sir. Don't worry about your car; I'll put a police notice under the windshield wiper, so no one will mess with it."

Karl, taking the stairs two at a time, was on the third floor in no time. At the desk, he asked in a labored voice, "Mrs. Vita, where do I go?"

The nurse, used to panic from expecting fathers, smiled, then pointed down the hall, saying, "No need to panic, Sir. She is still in labor; I believe your sister-in-law is in the waiting room with your son."

Karl walked quickly down the hall to the waiting room. Nick, seeing his father, ran out to meet him, his little arms reaching out. "Nick, slow down, and please, no squealing in the hospital." He looked up as Caroline joined them.

"God am I glad to see you, Karl. That was a scary drive, the passenger seat does not look the best. The main thing is that Claire is just fine. Leave Nick with me. Claire is in room #304; now, go see your wife. She was so worried I wouldn't find you." Karl kissed them with visible excitement before heading to the delivery room.

Quietly, Karl opened the door. There was Claire, propped up in bed with a labored smile on her face at seeing her husband enter. The nurse, seeing Karl, told him, "Your wife has insisted you remain at her side during this birth."

It was obvious to Karl that the nurse could see how much in love these two people were. Karl sat next to Claire, holding her hand and wiping her brow as the beads of moisture formed.

Claire kept her focus on Karl, his calm restraint helping her with each contraction. "Darling, how did you endure those long hours of being beaten by those Gestapo animals that tortured you while you were a prisoner?"

Karl kept squeezing her hand each time he felt her tense for another contraction, saying, "Focus on other things and places you have enjoyed. Close your eyes, darling, and try doing that. We have so many wonderful memories; focus on one only and try to picture yourself there. Feel the sun on your face and smell the sweet scent of the flowers swaying in the breeze. Claire, try doing that right now."

Karl, saying that, could feel her relaxing; her breathing was getting slower until a stabbing pain made her yell out. Doctor Burgess had entered, squeezing Karl's shoulder before sitting in front of Claire's draped legs in the stirrups. "Claire, are we ready to give your husband here another baby?" The soft, soothing voice of Doctor Burgess's Scottish voice influenced Claire; she trusted him implicitly. "Claire, the head is crowning; now, give me a big push when I ask you to do so." Karl could feel the excitement building. After all these months of guessing, they would know in a matter of moments if it was a boy or the girl they were praying for. "Claire, another big push; give it all you can the baby is almost out." With the skill of delivering hundreds of babies, Doctor Burgess delivered a beautiful baby girl. "Congratulations, Claire! It's a girl. Karl, swing around here and take your first look at your daughter before I cut the cord, then the nurse can clean her up before giving her to you both."

Karl was beyond words as he saw the bloody form of his daughter. With a tear of joy, he looked at Claire, whispering, "Claire, she will be your spitting image. No words can describe the feelings going through me right now. Thank you; thank you, darling. I love you and our children so much." With his arm around his wife, Karl waited patiently for the nurse to carry back their bundle of joy. Claire stretched out her arms to take the baby from the nurse, feeling her little hands firmly holding one of her fingers. Karl bent down and kissed his daughter, then he said softly, "Welcome to the world, Emily."

Claire's emotions were all over the place. Not at all like her, but today was no ordinary day for the Vita family. Looking up, she thanked the doctor, saying, "Doctor Burgess, thank you so much for making this the third happiest day of my life."

Still, with his arm around her, Karl smiled, knowing the answer to his forthcoming question. "What are the other two days, then?" asked Karl.

Looking so much better than half an hour ago, Claire squeezed his cheeks, replying, "The first was you, the second was Nicholas, and now, it's our daughter Emily."

The nurse opened the door for Caroline and Nick, saying, "Strictly against the rules, wouldn't you agree, Doctor? But this is a very special day for the Vita family."

Claire, seeing her son, called, "Nicholas, come here and kiss your mother and sister."

Doctor Burgess lifted Nicholas to sit on the side of the bed and said softly, "Hold your sister's hand; be very gentle doing so, Nicholas. She is less than an hour old." Doctor Burgess looked at his watch, saying, "Claire, I'll see you early next week then. Remember, if anything strange happens, call me immediately." Karl looked at Caroline, saying, "We better be going as well, so these people can do their jobs. Thank you again, Doctor, and to you as well, Nurse, for the excellent care you are giving my wife. I guess it's time for Emily to have her first breastfeeding. Nick, kiss your mother goodbye."

Caroline lifted Nick to kiss his mother and sister goodbye, then did the same, hugging her sister. Her tears were of joy, not sadness, even though she was remembering when Claire had a miscarriage while attending university; that loss shattered her world. Thanks to her husband, Karl, her world was now full and rewarding with two adorable children.

Returning home, Caroline made Nick some supper, then tucked him into his bed, returning to the sitting room. Karl sat in front of the fire, enjoying a glass of port, reliving the days' excitement. "Caroline, thank you for making supper and taking such good care of Nick. It's hard to believe you have decided to move back here, giving up the life you have enjoyed in Oxford. Are you sure this is the best for David, you, and the kids?" Karl was simply making small talk.

"Karl, I grew up in this very house; my roots are deeply embedded in its sturdy foundation. Years back, we thought moving to Oxford was the best opportunity for us and our children. That was then, and this is now. I told David that once the children are established here, I would like to restart my career. I really miss working." Karl, listening to her, nodded his head in agreement. He was also thinking of how he had longed to return to the sea when he was in the BIS. Thanks to Claire's pushing him, it had happened. As far as a move back to Vienna, that would never happen. Over the next two hours, they sat by the fire, watching it slowly die. "Caroline, I don't think we have ever sat and talked so frankly to each other. I'm really pleased we had this time. There's a side of you I frankly did not know existed. Thank you for sharing those sensitive moments in your earlier years with me. It's time to hit the sack; you must be tired, are you?"

Karl stood up, extending a hand to help Caroline off the couch. Later the following morning, they dropped Nick off at Sheila's house. Caroline was excited to see Sheila again after so many months. Karl was becoming anxious to get to the hospital, and Caroline could see it on his face. "Well, Sailor, what say we head to the hospital? My big sister will be wondering where we are by now. Sheila, I'm really looking forward to seeing you more often now that we are returning home to Hitchin. Well, let's say that could be Baldock, right Karl?"

Karl parked the car while Caroline waited for him inside the lobby, "Blimey, that wind is very strong," said Karl as he entered the lobby, stroking his hair back into place.

"Visiting hours started at 11:30 a.m., so we can go straight upstairs. Let's climb the stairs if you don't mind?" said Caroline. Walking down the hall, they saw the door to Claire's room was closed. At the nurses' station, Caroline asked if it was all right for them to enter.

"If you could wait a few more minutes for the attending nurse to leave her room, then you can join your wife," answered the nurse. Karl paced back and forth as Caroline watched him, pretending to look at a magazine. "Mr. Vita, you can go in now; the nurse is done."

Claire was sitting in a reclining chair, Emily sleeping in her arms. She spoke softly with a beaming smile across her face, "I was wondering where you two were. Papa, come look at your daughter; she is so beautiful, even if I say so myself. I'm all packed and ready to be discharged after lunchtime, so make yourselves comfortable while we wait."

A young intern entered the room to take the baby's vital signs and give Claire the once over. Satisfied, he announced, "Ready to return home, Mrs. Vita? I see you are packed and ready!" Shaking hands with all three, he left the room.

"Caroline, can you take Emily while Karl helps me up? I'm still sore down there, but I suppose that's to be expected."

Caroline, an expert mother of two, carefully lifted Emily from Claire's arms, softly saying, "God, she is really beautiful. It makes me feel like having another one."

After muffling a laugh, Karl replied, "It's never too late." Karl suggested he should leave to drive the car around to the lobby entrance. Taking Claire's overnight case, he hurried down the stairs and out into the crowded car park. Waiting in front of the lobby doors, he sat watching the doors for Claire and Caroline to exit with the baby. Sitting there, he thought back to another time when Claire had dropped him off in London for surgery resulting from an injury to his left eye after brutal torture at the hands of the Gestapo during the war. The doors opened, and out came Caroline, followed by Claire being pushed in a wheelchair by a friendly older gentleman volunteering at the hospital. Karl walked around and helped Claire with the baby into the back seat, then opened the front passenger door for Caroline, thanking the older gentleman for his assistance.

Back at the house, Claire entered the kitchen, taken aback by all the flower arrangements that had arrived yesterday and earlier that morning. With her arm around her big sister, Caroline said, "Claire, there are so many people who love you so very much. I called everyone on that list to give them the news. There were a few I couldn't get through to; if you give me their addresses, I'll drop them a line with the wonderful news about Emily."

Karl finally got through to his mother and family in Vienna. Everyone was excited that Claire was all right and ecstatic at hearing about baby Emily and how good she was. At 6.4 pounds, she was the icing on the cake for the Vita family. "Mama, it feels like Christmas; how strange it feels not having you here to enjoy Emily. I feel saddened that we cannot be together, and the time cannot go fast enough until we are home in Wien next summer. Emily will be over ten months old by then. You are going to love her."

Next, Karl talked to his sister, almost repeating the same things he had told his mother, also adding he would like to spend a Christmas in Wien maybe in a couple of years. Karl called Claire to the phone so that she could catch up with Mama and Frieda. The tears of joy and sadness on Claire's face told Karl his wife was missing having the family there.

Claire had convinced Caroline to remain in Hitchin for another week; it seemed senseless to return to Oxford so soon. Caroline, agreeing, called David for his approval. He, of course, was pleased that his wife could spend more time with her sister, saying he and the children would be fine until she arrived home again. Karl had stayed in touch with Jim McGinley, conveying the latest news on the baby and how hectic things had become since his return to Hitchin.

Jim, of course, was delighted to hear Claire and the baby were both doing wonderful. "Karl, look for a delivery. It should be there in a couple of days. The staff and management all chipped in; we hope you two like it. See you in three weeks. Have a wonderful time with your new daughter, and please, convey our congratulations to Claire. Karl, you haven't told me the baby's Christian name?" asked Jim.

"I'm so sorry, Jim too many things rattling around in my head right now. Her name is Emily; best to all, bye for now." After returning the receiver to its cradle, for no apparent reason, Karl started thinking about Wien and the warm, balmy days down by the river; he was missing his home city of Wien.

Settling back into home life, Karl and Claire were enjoying their children and home. However, Karl had a job to do, and as much as it upset him, he had to get ready to return to Glasgow for six or maybe seven weeks. Claire dropped him off at the train station with the usual tears before he boarded the train, "Claire, at least this will be a quick trip for me. Arnold, that poor bugger, is the one you should feel bad for. He is the one who has to complete that contract to South America. Now, give me a kiss, then get going; Sheila must think you got lost," concluded Karl. With one last kiss, he boarded his compartment.

The Clyde Princess was fully loaded when he arrived at the docks, waiting for her captain to board. Their first stop was in Belfast for three days, then on to Dublin before sailing to Liverpool, their final stop before returning to Glasgow to change captains and crews before heading back out again on an extended voyage to Montevideo on the River Plate in Uruguay, South America.

Karl had not seen Arnold Simms for many months, so when they returned to Glasgow, Arnold was waiting on the docks to board, happy to see his relief captain. "Karl, old man, thank you for making the first leg of this contract for me. I'm feeling fine now, but that bout of flu really put me down. I'm now ready to set off in a couple of days. How is that new daughter of yours? Thank God you're not completing the remainder of this contract; it would have made me very unhappy to do that to you. Now, let's you and our first officers review the logs, shall we? Is there anything I should know about the old girl before you leave today?" Karl, feeling lighthearted, was more than ready to hand over the Princess to Arnold. Saying his farewells, he headed to the station and home to his family.

Time was going by too fast. November was cold and damp. However, for the Vita family, there was so much to be done. Claire had returned to work, even though Karl and Bill had begged her to wait until after Christmas to resume her position as head of the firm. Karl was also busy writing a new manual for the commodore. Promptly at 3:30 p.m. daily, he would drive to Sheila's house to pick up the children, then drive to pick up Claire at the office. Bill and Dorothy would join them at least twice a week for dinner at home, followed by an evening of cards. Life was settling into a comfortable, laid back routine.

Two weeks before Christmas, Caroline arrived on her own by train. She wanted some time in Hitchin before her family arrived for the holidays. David and the children would arrive by car on December 23rd, bearing gifts for the Vita family, especially Emily. This family gathering brightened everyone's day. Karl enjoyed seeing and being part of this reunion. Watching Claire with her family around, he realized it was the medicine she needed. Dorothy and Bill were frequent visitors, in addition to the constant visits from Claire's school friends, along with people from the office and some clients. It was so enjoyable but so tiring for Claire. Caroline insisted that Karl take Claire out for New Year's Eve. She and David would stay home to watch the children. "Karl don't argue with me. I insist you get my sister out of this bloody house. Anyway, David and I would like some alone time. Now, where do you want to take her?" asked Caroline.

Claire interjected, "Let me make that decision, Caroline, and thank you for kicking us out." Looking at Karl sitting by the fire, she studied his facial expression, then answered, "All right, Karl, you win. Let's see if I can get us into the George and Dragon, shall I?" Walking over to her husband, she leaned over, kissing him on the forehead. She asked again, "Karl, you may be able to second guess my thoughts, but then again, I can do the same with you. You're thinking the George at this time of year is a special place, so let me call Charlie, the manager, and ask him to squeeze us in, shall I?"

Karl didn't have to say a word; she knew his preference. Christmas day was cold and rainy outside. Inside, it was cheerful with the fire and sparkling tinsel reflecting the flames from the fire. Karl sat with David on the couch, watching excited children ripping open gifts and making a ruckus over the contents. Claire sat next to Caroline on the opposite couch, Emily cradled in her arms. The day was long but so gratifying.

After the children had been put to bed, the four adults relaxed, enjoying a glass of vintage port. Claire, on the other hand, sipped on a glass of white wine.

Karl looked at David with a nod, then stood up, saying, "Ladies, perhaps you think David and I had forgotten you both on this hectic Christmas day. Well, we didn't; some months ago, we decided we wanted to give you both a lasting gift, so from the both of us, here they are."

David walked over to the tree and, reaching behind it, he produced two identical boxes. Claire, looking at Karl, then at her sister, also looking confused, said, "I thought we all agreed only to buy the children gifts this year. Vita, this has your devious ways written all over it, and David, you are no better." With big grins on their faces, Karl and David stood facing their wives as the wrapping paper was ripped off. They looked at the two identical brown boxes with excitement on their faces.

"Well, open them," said David, urging his wife to open the box. Inside, a fine linked gold chain had a left hand cradling half a heart. Claire's box had the same, except it had a right hand cradling the other half of that heart. Both sisters, overwhelmed by such an unusual gift, gently put the two pendant's halves together, forming a heart with two hands around it.

Claire, clasping her sister, spoke first, "Caroline, our wonderful husbands have given us a family heirloom never to be separated." Claire put Caroline's around her neck, and Caroline did the same for Claire.

"Well, ladies, did we do the right thing having these made?" asked Karl, sitting on the arm of the couch. David did the same on the other arm. For once, neither sister could speak; they just sat there holding each other tightly.

"Well," said David, "what's the verdict?"

Caroline reached up, tears streaming down her face, and replied, "Darling, what can I say except how lucky we both are to have husbands like you two? What a unique and thoughtful gift."

David, cradling Caroline's face, replied, "It was your brother-in-law's idea; thank him." Claire, hearing this, looked at her husband, his eyes firmly on hers. No words were necessary; those looks said it all.

The week was flying by. Claire and Caroline took the time to visit old school chums and go shopping in Luton and Cambridge before Caroline started her new job. As for Karl and David, they found plenty to do, including David opening a bank account at Lloyds Bank in Baldock, then a drive by visit to his new work location, also in Baldock. New Year's Eve was the following day, so Claire announced to their husbands that they would celebrate this holiday early.

"Tomorrow evening, we will be separated, so Caroline and I went shopping to cook a scrumptious dinner for us all this evening, children included. Now, if you boys could assist, let's get the ball rolling."

Karl, his arms over his head, nodded in agreement, replying, "Aye, aye, Captain, your orders, if you please." David and Karl went shopping for fresh flowers, decorating the solarium with their beauty. Then, they set the table with Claire's finest China on Mama's hand embroidered tablecloth. The kitchen, however, looked like a bomb had hit it. Karl and David agreed they would volunteer to clean up later. After the children had been put to bed, their bellies full, they relaxed, enjoying several bottles of fine burgundy wine. Karl stoked up the fire, the four of them sitting in the glow of its embers, enjoying that glass of port to round out the evening and each other's company. It had been a delightful evening and a fitting ending to another year. The new year, however, would bring new fears for world peace.

On New Year's Eve, Karl, dressed in a dark brown suit, sat patiently waiting in the sitting room for his wife for their first evening out since before Claire gave birth to their daughter, Emily. This evening at the George and Dragon would be very special; it was the place where Karl fell for Claire hook, line, and sinker. David and Caroline were still upstairs, telling bedtime stories to their children. They were looking forward to a relaxing evening in front of the fire with a bottle of wine and, most of all, being alone. Hearing footsteps on the stairs, Karl turned his head to see his wife in the doorway. The light from the hall backlit Claire, no longer in maternity clothing a little overweight due to her pregnancy, but to Karl, she still could take his breath away.

Wearing a flared burgundy skirt and matching top, she was everything Karl had fallen in love with. "Oh, my God, Claire, what a transformation! You look stunning; it's so nice to see you back in high heels. Those legs of yours are starting to get me excited."

Glowing with the praise she was receiving, Claire answered him by saying, "Darling, thank you for making me feel like an attractive woman again. Nine months is a long time to carry all that weight. Tonight, we can relive those early days of dining and making love to welcome the new year; how does that sound, lover boy?"

The bar at the George was packed; the dining room, however, was full but not as noisy. "Captain and Mrs. Vita, so pleased you are spending tonight with us. And may I say, Mrs. Vita, you look stunning, but then again, you always do," said the cheerful maître d' as he led them to their table nestled in a quiet alcove.

Karl ordered a bottle of burgundy wine, Claire reminding him, "Just a half glass for me, darling; remember, I'm still breastfeeding."

"That is true, darling, but one glass on New Year's Eve won't make a big difference, I'm sure," replied Karl. After a dinner of wonderful crispy duck, followed by a French dessert, the maître d' escorted them into the lounge, seating them in their favorite chairs by the fireplace. "Claire, I remember sitting here on that second day after we met. On that day, the Following Storm that followed me for so many years dissipated, never to return. And that was all because of you, my dearest Claire. This life we share and the beautiful children you gave us is more than I could have hoped for." Karl repeated what he had said so many times before to his wife. It had so much meaning and love that she thrilled each time he repeated it. When they returned home, the time was 1:00 a.m. Silently, they climbed the stairs; more than tired, they went straight to bed, in love and in each other arms, ready to face another year full of change and surprises.

CHAPTER 14

# 1949 A NEW YEAR, A NEW WAR

The house seemed very quiet after Caroline and her family left to return to Oxford. Ahead of them was the tedious job of packing to prepare for their move back to Hitchin. Karl and Claire took this time to clear the two guest bedrooms in anticipation of them staying with them until the bungalow became available. Hopefully, the offer Claire had given the RAF pilot and his family to terminate their lease early would allow Caroline and her family to move in sooner than the coming June.

The Second World War may be over, but saber rattling on the Korean peninsula would again start another armed conflict, or as the Allies referred to it, a police action. The latest world news was beginning to concern Karl as he read the morning paper concerning the escalating conflict between the North and South Korean governments. The North was demanding the South merge with them to unite the country under communist rule.

Karl was remembering why they fought World War II: to prevent further conflicts that could waste so many young men and women's lives. Yet, here they were again, facing another conflict. When will these political leaders ever learn? Feeling angry and vulnerable, he placed a telephone call to Clive at MI-5 in Slough.

"Karl, so nice to hear from you. How are Claire and Emily doing? You must be very busy about now. Julie told me that your sister-in-law was moving back home. Claire must be over the moon with excitement, but that's not what you're calling about, is it, my old friend?"

Karl knew his friend so well; they had relied on each other many times during the war. Karl, careful with his questions, asked, "Clive, are our forces preparing for the possibility of another war this time in Korea? The newspapers are all speculating that the English will join the Americans if this thing escalates into a full-blown conflict. When I saw Bill earlier today, he was not overly concerned that he would be recalled. On the other hand, I told him I was becoming increasingly concerned that I would again be recalled to wear the uniform of an intelligence officer."

Clive listened intently but refrained from commenting any further. His reply, "Karl, I wouldn't get overly concerned at this point. Don't worry; I will keep you informed. Best to Claire; I hope to see you soon. Bye for now." The phone abruptly went dead. Karl thought: Clive was probably annoyed at me for mentioning Korea on a non-secure phone line.

Claire continued doing work at home, even though her husband was not happy with her doing so. Sometimes, he would watch her, sitting hour after hour immersed in some case folder.

In the meantime, Caroline and David had changed their game plan. With Caroline and the children moving to Hitchin in early April, David would remain in Oxford until June, then join them. Hopefully, they could move into the bungalow soon after his arrival. On the Monday before her sister arrived home, Claire asked Karl if he would watch the children while she went to the farm to pick up groceries and other supplies. She needed to make stew and several other dishes that she would have ready for a house full of family.

Karl took this time to call Jim McGinley, asking, "Morning, Jim, hope all is well with you. I called you this morning to get your opinion on where we stand concerning the escalating political situation in Korea?" The phone went momentarily silent as Karl waited for Jim's answer.

"Karl, it doesn't look too good. We have been put on notice that our newer refrigerated ships will more than likely be requisitioned should England be pulled into this conflict. The Princess, I fear, would be one of them. She may not be fast enough, but I guess we will find out soon enough. I was going to call you tomorrow, but today is as good as any to discuss the political situation in Korea, and of course, your position in the event some of our ships are requisitioned. Karl, you are one of our most proficient captains, and God knows you have had more experience when it comes to operating a ship under enemy attack. If we are to send ships into harm's way, can we depend on you to skipper one of these vessels?

"Let me also add that no one here would blame you if you refused such an assignment. Think about that carefully before you give me your answer in a day or so will be fine. Now, another question for you, is there any possibility the Intelligence Service could recall you to active duty? Do you still have contacts in that service who could get you an answer? It would be useless for this company to make such an inquiry and expect a real answer, considering the sensitivity of the question."

Karl, listening, already suspected what that answer would be. Jim closed by saying, "Talk to you tomorrow best make it in the morning. I think that board meeting will take most of the afternoon; bye for now," concluded Jim as he hung up the receiver.

Karl remained sitting, thinking more about what could happen, then decided, I think I should visit Bill tomorrow morning, face to face is a better option, I'm thinking.

Bill was in his office, intently critiquing a report his secretary had just finished typing. He looked up as he heard a loud rap on the office door. "Come in!" he yelled. Karl opened the door, smiling as he entered, asking Bill if he could spare ten or fifteen minutes. Bill replied, "For you, as much time as you need; what's up?"

Karl sat down, draping his driving coat over the chair. "Let's get some coffee brought in, shall we? I can see you have a lot on your mind, am I correct?" inquired Bill as he buzzed his secretary for two cups of coffee.

"I can see your old intelligence habits are still as sharp as ever," smirked Karl. Once the coffee was delivered, Karl dove in with his questions. "Bill, you and I have spoken at length about the Korean conflict. My questions are simple. One, a question you have already answered, so sorry for repeating it: what are the prospects of you being recalled if a conflict erupts into a full-blown war? Secondly, which is my main question, do you think a recall could include me?

Let's face it; you're always talking with Clive about America's position should they be drawn into such a conflict. America is our closest ally; we owe them our support; wouldn't you agree? Could a general recall also be part of those contingency plans? Well, are they?"

Bill, rocking his chair, holding his mug of coffee with both hands close to his bottom lip, had a solemn look on his face. Nodding, he answered, "Karl, our old department is already gearing up in anticipation of war escalating sooner than later. I've already told you this, so I'm not sure why you are asking it again. Karl, this is highly classified, so anything I tell you now is off the record; are we completely clear on that?" Karl nodded in agreement while tensing himself, waiting for the answer.

"As you know, Clive has already accepted the position to reorganize our old unit that includes adding new agents. So far, most are relatively green when it comes to covert operations. It's very likely that some of the old timers could be recalled, bolstering the unit's effectiveness. Their immediate task will be to gather as much information as possible on how far North Korea and its Chinese allies are prepared to go in this conflict.

They are threatening the South Koreans with annihilation before firing the first shot. Our latest intelligence reports the possibility that the Russians could also join the North Koreans and China later. Will I be recalled? Well, I don't think so; my leg will keep me out of this conflict. As for you, my friend, it could become complicated. From what I've gathered, I believe if you're a servicing captain on a ship being used in this conflict, chances are that will take precedence over recalling you back into the BIS, better known these days as MI-5. Does that set your mind at ease?" Bill was searching Karl's face for a sign, but then again, Karl was a master of concealing his facial expressions well, most of the time.

"Thanks, Bill. I better call Jim McGinley with my answer. It looks like the best place for me to be is aboard a merchant ship."

Karl drove home, finding the house to be empty. He took advantage of this time by placing that call to Jim McGinley at the Clyde Shipping Company's main office. "Good morning; how may I direct your call?" answered Brenda in her strong Scottish accent.

Karl, recognizing her voice, answered, "Bren, it's Captain Vita. Nice to hear that wonderful accent. Is Captain McGinley still in his office?"

Karl patiently waited as Brenda dialed Jim's office, "Thanks, Brenda; I was expecting his call." He took a pad from his middle drawer and his favorite Parker fountain pen, placing them ready on the desk before pressing the flashing line on hold. "Karl, I was wondering when you would call me back. First and foremost, and by far the most important question for you today, can we rely on you to skipper a ship if the call comes to join the task force heading to well, you know the answer to that, don't you?" asked Jim, deliberately refraining from disclosing the destination.

"Jim, please accept that this was a difficult decision for me to make, but yes, you can count on me." Karl felt relieved at the commitment he had just made. On the other end of the phone, Jim waited before he responded, just in case Karl had spoken to him too soon.

"Karl, not to disrupt your time at home, especially now with the demands of a new baby, but have you considered that you could be away at sea for extended periods? You need to discuss that with your wife before we go any further. Now, Karl, we have another situation that has thrown a spanner into the works.

Captain Arthur Burns, as you know, has been working with the builders, getting the new Spirit ready for her final inspection before taking her out on her sea trials. Well, that is not going to happen. He had a heart attack last night, leaving our new ship without a captain."

Karl started tensing himself, already guessing what would come next. "You're scheduled to return to Scotland at the end of March. I have a request to make, and please forgive me for dropping this on you like this. We would like you to return in early February. The board has asked me for my recommendations to assign one of our captains to assume the command of that brand new fast passenger freighter, the Spirit of Clyde Side. She is being launched ahead of schedule. Captain Burns has been with her since her keel laying ceremony, but his heart condition has put us in a real bind. I have been tasked with replacing him at the earliest opportunity.

"This task is limited to candidates with a maritime engineering background like Captain Burns had in shipbuilding. However, the urgency to have such a candidate at the builder's yard during these final stages and signoffs prior to the launch date including the first sea trial is putting us in a predicament as most of our captains do not have engineering backgrounds like you and Burns have." The phone went quiet as Jim gave Karl a few minutes to absorb what he was leading up to. "Karl, I would really like that replacement captain to be you. Assuming you agree, we must move quickly, getting the Spirit signed off and made ready for her first scheduled voyage, which has already been posted. That trip will be to Montevideo. I know; I know; Uruguay is a long voyage, but I will feel so much better if you say yes to taking command. As for your staff and engineering officers, that will be your call. I have already given the board my recommendation, subject to your approval." Jim let the line go silent once again, waiting for Karl to digest all that had been said.

Finally, he answered, "Well, Captain McGinley, that's quite a load you have dumped on me. I guess you want me to say yes, correct?" Karl, saying that, felt those pangs of guilt, knowing what he was asking Claire to endure. "Jim, if I were making the decision for myself, well, that's a no brainer. However, I have a wife and two kids to consider. Let me talk to her tonight, then I'll call you in the morning. How does that sound?" Jim agreed that was the right thing to do, giving him the time to explain to his wife about the new ship and maybe the more extended time away from home.

"Karl, of course, that is the right approach. Call me after 0900 hours, alright? Good luck tonight." Karl returned the telephone to its cradle. Still sitting at the desk, he started to write down what Jim had just asked him to consider. You idiot, Vita, start putting your family first. Remember all those years when Claire sat alone, worrying if she would become a widow for the second time? Then again, after the war, the long months waiting for you to return from sea? You must say no to Jim tomorrow!

The sound of the car horn in the driveway meant Claire would need a hand with the groceries she had just purchased. Opening the outside door to the kitchen, Karl smiled as he walked over to the car. Claire was already lifting shopping bags off the back seat. Karl protested by saying, "Claire, let me do that, or have you already forgotten it was only a few months ago you had a baby!" taking the two heavy bags from his wife.

"Darling, I'm not handicapped. Why don't you take the ones in the boot? They are much heavier." Claire, always the independent woman, had many years of relying on her own abilities while her husband was away. Looking at Karl's face she asked, "Are the children still upstairs sleeping? I think that blast of the car's horn surely woke them. I'll go upstairs and bring them downstairs, shall I?"

Karl nodded in agreement. Back in the kitchen, he put the remaining bags on the table, his mind racing to explain his telephone call earlier with Jim. While Claire made supper, Karl fed and bathed the children, allowing them to play on the sitting room floor. Claire entered and announced, "Supper should be ready in about forty-five minutes; hope you're hungry, Sailor?" The heat from the fire was wonderful; Claire and Karl sat on the floor with their children enjoying this family time. Later, after putting the children to bed and cleaning up the kitchen, they returned to the sitting room. Lying in front of the fire, Karl quietly sipped a glass of whiskey. Claire knew her husband so well. If he was this quiet, there must be something going on in that head of his, but what could that be? Putting her arm around his shoulders, she kissed the back of his hand before asking, "Darling, what is troubling you? Remember, a problem shared sometimes is a problem spared. Do you have a problem you would like to share with me, my sensitive sailor?" Karl slugged back the remainder of his drink before taking both her hands and holding them tightly. He started telling her all about what had been asked of him. The mood was becoming solemn, Claire not saying a word as she listened intently to Karl, laboring with each detail before waiting for her response.

Claire fought back the tears before replying, "My darling man, I am not surprised at what you have just told me. I married a career officer with no illusions that, until he called it quits, he would be away for long periods, first as an intelligence spy and now a new objective launching this bloody new ship. But then again, I also agreed to do this for three years, and almost half of that time has already passed. Karl, if this is something you feel compelled to do, then we, as a family, must support you, remaining strong until you retire. One blessing is my sister and family will be right up the road in Baldock, as well as Dorothy and Bill only a few miles away in Letchworth. That's a good situation for the kids and me."

Claire stood up, reaching for his glass. She smiled, then threw him a kiss that told him she wasn't happy with the news but understood this was a task he was compelled to undertake.

Tomorrow morning, he would call Jim with his commitment. Claire returned, carrying two glasses of port. Karl, in the meantime, put more coal on the fire, banking it so it would last all night. Lying there in each other's arms, watching the flickering of the fire changing the reflections on the wall and ceiling, neither said much until Claire broke the silence by asking, "Karl, I hope in all your planning you remembered you promised me a holiday next summer taking a road trip to visit Mama in Wien. Please, say yes; that will give me something to look forward to."

Karl's heart was aching at what he was putting his family through. Hearing Claire ask that question, he wrapped his arms around her, tears of sorrow on his cheeks. He replied softly, "Of course, we will drive to Wien next summer, and Claire, I intend to resign before we take that trip next summer. I was going to resign anyway; my family needs me here. There are two kids upstairs; I want us to watch them grow together. Being an absent father is not going to work for you or me. As much as I will always love the sea, it must take a back seat to our family's future. But Claire, what am I going to do? You may have to support us until I find a land job. I guess I better start being nice to you."

Turning her face toward his, Claire kissed him before he could continue. "Karl, I would work, day and night to have my husband here under my feet all the time. And darling, why are you fretting? Remember, we have more than enough money and assets put away for our retirement, so don't worry yourself if that's what concerns you. As far as I'm concerned, after this next voyage, if you really want to stop working altogether, well, it will be your choice. God knows you have done more than your share during this last war. Look at all you have accomplished in your lifetime and how many times you have faced danger. Retiring while you're still in one piece and young enough to enjoy life is a wonderful idea. Perhaps I can convince Bill to remain in the position of senior partner, giving me a lot more freedom to enjoy our senior years. How about that idea?"

Karl, his mind in turmoil, was absorbing what she had just suggested. Retiring to enjoy their life together was starting to make sense to him. Those storm clouds hanging over his head were thinning, allowing the rise of bright sunshine to brighten his day. "Come on, old girl, let's go up to bed. You look really tired, and I'm not helping your state of mind, am I?"

Helping his wife off the floor, he caressed her backside, which made her giggle. "Careful, you dirty old man. What am I going to do with you?" Claire kissed him passionately, so in love with her sailor.

Caroline and the two children would be arriving mid-week. The time was going by too quickly. Claire and Karl spent time making sure the upstairs bedrooms were ship shape, ready for Claire's sister arriving Wednesday afternoon. Claire was in a wonderful frame of mind, excited about her sister returning home. "Darling, I've just called Sheila about watching Emily for a couple of hours. She is tickled pink; you know how she adores our little princess. Nick, let your papa put your coat and wellingtons on; we are going for a walk in the fields behind the Fox. The fresh air will do us good. What do you say, young man, ready to stamp in the mud?" asked Claire, laughing loudly.

Dropping Emily off, they drove toward their favorite pub in William. The Fox had a very special meaning to Claire and Karl; it was the place they both realized they had met their soul mate. After all these years, that love was stronger than ever. The day was sunny but cold enough for a warm scarf and gloves. Karl parked the car almost in the same spot he had parked Claire's MG sports car only hours after meeting her for the first time. Claire started to smile, her eyes focused on Karl's face.

Turning toward him, she said quietly, "Karl, you old romantic Austrian, parking in the same place we parked my MG. So much has happened since that first day, hasn't it? Over the years, that image has been my comfort each time you left to go off on some dangerous intelligence mission. I think back to how it all started. I was in a dark place; since then, so many things have changed for the better.

That happened in only a few days when I placed that newspaper advertisement to sell Patrick's MG and start a new life. He was a brave pilot who lost his life, but I had mourned long enough. My prayers would be answered when Ronny called me that morning about the advertisement. Karl, on that day, God gave me you and now two wonderful children."

Karl, absorbing what she had said, was quietly thanking his Creator for saving his life so many times and guiding him to Claire, feeling guilty about ever doubting his Creator. Hand in hand, they walked up the field, swinging Nicholas between them. Later, Nicholas started getting cold, and Claire looked at her watch and said, "Darling, our little lad is getting cold. Let's turn around and have lunch at the Fox; what do you say?"

Karl nodded and looked down at his son, asking him, "Nick, would you like a chip sandwich and a cream soda before we head home?"

Jumping up and down, Nick pulled at his father's hand, yelling, "Now, please, Papa." Claire started laughing; her little man was a chip off the old Vita block. Entering the inn, Claire greeted Harry as he opened the bar.

"Captain and Mrs. Vita, so nice to see you both, and is that little Nicholas hiding behind your coat, Claire?" Harry always spoiled Nicholas when they brought him into the pub.

"Nicholas Vita, stop acting and give Harry a big hug because, if you don't, he will not get you a cream soda." Claire was trying very hard to keep a straight face.

Nicholas, hearing this, ran over, hugging the old man's leg. "Well, that's more like it, young man. Follow me; I'll show you how to draw a glass of soda," remarked Harry, loving every minute.

Karl, enjoying his mild and bitter beer, looked at Claire and pointed to his watch, saying, "We better get going, or we'll find your sister sitting on the front steps of the train station." Claire nodded in agreement.

Harry gave Nicholas a big hug before they said their farewells. "See you in a couple of days, Harry. We'll bring Claire's sister along as well. They will be staying with us till the bungalow is vacated in

Baldock; they are moving here permanently from Oxford. I dare say they could become regulars," said Karl, lifting Nick onto his shoulder. Claire went into overdrive back at the house, making sure everything was ready for their houseguests. Karl and Nick took this time to drive to Sheila's house to pick up Emily.

The loud train whistle announced the arrival of Caroline and her children. "Caroline, come here and hug your big sister; we are so thrilled you're finally here to stay. Karl and I have spent the last couple of days getting the house ready for your arrival. We are so pleased that when you finally move into the bungalow, it will remain in the family."

Karl and Nick hugged Caroline's two children before saying to Caroline, "Come here, you good looking woman, and give your brother-in-law a big hug and a real big kiss on the cheek."

Caroline, who thought the world of Karl and always teased him, replied, "I'm ready, Sailor."

Arriving at the house, Karl laughed at seeing the children playing as if they had been together for longer than a few hours. He said, "Caroline, let's you and I unload the luggage, shall we?"

Things were hectic during the following week. Karl kept the children occupied while the two sisters started shopping for decorations for when they would finally move into the bungalow. Unfortunately, Karl would not be there for that move. He would be back in Scotland by then.

All good things must come to an end, and Karl now faced leaving home earlier than initially planned. His new command was moving along ahead of schedule. As much as he resented leaving his family and friends, he had a job to do. On a dreary, wet Sunday morning, Claire and their two children drove him to the train station for that long journey back to Glasgow. Karl got out of the car, telling Claire, "Darling, please drop me off in front of the station. With two kids, it will be a real hassle going with me up onto the platform, and it is still raining. There's no need to get these two wet, is there?"

For the first time in their marriage, Claire agreed. As much as her heart was breaking, she knew he was right; holding back the sorrow and tears, she said, "Nick, say goodbye to your papa and give him a big hug. With the back door open, Karl reached in to hug his son, kissing his cheeks, then gently kissing his daughter Emily in her car seat.

"Nicholas Vita, you're the man of the house now; take good care of your mummy and sister until I return home. Will you do that for your papa?" Karl chuckled at his son nodding his head, not really understanding what his father had just asked.

"Claire, I guess this is it. Do you have a kiss for this departing sailor?" Claire slid out from behind the driver's seat.

Throwing her arms around Karl's shoulders, she kissed him with all the love she could muster, saying, "Darling, call me once you arrive in Glasgow. I'm heading to Dorothy's house with the kids for a few hours. If you need to call me from King's Cross, try there first. Karl don't worry too much although saying that to you is a total waste of time. You're my world, darling; make this next trip, then hurry home to me and these two terrors. I meant every word I said about both of us retiring when you return home. Let's enjoy life and our family. Now, go get that train before it leaves without you. Kiss me again, Karl, and make it a good one. It will have to keep me going for a least the next five or six months."

Karl took his two cases and his briefcase from the boot, then, taking one last look, he entered the station with a heavy heart. Sitting on the platform bench, he thought about what Claire had reiterated about them retiring. Why not? It's not like we don't have sufficient things to do. She is so right; whatever time we have left should be spent together with no more long separations. His mind returned to the task at hand. Well, I can add to my list of accomplishments being the very first skipper of the brand new Spirit of Clyde Side, a fitting end to my career, retiring after her maiden voyage. Jim is not going to like this!

# CHAPTER 15

# THE SPIRIT OF CLYDE SIDE

Jim McGinley met Karl at the station. Smiling, he grasped Karl's hand, saying, "So pleased to see you, Karl; come, let's drive back to the office. I have some wonderful news to share with you. Yesterday, the board officially made me the fleet commodore. The downside to that is I'm on the beach from here on; what do you say to that, Karl? I think they gave me that position, fearing I was about to retire. I hope you're ready for a day of boring meetings. It can't be helped, I guess. Like you, I'm not a big fan of repetitive meetings."

"Jim, congratulations! They picked the best man for the job. I'll make you this promise: I'll stay out of your hair. This is wonderful news!" Karl was happy to see his friend receive the recognition he deserved. After a series of meetings with the company's board of directors, Commodore McGinley asked Karl if he was ready to start recruiting his officers. In Jim's office, Karl presented his list of officers and crew members, most already in the employment of the Clyde Shipping Company. In the back of Karl's mind, he wanted men he had served with before, knowing their strengths as well as their weaknesses. This, of course, was based on their availability. Confidently, he started calling and telegramming key personnel, hopeful of enticing them to join him. After two days, the crew list was approved by Karl, Jim, and the personnel manager, except for the first officer and chief engineering officer. "Jim, you did authorize me to hire from outside the company for these two positions, did you not?" asked Karl.

"Of course, Karl, your judgment is never in question. Please, share with me; who are your first picks? We're going to have to move fast. Are they available for immediate hire?" Jim wondered what was going on in Karl's head.

"Remember Dunkirk? Well, I had two officers that saved me and most of the crew before our ship, the HMT Reese, went down. Well, if they are available, they will be my first choice," replied Karl as he opened his file.

"Well, Captain Vita, I suggest you start recruiting post haste," replied Jim, also wondering about the timing.

Karl first called the telephone number Arnold Adams had given him after they parted company at the hospital rehabilitation center back in 1940. The phone kept ringing, and Karl was about to hang up when a charming voice answered, "Adams residence, Gloria speaking."

Karl introduced himself, telling her he was looking for Arnold and asked if he was home.

"Well, Captain, he should be home in about fifteen minutes or so. Would you like me to have him call you when he arrives home? May I have your telephone number, please?"

Karl gave her the number and concluded by saying, "Gloria, someday soon, I hope to be able to meet you. Arnold spoke of you often when we both served on the HMT Reese. It's been nice speaking with you; bye for now." Next, Karl placed a call to the engineering officer on the Reese, Scott McDonald. Waiting patiently for someone to pick up, his mind wandered back to the first time he met Scottie. His Scottish accent was a challenge for Karl, but with time, this would no longer be a problem.

"Hello, who's calling?" came that familiar brogue. Hearing this made Karl feel relieved he had made contact. The question now was, would Scottie be receptive to joining the crew of the Spirit on such short notice?

"Scottie, it's Karl Vita. I'm so pleased I found you at home. Are you able to talk with me about a contract you won't be able to refuse?"

Scottie was more than delighted to hear from his old skipper after all these years. "Well, Captain Vita, I'll be damned, or is it Mister Vita now? What a surprise! How many years has it been? The last time I saw you, they were loading you into an ambulance in Folkstone, still unconscious and in bad shape. I'm glad you recovered all right. The lads kept us abreast of your recovery. Sorry you did not hear from me, Skipper; you know what a sailor's life is like."

Karl listened intently, then hearing Scottie's last statement, replied, "Scottie, this is why I'm calling you. Are you still employed, or are you on the beach? As for me, well, I work for the Clyde Shipping Company. Until recently, I was a captain of the Clyde Princess." Karl spent the next thirty minutes detailing what he had been tasked with, his last comment being, "Scottie, I have been given a free hand to pick my first officer and chief engineer. Can I convince you to come out of retirement and join me? I'm assuming your union card and ticket are still current, aren't they?"

"Well, Skipper, I guess I won't be planting my garden if I say yes. It sounds like a dream come true a brand new fast merchant ship. I will have to clear it with the Mrs. first, but I don't think she will disagree when I tell her what you offered me. Call me later today. When will I have to report to the shipyard?"

Karl knew Scottie so well a chance to launch a brand new ship with the latest in engine room technology was too big a temptation to say no to. No sooner had Karl hung up the phone than Bren rang through, telling Karl he had a call on three from an Arnold Adams. Once more, Karl gave Arnold the details of the position he was trying to fill, followed by, "Arnold, are you interested? I'm not trying to push you, but we are under a deadline to get this ship commissioned. I would love to know I have you and Scottie working with me again. What do you say?"

Arnold listened intently while weighing a decision that contradicted what he had told his wife five months before, which was to take a year off and stay home with family. "Skipper, if it were just me, I would already be on a train heading North. How long do I have to get you an answer?"

Karl took his time answering, "Arnold, no later than tomorrow morning. You will have to leave home no later than the end of the week."

Arnold swallowed at hearing Karl's answer. "I will call you at 0830 hours' tomorrow, Skipper! The chance to sail with you and Scottie again is too big an opportunity to pass up. Have a nice evening, Sir." The phone went dead, and Karl felt pleased with the responses he'd received. What are my options should they say no, he thought?

Later in the day, Bren rang Karl, announcing a Scott McDonald was holding on two. "Thank you, Bren," replied Karl, hesitating momentarily before picking up the receiver. "Scottie, glad you're calling me with good news, are you?"

Scottie, in high spirits, simply answered, "I'm all yours, Skipper. Give me the details of where I need to travel to." Karl felt relieved that the engineering position was filled.

"Scottie, that's wonderful news. See you in a couple of days. Call Bren back with your arrival time, so I can send a car to meet you at the station. Now, if I can get Arnold on board, our crew for the Spirit will be complete. Later that day, he told Bren to hold calls, excluding Arnold, while he called home.

The phone rang, and Karl expected Claire to answer. Instead, Caroline picked up the phone, saying, "Vita residence, who's calling, please?"

How wonderful it was to hear his sister-in-law on the other end of the phone. Karl said, "Caroline, it's nice hearing your voice. How are you and the children settling in? Even though it's only a couple of days since we saw each other, it feels like a week or more."

Caroline gave Karl a condensed update before asking, "As much as I love talking to you, dear Karl, I believe it's my big sister you're looking for, right?"

Karl laughed and answered, "Correct, is Claire home, or is she at the office?"

Caroline answered, "She had an important meeting this afternoon, so I volunteered to babysit. As for David and the bungalow, we are still on schedule thanks for asking. Right now, Claire is upstairs having a bath. Can you hold while I let her know you are holding?"

Karl sat back, drinking a fresh mug of coffee, his spirits very high about how things were turning out. "Karl, darling, nice timing. I was just taking a bath. I'm standing here dripping wet with only a towel around me. How's it going? Did you manage to connect with Arnold and Scottie? You sound like you're in a good mood. I'm assuming your key people are on board; is that correct? Captain Vita, have you had time to miss your wife and kids yet?"

Hearing this was like the calming therapy he needed. "Claire, you and the kids are with me every minute of the day. Remember what I told you? Once this contract is up, I'm retiring another reason I want Arnold to be my first officer, as he will be in line to become the Spirit's next master unless the big wigs at the Clyde Shipping company have other plans. I'll share that with him when he calls me back in the morning. Scottie will be here the day after tomorrow. Claire, is that towel secure, or is it close to falling off? I'm visualizing that picture right now, and when I arrive home, you better have dropped the kids off with Shelia or Caroline because I'll need you all to myself. What do you think of that, you vixen?"

Thrilled at hearing this, Claire knew he was missing her very much. "Darling, I miss you so much! I'm counting down the weeks until you are here again with me, and Sailor, you better rest up on that return train ride. It's been too long since you made love to your wife. Stay safe, and pass along my congratulations to Scottie and Arnold, will you? By the way, Nick keeps asking where his papa is. Poor little tyke, he's too young to know his dad is a sailor. Bye for now, darling, must go; my towel is about to fall off." Karl remained in his office, staring at the color photograph of Claire and the children, thinking, in six months, you will be begging me to return to sea. Why do I not believe that? Karl laughed while putting his files into his briefcase.

The following morning, Karl arrived at the office promptly at 0745 hours. The clerical staff had not arrived yet, which suited him fine. I think I'll go down the hall to the cafeteria for coffee and maybe some toast. Brenda had just arrived at her desk when he returned to his temporary office. Seeing Karl enter, she smiled, saying, "This is a great way to start the day, seeing the handsome Captain Vita carrying his own coffee."

Karl smiled at her before allowing his flirtatious side to comment on Brenda's appearance. "Thank you, Bren. I must say, you look especially smart this morning. I hope it's for my benefit, is it?"

Brenda started blushing at Karl's comment, answering, "It could have been, Sir, but you're married with young children, so thank you anyway. Are you expecting that call this morning from Mr. Adams?"

Still smiling at this feisty Scottish lass, Karl replied, "Yes, I am. Make sure you find me if I'm not in the office when he calls." Entering his office, he closed the door behind him. Promptly at 0830 hours, Bren announced that Mr. Adams was holding on one.

Karl picked up the receiver, anxious for a positive answer. "Arnold, I hope you're calling me with some good news, are you?" Karl tensed up for Arnold's response.

"Skipper, you can count on me. Last night, I was not so sure. My wife was quite upset when I shocked her with your offer."

Karl, listening, asked, "Would you like me to talk to her, Arnold? I recently went through the same reaction, so I know first-hand what you went through. What changed her mind?" asked Karl.

"When I refreshed her memory about what had happened on the Reese and the loyalty I still have for you, she started to understand why I wanted to sign up as your first officer," explained Arnold.

"Arnold, it's more than that. What I'm about to tell you is confidential. Only my wife knows at this point. I will be retiring for good when we return from this maiden voyage. As the first officer, and with my recommendation, you could well be the Spirit's next captain."

The phone went quiet, Arnold absorbing what Karl had just told him. "Skipper, I don't know what to say except thank you for considering me as your number one. Surely, you must know that's the real reason I'm signing on, don't you? When do you need me? I can be there tomorrow afternoon if that fits into your plans, Sir?"

Karl replied, "I'll see you tomorrow then, Arnold."

Jim McGinley was at his desk, weeding through a pile of maintenance logs when Karl entered, knocking on the door frame as he entered. "Morning, Jim; ready for some wonderful news? Both positions for the first officer and chief engineering positions are filled. They will both arrive tomorrow, so please make time to interview them and make the appropriate introductions. I think you will be suitably impressed."

Jim walked around the desk, signaling Karl to sit next to him. "Karl, you are positively enjoying yourself this morning; I think I like these chaps already. They must be excellent officers to pass muster with Karl Vita. I'm looking forward to getting them signed up," replied Jim, smiling at the look on Karl's face.

As luck would have it, Scottie and Arnold's schedule had them arriving within an hour of each other, Arnold arriving first. Karl decided he would meet them at the station instead of sending a driver. Standing by the platform gate, he watched as the iron monster puffed slowly toward the buffers at the head of the platform. Like so many times before, he watched as passengers made their way out of the station. Straining, he looked for a tall fellow, his head above the other passengers, heading to God knows where. "Arnold," yelled Karl, "Over here! So good to see you again after so many years." Shaking hands followed by hugging each other, Karl continued, "This is wonderful, working together again. Let me take one of those heavy suitcases from you. Scottie should be arriving in about an hour. Feel like grabbing some coffee while we wait? It's a wonderful day! I haven't seen you since that fateful day during the Dunkirk evacuation. You look the same; it must be that good living, I suppose." Karl was in a wonderful mood, reconnecting with his first officer.

Over coffee, Karl told Arnold all about how Captain Arthur Burns had a sudden heart attack, leaving the Spirit without a captain. That course of events landed Karl with this opportunity to skipper the brand new Spirit of Clyde Side. "It took some convincing by Captain McGinley for me to accept this position. Little did he know I was planning to retire within the year, which brings me to now. While I'm so pleased you accepted the position as my first officer, it's the perfect position for you to be in.

Remember what I said on the phone; this information must be kept strictly confidential between the two of us. I'll find time later today to update Scottie. I think he will be very pleased to hear about this, don't you agree?"

"Crikey, look at the time. Scottie's train will be arriving in less than five minutes. We need to get going," said Arnold, glancing at his watch. Once again, Karl waited this time with Arnold at the platform gate.

Searching through the stream of passengers making their way through the gate, Arnold spotted the short, stocky image of Scott McDonald.

"Over here, Scottie. God, you haven't changed that much, have you?" yelled Karl.

"Well, blow me down; you two haven't changed much either, other than a little pudge. Arnold, it must be that home cooking," joshed Scottie as he hugged Karl, then Arnold. They were three former comrades who suffered the worst the Nazis could throw at them, but they survived, their friendship stronger than ever.

Walking to the car, Karl reiterated what to expect once they arrived back at the company offices. "Chaps, I hope you have brought your uniforms with you for tomorrow morning, have you?" asked Karl. "Commodore McGinley's secretary, Brenda, has new insignias for you, so give her those uniforms jackets as soon as you meet with her. The tailor will have them ready before we leave later today for the ship."

Meeting Commodore McGinley was upbeat; however, that meeting was short due to the schedule that had been planned for them. Finally, their last meeting was to meet with the director for staffing to process their employment documents, making them new employees of the company. Karl had returned to his temporary desk to continue the paperwork that needed to be completed before the day's end. At the hotel and over dinner, they made merry, continuing to share stories of what they had done since that last day aboard the HMT Reese. Both Arnold and Scottie had continued to serve in the Merchant Marines, crossing the Atlantic many times during the early years of WW2, never sure they would not become a fatality of a U-Boat torpedo attack. Scottie described in detail being attacked while sailing in a convoy heading to Gibraltar. An Italian bomber raid attacked them; his ship was badly hit but managed to limp into Grand Harbor under its own power.

"I told the captain later when we were tied up that I lost one ship, and I'll be damned if I was going to lose another after losing the Reese off Dunkirk." Karl smiled at Scottie's humor about losing another ship. Continuing over coffee, the conversation turned more serious as they discussed the enormous amount of work to do and the lack of time to do it. First on the priority list, familiarize themselves with the ship's equipment and so many manuals. Getting to know the crew would add additional challenges prior to the sea trial and finally, acceptance by the Clyde Shipping Co.

The following morning, Jim met them promptly at 0730 hours for the drive to the builder's yard, taking almost an hour before they entered the enormous shipyard. The driver knew exactly where to go, having driven others from the company to this yard on many occasions.

"Alistair, wait for me by the main entrance when you drop us off. Here, take this money to buy yourself some breakfast. Once I've made the introductions, I will be returning with you to Glasgow. I don't think I'll be too long," instructed Commodore McGinley.

The first stop was the office to meet with the project manager, Angus Freeman. "Morning, chaps, so very pleased to make your acquaintance. I will be with you until the ship is turned over to the Clyde Shipping Co. I'm confident all will go smoothly until that time. Commodore McGinley, will you be accompanying us aboard? Or will you be returning to Glasgow?" asked Angus.

"No, Angus, I will be returning to Glasgow. From this point on, Captain Vita and his officers will be your interface. I will be back before the week's end to spend more time with you all. Captain Vita, do you have any questions for me before I depart?" asked Jim McGinley, keeping his line of sight on Karl. Seeing Karl's radiant look of confidence, he knew their new vessel was in the best of hands.

Climbing the boarding ramp, Angus looked back, thinking, these chaps are trying to conceal their excitement. It makes me feel good watching them. "Chaps, as you can see, we still have sizable construction gangs aboard, so please don't get in their way. They are all acutely aware we are up against a deadline. The Spirit has been here at the fitting-out basin for over two months now. Please, follow me to the wardroom; that area is complete and a great place to set up shop. Virtually all your crew are aboard. We're still waiting on a few key people, such as your navigation people and wireless operators.

"First thing tomorrow, I would suggest we interface with the crew. Like you, they have much to learn about this new vessel and its equipment, as you will soon discover. Mr. McDonald, the yard's engineering people will be on board until after the sea trials, so gleam as much as you can from their wealth of knowledge. Remember, you will be on your own when they disembark for that last time."

Jim was following behind, not saying much. Looking at his watch, he realized it was time to depart. "Chaps, I hate to leave you so soon, but I must return to the office. Angus here will introduce you to your department heads. By the look on Scottie's face, he is anxious to see those new engines. Your team, along with the builder's engineering staff, are waiting for you down below. Don't worry about your sea bags. By now, they should already be in your cabins. I think you will approve of how those cabins have been appointed. Captain, one other point, we have installed a landline in the wardroom, another on the bridge, and one in your cabin, so please keep in touch." With that, Jim left the ship.

Angus asked if they would prefer to meet their cabin steward and see their accommodations before splitting up to meet their department heads. "Angus, I think that would be a good start; are they close by?" asked Karl.

"Follow me; they're at the head of this corridor next to the bridge entrance." The Spirit was designed as a passenger carrying cargo vessel; the ten passenger cabins were also on this same deck at the end of the corridor, separated by a locked crew door. Karl entered his cabin, surprised at how roomy it was and well-appointed compared to older merchant ships. The convenience of a large desk, positioned under the porthole with three colored telephones to one side, made it look very business-like. His berth was larger than he was used to, with a nice spring mattress. Stepping back into the corridor, the smiles on his officers' faces confirmed their approval as well.

Angus smiled at their reactions, saying, "If you are pleased with your berths, the rest of the ship will impress you even further. Shall we continue to the bridge?" Unlike the Clyde Princess, the Spirit did not have a captain's day cabin. The close proximately to his quarters made it convenient to eliminate that space. Karl liked this arrangement, thinking that having two cabins wastes valuable space. Entering the bridge, they were again surprised at all the latest equipment and the functional layout. "Gentlemen, the department heads will join us momentarily, so please look around the bridge while I call for some tea and coffee to be delivered."

Like schoolboys, they examined the new equipment, especially the new Marconi radar system. To one side of the bridge, in an open alcove, Karl and Arnold were favorably impressed by how neatly arranged the radio instrumentation had been laid out. Eliminating the bulkhead wall made conveying commands and radio messages much easier, and the added space provided two operator stations instead of the traditional single station. The bridge door opened, and in walked the department heads, eager to meet their senior officers.

Angus cheerfully announced the new captain, first officer, and chief engineer, then introduced the department leaders by name and department. Over the next ninety minutes, the conversation was spirited, everyone adding to the free-flowing discussion.

Feeling comfortable with how the group was finding common ground so quickly, Angus decided he would leave them by loudly announcing, "Gentlemen, I believe my job of making the introductions has gone splendidly, so I will take my leave unless there is an objection to me doing so? Your third officer, John Richardson, has been on board long enough to know his way around the Spirit, so I'll leave you in his capable hands." Angus had already stayed longer than planned, so bowing out at this point was appropriate.

The third officer thanked Angus for making the introductions, then announced, "Gentlemen, if you're ready, we can commence our tour. Shall we get started?"

Scottie was more interested in the engine room, so he politely said, "With your approval, John, I would prefer to head down to the engine room. I have a lot to cover with these new blokes. Can I take that tour of the ship later?"

Karl smiled at John with a simple nod of his approval. Seeing the eye play, Scottie touched the tip of his cap and followed his engineering officer, Alan Cooke, out through the bridge door.

John, a little confused, waited until Karl spoke. "Well, John, I think it's safe to assume Mr. Adams and I will not abandon you, so lead on, please." The day was flying by as they toured the ship bow to stern. Arriving back in the wardroom, they were more than ready for afternoon tea. "John, you know the ship really well. Let me congratulate you on the amount of information you have. She is really state of the art in maritime design. I can't wait to stretch her legs," remarked Karl, pouring a large mug of tea. "What are your thoughts, Number One? Did we make a good choice signing on with the Spirit?"

Grinning from ear to ear, Arnold replied, "This is pure luxury, Skipper. She is so beautifully designed. Shall I call down for Scottie to join us?" Karl nodded in agreement.

"Gentlemen, while we wait, please excuse me; I have a call to make from my cabin." Looking at his watch, Karl knew Claire and her sister would be home, preparing the children's supper.

In his cabin, he dialed his home number. Hearing it ring, he smiled, waiting for Claire to answer. At the house, the phone rang; Karl visualized Claire walking over to the kitchen wall phone and answering, "Hitchin 4567, who's calling, please?" knowing it could only be Karl.

"Claire, my adorable English Fraulein, I miss that sweet voice. How is everything at home, love? And how are our two rascals behaving themselves? I hope they are?" asked Karl, knowing once Claire started telling him all the news, he was better off just listening.

Sure enough, Claire spared no detail, giving him an update on David's new position as project engineer. He is taking an early exit from his present position, so he will be driving here in two weeks just in time to arrange their furniture at the bungalow. "Everything is working out so well for them. Caroline found out earlier today that she has been offered a research position at the Kaiser Bondor in Baldock. Karl, have you heard from Bill? He is such a workaholic. I wish he would listen to me about cutting back."

Karl, hearing this, replied, "Let me talk to him. He's still in military mode. By the way, Claire, if you're wondering about the new ship, well, let me put it this way: I always thought the Tristian was one notch above most merchant ships. This new Spirit is so much more than I could hope for. We should be on schedule for our first sea trial in a couple of weeks. This greyhound, I think, is going to surprise us all. Claire, have you heard from Frieda or Mama? I hope you're sending my apologies when you write them. You know how my schedule leaves very little time for writing letters."

Karl was feeling guilty at his lack of staying in touch. "Must go, Claire; the lads are waiting for me in the wardroom. Please, kiss the children, and this next kiss is only for you. Be creative by putting it anywhere you please!" Karl laughed as he said that.

"Well, darling, that's an easy one to imagine. Good night, my world traveler." The phone receiver went dead. Still holding the receiver close to his ear, Karl thought about how he had changed from that carefree sailor to the new Karl who preferred being home with his family. Within six months or so, this chapter in his life would come to an end. The sea would always remain close to his heart, but that's where it would stay a lifelong memory.

Looking at his LeCoultre watch, he smiled, remembering that Christmas so long ago when the family had given him this watch as a Christmas present. Sadly, that holiday would always be associated with his first fiancée, Lieutenant Kitty Johnson, who sadly lost her life. Shaking his head, he redirected his thoughts; better get going before they come looking for me.

The weeks flew by, the crew working with the builder's staff, making last minute changes prior to tomorrow's big day and the initial sea trials, followed soon thereafter by the first voyage of the Spirit of Clyde Side. The quiet of dawn was broken by the sounds of the ship's many systems coming alive. On the horizon, the day was sunny with a chill in the air, typical for this time of year, perfect conditions, though, to take out the new ship. A blue gray stream of smoke curling away from the funnel announced that the main engines were running; a slight tremor could be felt through the deck plates, which sent a clear signal that the Spirit was coming alive. The engines had been run up frequently, but today, they would run in preparation for the first annunciator signal from the bridge.

Karl called down to the engine room, "Chief, it looks like we're ready for the trials. How are the generators working? Check them one more time; we must be sure the refrigerator compartments are remaining at their set point. Also, have your chaps check to see that leak we found was taken care of. Sparks, fire up your radio gear; send a message to the Clyde Princess, wishing them a successful trip to Boston and Halifax. Once they respond, will you let me know the clarity and signal strength?

Officer of the Deck, exercise all the navigation equipment. Even though the radar will have harbor clutter, we need to know there are no glitches, then stand by."

Karl, in his element, strutted back and forth across the bridge. The bridge was besieged with representatives from the builders, the United Maritime Shipping Company, Ltd., and representatives for the Clyde Shipping Company. Karl was becoming irritated with people getting in the way as the bridge crew prepared for maneuvering.

"Mr. Richardson, are your deck gangs in position? If so, would you clear the bridge of nonessential personnel? With my apologies, of course. Mr. Adams are you ready to take her out?" asked Karl, holding back his own excitement.

"Ready and awaiting your command, Sir," came the response from his equally excited first officer.

"Very well, Number One, proceed. Let's show everyone what a first-class crew we have aboard this beautiful new ship, shall we?"

Arnold issued his first command, "Helmsman, make your helm twenty degrees left rudder and stand by; Mr. Richardson, proceed with clearing the mooring lines."

"Aye, aye, Sir." Like a well-rehearsed team member, John walked out onto the starboard wing deck, carrying his shiny new bull horn. Loudly, he instructed the stern maneuvering gang to single up on the heavy mooring lines, then, yelling into the bull horn again, instructed the gang stationed at the bow to do the same. His next command was to let go the forward spring lines. Inside the bridge, Adams ordered the port engine to remain idle before the command was made to make revolutions for two knots on the starboard engine, followed by a single blast of the ship's horn to release all remaining mooring lines. That blast also signaled the two forward tugs and the single tug positioned at the stern to commence pushing the big ship away from the dock and out into the center of the harbor.

Ships throughout the harbor commenced a crescendo of good luck and congratulations, blasting their ships' horns. The Spirit replied with numerous blasts of thanks. The three tugs now took up stations, waiting for a sign that the Spirit was getting underway. Slowly, the Spirit's two massive Perkins engines turned both propellers, kicking up the dirty waters of the harbor.

"Sparks, make to the tugs for them to take up stations on either side of the bow." The sailor stationed at the annunciator waited patiently for the order to ring down the order to start forward movement.

"Mr. Auburn, make shaft revolutions for slow ahead both until we clear the harbor entrance, then all ahead one third once we have passed the outer markers."

The first officer now turned his attention to his captain, asking, "Your instructions, if you please, Sir?" He was beaming from ear to ear.

"Nice going, Number One; you and Mr. Richardson are making my duty as captain so very enjoyable." Karl stood in front of the bridge's center window, his binoculars around his neck. He looked out toward the bow; in those fleeting moments when he had time to relax his mind, he thought back to taking his beloved Tristian out to sea as a junior officer for the very first time. His last thought was; I wonder if she survived the war.

Standing quietly at the rear of the bridge, Commodore James McGinley observed how Captain Vita and his officers firmly guided their new ship out to sea to commence the many maneuvers needed to prove the seaworthiness of the Spirit. Karl, his clipboard in hand, stood without expression, watching the land slip away astern. Loudly, without warning, he yelled, "Starboard engine full ahead; port engine reverse one third; Helmsman, right full rudder." Reaching for the PA, he announced that emergency maneuvering had commenced and asked everyone to please grasp something firmly attached to the ship.

The Spirit of Clyde Side violently shuddered as she resisted the right full rudder; heeling to starboard, she held her heading until Karl yelled, "Helm amidships, reverse starboard engine to one third." Karl stood firm, his eyes fixed on the ship's compass. A few moments passed as the ship, in reverse, threw up a wall of saltwater, frothing angrily at her stern. "Mr. Arnold, all ahead full both engines, if you please. I would like to witness the maximum speed listed on this clipboard."

The bridge door flew open, and in walked the very angry general manager, Mr. Reginald Dooly, of the United Maritime Shipping company. "Captain Vita, I must object to these violent maneuvers you are subjecting this brand-new ship to. Many of its systems are still untried; now, let's continue with the schedule on your clipboard."

Looking up at this tall figure of a man, Karl waited until his anger was under control before replying, "With your permission, Commodore McGinley, I will address this intrusion of our extreme maneuvers trials." Karl had turned to face Jim, and his facial expressions told Karl what he needed to know. "Mr. Dooly, let me first compliment you on building a very strong ship; an older ship would have failed that maneuver, but the Spirit did exactly what I expected. What I didn't expect was to have you barge onto my bridge, mouthing off and telling me how to handle my command. During the build, all those systems should have been rung out completely and, therefore, able to handle those violent commands I issued. My job, for my employer, is to make sure this grand lady will not come apart should we find ourselves in a force ten gale. I can assure you, Sir, the safety of this crew comes before your barking criticism on calm seas such as today. If you believe I'm out of line, then I would suggest you ask my superior behind me, Commodore McGinley, to relieve me of this command." Karl stopped short of screaming louder at this arrogant landlubber. "Commodore McGinley, I'm prepared to stand down if so ordered by you, Sir?" Karl felt his legs trembling with anger as he waited for Jim's response.

"Reginald, old man, I must request you leave the bridge immediately; please, no more disruptions. Captain Vita is doing exactly what he should be doing: to see if this beautiful ship will be strong enough to weather the worst sea conditions and keep his crew from drowning. I will submit to my management a report on this episode. I have spent many years sailing ships and have commissioned a few new ones, and I can assure you, Captain Vita has been given the task of finding the weak points on the ship. Any captain worth his salt would perform similar maneuvers. Look, I know you're new to the shipping business, and this is your first sea trial. Believe me; we call them trials for a reason. Now, unless you have any further remarks to make to Captain Vita, please leave this bridge. Captain Vita, continue with your schedule; that last maneuver was skillfully executed."

Jim McGinley walked over and spoke to Karl, his mouth close to Karl's ear, saying, "Pity we couldn't throw him overboard. Don't let that bastard get to you; we gave you this ship because you are the best at what you do."

Karl turned to Jim and, with a nod, thanked Jim for standing by him. They performed function tests on all systems for the rest of the day. Later in the day, they trooped down into the very hot engine room. "Scottie, any issues we need to address?" asked Jim.

"Well, that first maneuver made the rudder bearings start to bind up under that pressure, so when we return, I would like them replaced with heavier duty ones and reseated. Can you imagine if that would have happened in a really bad storm? In addition, Captain, the starboard shaft lubrication gland could not supply enough coolant when we were at maximum RPMs; opening the orifice should take care of that nicely. Other than that, I'm satisfied we will be in good shape for our maiden voyage," concluded Scottie. By late afternoon, Karl made the call to return to the shipyard, his clipboard of testing requirements covered in notes for later review.

With the ship secured, Jim invited all the guests to join the ship's officers in the passenger's lounge for light refreshments and well deserved cocktails. Karl and his officers mingled with company executives and the builder's upper management. The conversation was spirited, with many comments on that first maneuver.

"Excuse me, Captain; may I have a word with Commodore McGinley and yourself?" asked a sheepish Reginald Dooly.

Jim responded before Karl could answer. "Of course, Mr. Dooly, why don't we take that table by that porthole? It will give us a little more privacy. Still with a stern look on his face, Karl placed his glass of Champagne in front of him, both hands at its base. Looking at Karl's face, Jim jumped in with some diplomatic small talk, then asked, "Mr. Dooly, I'm assuming we are here to discuss the incident on the bridge, correct?"

Reginald Dooly, taking a slug of whiskey, replied, "Captain Vita, I owe you an apology, and thank you, Commodore, for stepping in to defuse my heated abuse of your captain. Gentlemen, as you know, I'm somewhat new to shipbuilding. This was the first time I had been exposed to a sea trial. I never imagined or considered why a new ship would be put through such severe maneuvers. What I did was inexcusable and not like me in any way; will you accept my apology? Hopefully, we can make a new start right here and now." Reginald extended his hand toward Karl, still sitting without movement or emotion. Jim looked at Karl silently, hoping Karl would accept the apology and the hand of friendship.

"Apology accepted, Reginald; maybe another captain would have preferred to throw you overboard! All kidding aside, I'm assuming you now understand the importance of pushing a ship to its limits. Today, we had calm seas, so simulating severe conditions could only be achieved by that maneuver. Shall we return to the others unless the commodore has something more he wishes to add?" Karl stood up first, a confident smile on his face, followed by Jim and Reginald. They returned to the party, feeling better that a festering confrontation had been avoided.

# CHAPTER 16

# CLAIRE IN SOUTHAMPTON

It had been almost three weeks since the sea trials. Karl and his crew were feverishly completing the final preparations before departing on the Spirit of Clyde Side's maiden voyage, and the mood throughout the ship was charged with excitement. Karl and first officer Arnold Adams had spent most of the previous day at a meeting held at the company's main offices, going over last minute details such as the final manifest, projected fuel requirements, and the passenger list, which might change with each leg they would make.

"Well, Jim, I believe the crew is about as ready as they'll ever be," said Karl, aware of the strange silence displayed by those in the meeting. "Making that first stop in Southampton came as a surprise. However, the revised orders you just described are really a shock. Until this morning, we assumed we would be heading directly south to the River Plate and Montevideo, Uruguay," remarked Karl, irritated at this last-minute change.

Pulling two binders from his desk drawer, Jim responded by saying, "Unfortunately, these orders were only shared with me last night. Your revised itinerary, Captain, will be to load arms and military personnel in Southampton before making the long trek to Busan, South Korea."

Arnold displayed his objection by saying, "South Korea?" Surprise was written all over his face.

Jim's response to that remark was, "Your ship has the largest cargo capacity in the fleet, and those refrigerated holds are the largest of all our ships. Believe me; they will be at full capacity with food supplies when you depart Southampton. In addition, eight senior military personnel will also be boarding in Southampton."

The company's fleet loadmaster asked them to turn to the page in the manifest that referred to the cargo. "Commander Adams, your concerns are well taken. Things are heating up faster than we expected. A little more than a week ago, we received a ship requisition for a priority shipment, further detailed in that route sheet in front of you. The Spirit is the only ship in our fleet that can accommodate the Ministry of Defense's requisition. Her capacity and speed make her the logical choice," concluded the loadmaster.

"Number One, what do our orders say about a departure date?" asked Karl, opening his binder of documents and removing the folder labeled Montevideo. "I'm assuming this folder has no further validity; is that correct?" Karl placed the folder directly in front of Jim McGinley.

"Captain Vita, once you have unloaded in Busan, your orders are to proceed in ballast to Darwin, Australia, to refuel and load a cargo of frozen lamb. Then, Captain, you can head home to England, unloading your cargo in Southampton before heading North to Glasgow. Any additional questions? The binder I just gave your first officer is the same as the one I'm giving you now. The level of security prevented us from giving it to you any sooner. Captain, you will rendezvous with the destroyer HMS Albion upon entering the Yellow Sea off the island of Jeungdo. All going to plan, that will be in approximately twenty-nine days with the right conditions; that time could be dramatically reduced, plus a refueling stop in Singapore, from the time you depart Southampton. Those details are also in that binder.

"Captain Vita, we are experiencing an increase in Chinese activity in the Yellow Sea. The navy has mandated that a Royal Navy warship escort any English merchant ship. It is essential we protect our merchant assets in the region, both in and out of the danger zone." Jim did not wish to add more at this juncture other than the fact that there had not been an attack on any Allied shipping to date, although the probability of such an aerial attack could happen at any time.

"Thank you, Commodore. It's not like we haven't been in similar situations during the last war, correct, Mr. Adams?"

Arnold, looking at Jim, simply replied, "That is correct, Captain."

"Gentlemen, we are truly sorry for springing this on you like this. Believe me; it was never our intention to surprise you in this manner," answered Jim sheepishly, reading the expressions on Karl and Arnold's faces. "Chaps, I'm truly sorry in advance for adding one additional piece of business, which I was just made aware of a few hours ago. The chief executive officer, the president, the chief financial officer, and I will board the Spirit for that first leg down to Southampton. Please, have the steward prepare those guest cabins." Jim concluded by standing, facing Karl and Arnold, saying, "Until later, then."

The meeting ended abruptly, Jim shaking Karl's and Arnold's hands, "Again, my deepest apologies for dropping these changes on you like this. Believe me, it was not my idea or doing. My wife is still rattled to hear I was not going to be home for those few days with no advance notice. Bye for now." Jim walked with them to the main lobby, then, with a smile, headed back to his office.

The drive back to the ship was solemn, neither conveying their thoughts too well until Arnold said, "Well, Skipper, no one said a sailor's life is always blue skies and calm seas, did they?" That broke the tension, and they both laughed loudly.

Back on board, they immediately met with the ship's officers, updating them on the revised itinerary and the guests arriving later that evening. "Number One, make ready for a 0700-hour departure. File that with the port authorities if you please. I think only two tugs will be required, so I will retire to my cabin if we have no further business. See you chaps later in the wardroom," concluded Karl. In the privacy of his cabin, he studied the entire binder and other confidential directives for his eyes only. Closing the binder, he locked it in the small wall safe. Karl sat at his desk, thinking, if we are scheduled for two or three days in Southampton, that's a doable drive from Hitchin.

I wonder if Claire would be interested in driving down to spend some time with me before we depart. I think I'm going to give her a call right now. Picking up the landline telephone, he made the call, receiving an immediate response that made his heartbeat faster; he heard his wife's voice saying, "Hitchin 4567, who's calling, please?"

Claire, saying that, knew it would be her husband. He always called before leaving the dock. "Claire, it's your homesick husband. Throw him a big wet kiss!"

Claire was thrilled at hearing him talk like this, knowing he would always say that if he had good news to share with her. "Claire, we set sail tomorrow at 7:00 a.m., first stop Southampton to load cargo and fuel. Claire, I have no right to ask you this, but any chance you could drive down to see me before I leave? It would mean the world to me."

Karl was cut short by Claire with an immediate response, "Give me the details and your arrival time. I'll leave on the first train tomorrow morning. I will have Bev book me a hotel close by. Karl, I know seeing the children would mean the world to you, but darling, it would be too much for them. When I hang up with you, I'll call Sheila to see if she will take care of them for a few days; sorry, darling." Claire could sense his excitement at seeing her, as well as the disappointment at not seeing their children.

"Darling, call me with your hotel information. I can't wait; this is such a bonus. Hugs and kisses to the kids, and a special kiss for you. See you in Southampton." Hanging up the phone, Karl put his jacket back on. Walking out onto the empty bridge, he gazed at all the instruments and equipment. Placing his hand on the varnished wooden ship's helm, his thoughts drifted to how his family in Vienna was coping, thinking that he felt a pang of guilt for not staying in touch more often. In a flash, he knew what he had to do before the landline was disconnected.

Spinning on his heel, he headed back to his cabin to place a call to his mother in Vienna. With luck, he would find her at home. International calls had to be placed through the company's switchboard operator. "Go ahead, Captain Vita; your party is on hold."

Brenda had made the call. Not understanding German, she asked in English, "Good afternoon; I have Captain Vita holding for Mrs. Vita; is she available?"

She was surprised at an immediate answer in English. "Go ahead, Mrs. Vita; you have Captain Vita holding for you; thank you."

Mama could not believe her youngest son was calling only minutes after she had gotten off the phone with her daughter-in-law, Claire. "Karl, this is so wonderful to hear from you, only minutes after Claire called. It must be my lucky day. Claire mentioned you were taking your new ship to Southampton tomorrow morning. She was so excited to be able to see you on the spur of the moment like this. You must be so happy, knowing you will have that opportunity." Karl and his mother spoke for about forty minutes before Karl forced himself to say goodbye. Mama, with a heavy heart, wished him a safe voyage.

In the wardroom, Karl joined his officers, Arnold making space for his captain. "Sir, I was waiting for you to finish your phone call to tell you our guests will arrive in about an hour. We have been asked to join them tomorrow evening for dinner, and if it's not too late this evening, cocktails in the guest lounge at 1830 hours. Commodore McGinley was calling for you. I took the liberty of answering for you. Once again, he apologized for these last-minute decisions on this maiden voyage."

As early evening set in, Karl and Arnold stood at the head of the boarding ramp as two company Armstrong Sidley cars approached the dock. "Here we go, old man," said Arnold, receiving a chuckle from his captain. One by one, the two officers welcomed their passengers. The steward stood, waiting to direct the seamen carrying the luggage to their staterooms.

"May I suggest we get settled in, then meet up for light refreshments and cocktails? I think you suggested 1830 hours, did you not, Mr. Adams?" asked Commodore McGinley.

Karl replied, "Excellent, we are looking forward to this evening. Tomorrow, while we are underway, Mr. Adams will guide you on an extensive tour of your wonderful new vessel." Promptly at the requested hour, Karl, his first officer, and engineering officer waited to entertain the directors of the Clyde Shipping Company.

"Here we are," said Jim as he entered the lounge. Karl stepped forward, introducing his officers to the company directors.

"Gentlemen, welcome to the Spirit. I hope your accommodations are up to your expectations. This informal get together is perfect, as it gives my officers time to mingle with the steering members of this company. Commodore, I understand she is the first new ship to enter the fleet since before the war, is that correct?" asked Karl.

"It most certainly is, Captain," replied Jim. "If I may have your attention for just a few minutes, I'd like to explain my relationship with Captain Vita. Back in 1936, while dockside in Ostend, Belgium, I was approached by the harbor master to allow a fellow maritime officer, previously with the Langstaff Shipping Company, and members of his family escaping to England from Vienna, Austria to be granted passage on my ship to England, leaving the life they had until they boarded the Clyde Princess.

That officer stands before you today as the first captain of this ship. Let me also add, up until recently, he was also the captain of my favorite ship, the Clyde Princess. Please, join me in toasting our own courageous sailor, Captain Karl Vita."

Karl stood humbled by the accolades being showered upon him. "Commodore, I am humbled by your introduction, but please, I must add, with your permission, a brief introduction for these two officers standing quietly by my side. They are not only heroes and survivors of the evacuation of Dunkirk but lifelong friends to whom I owe my life. When the ship I was in command of was attacked by German aircraft off the beaches of Dunkirk, in those hellish moments, I was mortally injured and remained unconscious for several days. These two officers took control of the sinking HMT Reese, saving my life and those of the remaining crew. Your new ship could not be in better hands. Please, raise those glasses once again as I thank them for allowing me to badger them out of retirement to join me on this new vessel. To both of you, my eternal gratitude." To their surprise, these three officers enjoyed mingling with the company directors until the gathering ended at 1930 hours.

"I think we should get a good night's sleep; what do you say, chaps? Tomorrow will be very busy; good night, all," said Karl, shaking everyone's hands before they headed to their cabins.

The dark of night slowly and reluctantly gave way to a cloudy, gray morning. At their stations, the crew of the Spirit waited for the commands that would take the Spirit out of the builder's yard that gave her life. It would be more than three years before she returned for maintenance. Standing by the helm with his old reliable binoculars around his head, Karl watched as the ship cleared the outer markers. Karl issued his next command, "Number One, ring up revolutions for ten knots and maintain the current heading until we turn into open waters, then increase revolutions for sixteen knots, followed by the course correction."

Arnold answered, "Aye, aye, Sir."

Karl walked over to the navigation station, asking, "Mr. Phillips, can you update me on an estimated arrival time in Southampton?" John Phillips had transferred from the Northern Lights, tickled pink he would be the first navigation officer of the Spirit.

"Let me plot that, Sir, and get you that approximate arrival time. Will you be remaining on the bridge?" asked Phillips.

"Yes, I think so; well, until our live cargo gets up, anyway." The crew on the bridge quietly laughed at their captain's last sarcastic remark. About thirty minutes later, a sailor entered the bridge to inform Karl the guests had gathered in the passenger's lounge for breakfast.

"Morning, Sir; the commodore sends his compliments and asks you to join the company directors and himself in the guest lounge."

Karl turned to address the sailor. Looking sarcastically at Arnold Adams, he replied, "Thank you; would you please convey my apologies to the commodore that I'm tied up on the bridge and that the first officer will be down shortly?" Karl had a smirk on his face as he replied to the sailor. "Mr. Adams, those guests are all yours; have fun."

Looking at his captain, Arnold replied, "Rank sometimes has privileges, this last order being one of them. Thank you, Captain." Karl enjoyed that last remark. The ship was exceeding Karl's expectations. "Well, chaps, I think we can say our new ship is everything the builders said it would be. At sixteen knots, we still have a healthy reserve of available power to push her comfortably over eighteen knots, which is unusual for this type of merchant ship." As much as he hated the idea, Karl gave in to making an appearance in the guest lounge. "Number Two, you have the con. Maintain course and speed. I should be back in an hour or so." With that, Karl left the bridge.

The day quickly turned to late afternoon. Karl, back on the bridge, was surprised at the navigator's E.T.A. "Sir, if we maintain this speed, making allowances for wind and currents, I have calculated we should be laying off Southampton at 0630 hours in two days. Sir, we are making amazing time; she is really a marvelous ship." That evening, the chef surprised them all by making a dinner fit for a king, amazing Karl, Arnold, and the company executives. The evening was finished with a glass of vintage port, a gift from the company president.

Two days later, Karl lay half asleep in his bunk; sitting up, he felt the silence of the ship. She wasn't moving, nor were there any vibrations from the propeller shafts. Surely, we cannot be off Southampton yet, or do we have a mechanical problem?

Reaching for the green phone, he called the bridge. "Lindsen, is everything alright? We appear not to be moving," said Karl, reaching for his shirt.

Mark Lindsen, a junior officer, had the watch, answering. "Morning, Captain; before he turned in last night, the navigator told me we should arrive ahead of schedule. In that event, he plotted a position to lay off the Solent until you or Mr. Adams were on the bridge. Presently, we are thirty miles due southwest of Nat Island, off the Isle of Wight.

"That is very good news, Mr. Lindsen; I'll be up in about twenty minutes, thank you." Karl washed and shaved, then after dressing, he headed to the wardroom for some hot coffee and toast before heading to the bridge. Karl opened the bridge deck to find his number one already studying the charts. "Morning, Number One; it looks like we have a beautiful day to enter Southampton. Have you been in contact with the harbor pilot yet?" asked Karl, gulping his coffee.

"Yes, we have, Sir. When we get underway, we are instructed to enter the Solent Port side of Nat Island, then contact them again at marker 4A. Karl was getting excited, knowing he would be with his wife within a few hours.

The bridge door opened once again, and in walked Commodore McGinley. With a big smile, he announced, "Morning, all; thank God we are not in a race with the Clyde Princess because she would have lost for sure. This ship is very quick! Captain, our guests are having breakfast. I have explained that your wife will be waiting for you when we dock. I would suggest you say your goodbyes while they are in the lounge. Mr. Adams and I will take care of securing the ship, so off you go."

Karl, returning a casual salute, moved toward the door. Doing so, he thought about when and where he would tell and deliver his letter of resignation to Commodore McGivern. "Excuse me, Commodore; may I have a few minutes of your time while we are underway?"

Jim replied, "Of course, can we talk here, or would you prefer a little more privacy?" Karl suggested that his quarters were close, so they should talk there. In the cabin, Karl sat at his desk, Jim taking a seat on the adjacent couch. "Karl, what's on your mind? You look a little uptight," said Jim, becoming somewhat suspicious.

"Jim, you and I have a history and a friendship that is very close, so what I'm about to tell you is not easy for me, but this may be the ideal time to tell you of my decision to resign from the maritime service, effective at the end of this contract." Handing Jim an envelope, he waited while Jim read its contents.

Jim nodded as he slid the letter back into the envelope. "Karl, am I disappointed by reading this? No, I'm not more like saddened at losing a first class captain. Look, I know trying to talk you out of this would be pointless; your mind is made up. I wish it could have been later instead of on this maiden voyage. I know how you are once your mind is made up. Is this why you were so adamant about having Arnold?

Adams join you as your first officer on this long voyage. Quite honestly, I suspected your motives when you first brought him to my attention. He's a fine officer and will be an excellent captain for the Spirit. I may run into a few complaints from other captains who have been with the company a long time and believe seniority should be considered, but I think it will work out fine in the end." Jim stopped, waiting for Karl to answer him.

"Jim, I have agonized over this. I wasn't quite sure if I should wait until after we returned to Glasgow or tell you before we headed out on this first voyage. By telling you now, it will give you two to three months to build a case for Arnold to assume command. Why am I doing this now? Well, I have a wonderful wife and two adorable children. I need to be there for them, watching them grow up and perhaps influencing their direction in life. Jim, I also feel very guilty about my timing. It's like I'm letting you down."

Jim stood and moved in front of Karl; he put his hand on Karl's shoulder, saying, "Nonsense, I was the one who asked you to ring out this ship, and what a first-class job you and your crew have done. If you don't mind, I would like to keep this between us until you return, that way I can have my plan honed and ready. Is that all right with you, Karl? Would you mind taking over the watch and ask Arnold to meet me here, in your quarters? He needs to be aware of this meeting and my endorsement for him to assume command."

Karl shook Jim's hand and felt relieved that he had made the difficult decision to inform his superior, Commodore McGinley. Back on the bridge, Karl announced he was assuming the watch, then quietly said to Arnold, "The commodore would like to meet you in my quarters." Then he said out loud, "Officer of the Deck, please give me our current position and how long until we rendezvous with the pilot boat." Karl smiled, feeling the relief of making his intentions clear. "Make turns for three knots; I have the pilot boat in sight," ordered Karl. The bridge door opened, and in walked Arnold and Jim, smiling as they watched Karl.

"Gentlemen, just in time to witness the Spirit's first docking in Southampton. I'll take her in, Number One, if you conduct the maneuvering."

Arnold responded, "Aye, aye, Captain." With a beaming smile, Arnold walked out onto the wing deck.

Jim approached Karl and, in a whisper, said, "All is well, Captain. Safe travels on this, your last voyage." After saying that, the commodore left the bridge.

With the ship secure, Karl said his goodbyes, then waited for the boarding ramp to be connected. From the building opposite the dock, Karl noticed his wife walking out toward the ramp, receiving numerous whistles from the dock workers as she passed. Waving madly, Karl, half running, moved down the ramp before the lines were totally secured. He closed the distance to Claire in seconds, yelling, "Claire, this is more than I could hope for."

Immaculately dressed, Claire knew what to expect as Karl swung her off her feet and, as usual, pushed her skirt high up her legs. Sailors, being sailors, started whistling and yelling at this show from their captain and his wife. "Darling, you always do this. What on earth do you think those sailors are thinking?" Claire laughed as she said that.

"Excuse me, Captain; can we meet your wife before we depart back to Glasgow?" asked Jim, accompanied by the company officers.

"Of course, Commodore. Will you make the introductions?" Claire, the ever-confident wife and solicitor, shook hands and conversed with the directors until Jim interjected, "Gentlemen, we really should be heading to the station. We don't want to miss our train, do we?" One by one, the directors thanked Karl and his First Officer Arnold Adams for an enjoyable trip from Glasgow. Arnold had joined them dockside to make his farewells and meet Claire as well. With a last wave, they walked over to the small coach that would take them all to the station. Being the last to leave, Jim kissed Claire on the cheek, saying, "My dear, we are so fortunate to have these two officers working for the company." With a smile and a wink to Karl, he walked over to board the coach.

With her arm looped through Karl's, Claire made a final wave to the coach as it drove down to the dock entrance. "Darling, what a nice bunch of chaps your bosses are; wouldn't you agree, Arnold?"

Arnold, nodding his head, asked Claire, "Wouldn't you like a tour of our new ship? Captain, with your permission, of course?" Karl was grinning from ear to ear.

"Lead on, Arnold; I believe the third officer has the loading under control. The commodore advised me to expect our passengers later this afternoon. Once we have made the tour, I would like to take my wife out to lunch, as it's going to be a few months until we see each other again. I hope you understand, Arnold?"

Arnold nodded his approval saying, "By all means, Karl! Take the rest of the day off. Claire, what time does your train leave today?"

Claire realized they only had until 4:00 p.m. to be alone. Claire enjoyed the tour, getting whistles in a few places as she climbed down the steep ladders. Laughing, she enjoyed the attention and the show she was giving the sailors, regardless of the captain's presence. The time was approaching 11:30 a.m. Karl looked at his watch and thanked Arnold, then said to Claire, "Well, lady, now that you have rattled my crew, shall we go ashore and take advantage of what time we have before I take you to the train station?"

On the deck, Claire shook hands with the officers gathered around to say goodbye. Walking arm in arm down the dock, Karl was on a cloud of happiness, having a few brief hours alone with his wife. "Darling, I extended the checkout time until 3:15 p.m. That gives us a few hours to be alone. Let's get a late breakfast before we make use of that hotel room; how does that sound to you?" Claire squeezed Karl's arm as she said that.

The hotel was an older structure from the late eighteen hundred, and it had gone through a major renovation after the war. Inside, the lobby and lounge area were tastefully decorated, and two small lifts had been added as part of the upgrade. They ate breakfast quickly, then went up the stairs to the room. Claire removed the room key with its big wooden tag attached. Laughing, she said, "No way I can lose this bloody thing. Come on, lover boy, let's see how soft that mattress is, shall we?" Claire was not wasting any time; 3:15 p.m. would come all too soon. The room was larger than Karl expected; many older hotels made provisions for a sitting area in their better rooms.

"Very nice, darling; thank Bev for me when you get home, will you?" Before Karl could remove his jacket, Claire wrapped her arms around his neck, kissing him like there was no tomorrow, simultaneously pulling at the sleeve of his jacket. "Steady, old girl, this jacket has got to last me for at least the next six months," said Karl as he cupped her left breast, still restrained under her blouse. "Darling, let's get comfortable, shall we, before starting anything?" asked Karl.

Claire agreed; crossing to the couch, she took off her blouse and skirt, then turning, she returned to her husband. "Let me help you, Sailor, shall I?" Kneeling in front of him, she untied his shoelaces, removing his shoes and socks. Slowly and deliberately, she moved up to his belt, then unbuttoned his trousers, breathing much faster as she helped him undress, feeling like this was a gift she would not waste. Looking up, she kissed his naked thigh, saying, "Darling, how I miss having you alone like this. Please, don't tease me like you always do. Make love to me; it's got to last me a long time."

Karl lifted her, carrying her to the bed and laying her down carefully. Watching her breathing heavily, he thought, God, she is a beautiful woman, and she is all mine. With that, he laid between her waiting thighs. Both spent, they lay in each other's arms, saying very little until Claire asked, "How long will it take to reach Montevideo?" It was like an electric shock; she had asked Karl the question he was trying to hide from her.

"Claire, we are not going to Montevideo. Our orders have changed. Unfortunately, I cannot tell you more, as it is top secret, but don't concern yourself, darling. We are only delivering some passengers and their cargo; then we sail to Northern Australia to load a cargo of frozen lamb. Then, my love, we sail for home and into my retirement." Karl was skirting the prospect of being attacked by hostile aircraft. Karl looked at his watch, feeling the tension building. It was almost 1430 hours. "Claire, how far is the train station from here? Should we be thinking of leaving soon?" Karl looked at his wife cuddled close to him, her arms firmly around his waist. Claire sat up, reaching for her bra. Karl bent over her, kissing her breasts one last time. It would be a long time before he could lay his head between them once more.

At the station, Karl paid the taxi driver before picking up Claire's overnight case, then with his arm around her waist, they walked up the ramp to the ticket booth. Claire presented her return ticket, receiving the platform number from the clerk.

They walked arm in arm, saddened that it was almost time to say goodbye again. "Karl, this is the part I hate. It reminds me of all those times we only had a few days together, but this time, it's me leaving. At least we had today before you leave to, where did you say?"

Karl, smiling and kissing her cheek thought, I knew she would try to trick me into telling her where we were heading. If she only knew. The public address announced that the train for Victoria Station was boarding, "All aboard, please."

Claire, hearing this, wrapped her arms around Karl, tears flowing freely. It was time to part. "Claire, write to me often. I will do the same when possible. I will try to phone you, but I'm not sure of the frequency. I will call once we land. Claire, I love you and our little terrors so very much; now, let's get you into that carriage, shall we?" Kissing her once again, he helped her climb into the compartment, giving her backside a love tap.

"Karl Vita, you're embarrassing me again. You will pay for that, Sailor, when you get back home." Leaning out the compartment window, Claire reached down to kiss her husband one last time as the train lurched forward, blowing its whistle.

Karl walked alongside until the gathering speed made him release his wife's hand. "Claire, will you marry me again when I get back?"

Claire, hearing this, threw him a kiss, yelling back, "Every week, if you like." Karl stood there, waving until the train was speeding out of the station toward London. Walking back, he felt very much alone. He thought this is how Claire must have felt each time she saw me off at the Hitchin Station.

# Destination Busan, South Korea

The Spirit had been tied up in Southampton for three days. They would leave on the afternoon tide, fully loaded and much lower in the water. Karl, as the ship's captain, welcomed the army officers aboard. Other than that brief interface, they kept mainly to themselves. Karl and his officers had met earlier in the morning to go over the final details for the long voyage to South Korea. Instead of joining the others for lunch, Karl, alone in his quarters, made his last call to Claire before the landline was disconnected. He called the office, Beverly connecting him to his wife.

"Darling, I just wanted to say goodbye before we cast off in a few hours. All going well, I should be able to call you in a few weeks. Claire, I miss you so very much; these next few months are going to be torture. Throw me a kiss, you good looking woman."

Claire replied, "That's good; no looking at those Asian women, Mr. Vita. Your English wife knows that look of yours." Karl, quietly laughing, knew his wife, the solicitor, had figured out his destination by that last remark.

"Claire, kiss the children for me. Always tell them that their papa will be coming home soon. Must go, darling; it's a busy day. All my love. I'll write you when we make our next stop." Hanging up the phone, Karl returned to the bridge.

"Mr. Adams, I'm assuming the watch. The port authorities have cleared us for departure, is that correct?"

"Yes, Sir. We will have tugs alongside in about thirty minutes," replied the first officer.

Calling down the voice tube, Karl asked, "Scottie, are your engines ready?"

Scottie replied, "Awaiting your orders, Captain."

"Mr. Phillips, let's review the course notes one more time before we cast off our lines, shall we? Adams and Duncan, please join me over here." Karl was once again exercising his authority as captain.

"Tugs coming alongside, Sir," called Adams.

Karl moved out to the wing deck, instructing Adams, "The ship is yours, Mr. Adams. Proceed with maneuvering, if you please." An hour later, under her own power, the Spirit was underway, heading down the Solent Estuary toward the Isle of Wight. Following the channel, the two tugs escorted them out into the open waters. With a long blast from their horns, the tugs peeled off, returning to Southampton. Passing the last channel marker, the Spirit made its first course correction out into the North Atlantic. This first leg would take them south through the Bay of Biscay toward the Straits of Gibraltar. The weather conditions remained warm, with clear skies as they entered the Mediterranean, then southerly toward the entrance to the Suez Canal. Clearing the canal, they entered the Indian Ocean. The sea conditions were lumpy; the Spirit, however, handled them effortlessly. Scottie informed Karl that a fuel stop in Singapore would not be necessary. However, the cautious captain was thinking ahead. Having full fuel bunkers would be the prudent thing to do. So, refueling in the very hot port city of Singapore would be his instructions.

Once the ship was secured, Karl and Arnold went ashore to visit the agent for the Clyde Shipping Company. Their main concern was the present conditions in the Yellow Sea and any updates for the ship's safety once tied up in Busan, South Korea. Returning to the ship, Karl and Arnold joined their passengers in the lounge, sharing the information they had on and around Busan.

"Gentlemen, when we leave Singapore, we will be heading northeast, maintaining approximately one hundred fifty miles abeam of Vietnam and Hong Kong to our port side. In all, we expect to travel twenty-eight hundred miles before docking in Busan. Having already traveled from Southampton, I can only imagine how bored you must be. Take comfort in this; we are on the last leg of this voyage. Perhaps you would like to join me on the bridge tomorrow morning as we depart. I think it might be a welcome change for you all?"

Looking at the faces of these senior army officers, he couldn't help wondering why on earth they didn't fly. There must be some high security stuff in those large crates we are carrying. It makes me recall my time in the Intelligence Service. At 0730 hours, the Spirit departed Singapore, her fuel bunkers completely full. Her new heading was northeast to rendezvous with the Royal Navy destroyer, HMS Albion.

Karl was sitting in his bridge highchair, sipping hot coffee, looking ahead at the small image coming over the horizon.

Sparks announced he had received a signal from HMS Albion, "Captain, HMS Albion requests you maintain course and increase turns for fifteen knots; she will take up her station on our starboard side. Oh, Captain Riley also sends his compliments."

Karl continued to watch the sleek greyhound as it passed astern of them, heeling as she made the sharp turn to take up her escort position on the starboard side of the Spirit. "Sparks, make to Albion. I request a private discussion with Captain Riley.

Notify me when he's on the line if you please." Karl walked to the radio room, waiting until the Albion's captain spoke. "Captain Vita, nice to make your acquaintance. Are you capable of maintaining this speed until we clear the island of Jeungdo on our starboard beam?"

Karl, smiling, could not resist a sarcastic reply, "Captain, we only slowed down so you could keep up with the Spirit." Both captains enjoyed this jovial remark.

"Captain, be advised; we have observed some low flying Chinese Mig-15 fighter jets for the last several days. One buzzed us very low this morning. Now that we are escorting you into Busan, we expect continuous surveillance by these pests, so don't get too alarmed. Our guns are armed and ready should an intruder get too close. We have been on station, escorting merchant ships for the last three weeks. At this point, we look forward to each incident, so we can give those pesty buggers a hand gesture as they fly down our flank. Bye for now, Albion clear."

Karl returned to his bridge chair, then casually updated everyone on the bridge, "The captain of the Albion told me not to get too excited if we see Chinese Migs flying dangerously close to the ship. If that happens, give them a victory salute to piss them off." Laughter erupted from the bridge crew, one sailor suggesting they direct a high pressure hose in their direction. "That would be comical, but perhaps we would be better off ignoring them. No need to start an international incident just yet," replied Karl, thinking that would be a great idea, though.

The Spirit and its escort arrived ten miles off the entrance to Busan Harbor. "Jones, signal Albion we are reducing turns for three knots, awaiting the pilot, and thank them for the escort."

"Aye, aye, Sir, shall I wait for a reply?" asked Jones as he walked to the wing door where the signal lamp was mounted.

Returning, he announced, "Return signal from the Albion, Sir. Once we enter the harbor, they will return to their patrol. When we depart Busan, they will be waiting three miles out."

Hearing this, Karl thought that captain is deliberately being vague, not mentioning dates, of course. We can't be sure who is watching, I suppose. Karl joined the military contingency standing on the deck, looking at the harbor becoming clearer as they closed the distance. The Spirit docked at a long pier, ahead of two other merchant ships unloading their cargoes. "Gentlemen, this is where we say our farewells. I hope you are relaxed, or should I say bored stiff after all that time at sea? We expect to have you dockside in less than thirty minutes. I wish you success and safety while you're here in South Korea," concluded Karl, shaking each officer's hand.

Things were now proceeding very quickly, with large derricks moving alongside, ready to start offloading the guarded cargo from the ship's holds. The last of the cargo was the refrigerated food pallets. By 1900 hours, the holds were empty, and the Spirit was now riding high in the water. Scottie would start the process of ballasting the ship in preparation for departing in the morning. Karl spent the evening writing a long letter to Claire, not mentioning their present location but including their next port of call in Darwin, Australia, to take on a shipment of frozen lamb before commencing the long journey back to England. Sealing his letter, he walked down the boat ramp, heading toward the port office. Powerful searchlights penetrated the fading light as he walked along the dockyard; military patrol boats circled the harbor, searching for intruders wishing to harm the merchant shipping docked there.

Karl started to consider that this conflict would get uglier sooner than later. Right after World War Two, the Russians pushed the Japanese out of the North in 1945. Thank God President Harry Truman declared the 38th parallel as the separation between American and Soviet influences in Korea. It would be referred to as the neutral zone until a formal truce document could be signed, after which it would become known as the Demilitarized Zone (DMZ). This division divided the communist state that would become the Democratic People's Republic of Korea (DPRK) under the leadership of Kim II Sung. South Korea, influenced by the Americans and Western allies, established the Republic of Korea under Syngman Rhee. In 1949, when the Americans and Russians withdrew, the conflict between the North and South intensified with no means of reuniting. In 1950, the North Korean People's Army invaded the South, making rapid progress toward Seoul, overrunning the capital city and remaining there until driven out by a superior force of Allied forces that would become permanent.

Walking back to the ship, he stopped in front of one of the American ships, an old, tired liberty ship designed and built in the hundreds by Henry J. Kaiser and his workforce of over 20,000 ship workers. These welded utility ships revolutionized how ships could be mass produced. Standing there, Karl smiled, thinking when the Yanks have their backs against the wall, they usually come out swinging with new inventions. This old girl is an outcome of one of those inventions; she will more than likely soldier on for years to come.

The following morning, Karl had a quick breakfast, anxious to get his ship underway and back out into the Yellow Sea. "Sparks, make to Albion, will rendezvous with you at the designated time at the appointed coordinates; Spirit out." Clear of the harbor entrance, the two tugs broke off, flashing a parting signal as they headed back into Busan Harbor.

"Captain, the Albion is taking up position on our starboard side." Karl nodded a response as he walked over to Phillips, studying the charts.

"How do we look, Phillips? How many hours until we dispatch HMS Albion?" requested Karl.

"Well, Sir, a lot depends on this depression directly ahead of us. My fears are it will develop into a very ugly tropical storm. I'll update you once I get the next weather transmission in sixty or so minutes." Karl searched Phillips' usually friendly face, now replaced with fear, plotting the forward movement of the tropical storm directly in their path. "Captain, from Albion, she is breaking off and returning to Busan. Her captain suggests we take evasive action by altering our present course to a more easterly route, away from the center of that storm."

Karl motioned to Adams to join him and Phillips at the chart table. "Chaps, let's consider our options now that the HMS Albion is breaking off, shall we? Arnold, share with us your opinion on what you think we should be doing, please? If the Albion is withdrawing, its captain must be worried about being caught out in the open like this. I'm sure you both concur?" asked Karl, his mind already made up.

"Sir, we have delivered our cargo and military personnel, and we are under no time restraints as to when we need to be in Darwin, Australia. So, if you're asking for my opinion, I think we should ring up maximum speed and head directly away from that storm."

"Mr. Phillips, how far off our course do we need to travel to get around this heavy weather?" Karl knew Adams would agree with him about getting their new ship away from the prospect of suffering storm damage. "Good, it sounds like we agree. Helmsman, come left on a new heading of one two zero. Yeoman, ring down to the engine room for maximum revolutions, please.

Sparks, send to Albion, taking your advice. Safe return to your home port; thank you for the escort, Spirit clear."

Shortly after that last request for maximum speed, Scottie entered the bridge, yelling, "Will someone explain to me what the bloody hell is happening?"

Karl beckoned Scottie to join them at the chart table. Once again, he explained the pending danger of the tropical depression. Scottie, paying close attention, shook his head at that course of action. "Permission to speak freely, Sir?" asked Scottie.

"Of course, speak your mind," answered Karl.

"The Spirit can maintain close to twenty knots. For how long, I wouldn't venture to say. My suggestion is to decrease turns for eighteen knots for three to four hours, then come about, reducing speed to a mere five knots. It will be difficult to come about in a driving following sea. That's my suggestion, Sir. This action will give us time to prepare the Spirit and ourselves."

Karl and his officers looked at each other before nodding in agreement. Karl asked, "It looks like we are all in agreement with Scottie, but why wouldn't you try to get as much distance as possible between that storm and this ship?"

Karl called out to the yeoman, standing next to the annunciator, "Yeoman, ring up eighteen knots if you please."

"Thank you, Captain; I knew you would see it my way. With your permission, I would like to lock down as much of the ship as possible while we still can."

Karl was thinking; I always thank God that Scottie is my chief engineer. "Mr. Adams, have the galley prepare as many sandwiches as they can; also, fill those large thermos containers with tea and a small one of coffee for me, and why don't we commence feeding the crew a hot meal in shifts? It's going to be a long night. While doing that, have the stewards stow all loose items in the guest cabins and lock all the port light shutters before locking the cabin doors. Mr. Wriggles, it will be your job to direct the deck gang in securing all deck equipment. Also, ensure the lifeboats are inspected for equipment and supplies, should the need for their use arise. Oh, and have the crew put extra lines over the lifeboat covers. Mr. Wriggles, I know this is only your third cruise, but you are a junior officer, so take that look of fear off your face. You're scaring me." Hearing Karl talk like that broke the tension on the bridge, everyone laughing at the petrified junior officer.

"Mr. Wriggles, this is standard procedure when faced with the prospect of becoming a cork in an angry ocean. We are fortunate we have a very strong ship and a seasoned crew, so be off with you." Karl was trying to make this young man regain his confidence. Even though, as the ship's captain, he was becoming very concerned himself at what lay ahead of them later that day and into the nighttime hours.

The wind continued to pick up as the sky turned dark with menacing, swirling black clouds. The seas continued to build, and everyone on the bridge was strangely quiet, each one visualizing what was stirring not that far away from the Spirit as she continued putting distance between the storm and themselves. "Mr. Phillips, our position, please? The seas astern of us are building faster than we anticipated. If we keep surfing like this, it's going to be difficult to come about," announced Karl.

"Sir, we have covered approximately one hundred twenty miles since our course correction. Now is a good a time as any to make that turn, Sir."

Karl picked up the general intercom and informed the crew of their next action in an authoritative voice he announced. "Attention, this is the captain speaking. As you are aware, we have been running from a very powerful storm astern of us. I am concerned that we are out of time to run any further; therefore, I am ordering a speed reduction to commence a 180 degree turn to port in preparation to ride through those waves head on. Please, brace yourselves as we conduct this maneuver. We don't need any broken bones or cuts at this point. All the off-duty crew, wedge yourselves on the floor, staying out of your bunks, and please, try to relax. Our ship will get us through this, Captain Vita out."

The 180-degree turn was far from easy, heeling the ship as she fought to come about. The wind and waves were slamming into the bow, and the Spirit was making no headway, which was their plan. The daylight was fading fast, increasing the tension throughout the ship.

"Mr. Adams, add additional sailors to assist the helmsman and have relief helmsmen standing by. Those waves are trying to turn us abeam to that breaking sea. Would you also confirm the secondary steering station is manned and ready should we lose the bridge helm?"

Karl held on tightly to the rail, looking forward toward the bow as it reached for the sky before dropping down into the trough between those angry white capped waves. Watching, he was also thinking, this could well be the worst storm I have been in. The hours dragged by as the Spirit yowled and pitched from bow to stern. "Sparks, make to any vessel ahead of us for a weather update. Gentlemen, this is more like a typhoon than a heavy storm." Whistling into the voice tube, Karl called down to Scottie in the engine room, "Scottie, can you talk?"

"I'm here, Captain; no need to worry about us lads down here. We're fine; glad to see we reduced turns for five knots. Our shaft bearings are running hot, but that's to be expected." The constant banging, pitching, and rolling continued throughout the night.

Dawn was breaking, and there were signs that the worst of the storm was starting to diminish, thankfully, behind them. The crew, still at their stations, were worn out and in need of sleep, most still holding tightly to a solid object, silently waiting for normal conditions that would allow them to climb into their bunks.

Looking ahead at the angry sea and solid black clouds, Karl could see a thin line of dark blue expanding between them. "Number One, do you see what I see up ahead?" asked Karl.

"Yes, Sir, I do. That last transmission from the American ship, Tidewater, indicated they were almost back into moderate sea conditions. It won't be long now, Sir."

No sooner had Adams said that when an enormous rogue wave slammed the port bow, sending most of the bridge crew careening across the deck as the Spirit violently rolled to starboard. That wave buried the forward part of the ship as it slammed back into the angry ocean waters, lifting the bow again before it to slammed back down into the deep trough between the cresting waves, sending the stern high out of the water, both propellers thrashing the sea in protest before slamming back into the surf. For a moment, the silence was deafening before crew members struggled back to their feet and returned to their stations.

"Is everyone all right? Do we have any injured? All stations report," yelled Adams over the P.A. In the middle of that announcement, a noticeable tremor from the stern stopped him from saying more.

He turned toward Karl, already whistling and yelling down the voice tube to the engine room, "Engine room, report. What in God's name is happening, Scottie?"

Scottie immediately responded by yelling, "Sir, we have thrown a bearing on the starboard shaft. That side has given us grief since leaving England. I have shut it down and reduced the port shaft to two knots. Will report back once we can assess the damage. With the seas now subsiding, it should make repairs much easier. Although, that last wave would not indicate that, Sir." Scottie was making light of the task ahead of him and his engine room crew.

Karl shook his head, thinking nothing rattles that little Scotsman. Picking up the mike, Karl made a general announcement. "To all hands, this is the captain. That last wave hit us very hard, causing the starboard shaft bearing to fail. There is no need for alarm; the chief engineer assures me they can have it repaired by late morning. The good news is that the storm is pulling away very quickly. We will maintain steerage at two knots or three if needed. During this time, try to relax. One last announcement, the chief engineer is asking for at least six men to handle the chain and tackle needed to lift the shaft out of the lower bearing shoe. I know you are tired, but the sooner they can repair that shaft, the sooner we can get underway again. If you can help, just report to the chief engineer, bridge out."

By 1130 hours, Scottie called the bridge, saying, "Repairs are done, Sir. We'll need to run the shaft at low RPMs for about thirty minutes or so while the new bearing gets seated. By the way, Sir, we have a wonderful crew. I had over ten volunteers manning the hoist. Think you should thank them for working like they did." Scottie was always ready to praise fellow sailors.

"Engine room, Bridge, Sir, I forgot something." Karl answered, "What do you need?"

Scottie answered, "My boys are completely knackered, Sir. Permission to go on a skeleton crew for a couple of hours?"

Karl, hearing this, thought quickly before answering. "Scottie, once you have the ship shape, idle the engines. Our crew needs to rest. The nearest ship to us is over five hundred miles away. The current will carry us in the right direction, so other than a skeleton crew, you have my permission to close down. Now, go get that well deserved sleep."

Scottie chuckled as he listened to his captain. "Thank you, Sir, will do."

Karl looked at Adams, saying, "Number One, you look terrible; report to your bunk, and that's an order." Adams, nodding his head, was more than ready to leave the bridge.

"All hands, this is the captain again. Now that we are clear of that storm, I'm very aware you're all exhausted, so please, retire to your bunks for some well-deserved sleep. See your section leaders for a rotation schedule, bridge out."

Arnold relieved Karl on the bridge at 1400 hours. He looked so much better; his clean-shaven face made a new man of him. "Sir, it's time for you to have a shower and some sleep. It's amazing how calm the sea is now. Last night seems like a bad dream; wouldn't you agree? What time should I call down to get underway again?"

Karl, his jacket over his arm, thought about that question, then answered, "Arnold, let them have another couple of hours. They deserve the sleep." While nodding, Arnold noticed that the helm was not manned but locked. As he headed for the door, Karl called back, "Arnold, old man, other than the radio shack being manned, you have the bridge all to yourself. See you in a couple of hours."

The voyage to Darwin was delightful calm seas with mainly blue skies and a vast empty ocean all around them. Besides a bent bow rail and the shaft bearing issue, the Spirit had weathered one of the worst tropical storms to hit the area in many years. Karl had started to let Adams take more responsibilities in the ship's daily operations, preparing him for when he would assume command after his retirement. Their time in Darwin was short; refueling and loading the many hundreds of frozen sheep carcasses into the massive freezer hold would not take long. The ship's crew had little interest in going ashore other than to buy a few souvenirs. They were more intent on getting underway again on the final long leg back to England.

Karl had written four lengthy letters to Claire while on that last leg, careful not to mention how dangerous that storm had been. Once he was home, maybe he would share that story with her over a glass of wine. Entering the agent's small office, Karl asked the receptionist to stamp and mark his letters for air mail. He wanted these letters to arrive before he did.

Once again, they made ready to cast off. "Skipper, on your command, we are ready to cast off," Adams said.

"Very well, Number One. Why don't you let our second officer take her out under your supervision of course?"

"Aye, aye, Sir," came the response.

Karl was enjoying his bridge highchair. Sitting there, he started thinking of all the other captains he had known who had sat on a similar high throne, now adding himself to that list as he thought ahead to disembarking for the last time in Glasgow.

Cruising at eighteen knots in a following sea gave them an over the bottom speed of over twenty-two knots, putting them ahead of schedule as they entered the Red Sea from the Gulf of Aden. The ship traffic bound north into the Suez Canal was light, which delighted Captain Vita.

"Chaps, it looks like we will not be anchoring long, waiting for a transit time. This latest message from the canal authorities is telling us to proceed. There are only two ships behind us. I guess we timed it right. Steady as you go at eight knots." Karl had made this transit of the canal so many times before. It was narrow, so traffic was one way until reversed, with shipping heading in the opposite direction. Exiting the canal into the Mediterranean, they followed a new course, northwesterly heading toward the Straits of Gibraltar. Karl had instructed the off duty sailors to take advantage of the wonderful weather and relax on the forward deck.

"Captain, receiving a wire from Glasgow," yelled Sparks. "Very well, print it out for me," answered Karl. The wire read: when you dock in Southampton, the commodore and two other officers will join you for the return trip to Glasgow. Will tell you more once we can talk freely. In his highchair, Karl started to think about what this could be all about. Why would the commodore be joining them? The more he thought about that message, the clearer that wire became. They will be evaluating Arnold Adams as a candidate to assume command of this ship, so who are the other two officers?

"Number One, please join me in my cabin." Karl wanted to prepare his friend for the evaluation they would be conducting on that final leg up to Glasgow. After the steward delivered refreshments, Karl told Arnold about the wire and his assumption of what it could mean. "Arnold, in one way, this is terrific news. Those blokes will watch how you handle yourself and this ship, along with how you interface with the crew. You must act as if you have no idea of their being aboard. I, of course, will not interfere with you or them, agreed?"

Entering the North Atlantic, the weather was brisk, even cold at times. "Number One, you have the con for the rest of the trip. This could be a good time to whip your second officer into shape." Karl winked at Arnold, grinning from ear to ear.

"I'll be in my quarters if you need me." The Spirit plowed onward to England and, for the crew, a welcome leave before heading out on another journey with a new captain in that high chair. Karl sat on a chair next to the navigator station, watching Arnold giving orders as they slowly inched toward their berth in Southampton. Guided by three powerful tugs, Arnold made his last command, "Done with engines; secure the helm." Arnold, removing his cap, walked over to Karl, sipping coffee. "Well, Skipper, how did I do?"

Extending his hand, Karl answered, "Bloody marvelous, Adams. Now, get the logbook up to date because that will be the first thing to receive attention." The bridge was quiet just two friends sitting, enjoying each other's company, wondering when the company people would be arriving. The bridge door opened, and Karl and Arnold expected to see the commodore or maybe one of his officers to enter. Karl nearly dropped his coffee cup when he saw someone he did not expect to see. There, smiling in the doorway, looking immaculately dressed, stood Mrs. Claire Vita, trying very hard to hold back the laughter, then the tears at seeing the look on her husband's face.

"Well, Sailor, is this the way to welcome your wife after all these months?" Claire crossed over to Karl, squeezing Arnold's arm as she passed by him, saying, "Thanks, Arnold, for keeping this a secret."

Arnold laughed and shook his head as he walked toward the bridge door; his parting words were, "Hey, you lovebirds, we will be in the lounge waiting for you. Take your time; you have a lot to catch up on."

Claire stood in front of her husband, and for once in his life, Karl was utterly dumbfounded. Without saying a word, he wrapped his arms around his wife. Holding her in silence, he realized he would never again leave her and their children for this long. "Claire, how did you know we would arrive today? Did you come down by train again?" Karl was firing rapid questions, one after another.

"Well, darling, I have stayed in touch with Jim regularly. He's such a sweetheart, and he kept me informed about your trip. A couple of days ago, he called me to say you would be docking today and that he and two company officers would be joining the Spirit in Southampton for the final leg up to Glasgow. The purpose was to evaluate Arnold Adams as the replacement captain. While Jim was talking, he stopped speaking, then said out of the blue, 'Claire, this is Karl's final voyage back to Glasgow. Arnold will be in command, so Karl has little to do but watch.' Like a bolt of lightning, he asked me, 'What a wonderful way to end his career as a sailor, by having you, his wife, accompany him on this leg back to Glasgow. Think of it as our way of thanking Karl for commissioning the Spirit, then taking her on such a strenuous and, at times, difficult maiden voyage.'"

Claire continued by saying, "You don't have to ask me twice. When do I have to be there? These next couple of days will give me time to arrange for a babysitter. Jim, I can't thank you enough." Claire stopped talking. Then, kissing her husband, she continued, "Darling, I have never stayed on board a big ship before. This will be a first for me; think of it as a mini honeymoon for us, Karl!"

With his handkerchief, Karl wiped away a tear on her cheek. "Claire, I'm still in shock. In my wildest dreams, I could not believe Jim would think of doing this. Shall we join the others in the lounge? Wait, did you bring an overnight case with you? If so, where did you leave it?"

Claire giggled, answering, "Darling, Jim had it put in your stateroom." Arm in arm, like honeymooners, they walked off the bridge. Karl's final thought as he did that was, I will never again walk onto this or any other bridge as a ship's captain.

Holding the lounge door open for Claire, a sea of dark blue uniforms greeted them, clapping loudly as the couple entered. Jim stepped forward and slid out a chair for Claire, pointing to the one next to her for Karl. The steward had decorated the table, placing two decanters of red and white wines in the center, with the ship's engraved tumblers arranged around them. For those preferring other than wine, the table at the side had a supply of beer.

Jim, his hand still on Claire's chair, announced in a cheerful voice, "Captain Vita, in light of this being your last contract, we decided to have a small gathering tonight instead of waiting to have one in Glasgow. Claire, having you here adds so much to this party for your husband. All of us present would like you to accept this parting gift. Hopefully, it will always remind you of this time, even though your time with us was short as one of our fleet captains."

Jim reached under the table, bringing up a beautifully varnished box. He placed it in front of Karl. "My officers and I carried this with us from Glasgow yesterday."

Karl, never one for surprises, thought this was all prearranged; I've been blindsided again. Looking at Claire's face was proof they were all in on it. Commodore McGivern continued by asking, "May I suggest we dispense with the formalities of rank for the time being, if that's acceptable to you, Karl?"

Smiling back, Karl nodded in agreement. Jim continued, "As I said a few minutes ago, originally, we had planned this going away party to be held in the company offices. However, the Managing Director, Malcolm Finley, suggested it would be more appropriate to have me travel down with these two chaps on my right for this party and the last leg home. Being surrounded by your fellow officers would mean more to you and your wife. By the way, your entire crew would like both of you to join them on the foredeck in about two hours, after the unloading of the ship has been completed. Now, why don't you open that box in front of you? Although most of the employees can't be here with us tonight, that gift carries the best wishes from the company directors and the entire staff of the Clyde Shipping Company. We hope it will receive a prominent place in your home and always in your heart."

Jim sat down; reaching for his wine, he toasted the outgoing captain of the Spirit of Clyde Side. With both hands on the box, Karl was choking back his emotions, humbled by this gathering of fellow officers he so admired. Claire, her attention on her husband, knew he was having a hard time. She slid her hand over his, then with a smile, quietly said, "Well, darling, I think these fine gentlemen are waiting for you to open that box. Shall I help you?"

Karl removed the lid, parting the wrapping paper; a surprised look crossed his face, looking at the very familiar funnel of the Spirit. Placing both his hands under the ends of the stand, he carefully removed the beautifully detailed model of the Spirit.

Claire gasped at this museum quality model, saying, "Oh, my goodness, Karl, it's so beautiful. Look at those covered lifeboats, so much detail!" Claire could see Karl was still gathering his composure, so she stepped in by saying, "Gentlemen, Karl is still speechless. So, if I may, let me thank you all for the support and friendship you have given my husband during the time he has served with you all. This model will be the centerpiece on the living room mantle." Placing her hand on Karl's shoulder, she sat down, waiting momentarily for Karl to respond.

"Chaps, my wife always knows how to read me, and today is no exception. The honor I feel for being the recipient of such a lavish gift is overwhelming to me. I have been fortunate enough in my time as a merchant sailor to have served on two ships that will forever have a special place in my heart the first being the Tristian and this wonderful vessel, The Spirit of Clyde Side. I was fortunate enough to be a commissioned officer on both vessels during their sea trials and maiden voyages.

Standing here, I truly believe there is a very special bond between seamen; all of you here are, without question, the closest I will ever have." Karl winked at Arnold, Scottie, and Jim as he said that.

The rest of the time was festive, all enjoying this gathering. While watching the time, Jim pointed to his watch, so Karl knew they had to leave. "Chaps, Jim here is telling me that Claire and I must leave you all to join the crew on the foredeck. Again, thank you for making this such a marvelous time."

Helping Claire, he lifted the wooden box with both hands. Claire also thanked them all for this wonderful party. Walking toward the companionway leading down to the main deck, the crew started clapping loudly while watching them navigate the steep stairs. Karl made sure Claire did not have a problem with her high heeled shoes.

Scottie, who had left the officers gathering to joining the crew on the main deck, stepped forward and yelled for everyone to be quiet before speaking. "Today, we all are celebrating our captain's retirement; please, join me in wishing him and his wife, Claire, Godspeed, safe travels, and long and healthy lives!"

"Hip, hip, hooray for Captain Vita," came a shout from the back of the group. One by one, they stepped forward to shake hands with Karl. After shaking Karl's hand, one cheeky junior stocker turned to Claire, kissing her on the cheek.

"Ere, mate, steady on; that's the skipper's wife your kissing," yelled another sailor. Claire first had a look of shock, followed by a beaming smile. Looking at the young man, she broke out laughing, kissing him right back on his left cheek, taking him totally by surprise.

Taking a wrapped gift from his assistant, Scottie extended it to Karl, saying, "Captain, please accept this token of our appreciation. Think of your crew when you wear it."

Karl stood quietly with a smile that expressed his affection for his crew. Inside, neatly folded, he opened the inner wrapping to find an American style windbreaker. Over the left breast, a yellow embroidered ship's shield and name, with its hailing port around the bottom in a semicircle. "Sir, we also had a matching cap made for cooler days when you take the MG out for a drive."

Claire reached out, taking the cap from Scottie, saying, "Scottie, I think this looks better on me. Mind if I wear it?" To the crew's delight, Claire arranged her hair to fit under the cap, placing it on her head. She entered their ranks, hugging and kissing a few as she strutted between them. Karl, wearing his windbreaker, stood, slowly nodding, thinking, I can always rely on Claire to rally the crowd. God, I love her ways.

Karl turned to Scottie, asking, "When on earth did you find time to have this made?"

Scottie answered, "Well, my old friend, the commodore had them made in Glasgow, bringing them with him yesterday." Finally, Scottie, looking at his watch, put his hands in the air, breaking up the boisterous group. Karl, Claire, and Scottie waved goodnight to the remaining crew members still lingering around.

Making their way to the officers' mess, they joined the spirited group already enjoying their evening meal. Starting tomorrow, things would change very quickly for Karl, but was he ready to bid farewell to his career in the merchant marine?

Most of the night, Karl kept rolling memories about his time in the maritime service, coming to an end in just a few short days. These thoughts kept him awake. Looking at his watch, he saw it was almost 0530 hours, so rather than disturbing his wife, he quietly got out of bed. Dressing stealthily, he quietly closed the cabin door behind him as he walked out into the corridor leading to the bridge.

"Morning, chaps; it looks like we are ready to cast off, correct?" Arnold replied, "Morning, Skipper, should be ready momentarily; glad you got up early for this one. Would you like to take her out?" asked Arnold as a gesture for Karl to command his ship for what would be the last time.

"No, Captain, I'll stand back here out of the way. Thank you for asking anyway." The Spirit quietly cast off her lines, departing before dawn broke. Karl stood at the back of the bridge, observing Arnold giving precise orders to the bridge crew.

Sipping his coffee, he was feeling melancholy, that feeling of leaving the merchant service for the second time was the reason for his sadness.

"Gentlemen, if no one objects, I will take my leave. I need a walk around the deck. Nice maneuvering, Captain; catch up with you all later." Karl exited the bridge; walking slowly down the deck, deep in thought, he turned to face the water. Placing his hand on the railing, he solemnly watched the channel marker for Southampton slide astern of the ship. His mind was wrestling with becoming an observer instead of the captain. Staring at the land as it slipped over the horizon, the turmoil he was experiencing continued taking him back in time, reliving the events that made him the person he had become today. With difficulty, he was trying to accept that his life as a seaman was almost at an end, closing yet another chapter in his life.

With a long sigh, he finished his now cold coffee, turned around, and slowly walked back.

As he entered the bridge, a sailor standing by the door announced loudly, "Captain on the bridge." Hearing this lifted his spirits, even though it would only be repeated a few more times. Arnold was busy with Phillips, studying the upcoming weather.

The commodore and his two company men had not yet arrived, which surprised Karl.

"Chaps, how are we looking for the rest of the day? It's starting off really nice; wouldn't you agree?" remarked Karl, making small talk.

"I think you're right, Captain. I hope it stays like this for the rest of the trip. I'm assuming you will be taking her in, am I correct?" Arnold looked at Karl for an answer.

"No, Captain, the Spirit is yours for the rest of this trip; at this point, I'm only an observer. That walk this morning did me some good cleared my head, you could say. Please, return to your planning. It sounds like it will be a calm trip north, correct, Mr. Phillips?" Nodding in agreement, the navigator, smiling, returned to his charts, thinking, poor chap, he's lost right now.

Walking back to his quarters, Karl could see the steward had retrieved his suitcases from the storage room, placing them next to the door. As he entered the cabin, he saw Claire had gotten herself ready, wearing sensible tweed slacks and a cardigan.

"Morning, you gorgeous thing, you slept like a log, so I let you sleep. Ready for breakfast?" asked Karl as he squeezed her tightly.

"You look nice, Mister Vita; is this your new attire, wearing that new windbreaker?" answered Claire, grinning at his reaction to being called Mister. Over breakfast, they talked about the motor trip to Vienna and the places on Claire's list to visit once they landed in Ostend, Belgium. Karl reiterated that they should head directly to St. Sebastiana in Germany. Then, they could cross over to Switzerland for some sightseeing before heading to Vienna. Karl, the seasoned sailor, felt the slight vibrations coming from the engine room.

"Looks like Scottie has been given the signal to wind her up." Claire could sense his discomfort at not being on the bridge.

"Darling, you belong on the bridge. Now, go; I'll be fine." Claire watched him as he walked out the door. She could feel his sorrow, even though he was trying very hard to be cheerful. She knew those signs he was trying hard to cover up.

"Poor chap," she concluded, closing the cabin door to finish her makeup.

Back on the bridge, the commodore and his staff officer conversed with Arnold and Phillips about the trip north. Taking a seat near the navigation station, he continued to observe the bridge crew, busily attending to their duties before relaxing at their stations. Conditions were perfect; it would be a long day with little to do. "No need to remain now that we are on our rhumb line," remarked Karl to Phillips. Moving over next to the commodore, Karl spoke quietly, saying to Jim, "Everything appears to be running smoothly, so I'll take my leave unless you need me to stay?"

Looking at Arnold in jest, Jim said, "Captain Adams, will you require Captain Vita to remain on the bridge?"

Arnold lowered his binoculars, turning to Karl and replying, "If I were you, I would not leave a striking woman like Claire sitting in a deckchair alone. See you for lunch." Karl got the message that he should join his wife on the passenger deck.

Changing into casual clothing, he joined Claire on the deck. "Wow, Claire, no wonder there are sailors walking around on the main deck. You're flustering me; never mind those blokes down there." Claire had changed again to take advantage of the bright sunshine on the passenger deck. In a short white skirt and yellow and blue striped blouse, Claire looked like she belonged on a cruise ship, not a merchant ship.

"Karl, you're back early. I didn't expect you until lunch. These chaps can't do enough for me; I feel like a princess."

With a smirk on his face, Karl shook his head, saying, "Claire, the way you're lying in that deckchair, with an unobstructed view of your luscious thighs and legs, is creating quite the stares from those poor blokes."

Sitting down next to her, Karl could not pass up the chance to let his wife know that the way she was looking was giving him ideas about some quiet time this afternoon a luxury they had not had in a long time. "Why, Karl Vita, I do believe you have ideas of ravaging me back in the cabin. You better be a good boy, or you'll be putting me back in the maternity ward, and we don't need that, do we?" Claire started laughing, feeling special about the saucy way her husband was flattering her. "Come here, Herr Vita; you need to kiss your wife. She has waited so long for this."

The next few days were like a second honeymoon, spending most of their time sitting outside on the passenger deck, soaking up the sunshine and filling their lungs with fresh salt air. Looking at Claire, Karl could sense she needed this break from family and office commitments. On the last night, after a wonderful dinner in the officers' mess, they took a walk around the deck before retiring to his quarters. Closing the door, Karl opened a bottle of Pinot Noir. Pouring two glasses, he joined her on the small couch. Kissing her softly, he spoke, "Never thought in a million years I would be enjoying time alone in my quarters with my sexy wife. Claire, it's my last night as the captain of this grand lady. I think I will always remember this as the night my vixen of a wife gave me a going away night to remember."

With a girlish smile on her face, Claire took a gulp of her wine, then placed it on the side table, saying, "Come here, Sailor. I know precisely what you need, and we have all night to get it right."

Karl put his wine down, and, taking Claire's soft hands, looked intensely into her eyes, mentally removing each piece of her clothing. Claire knew exactly what he was doing. Placing her cheek against his, in a soft voice, she said, "Darling, I know that look. When we first met, it would scare me, turning me into a babbling idiot. But now, I embrace that look and the way you touch me. Karl, I love you so much. My adult life did not start off very well, but my life has been beyond marvelous since we met. Here we are, acting like young lovers, with two beautiful kids waiting to see their mama and papa in a few days." Claire, talking like this, was working herself up; she could not wait any longer. Sliding her hand down inside his trousers, she felt his erection.

"Darling, I don't think you need any enticing. Maybe I need to feel you someplace else?" Claire, sliding down onto her knees, pulling his trousers and shorts down, wasted no time burying his erection deep in her mouth. With other ideas, Karl pulled her up alongside him, then, with slow, deliberate movements, slid his hand up her skirt, stopping at the bottom of her underwear.

Slowly, he slid his hand under the silky material. Claire twitched her thighs, trapping his arm in doing so. "Karl, whatever you're going to do, please do it now. You know you're driving me mental."

Karl reached up, sliding her underwear down around her ankles. Then laying her down, he pushed her skirt up high. Claire trembled as she waited for him to enter her. With all the restraint he could muster, he touched her, moving his penis back and forth. Feeling that this stimulation was getting her very moist, Claire was just about to plead with him when he thrust deeply into her. She had waited long enough. More than sexually charged, Claire erupted into a mind-blowing orgasm almost immediately, whispering, "Darling, don't you get carried away. Remember, two kids are our limit. I think you should pull out. Come on, Tiger; you're too close, and that could be dangerous."

Karl knew she was right. Taking risks at this point would be foolish, so reluctantly, he did what she asked. Claire moaned as he did so, knowing they would be safe for another day anyway.

Spent, they lay back on the couch, content at being together. The Spirit, after a long maiden voyage, was almost home.

Sailing along the coast, one of the lookouts announced loudly, "Pilot boat in sight, Sir." The officers and bridge crew craned their necks to see.

"Reduce turns for five knots; Helmsman, maintain your course!" barked Arnold. Jim was standing with Claire, Karl, and the two company officers, waiting for the pilot to enter the bridge.

The pilot smiled as he entered, saying, "Morning, gentlemen, and you too, madam; I take over from here." He began making precise instructions to the crew. Ninety minutes later, he bid farewell, returning the ship's command to Captain Adams.

Approaching the commodore, Arnold asked, "Commodore, with your approval, I think we should ask Captain Vita to return his command back into her berth."

Karl stood there motionless for what seemed like an eternity before answering, "Captain Adams, it would be my pleasure. I think

I remember how to do this." Kissing Claire on the cheek and shaking Jim's hand firmly, he moved over to the center window.

Adams took up a position at Karl's side, smiling, "Your instruction, Captain."

Maneuvering was seamless; they had done this so many times before. Karl's last command as the ship's captain was, "Helmsman, secure the helm; done with engines. Thank you, Number One sorry, meant Captain." On the bridge, an eerie silence hung over them momentarily before everyone started clapping, turning to face Karl; their love and respect for their captain on his last day was so evident. Karl went around shaking hands with everyone until he stood in front of the commodore. Coming to attention, he said, "Sir, with your permission, my wife and I will take our leave and head ashore. I will always cherish the trust you had in my abilities over the few years I have served with you.

Before departing, I have a last entry to make in the ship's log." Claire moved to Karl's side; he would need all her strength as they made their farewells.

"One moment, Captain Vita the board of directors is waiting on the dock for the boarding ramp to be attached. They would like to add their goodbyes; it shouldn't take long," said Jim, knowing Karl was anxious to leave before his emotions took control.

Karl turned to face the assembled officers, saying, "Arnold, Scottie, she's all yours now; send me pictures from wherever your journeys take you." As Karl was saying that, the company board of directors came aboard, enthusiastically shaking Karl's hand, then introducing themselves to Claire. "Gentlemen, thank you for the trust and support you have always given me. I appreciate the trust you extended to me by allowing me to make my last trip on the Spirit's maiden voyage. She is an amazing vessel. Sorry about the bent bow rail; it couldn't be helped. Commodore, what can I say other than we will always have this bond; stay in touch and visit us in Hitchin whenever you can make it."

Claire softly pulled him away, saying, "Time to drop your anchor, Sailor, and head for the station." Many of the crew had assembled on the dock to make their farewells. Karl held Claire's arm tightly as they carefully proceeded down the boarding ramp. About halfway down, that old pulling feeling and memory made Karl stop. When he turned back to face the ship, his friend, Jim McGinley, stood alone at the head of the boarding ramp, tipping the peak of his cap and sending a silent goodbye. On the other hand, Karl was reliving his departure from the Clyde Princess, docked in Dover back in 1936. Looking back at his friend, he started choking up. Coming to parade attention, he saluted Jim one last time.

Changing trains in Edinburgh, they decided to have dinner on the Golden Arrow Express. Over dinner, Claire could see the turmoil her husband was experiencing. Reaching over the table, Claire clasped his hand, finally saying, "Darling, I can see by the look on your face that saying goodbye to long term friends was hard for you to do. You have not deserted them; they will always be there, but staying in touch is up to you. Your decision to leave was not easy for you, nor was it easy for me to retire, but you and our kids will always take precedence over everything and everyone else. Karl, you left on your own terms, your head held high, revered by all that met you; take comfort in that. Now, I think we should retire to our compartment, don't you agree?" Karl was lying in the darkness of that compartment, his brain churning over the last few days. With the emotions of this last day finally completely exhausting him, he fell asleep.

Changing trains again, they took a taxi to King's Cross Station for the short train ride back to Hitchin. Karl could not let go of all those memories, reliving those times he had returned home. Looking at Claire, he finally spoke as they waited by the platform gate, "Darling, stay here on this bench; there is one thing I must do." Karl hurried off quickly, Claire thinking he can't let go; he is still reliving those times gone by. Right now, I feel so sorry for him; it's like he is lost and looking for the way home.

After about fifteen minutes, she saw Karl walking swiftly around the corner. He held a big bunch of flowers in his right hand, and an envelope was in the other hand. Karl had a big smile on his face as he approached his wife.

With his arms outstretched, he wrapped them around Claire, saying, "I did this so many times when I came home to you. Today is no different, with one exception. Today is the start of our next chapter in retirement and never to be separated again."

Claire was utterly shocked. With tears of excitement in her eyes, she hugged her flowers. People around them passed by with cheerful remarks, smiling at the sight of two people so much in love. "Darling, what's in the envelope?" asked Claire, looking at it still in Karl's hand.

"Oh, I nearly forgot; this is for you as well, darling." Claire sat back down, looking at Karl's face before she opened the envelope. The card read:

***My Darling Claire,***

***Today starts the next chapter in our life together. This next train will be the last time I return home in uniform. From here forward, any train trips will be together as a family, no longer separated.***

Arm in arm, they followed the porter down the platform to the first compartment, which looked empty. The friendly porter stowed their luggage overhead. Karl made the porter's day by tipping him with a five-pound note, setting him back with the generosity of this kindly merchant officer. Holding hands, they watch the countryside flash by. Claire occasionally looked at Karl with a smile that reflected her new happiness. Leaving Welwyn Garden City, Karl stood, saying, "The next stop is ours, darling; we're almost home." Lifting the heavy suitcases down from the overhead rack, Karl did little to block the stream of memories that continued flowing through his mind. The squealing from the wheels as they rounded the bend in the track was like music to this returning sailor, followed by the bumpers banging as the train slowed to a stop. Like those times before, smoke mixed with steam curled around the carriage, giving off a distinctive odor. "Claire, why don't you find a porter while I put all this luggage onto the platform?"

Claire, nodding her head in agreement, replied, "Will do, Captain." Karl was standing on the platform, waiting for his wife to return. The high-pitched train whistle made Karl react as the conductor waved his flag, signaling the engineer to release the brakes. It made Karl turn to watch the iron beast pulling out of the station; as he watched, he quietly thought, this was.

## THE LAST TRAIN HOME.

# CHAPTER 18

# A New Life

The taxi pulled into the driveway of Hemmings Way. Karl jumped out to help the driver with the heavy suitcases.

Karl heard his son, Nicholas, from the front door, yelling, "They're home!" Nick ran toward the car and wrapped his arms around his father's legs.

Claire laughed as she stepped out of the taxi; she reached down to her excited son, saying, "Well, young man, how about your mother? Now that your papa is home, I don't get my usual hugs?" Sheila, carrying Emily, was having difficulty holding onto the energetic little girl as she waved her arms with excitement and reached for her mother. "Emily, look who I brought home for you. It's your papa."

With his arm around Nick, Karl said to Sheila, "Let me hold her, Sheila; it's been such a long time. I think that look on her face is telling me she's not really sure who I am." Seeing that look on her daughter's face, Claire took Emily from Sheila, receiving a big hug and kisses on her cheek. Her eyes fixed on Karl, Emily slowly reached out her little arm toward her papa.

Karl, feeling a little saddened, slowly took her little hand, kissing it softly. With a loud, shrill, Emily yelled, "Papa!"

Claire paid the driver, waving a cheerful goodbye as he drove down the driveway. Leading the children back into the house, Claire held Emily under her arm while Sheila held Nicholas's hand. Karl picked up one of the two big suitcases and the box containing the model of the Spirit. Inside, he could feel the house all around him that comfortable feeling of home and safety.

Placing the box on the desk, he went back outside for the rest of his luggage. Claire reached for her handbag to pay Sheila, then asked Karl to drive her home while she fed the children.

"Of course. Are you ready, Sheila?" replied Karl. In the car, Karl asked Sheila how her husband was doing with his bad dreams.

"Thanks for asking, Karl. He is almost his old self; he still has the occasional nightmare, but he always says you and your fellow officers were responsible for leading him out of the hell he was in. Twice a month, he attends therapy, and as I said, he is almost his old self."

Karl pulled the car in front of their house; with a parting comment, he said, "Here we are, young lady. I'm so pleased to hear your life is returning to normal again. We will have to have the family over really soon," concluded Karl as he helped Sheila from the car.

Arriving home, he entered the kitchen to find Claire preparing dinner. "Darling, why don't you put your luggage upstairs; use the left bedroom, we can unpack everything in the morning." After dinner, the Vita family moved to the sitting room, sitting on the floor. They enjoyed watching their children playing. Karl had placed the model of the Spirit up high on the bookshelf, knowing it would be an enticement for Nicholas if left on the desk. Quite settled in, after the children had been put to bed, they returned to the sitting room for an evening glass of port.

Claire reminded her husband, "Karl, in two weeks, we have reservations at the Charter Arms for Clive's BIS reunion party.

Julie mentioned that most attendees plan on wearing their uniforms; will you also wear your uniform?"

Looking at his face, she knew instinctively what the answer would be. "Well, Claire, officially, I'm still a serving officer for the Clyde Shipping Company until the middle of next month, anyway. In light of that, I think it appropriate to wear my maritime dress uniform; it will need to go to the cleaners before then, though."

With her arm over his shoulder, Claire smiled at him, saying, "Darling, I knew you would say that but needed to hear you confirm it first. No need for you to drop it off; I'll do that when I have lunch with the girls next week. I told Julie to expect a navy-blue uniform amongst that sea of khaki. By the way, I invited Bill and Dorothy to stop by tomorrow evening; they're both anxious to catch up with you." Claire took his hand; kissing it, she looked at her husband, saying, "We are about to start another chapter, darling. I still can't believe you're almost out of uniform a civilian at last. I'm sure it will seem very strange to you at first."

The following morning, Karl unpacked, then caught up on loose ends. At 1900 hours, the Lowes arrived, carrying a large bottle of Champagne. Excitedly, Bill hugged his old friend, followed by Dorothy. In the living room, Bill made a toast to new beginnings.

The next two weeks were hectic for Karl, catching up on home projects and servicing the family car to prepare for the long road trip to Vienna. In preparation for that trip, Claire had sent away for an RAC (Royal Automobile Club) travel package. Karl enjoyed studying the route they would travel, the stops they would make, and the changes he made, noting them on the route sheet. While Karl laid out their trip, Claire was busy assembling the items they would take with them: the children's clothes, toys, and her and Karl's clothing. This she did in one of the spare bedrooms. Karl was feeling very relaxed, enjoying the freedom of retirement.

Bill and Dorothy occasionally stopped over, sometimes to babysit, giving Claire a chance to get out of the house. Julie had told Claire that her two daughters had volunteered to babysit at the Charter Arms, giving the adults peace of mind that their children were well cared for. Time flew by, and now it was time to drive to Slough for the reunion. Karl drove the familiar roads he had driven on so many occasions during the war years.

"Claire, you have been smiling since we left the house. What is going through that head of yours?" asked Karl.

Claire reached over and, placing her hand on his arm, replied, "Probably the same thoughts going through your head, darling." Karl nodded in agreement.

When they arrived at the Charter Arms, the porter unloaded the luggage, taking it inside. "All, right, you good looking woman, it's Showtime; are you ready? What time do we have to be downstairs?"

Karl was surprising himself, feeling the excitement of seeing old friends. Then a thought crossed his mind was some of that excitement caused by seeing his old flame, Hazel? Before heading upstairs, they walked into the ballroom to see the decorations for this evening's event and maybe a few lingering BIS attendees.

Holding Nicholas's hand, Karl walked into the ballroom to see the hotel staff decorating the tables. A big banner had been hung over the stage that read: Welcome to the British Intelligence Service REUNION. Over by the back door, Karl noticed Clive talking with the hotel banquet manager, his clipboard in hand. Excusing himself, he walked over to his old boss and clasped his hand on Clive's arm.

"Major Vita, reporting for duty, Sir!" Karl reached down to show Nicholas how to make a salute. Clive broke out laughing, looking down at the comical picture of little Nicholas saluting him.

"Private Vita, you salute better than your father does. Welcome, old friend; just making sure we are well stocked for tonight. I'm so glad you could make it. I'm assuming Claire has found the girls in the lounge, let's go join them, shall we?" Clive slowly led the way, enjoying holding Nick's hand. Entering the lounge, they found a sizable group milling around the bar area. Karl scanned the faces until he noticed a striking woman looking in his direction. Smiling, Karl walked over to his old flame, Hazel.

"Karl, it's so good to see you. The last time I saw you was in Canada; Claire keeps me abreast of your voyages. When the war was over, I always thought you would return to your first love the sea, not me."

Karl was ready, knowing Hazel would zing him somehow. "Hazel, it really is good to see you again. How is married life treating you?"

Hazel shrugged her shoulders, saying, "These days, I miss living in England more and more. Unfortunately, that has become a topic of contention for Steven and me. I told him I'm going to move back, so he better accept the posting in London."

Karl, changing the subject, reached down to Nicholas, saying, "Nicholas, are you going to say hello to this pretty lady before we join the others?"

Nicholas, showing his shy side, kissed Hazel's cheek as she bent down to his level. "I have a feeling when you're older, you will be very much like your father leaving broken hearts all over the place." Hazel looked into Karl's eyes as she said that. Kissing Karl on the cheek, she said softly, "It still hurts, Karl, but that's not your problem, is it?" Joining the group, Karl and Hazel mingled but not together. Claire, the observant attorney, had watched from a distance, and for once in her marriage, she felt a little jealous, knowing Hazel still carried a torch for her husband, Karl.

The day flew by, and now the ballroom was starting to fill up. Clive and Julie greeted each couple as they entered. In their room, Karl had dressed in his merchant navy uniform, the gold bands on his sleeve indicating he held the rank of captain. He was pacing the floor, feeling a little nervous about being the only officer at the party not in the uniform of the BIS.

"Claire, are you almost ready? We were supposed to be downstairs at 1800 It's now 1812." Claire, still in the bathroom making the final touches to her makeup, deliberately delayed her exit. She wanted Karl to remember the first time she appeared in this evening dress.

"Almost ready, darling," she replied. Karl was standing by the door, ready to make a quick exit; he continued staring at the bathroom door. He was just about to remind her again when the door opened, and out walked Claire, asking, "Well, Sailor, does your wife pass muster?" Claire was in that black evening dress she had worn to meet Karl's friends before they were married.

Karl stood, staring at his wife before saying, "Claire, you look the same as that first time here at the Charter Arms. God, you still take my breath away. All eyes will be on you tonight, not my bloody navy-blue uniform."

Holding back her nervousness, Claire smiled at Karl as he wrapped his arms around his wife, flooding his senses with her looks and that same perfume. "Darling, I thought you were in a rush to go downstairs or has this memory stirred old visions of the woman that captured your heart, taking precedence over the reunion?"

Karl was more than excited; Claire was always well dressed, and since his return, they had been too busy at home, but tonight, she was the most striking woman he had ever seen. This vision of a mother and housewife had faded. "Claire, forgive me. For a while, I have not looked at you as the woman I first met, but seeing you like this reminds me how lucky I am."

With a big sigh, Claire kissed him with all her might before saying, "My darling, Karl, I must admit, earlier today, I did not feel so sure of myself. What a fool I am. Why would I ever doubt what we have? Let's get going; you can strip off my wrappings when we get back upstairs, but not before putting our two lovely, adorable children to bed."

Karl, with a confused look on his face, thought this is so not like Claire. She is always confident and so very sure of herself. I think I hit a nerve when she saw me with Hazel. I won't make that mistake again. God, she is so amazing. Arm in arm, they walked down the stairs; that spark was back the love they shared stronger than ever.

At the entrance to the ballroom, Julie and Clive continued welcoming everyone attending. Julie, seeing them first, reached out to Claire, saying, "My goodness, look at this striking couple! Claire, you look marvelous in that black dress! You're so lucky to have kept your figure after two children. You need to share your secret."

Laughing out loud, Claire pointed to Karl, saying, "When you marry a bloke like this one, you never know what to expect. That's my secret."

Clive hugged Claire, then looked at Karl and said, "Well, old boy, you were wearing a dark blue maritime uniform when we first met you. I suppose it's only fitting you would return to that same uniform. Welcome, old friends, enjoy the party. If I were you, I wouldn't take my eyes off this woman of yours; she looks stunning. Now, go have fun. Julie and I will join you in a little while. Karl winked at Claire, her radiant smile letting him know there was only one man for her. The happy hour was hectic, mingling at the bar just like in the old days.

A tap on the shoulder made Karl turn around quickly to face Gunther, Herbert, and their wives. "Well, we were wondering where you four were. Did you just arrive?" asked Karl as he and Claire hugged their friends. Karl also noticed that he was not the only one not wearing a khaki uniform. Herbert was now a one star general in the new German army. He also felt it was the right thing to do.

Looking at the numbered tables, Gunther yelled over the noisy bar crowd, "We are all sitting together; shall we find our table?" His arm was over Karl's shoulder, old friends who had faced the hell of war on more than one occasion. Once everyone was seated, Clive and Julie sat at the head table with General and Mrs. Jacks. Clive stood, facing the microphone, then asked, "Please, stand in silence for the invocation given tonight by our own company Chaplain, Captain William Regales. Standing with their heads bowed, Claire slowly reached over to take Karl's hand after listening to that touching prayer. Clive continued to stand, getting everyone to laugh by promising not to bore anyone.

"First, let me thank you all for making the effort to be here tonight. We are so fortunate to have in our midst this evening retired General Jacks, who always went the extra mile to support all our missions and, on many occasions, unauthorized operations. Join me now in thanking the general and his charming wife, Mary, for that support.

"Now, some of you here have traveled from distant places like Captain Hazel Collins, now Mrs. Steven Kowalski. She joins us from Newport, Rhode Island, in the United States.

"Another former BIS officer also here tonight; Captain Herbert Werner, and his charming wife Elsa, have traveled from West Berlin, Germany. After the war, they returned to Germany, playing a strategic part in rebuilding the new German Army. Would General Herbert Werner please stand to be recognized?

"Looking around the hall, I'm sure you may have noticed another non khaki uniform as well. Would Captain Karl Vita of the Clyde Shipping Company please stand to be recognized as a former Major in the BIS? Before the war, he served as the second officer for a German shipping company. Escaping with his family members to England, he joined us in the BIS in 1936. Both these officers are still in service with other entities, hence their uniforms tonight.

"Would former BIS Colonel Gunther Fisher please stand to be recognized? Colonel Fisher, after the war, joined the American State Department. Recently, he accepted a posting here in London with his family.

We're glad to have you back in old Blighty; both Captain Werner and Colonel Fisher were commissioned officers in the German Wehrmacht prior to the war. Like Captain Vita, they braved being shot as deserters, escaping to England."

With both hands in the air, Clive called for silence as he continued by saying, "Would Colonel Fisher and Major Vita remain standing, please? During the war, service awards were kept under wraps. Only commanding officers and close family members were allowed to attend these ceremonies. Colonel Fisher and Major Vita are the only officers from this command to be awarded the Military Star and the War Medal for service above and beyond the call of duty." Tonight, we honor them and many others who accepted the danger of serving in the Intelligence Service. Would you now all stand to congratulate these outstanding officers here tonight?"

Loud cheers and clapping filled the hall as Gunther and Karl stood there, then shaking hands, they sat back down.

"To all of you out there in khaki, thank you for dusting off your old uniforms. Mine must have shrunk a little at the cleaners, as I had a devil of a time getting the buttons to close."

Everyone roared with laughter at Clive's humor. Clive and one hundred and forty other BIS members cheered and clapped. Karl kissed Claire on the cheek, then reached out to Gunther and Herbert, shaking their hands, a silent nod recognizing their courage and commitment.

The reunion was over, everyone there enthusiastically exchanging addresses and promises to keep in touch. Karl was thinking: the road to hell is paved with good intentions. At least close ties will be kept amongst our small group. That reunion would be the only one ever to take place, and it would be the last time Karl would ever see Hazel, who returned to her husband and daughter in America. Heading home, Karl and Claire said little other than the occasional smile and touching hands, confident their children would continue the Vita name, following in their parents' footsteps.

# EPILOGUE

Karl and Claire kept their promise to make their first stop in the German village of St. Sebastiana to replace Kitty's headstone. She was buried under the assumed name of Gretel Manton back in 1937. Karl, on his return home after leaving the Clyde Shipping Company, had written to the Catholic priest in St. Sebastiana, explaining what needed to be accomplished before he arrived in that village. The priest, delighted to receive Karl's letter, knew sooner than later he would be contacted to have a new headstone made with the correct name inscribed on it. Karl asked if a local stone mason could provide a fitting black granite stone with an inscription etched into it. Further, he asked the priest to advise him how much it would cost, so he could arrange payment before his arrival. The inscription was to read:

*Lieutenant Kitty Johnson*
*July 16th, 1916 – October 11th 1937*
*British Intelligence Service*
*Left this world too early for her years.*
*Rest in peace.*

Loading the MG with the luggage they would need during the two months on the continent, Karl was excited to be going home to Wien. On the back of the car, he attached the white oval disc with black lettering GB, indicating the car was from Great Britain, which was supplied to him by the Royal Automobile Club. Two weeks before their departure, he received a reply from the priest in St. Sebastiana with the amount due for the new headstone.

Looking at the amount, Claire was amazed, telling Karl, "Darling, that is really reasonable. We should make a donation to the church once we are there." The crossing from Dover to Ostend gave Karl another chance to be out at sea; however, that crossing would be less than four hours. Driving off the ferry, Karl started noticing the amount of rebuilding in and around the harbor.

However, numerous buildings and equipment still needed to be demolished. The road to St. Sebastiana was full of commercial traffic, making the going slower than expected.

The village of St. Sebastiana was exactly what they expected: small and quaint. The accommodations they found were spotless, the room bright and airy. Claire proclaimed, "Darling, I am going to love staying here for a few days!" During those days, the Vita family enjoyed exploring the village and the beautiful forest surrounding it. Finally, the headstone was ready. The priest agreed to a private service, blessing the grave site. Claire and the children stood back, allowing Karl to make his own private farewell.

From his pocket, he took a film canister, scooped up some of the soil, then placed a few of the fresh flower petals they had purchased that morning into an envelope, sealing it before he took a step back, his hands clasped in front of himself. Quietly, he bid farewell, saying, "Kitty, finally, you are no longer an unknown person. I will post the pictures, canister, and petals to your mother once we arrive in Vienna. Life was unfair to you, my dearest Kitty. I hope you approve of my family; they are the reason for every day I live. Claire was the one that insisted we do the right thing here today. Until the day I die, there will always be a special place in my heart for you, my love, for what we shared." Karl reached back to Claire for her camera, taking pictures of the new grave site, then came to parade attention, saluting a fallen hero. As promised, Karl had the pictures developed, adding a lengthy letter to the package before sending it off to Kitty's mother in England.

Their time in Vienna was wonderful, Claire bonding with Mina, Karl's oldest brother's wife, and with Freida, her dear friend and sister-in-law. Karl took his family on a guided tour of the restored, magnificent buildings. Unfortunately, Mama was becoming frail, and her children recognized her time with them would not be much longer.

As promised, Karl drove his family to meet Annie Laurie and her parents. Claire and Annie instantly became friends, enjoying their brief time together. Annie, holding Emily on her lap, was enjoying the memory of her own daughter, Julie. Before leaving, Claire invited Annie to visit them in Hitchin, which never happened. With heavy hearts, they left Wien to make the long drive home to Hitchin, promising to be back the following year.

Arriving back in England, Karl started to consider his future. One night, having dinner in Cambridge with the Knights, Clive invited Karl to visit the Intelligence Service's new headquarters, now known as MI-5.

Karl enthusiastically accepted the invitation. Clive's primary function was to recruit new field agents; training would be a monumental task. Clive convinced his superiors to consider civil contractors with strong intelligence backgrounds and field experience to be hired to expedite that training. Karl was being given a second chance to be part of the new British Intelligence Force. Working an average of one to two days a week, he would travel by train to the Cambridge facilities for the next five years.

Most years, the Vita family would spend their holidays on the continent, always spending time in Karl's beloved city of Vienna (Wien). As their children grew up, Karl and Claire would continue making that trip on their own, usually flying to save time instead of the 1500-mile road trip. At the age of eighty-nine, Mama's health was failing her. Karl flew to Vienna, spending those last two weeks at her bedside, along with his brothers and sister.

As the years passed, Karl, no longer a contractor for the MI-5, would spend the nice weather working in the garden, maintaining the house, and driving his MG sports car on nicer days. On rainy days, he would enjoy time in the library and visiting old friends for a game of cards. He was, however, becoming increasingly bored. He needed to use his mind once again, constantly searching for new projects to occupy his time. On the other hand, Claire was busy with various committees and, from time to time, would assist at the law firm. One day, when they were taking a glass of sherry out in the garden, she suggested he start writing down all the experiences and things he had done during his careers.

"Karl, if for no other reason than to give our children a history of what you achieved in the Merchant Service and the Intelligence Service."

Nicholas continued to excel in school, always in the top five or six in his class. He would go on to join the Royal Navy, working hard to climb the ladder of command. As for his younger sister, Emily, she was all Claire, excelling in all she undertook. Following in her mother's footsteps, she attended the same university in Cambridge before attending law school. After she graduated, she joined her mother's law firm, McGivern, Tilbey, and Morrison. In later years, after Bill had retired, she would become the managing partner. Unfortunately, her father didn't live long enough to see that happen.

One day, Claire had come home from a women's club luncheon. Entering through the kitchen, she heard sounds from her old typewriter, the keys being banged by inexperienced hands. She entered the sitting room, thinking, what is he up to now? Walking up behind her husband, she inquired, "Darling, what are you writing? By the way, you're banging those keys. You need to press them lighter, or they will bind. What is it you are typing? It must be something special?"

Turning around, his face was full of the old Karl that sparkle in his eyes was back. "Well, darling, you gave me the idea of writing my memoirs, so I thought more about that and came up with the idea of taking those experiences and writing a fictional book series based on events that happened in my life."

Claire was relieved that Karl had found a new direction, awakening that cocky sailor she had fallen in love with. "And what will the title of this first book to be?" she asked.

Karl, smiling profusely, answered, "I would have thought you would have guessed that one, Claire. The first book title is:

"THE FOLLOWING STORM."

THE END

ALSO BY PETER A. MOSCOVITA

The Following Storm Series:
*The Following Storm*
*Beyond All Doubt*
*All That Ends Well*
*The Last Train Home*

# ABOUT THE AUTHOR

**PETER A. MOSCOVITA** grew up in England and had a love for exploring different countries, sparked by exciting family trips across Europe. His Dad's adventure stories from his early years as a ship's officer made him dream about discovering new lands far beyond.

**In 1966,** his dreams came true, when he emigrated to the United States of America as a design and development engineer. In later years he would enter medical device manufacturing.

**In 1982,** he met Martine, who shared his passion for travel, sailing, cruising, culinary clubs and the love of history.

**In 1986,** alone with two fellow engineers they founded a startup company that designed and developed a line of advanced Medical Vascular Diagnostic instruments. Once the instruments were ready for market he turned his attention to creating a National Sales and Marketing Division. As the company grew he convinced his wife Martine to join the company as its event coordinator.

When time permitted the couple continued their long distant traveling all over the world, exploring was in their blood.

**In 2010,** the partners agreed they would sell the company, now traveling and exploring had no boundaries.

**In 2011,** The couple moved to Florida in their boat, living on it in Sarasota before settling ashore in Lakewood Ranch. Since then, they've continued to explore distant lands and enjoy life to the fullest.

**In 2018,** the author wrote his first book, *'The Following Storm'* which readers loved, that first book turned into a series. The four thrilling books follow the life, loves and dangers of Karl Vita throughout World War II into the early 1950's. *'The Last Train Home'* wraps up Karl Vita's story.

Since then, his books continue to receive five-star reviews.

To review additional titles and updates please visit the authors website:

**www.petermoscovita.net**

Note: *'The Ultimate Sacrifice'* from the same period but not associated with The Following Storm series is available through various outlets like Amazon and Barnes & Noble and other online retailers. *'The Unexpected Encounter'* takes place in the 1960s during the cold war between America and Russia. This gripping story of espionage, romance and commitment will keep you guessing with its never-ending twist through numerous continents. Another book available during the first quarter of 2025 takes on a completely different story.

*'My Journey To You'* centers on two major characters, a high powered American advertising executive and a German superstar. Both very successful in their chosen careers but in their private lives they both lack that relationship they both crave to find. This story starts off with an online relationship you will embrace but don't get comfortable with. It will take you by surprise as you read on.

Am I considering another series? Stay tuned to find out!